C0-AWK-126

THE AELIAN FRAGMENT

By the same author:

A JOB ABROAD
FAIR GAME

George Bartram

THE AELIAN FRAGMENT

G. P. Putnam's Sons
New York

Published simultaneously in Canada by Longman Canada Limited, Toronto.

SBN: 399-11625-7

Library of Congress Catalog Card Number: 75-37113

PRINTED IN THE UNITED STATES OF AMERICA

Like stragglers from a lost battle
With the invader, the new Tamerlane
my people
my people's souls
Out of the Kora Kum, their bodies
forgotten in mass graves
fly, wailing.
And behind them, the smoke of Russian factories.
Crematoria:
We are their Jews.

—YOMUT, *The Book of the Dead*

Chapter one

"THANK you very much, Mr. Teck, and have a pleasant journey on Air India." The young woman flashed him a ludicrously intimate smile as she handed him his ticket; seconds later she would be dazzling someone else with the same flash of little teeth. Teck smiled a little sourly and looked around for a vantage point from which he could watch for the Princess, but he found her only fifty feet away, striding confidently toward him.

"All ready, Sam," she said crisply, "and please don't look so self-satisfied; I don't know whether it's because I'm not coming with you or because I'll be with you again in a week. And don't try to kiss me; it's just too tacky. Isn't that a simply impossible word, 'tacky'? I love it. Here, I bought you a magazine."

"Is your luggage checked?"

"Of course. I'm very capable." She grinned. Her eyes were hidden by gigantic sunglasses and her brow was covered by a wide-brimmed hat. The grin seemed that of a happy animal. Teck put his hand under her right elbow and began to walk through the terminal.

"I wish I were going with you," she said softly. "Smuggling is terrifically more exciting than visiting t'e fooks in 'Oxton." Her voice sank to a rough parody of her father's.

"It isn't smuggling," he said primly.

"Oh, don't disillusion me, Sam! Of *course* it's smuggling. If you're caught, the Turkish government will be livid and they'll put you away for years and pull your fingernails out."

"I haven't even bought the fragment yet," he said in the chilly voice he ordinarily reserved for students who asked awkward questions. The implication that he was going to acquire the Aelian Fragment as a lark distressed him, but of course, as he had had to remind himself before, the Princess did not understand the cool passion of the collector, which is quite different from the emotionalism of the simple thrill-seeker. "And I doubt that the Turkish government knows it exists—or cares."

"Oh, you're such a *stick,* Sam!" *Stick.* His ex-wife had used the same word, along with others that the Princess certainly knew, but that she ordinarily suppressed with all the other vestiges of Hoxton. "Do be a little excited about it, ducks. Allow the rest of us poor humans to believe that *something* matters to you!" Her tone was mocking, but under it was a hint of real feeling. He changed the subject.

They parted fifteen minutes later. They planned to meet again in six days at Antalya on the Turkish Riviera.

In four hours Teck was in Izmir. He had not forgotten the Princess—they had been lovers for only two weeks, after all—but he was able to file her away for the time being and thus prevent his being distracted while he did the thing that had brought him back to Turkey.

For two hundred yards along the seawall, the fishermen of Izmir line the quay as fishermen have, no doubt, for as long as there has been a wall there. Even the heat of the Turkish summer does not stop them, and for three hours on each side of the high tide they are there, wiry, muscled men with a leanness dictated by their diet, which is not learned from books, but from necessity. They are certainly not sportsmen—not "anglers"—but professionals for whom a place on the quay is the difference between life and starvation, and every day they take their places there, each man separated from the next by a spacing of almost mathematical precision, the space needed to whirl a heavily weighted line around a man's head before launching it out into the bay. The weights are half a pound or more, to hold the tackle on the bottom against the tidal pull; the hooks are big enough to hold a tuna, or a shark, or a man.

Teck kept to the shoreward side of the road, away from the whirling hooks. An occasional car passed between him and the fishermen. One car had to swerve almost to the sidewalk, and the driver turned in his seat to shout at the fisherman, his face contorted.

It was hot. In the interior it would be a hundred and twenty degrees; here on the coast it was in the nineties. And not one of the really hot days.

Teck regretted the necktie he had foolishly decided to wear.

He worked the knot loose as he walked, then slid the tie around the right side of his neck until it pulled loose and he could fold it into a fat bundle that would fit into the side pocket of his coat.

He stopped to shoot several pictures of the fishermen and the quay, wishing that he had brought a telephoto lens from the hotel.

Tomorrow. They would still be there tomorrow. And he was not really there to take pictures, although it was a convincing cover.

In the bay, freighters sat as stolidly on the water as if they were rooted to the bottom. Closer in, a brightly painted skiff chugged parallel to the quay, leaving behind in the still water a *V* so regular that it might have been a zipper opened in some soft, unwrinkled fabric. Teck took a picture. Idly, he thought how it might be captioned: *In the seafaring tradition of their Greek and Trojan ancestors, today's Izmir boatmen. . . .*

He heard a hoarse cry from the end of the quay. A fisherman had stepped back from the edge of the wall and was braced with his right arm extended toward the water; on each side of him his neighbors had turned to shout their encouragement. Teck trotted up the quay, stopping twice to shoot pictures.

When he was close enough to fill the frame with the fisherman's head and torso, the young man was pulling hard and his heavy line angled down into the water close to the quay. As he gained line, he wrapped it around his left arm from palm to bent elbow as Teck had watched women wrap clothesline in his childhood. This was very direct fishing, without any of the niceties of a more affluent world—no flexible rod to tire the fish, no reel to let it run against a controlled resistance—and the fisherman sweated heavily as he brought his prize in, his straining forearms like anatomical models of muscles and veins. Tech shot, focused, shot again, moved in still closer; the fisherman, noticing him, turned once and grinned quickly, then moved forward to the very edge of the stone seawall and bent down to lift the fish from the water to the stones at his feet.

The fish had a curious, almost pointed snout and vicious teeth. Blood seeped from the gill cover and Teck knew that the hook was lodged deep inside.

Deftly, the young fisherman spun the fish so that the top of its head was under his right hand, and then he pushed a sharpened screwdriver down through its brain.

"What kind of fish is it?" Teck asked.

"Kind?" The young man smiled happily. He had large, very white teeth and a melodramatic mustache.

"Yes, what kind of fish?"

"Is—" The young man's English was almost as limited as Teck's Turkish.

"Is—animal, you say—" He snarled, then barked.

"Dog?"

"No dog, is— No, is—" The young man put back his head and howled.

"Wolf."

"Yes! Wolffish, yes. Wolffish." He seemed extravagantly happy as he took a knife from his belt and slit the fish from vent to chin with a single long stroke that let the insides spill out like the contents of an overfilled suitcase.

"Can you eat this fish? The wolffish?"

But the young man had misunderstood. "Oh, eat, yes, he eat everything, this wolffish. Look!" And with another motion he groped among the fish's entrails and came up with the stomach, which he slit carefully; then he picked among the contents with the knife's tip. Teck recognized a whole silvery fish like a smelt, a piece of crabshell the size of a silver dollar, some large fish scales. The rest was unrecognizable.

"I meant—do *you* eat this fish?"

The fisherman answered as he finished slitting the jaw to free his line. "Oh, yes, very good. Wolffish is good." He put the knife down on a bloody stone. "Did you make that knife?"

"Yes, very good knife. Sharp." He retrieved his hook from the fish's gullet and laid it beside the knife. To Teck, it was more interesting than the knife—homemade, too, but of a type that would have been recognizable on the Danube or in the Baltic a thousand years earlier.

Teck spoke as he focused. "Did you make this hook?"

"Ah, yes. Me." He smiled again. "Very good, yes?" He pantomimed swinging a hammer, but Teck already knew that he had hand forged it on a charcoal fire; Teck could probably have told him more about the process than he knew himself.

"I'd like to borrow your hook."

The young fisherman severed the fish's head and threw it into the water.

"When you're through fishing? So I can take photos and measure it? I am a scholar—a specialist in old things."

"Pictures, okay."

He bent over the fish again, working with his knife on the pectoral fins. Teck backed away a step so that he could photograph the process, not because he wanted such a picture but because he did not want to lose contact with the man. "I'll pay you." He focused. He heard a curious, fluttering sound over his head, as if a bird had flown very close. "Could I pay you?" He backed away another step, crab-walking, crouched. The strange buzz came again, very close this time, and he ducked. When he looked up, the fisherman was frowning. Suddenly the fisherman swept his hand away from his chest.

"Go! Go away!"

Teck turned. Another fisherman had moved down toward him; his whirling tackle was passing the harbor end of its circle and continuing back toward the quay, toward Teck, and he scrambled into the road as the heavy weight and the big hook passed through the place where he had been.

Then the young fisherman shouted angrily at the newcomer and Teck saw two men get up from a café across the road and start toward them. The man with the whirling tackle called out something, of which Teck caught only the word "American." The men from the café were coming straight toward him, and they were scowling.

It was not like the old days. Not at all like those days before the Cyprus invasion when being an American was reason enough to be welcome.

"Go away!"

The young fisherman was trying to warn him off.

Teck would have turned away then, but suddenly there was a commotion fifty yards away and everyone's attention focused on an old man in a dark beret who was straining against his line. He turned sideways to it and tried to pull from that position, and the men on each side of him grasped the line and began to pull.

The two in the road gave Teck up with a scowl. Men from both ends of the quay were running, even the young fisherman.

Teck hesitated. Then, because the atmosphere of menace had dissipated, he started toward the excited group at the other end of the quay.

When he reached the fringe of the crowd, whatever was attached to the old man's line was almost at the surface.

Teck's camera came up. He focused on the water where the heavy line met it.

A white belly rolled under the water. *Flatfish,* Teck thought.

Just as it reached the surface he tripped the shutter, an automatic response that had nothing to do with what he saw.

He advanced the film and put the camera to his eye again.

He knew what he had seen in the instant before the shutter had tripped and the reflex mirror had blotted his vision.

It was a body, a human body, with the fishhook fastened in the left calf so that the leg came up first. The legs were spread apart and the head and torso hung downward in the water.

He had thought it a woman because of a raw place in the groin.

Now, looking again through the viewfinder as the body rose almost lazily to the surface, floated briefly, then started slowly to sink again until the men pulled on the line and the left leg lifted it, he saw that it had been a man. The scrotum had been cut away.

The shutter tripped.

Teck thought of the wolffish, of its predator's teeth and the unrecognizable mess in its stomach.

"American!"

The two men who had started toward him earlier were pushing their way out of the crowd. Other heads were turning and there was a murmur of angry voices.

The young fisherman who had caught the wolffish came at Teck from the side, striking him stiff-armed with his open palm so that Teck stumbled into the road.

"You go away!" The young man spat. The others slowed, content to let him handle it.

Teck was turned around by the shoulders and pushed across the road. The young fisherman hustled him to the sidewalk. His grip did not relax, but he put his lips to Teck's left ear and whispered. "Friend, okay? Okay? You know Gol Café? You go Gol Café, five o'clock, I bring hook. Okay? You pay, yes?" And without waiting for an answer he shoved Teck forward so that he stumbled and fell to his right knee, swinging sideways to protect the camera as he fell.

"Go away, American!"

The fabric was shredded where his knee had hit the stone

and there was blood on the skin that showed through the hole. Teck's face was a dull flush of red as he hobbled past the café. If there had not been an overriding reason for his being in Turkey, he would have returned to his hotel then and packed, because he could not abide being made a fool of. "You're a stick. A dirty little snob," his ex-wife had said.

An old man with no front teeth laughed at him.

It was not at all like the university, where the graduate students did not dare to laugh at him. (Teck refused to teach undergraduates.)

At the first street, he turned away from the harbor and headed into the city along the route by which Ataturk's army had fought its way to the port fifty years before. In the mass deaths of that battle, the body that had been hauled to the surface by the old fisherman would have gone unnoticed. The victorious rebels under Ataturk, driving on the city, its Greek inhabitants and its fleeing Greek army, had used heavy artillery, then mortars and machine guns, then bayonets and rifle butts and clubs and knives and bare hands. The harbor then had been littered with bodies—male, female, old, young—and the scavenger fish had grown fat. One mutilated body among so many would not have been worth turning a head for.

Teck passed a Russian tractor outlet where a huge banner hung over the showroom door. Inside were a single tractor and a great many farm implements scattered seemingly at random like a slovenly workman's tools. Farther along, a French appliance showroom and an English heavy machinery display seemed similarly understocked, but all carried large flags and signs. It was the week of the International Trade Fair.

Teck stopped to let a very young boy polish his shoes. His knee still hurt when he raised the foot to the brightly polished shoestand. He snarled at the boy when he asked some question in Turkish, and Teck, thinking of the old man's laughter, did not give the boy a tip.

When he turned into the bazaar, Teck put his necktie on again and knotted it with the help of a shop window. He crossed the intersection that divides the fresh produce stalls from the meats and fishes, then turned down a little covered alley and came out its far end into another street lined on both sides with jewelry shops. He went on, almost to the end of the bazaar, then plunged down three steps into the rank cool of a narrow passage between two buildings and came suddenly into a small square surrounded by curio shops.

On the right-hand side, Ashir Parduk's shop seemed barely able to squeeze a doorway between its two neighbors, but Teck knew that it was actually a T-shaped place that ran between and behind the others, and that its proprietor, Parduk, was their landlord. The falsely modest entrance was part of Parduk's approach to marketing; it did not pay to advertise. Not in his business.

Teck crossed the oppressive sunlight of the little square and, stepping around a display of brasses, pushed through the strings of plastic Italian beads that hung over Parduk's doorway. The motion set a little bell ringing. An instant later, a small, pale face appeared at the end of the narrow shop aisle.

"Yes?"

Teck smiled and moved forward.

"Mr. Parduk, it's Samuel Teck. We've been corresponding."

Parduk's face screwed itself up into a frown and then suddenly became bland and smiling.

"Of course. Mr. Teck, how very nice. Of course!"

But Teck had the distinct feeling that Parduk would have greatly preferred that it be somebody else.

Chapter two

IN a glossy apartment in one of the new buildings on Ankara's Çanakkale Street, an American-made air conditioner clattered in a window, the bent blade of one fan banging the vent on each revolution. Given the shortage of technicians, it was simply the sort of thing that one learned to bear.

As a wag from Aramco had said, the apartment was furnished in global bad taste—bright plastic French pieces, an Iranian carpet, some Turkish brasses, an American stereo-television in an anomalous Spanish console—and yet everything had carried a high pricetag, and so everything was suited to its owner. And it suited him the more because he had not paid those high prices, at least not in money, but had accepted everything as a "gift" for such little favors as he could perform.

Dignified and handsome, he faced an American visitor across a low glass-and-chrome table. They chatted of the hot summer, of the American's duties at his embassy. They sipped sweet coffee.

After thirty minutes the American rose and apologized for having to leave. His host was desolated but resigned to the loss. They parted.

On the glass-and-chrome table, the American left the keys to a new Chevrolet Impala. The car itself was parked in the garage under the building.

He walked a block to a rank of public telephones and selected one in the middle.

"Good morning, the Embassy of the United States of America, may I help you?"

"This is Mr. Burrell. Could I have my office, please?"

"Oh, yes, Mr. Burrell."

A near-silence, bordered with wisps of other conversation.

"Cultural Affairs, Miss Kerrigan speaking."

"Sally, it's Phil."

"Yes, sir, good morning."

Her voice cool and almost bored, giving no hint that they had been sleeping together for six weeks.

"Messages?"

A brief silence, a rustle of paper.

"Yes, there was a call about that literary matter. That literary acquisition you were hoping for?"

"Yes, I understand."

"Please call the author's agent at once."

He hung up, deposited another coin, and dialed. The call was answered in Turkish.

"You have some news for me about that literary property?"

"Yes, I think I have. There is a very strong rumor that it has reached Izmir. There are also rumors that there will be an attempt to suppress it."

"Is it moving?"

"Not just at this time, I believe. There has been some difficulty. One of the, ah, the preliminary readers has been found —in the bay, I understand."

"Thank you."

Burrell hung up. The news was not unexpected, but it

meant he might have to change his schedule. He was supposed to go into the mountains the next day with a shooting party that would include some valuable government contacts; that evening he had to visit two informants and a minor official in the Ministry of Defense. He would have to prepare to leave for Izmir on short notice.

"Greek. Nineteenth century."

Parduk spoke almost contemptuously of the object Teck was holding, a small metal box with an embossed cover showing Saint George conquering a rather flaccid dragon. "It's not even *that* old," Teck said unkindly.

Parduk shrugged and his little mustache twitched. "Before Ataturk, all right? Then, if you say before Ataturk, you might as well say before 1900. To many foreigners such, ah, antiquity makes a piece attractive." He smiled wryly, as if he and Teck shared a concept of antiquity that was incomprehensible to the casual tourist—and, indeed, their common interest was in an object well over a millennium old.

Parduk sighed. "However, it is such items as these that the government lets us sell abroad, you know. Even the Ministry of Export do not regard this as a national treasure." He sighed again. "Last week a Swedish tourist was held at Yesilkoy for possessing in her handbag a piece of funerary brass that I *know* was made by an old man near Ephesus within the last two years, because I gave him the pattern. Of course, it was a very good copy."

Teck tried to look sympathetic. "Not worth going to jail for."

"Oh, well—Turkish jails!" Parduk laughed and raised his eyebrows comically. Parduk, as Teck knew, was a resident alien who called himself a Levantine. He was one of a shrinking group of seemingly rootless merchants whose families had moved about the Near East, keeping ahead of revolution and invasion when they could, always seeking the country with the hardest currency and the most forgiving social system. Teck had first met the man five years before. He thought Parduk was a Jew, although this had never been confirmed and he had never tried to check it. It was certainly nothing he might hold against the man (as, for example, he most certainly held their Semitism against the three Jews in his academic department).

He looked around the shop. It had changed little in five years, although much of the stock was new, and some of it depressingly poor stuff, suggesting that Parduk had begun the slide toward mere touristic knickknacks.

"The world market has changed," Parduk said as if he had guessed Teck's thought. "Now, it has to be gold—anything gold. Or genuine antiquities, of course, but the new regime make it quite impossible to deal in them. Legally. May I offer you tea?"

He led the way to the back without waiting for Teck's answer, and Teck sucked in his belly to slide between a brass coffee set and a carved armchair, before ducking under an eighteenth-century censer that Parduk, who was barely more than five feet tall, avoided without effort. They passed through a doorway into a combined office and bachelor studio. Like so much of Parduk's life, the room was partly illusion: Teck had been told that Parduk was married and lived in a house nearby. The narrow cot against the wall, the little pantry that lay beyond the far doorway, were like the false patina put on a fake art object by one of the local artisans.

"Do you have the Aelian Fragment?" Teck said. He could never hold himself in check long enough to match the slow, almost ritualistic pace of this sort of negotiation. He perversely prided himself on his impatience, as if it were a mark of his caste, like his faint New England accent and his doctorate.

"Let me get us some tea." Parduk smiled. He vanished into the pantry. Teck heard the unmistakable sound of a refrigerator door opening and then closing, and a few seconds later its motor began to hum quietly. A dish clinked. Parduk's footsteps shuffled and the refrigerator opened and closed again.

Parduk's head appeared among the plastic beads.

"I remember your love of fishing, Mr. Teck. I have something that might amuse you. In the brown paper parcel there."

On an octagonal inlaid table in the middle of the room was a flat package wrapped in a coarse, flecked paper the color of dark mustard. Teck cut the elastic cord that bound it and folded back the heavy paper. Inside was a carved and painted slab of wood the size of a small headstone. Four round scars at the corners had once been covered by round brass bosses, Teck knew; he recognized the carved and gilded bas relief columns, the delicate tracery of gold leaves and flowers against a sea-green background. It was decadent Gothic work, not a copy, not a fake, but the pedestrian and well-meaning craftsmanship of a workman who had inherited a style that had no meaning for him, and in which he had no capacity to delight or surprise.

The thing itself was one of a pair of covers for a large manuscript book. He found the dark marks of leather hinges on the edge.

Teck sat down in a low armchair and propped the cover on his knee as he set about translating the Latin inscription on the center panel.

When Parduk returned with a brass tray, Teck was smiling ironically at the book cover.

"An interesting piece, Mr. Teck?"

Teck raised a fleck of paint from one edge with a fingernail. He put the book cover down and said curtly, "Not exactly a national treasure."

Parduk shrugged. Teck saw him glance at a clock on a far wall. "I have a permit to export it from Turkey, if you are interested in it. Tea?"

"Thank you." Parduk put a glass of dark tea next to him and began to spoon thin, almost liquid yogurt into another glass. "Perhaps you don't like our yogurt. One never knows. Americans do drink yogurt, I'm told, but flavored—like a sweet." He smiled and paused, the spoon hovering over the glass, and he appeared about to speak when there was a noise in the square outside—a barking dog, a man shouting—and he dropped the spoon and ran into the shop with a suddenness that was disturbing. Teck's impression of nervousness was greatly strengthened. Yet, when Parduk came back a minute later, he was as bland as before and took up the spooning of the yogurt where he had left off.

"Will you try some?"

"Thank you."

"There is honey."

"No, thank you."

It was refrigerator-cold and very tart.

"Delicious."

Parduk smiled. "And do you admire the book cover?"

Teck put down the yogurt glass. "Actually, Mr. Parduk, I'd like to talk about the—"

"It's an interesting piece, the book cover. You saw the fish in the design?" Parduk spread his hands slightly, palms up, almost in apology or supplication. "Fish are quite a rare motif. Mr. Teck. Very rare. I think rarity is more important than age, don't you?"

Teck put his fingers together and studied them with great concentration. "About the Aelian Fragment, Mr. Parduk. I have come a long way, all the way from Rome, just to—"

"Of course! I understand, Mr. Teck." Parduk sighed and looked miserable. "I am unhappy. *Very* unhappy. I do not have it."

"You said you'd have it on the nineteenth!"

"I did have it. The man from Anatolia who brought it went home again. He said he missed his family." He spread his hands again apologetically. "Actually, he's an opium buyer and he has to make his rounds. He will return in four days."

"But the fragment!"

"He has it; it is safe with him. I saw it. It is exactly as offered; the illumination is more beautiful than described, I can assure you; the three paintings of the fishermen are incomparable! Within my experience, of course."

"Byzantine?"

"Unquestionably. Certainly earlier than one thousand A.D. But, of course, I leave that to your expertise."

Despite himself, Teck smiled. He thought of the sensation he would make with such a find; perhaps "sensation" was the wrong word for an upheaval in a field where only a few hundred people worked, but within that tiny sphere it would make him famous. Once he had taken it out of Turkey, of course.

"When can I see it?"

"The man is very concerned. He is afraid that if you are—pardon me—if it is taken out of the country illegally and found out, it will be traced back to him, his opium business—you understand." Parduk looked more unhappy than ever, but when Teck was supposed not to be looking, he glanced again at the wall clock and frowned.

"Money?"

Parduk hesitated, his head tilted as if to listen to a sound from the shop rather than to Teck. Then, as if forcing himself to concentrate, he looked at Teck and said, "I beg your pardon?"

"Does he want more money?"

"Ah, well, I tried to reassure him. That you would give him a good price. But such people are suspicious, they—" Parduk stopped, his head again tilted, birdlike. His movements were usually smooth; now he jumped up and made a jerky exit into the shop. "Excuse me!" He was gone.

Teck followed quietly as far as the doorway.

The shop owner was standing, talking to an old man with his back to Teck. When Parduk moved, Teck had a glimpse of the old man's sparse white stubble and red-rimmed, almost weepy eyes; then the two were close together again and he could see nothing more.

When Parduk returned from the shop, Teck was sitting in the low chair again and he seemed to be studying the book cover.

"I am very sorry"—Parduk began drinking his tea—"an astonishing breach of manners, Mr. Teck. Please forgive me." When he put the glass down, his hand was trembling. His face seemed pale and there was an unhealthy sheen of sweat under his eyes. "I have had, ah—some—I have had a piece of news."

Teck stood up. "Maybe I'd better go—"

"No!" The voice was loud. Then, more softly, "No, please, I am a little—" He stroked his mustache between his right thumb and forefinger to hide his trembling mouth, which wanted to twist and droop into an expression of despair. "I have had a piece of news," he said again.

"I'm sorry."

"A death." Parduk stopped stroking his mustache and sat back a little, evidently under more control now. He looked at Teck. "Death," he said again absently, but his mind was on something else and he was studying Teck appraisingly.

On the quay, the fishermen and the men from the café were held back from the corpse by five uniformed policemen. The crowd was very quiet. Death was an unwelcome visitor at best, a tourist from a country with no hard currency to spend. Some of the men had seen death in Cyprus, and a few had seen it in Korea, but none was pleased to meet it again.

Inside the quiet ring, Inspector Esmen Arkadi of the Izmir police stood fifteen feet from the corpse, which was now covered by a gray blanket. His eyes remained fixed on it, although he was listening attentively to the old fisherman who had first hauled the body up. Hatless and in plain clothes, Arkadi did not look so much like a policeman as like some harried executive, some decent and responsible man whose face had been eroded into deep lines by the collapsing state of things. He was thirty-seven and he looked ten years older.

"That's all there is to tell, mister, that's all. I just pulled it up. I don't know it's a body until I see it. I know it isn't a fish because it's like a stone but sometimes we hook, you know, tires and things dropped over from ships—sometimes just by accident, you know, no contraband, I swear—but a corpse, I don't know—"

Arkadi waved the man to silence. He instructed a plain-clothes officer to take his statement and then moved to the corpse.

"Finished?" he said to the photographer, who was taking a picture of the soles of the feet.

"In a minute, in a minute," the man said irritably, trying to squint through a Nikon with his chin almost on the stones of the quay. When he had taken the picture he glanced up and, recognizing Arkadi, he apologized. The inspector said nothing.

"I'm done now, Inspector," the photographer said. "I didn't know it was you, sir, I truly didn't."

Arkadi bent to look at the bleached, water-wrinkled feet. When he glanced up at the photographer, the man knelt quickly next to him.

"Who told you to shoot the feet?"

After a pause the man said miserably, "Nobody, I guess. I thought it was a good idea." He looked around, as if for support.

Arkadi grasped the left foot just above the toes. He bent it down to the left so that the underside of the arch was exposed. "Did you get that?" He pointed to a discoloration inside the arch.

"Yes, sir. That's why I took the photograph."

Arkadi nodded. He pulled the gray cloth away from the legs and knelt to look at the groin.

"Whoever did it was in a hurry," a voice said above him. It was a sergeant from Violent Crimes. He bent down so that his face was close to Arkadi's. "This looks the worst, but they worked on the face—cut up the lips with some kind of tool, wire cutters or big scissors, I'd say. The, uh, the anus is torn up, too."

Arkadi kept his voice low. "You saw the feet? Beaten with a club of some kind, I'd say."

"I missed that." The sergeant cleared his throat loudly. "They'll find it all in medical, anyway." Arkadi did not point out that the sergeant should have seen it and that sometimes waiting for medical reports cost critical time.

The sergeant tried to seem helpful. "Are you interested in this body, Inspector?"

Arkadi shrugged. "There have been rumors for a week of something big coming through. From the East. And with the Trade Fair, everybody's nervous. Can you send me a copy of your report as soon as it's ready?"

The sergeant, who was older than Arkadi and would probably never rise above his present rank, frowned. He was reluctant to make any commitment to another department without approval from above. There was no point in telling him that his very timidity was one of the things that would keep him in grade.

"I'll go through channels," Arkadi said crisply. That would be time lost, of course; perhaps it was better to give in and resort to personal favors and contacts like everyone else.

"Cover it up," he said, and started to turn away; and then, remembering that it was really not his case, he told the sergeant that he was done and the body could be covered when he was through. The sergeant told someone else to cover it, his voice too loud and inexplicably annoyed.

At the edge of the crowd, a witness was telling a policeman about an American who had watched the finding of the body and who had taken a suspicious number of photographs.

"*Please* sit down again, Mr. Teck. The Aelian Fragment *will* be yours, I promise you that. Please. I know I have failed you; I do not have the fragment, but"—he held up a finger significantly—"but, I do have a tracing for your study. Your evaluation."

"Of the entire work?"

"No, I am sorry; of several panels, Mr. Teck." Parduk opened a cupboard in the wall behind Teck and reached in. He moved very quickly now. "There." He put a folded piece of paper in front of Teck. "The present owner allowed the tracing of only four panels."

"Did you study the original?"

"Studied, no, but I saw it—a glorious thing, Mr. Teck! Colors of such vibrancy! And the delineation—see for yourself on the tracing; note the similarity to the mosaics. Of course you will see that without my telling you. . . ."

Teck opened the folded paper. It was brittle but thin enough to trace through. One glance told him that it could have been traced from the fragment, a ninth-century, illustrated copy of Aelian's *De Animalium Natura.* Thirty-two leaves were in the Vatican Library, but until now the section on fishing had been lost. *Until I found it,* Teck thought. He gloated. What had he thought this morning? The "cool passion of the collector"? His heart raced and he knew it was an avarice as strong as any other.

"If authentic this would be the oldest illustration of fishing with the artificial fly in the world." His voice was steady.

"If you judge from the tracings that it is worth the risk, the man from Anatolia will bring the fragment here for your study—for a thousand dollars in advance."

Teck was about to object to the amount, but he was saying to himself, *I must have it; I must have it.*

"When?"

The telephone rang.

The conversation was very short and almost entirely one-sided. Parduk spoke a few words at the beginning, and then nothing more. Teck wanted to study the tracing further, but he found his gaze returning to the little man by the telephone who was so clearly receiving more bad news.

When he had hung up, Teck said, "Can I expect to see the fragment in four days?" When Parduk did not answer, he added, "I'll bring the thousand dollars, of course."

"What? Oh, yes, of course. A thousand. . . ." Parduk glanced at his watch. "In four days," he whispered. "Of course." He bolted into the pantry; the refrigerator door opened, and then, as abruptly as he had left, he was back with a black packet in one hand.

"I want to show you something, Mr. Teck. A fantastic find. You will never have such an opportunity again!" Now, his hands were trembling for a certainty and his voice was rising in pitch; he was becoming hysterical. Teck had the distasteful feeling that he was looking on at another man's nervous collapse.

"No one has ever seen such a thing before. This is—Mr. Teck, I insist you attend to this—this a most rare, a tremendous—no, a unique—" The hands tore at the black plastic wrapping, tried to unknot the string; something like a sob burbled up when the knot refused to loosen, and he clutched the string in both hands and snapped it feverishly.

"There! Such—an event, you an American—will understand—its importance; I will let you have it, Mr. Teck—almost *give* it to you—" The voice was pleading and demoralized. The rank odor of sweat struck Teck's nostrils when Parduk moved closer to him. "*Look* at what I have! Look. Do you know what this is?" He held up an inch-thick pile of small pages no larger than a paperback book, covered with small, precise writing.

"It's a manuscript, I take it."

"Yes!" Parduk giggled. "And what a manuscript! Look at it!"

Teck looked. "It's Cyrillic, isn't it? I'm afraid I don't read it."

"Russian. It's Russian." Parduk seemed to be panting. "It's stolen, I don't mind saying that, let's be frank between the two of us because you know what kind of business I'm in, what business I've been driven to, God forgive me! It was got out of Russia illegally, but you understand that is all right, yes? I mean, the author lives in the West now."

"Is it about fishing?"

"It's by Vladimir Nabokov!" Parduk almost screamed. He sounded as if he wanted to call Teck an idiot.

"Well, I'm afraid that wouldn't be my field. You see—"

"An unpublished Nabokov!" Parduk moved between Teck and the door. "Untranslated, maybe the author himself has forgotten it, but the importance—you're an educated man. Mr. Teck, you must understand, yes? It is your *duty* to take this manuscript."

"I really have to go—"

"*Look* at it!" His finger, the nail polished but not lacquered, the manicured tip as neat as a woman's, followed a line of small letters on the topmost page. "*The-Snow-Is-Black*-by—" He paused. "Well, it is Nabokov's name, but he used a different name, I mean a familial, a variation. It was long ago. In

Russia. You do understand?" He looked at Teck, his forehead shiny with perspiration, his breath coming shallowly. "*Black Snow* by Nabokov? You don't think that's a find?"

"Is it a novel?" Teck began to turn the pieces of thin, shiny paper, like pieces of cheap hotel toilet paper.

"Yes, a novel." Parduk swallowed. "About a young girl, adored by an older man—you know the theme, yes? Very, very sensual, once thought obscene—Girodias in Paris would give a fortune for this—"

Teck looked at the page. Down the left-hand margin, heavily underlined, were short groups of characters; opposite them were what looked like brief verse paragraphs.

"But this looks like a list. And verse."

"Yes, it is. A list. Lists. Yes." Parduk looked at the clock. "The protagonist compares his beloved to a—to butterflies. He makes lists of her body. The parts of her body. He gives each a butterfly name. Erotic, and—Nabokov loves butterflies, you know. It is most ingenious. Artistic."

They looked at each other.

"Take it on approval, Mr. Teck."

Teck stacked the pages neatly together.

"I'm afraid I'm not interested. You'll get a good price from somebody who appreciates that sort of thing. I wouldn't know what to do with it."

He expected Parduk to argue, to wheedle and cajole as he might when a deal needed pressure, but he merely shrugged and began wrapping the thin pages in their plastic covering again. His body sagged and his voice seemed faint.

"It is a rule among—among people like me, Mr. Teck; one must know when there is no hope. I am very sorry for imposing on you." He became calmer. "But as a good Levantine merchant, I must sell you *something!*" He turned a false grin to Teck, upon whom it had the effect of a death's-head. "My Swedish refrigerator, perhaps! No? My yogurt glasses? No? Ah, the book cover, Mr. Teck! Can't I sell you my lovely Gothic book cover?"

The man's disintegration annoyed Teck and he wanted to be out of the place as quickly as possible. He looked at the book cover again. Perhaps his sister would like it as a gift, something to hang in the "music nook" with her musical daughter's recorder and her musical husband's viola da gamba. He said he would buy it for twenty-five dollars.

Parduk beamed. "I'll wrap it up for you."

"No, no, please—"

"I insist."

"Mr. Parduk—"

"The paint chips so easily; only a moment."

So Teck waited, at first in the room where they had had tea and then in the shop, going desultorily through the mediocrities that filled the cramped space, wondering how many of the wretched things Parduk would ever sell.

Outside the beaded curtains, the far side of the square was in shadow and a single figure leaned in a doorway there, escaping the sunlight. Teck paid no attention to him. He was thinking of the Aelian Fragment.

"Your package, Mr. Teck."

Parduk slipped the bundle under his arm. He had padded the book cover heavily with cardboard and then wrapped and tied it.

"It *will* go through customs?"

"Oh, *yes!*" Parduk sounded almost hurt at the suggestion that the export license was invalid. "There is the form. See?" He pointed to the yellow paper.

"And your man will be here in four days with the fragment."

"Yes, and you will be here with one thousand dollars."

They shook hands. "I'm at the Turisti Pallas," Teck said. He felt expansive. "I'm sorry about the Nabokov thing, Parduk."

The shop owner shrugged. "Nothing, nothing at all. I will find another buyer. I always do. We will laugh about it, you and I." He giggled to show how they would laugh. "*The Snow Is Black.*" He giggled again. "It will be our joke—our password, how is that, eh? *The Snow Is Black.* You will hear that whispered in your ear one day, and you will think of me, eh?" He whispered the last words in a throaty croak and both men laughed uncomfortably.

Teck hurried away from the shop with the bundle clutched under his right arm, but when he had gone a hundred yards he became acutely conscious of the ovenlike heat and the sweat soaking into his shirt where the book cover pressed against his side. He slowed, then stopped to rest in the shadow of a wall.

He tried to keep on the shady side of the streets as he made his way out of the bazaar and up toward the center of the city, where the young fisherman with the handmade fishhook was to meet him.

He walked very slowly, too hot and too absorbed in pleasant daydreams of owning the Aelian Fragment to notice that he was being followed.

Chapter three

OUTSIDE Washington, D.C., set discreetly back from the ring highway that circles that traffic-strangled city, is a large and handsome building. Its architecture is like the faces of its principal occupants, bland and characterless; given a neon sign, it might be a very large motel. The lack of distinction, however, serves it well.

On the third floor, two men sat in a corner office, the set of their heads and the expressions of their faces expressing the roles they played—one deferential, polite, the other brusque and dominant.

The superior spoke. "Now let me get this straight. We inherited this project *in toto*, isn't that right? I mean, it's going to be clear upstairs that we aren't responsible for it? Except in stage managing?"

"Yes, I'd think that was accurate, sir."

"When did the manuscript come over?"

"Well, we think last week, last Wednesday to be exact—" The younger man consulted a notebook no larger than a deck of playing cards. "Probably in the mountains near Kagizman."

"Y-e-e-s. Well. Of course, it may go through without a hitch, just turn up somewhere and we'll be home free. But just in case, you know, in case of—"

"—something going wrong, yes, sir—"

"—right, I want it clear this was not, repeat not, our creation. For instance, in your progress report, you could say, uh, 'The *Book of the Dead* Project, uh—"

"—originated by Mr. So-and-so in nineteen, uh, well whatever it was, I'll have to check, sir—"

"Yes, that would be good. In passing, as it were, just kiss the fact that we didn't create it, right?"

"Yes, sir."
"Who's the local honcho there?"
"Well—our Ankara man—Phillip Burrell."
"He was in on it from the beginning?"
"I believe so, yes, sir."
The older man looked warily at a small painting on the wall. "What d'you make of Burrell?"
The younger man glanced at the notebook, not because he needed to study the data there, but because he wanted to give the appearance of careful deliberation. "One of the hard-line spooks, sir. Cold warrior, flags flying, black bag whenever you can."
"Mmmm." He studied the painting again. "I don't think it would be smart for us to get too closely associated with him, Ken."
"No, sir."
"Keep him at a distance. A loose rein. If he's going to get cute, let it be on his head, not on ours."

Samuel Coffin Teck was, at forty-one, a successful academic and an unhappy man. He was acutely aware of his success and almost arrogantly pleased with it; he was less aware of his unhappiness, which he identified as a treasonable feeling of self-disappointment, associated most often with moments of remembering his ex-wife's desertion. Born in Newburyport, Massachusetts, the city of John Marquand and Towle silver, once one of the great ports of the East Coast and still one of the finest federal cities in the country—he had spent much of his life in a restless migration, as if groping for some green happiness that had escaped him or that he had missed by some accident of history. His father, just before his death, had warned Teck that he was turning into "a three-year man," an Ishmael who could stay no longer in one place than that.

He had gone to college in Boston, to graduate school in California; he had worked for a year in the Northwest and spent three years in the Navy in Rhode Island, Virginia, Florida, and Turkey. He had put in one year with a New York advertising agency before surrendering to his education and entering academic life, which had taken him to the Midwest, down to Arizona, and south to Kentucky before his father died. That death had left him with a house in Newburyport and a permanent income, and at forty-one he was envied by his colleagues for his financial independence, his lack of a wife, and his small museum of privately, sometimes illicitly, collected artifacts.

Now, walking up Vasifcinar Bulrari on a hot day in Izmir, he seemed professorial still, a lone, somewhat introverted man whose eyes were focused on a point in the distance as if he were still searching for permanence. Two inches under six feet, with a layer of subcutaneous fat around his middle that showed only when he wore bathing trunks—knowing of the bulge, he never appeared at beach or pool—he still seemed younger than he really was, perhaps because he had kept his hair or because he was unencumbered and restless.

Teck strode along by a featureless wall that gave its small blessing of shade to a scant foot of sidewalk. Behind that wall in the old days, female convicts had worked out their prison time as prostitutes; now, it was deserted. In their absence, the New Turkey was considering legalizing prostitution, since without the prison brothels free-lance whores had sprung up like shoots in spring.

But Teck was not thinking of such matters. Rather, he was nagged by recurring thoughts of the mutilated corpse he had seen in the harbor, the vivid memory of it coming unbidden as if it had an independent and vigorous life in his brain. He thought, too, of Parduk's odd behavior, the man's near-hysteria and his nervousness.

Ahead of him, an arched gateway into the Culture Park was achingly sunlit. In front of it was a little square where, during a visit in his Navy days, three thieves had been publicly hanged from portable gallows and their bodies left as examples to others; Teck wondered idly how many of those who had seen them were now thieves themselves, or worse. Where the temptation to break the law was sufficient, no deterrent seemed to function. (Teck was thinking of lower-class Turks, of course, not of genteel Americans like himself.)

He turned into the park and sought the shade of the trees there, heading off on a path he thought he remembered. The cinder surface crunched underfoot, the black, glassy lumps hot under his shoe soles. The hoofprints of a single horse went on ahead of him. For thirty yards there was no shade and he could feel the sun shriveling his face and throat, feel it like a weight on his eyelids. The package under his arm was leaden. When he had crossed the bright space and rounded a curve in the path, he stepped to the grassy edge to rest himself against a tree, and it was in that interval of weary silence that he heard other footsteps on the cinders behind him. They stopped abruptly, as they might have if someone had stopped to listen, and Teck's heart pounded. He realized that whoever it was must be standing in the open, sunlit stretch, and he was aware of voices off to his left and the grind of traffic in a street not far away. The path ahead of him seemed to close down into a green tunnel, and the place looked suddenly sinister.

Teck stepped softly back along the route he had come, keeping on the silent grass, and after he rounded the curve he confronted, at a distance of twenty feet, a young man with no tie and a soiled, limp jacket, a fiercely frowning young man who looked not unlike some of Teck's students.

"Did you want something?" Teck said sternly; it would have been ridiculous to have turned and run, futile to have stood there and simply stared.

The man hesitated for one, two, three full seconds, breathing heavily as if he were winded or frightened, and then he turned and hurried away.

Teck could not be certain that he had been followed. The very opposite might be true—that the young man thought that he, Teck, was somehow threatening him! The possibility made Teck smile, but to be safe he turned away from the path along a paved track and walked quickly toward the sound of voices. He passed the buildings of the Trade Fair, where workmen were finishing displays. Several people stared vacantly at him. His fear evaporated.

The Gol Café was a teahouse sited on an island in the middle of an artificial lake, reached by a ridiculous bridge that seemed to have been inspired by a comic-opera idea of the Orient. Teck crossed over it and sat at one of the outdoor tables, shaded by a large umbrella whose stripes of green and yellow had faded to the colors of dried grass.

"Tea, please." The elderly waiter flicked a cloth across the table; dried buds from a nearby tree fell to the ground. The waiter asked him something in Turkish, but he did not understand.

"Just tea." *What was the word? "Cay."*

The waiter gazed sadly over his head at the lake, where a bird flicked across the water and dipped into it once to pick up an insect, leaving a widening circle as if a fish had risen there.

Then he moved away among the other tables, going slowly from table to table, flicking his cloth and straightening chairs that were not crooked.

Half an hour later, when a dark mass came between his table and the sky, Teck still had not touched the tea.

"I come." Teck turned quickly, startled. "This day—before—with fish, I—fishhook, yes? Fishhook?"

Teck stood up quickly. His head struck the edge of the awning, which was tilted down on his own side of the table. "Of course, I remember; I was thinking of something else. Sit down, please. Sit down." He gestured at a chair.

"Okay." The fisherman smiled and sat down as obediently as a child.

"My name is Samuel Teck." Teck put his hand out.

"Ah." The fisherman stood up again. His hand came forward. "Hakail, Sayid."

"Yes, how do you do?" Teck sat down. "I'm sorry—is Hakail your last name? Would I say Mr. Hakail?"

The young man laughed. "Yes, Mr. Hakail. Very good, very good!" His open hand hit the table with a loud slap, and the waiter appeared from the teahouse. "Very good, yes?" Teck smiled. "I bring hook." The young man took a newspaper-wrapped bundle from his pocket, and, when he had finished ordering from the waiter, unwrapped it to reveal the hand-made hook, a crudely cast lead weight, and about ten feet of line the size of sash cord.

"You pay, yes?"

"Yes, I said I would. Fifty liras."

"To buy?"

"No, no; I just want to borrow it to photograph."

Hakail looked at Teck's camera.

"Here?"

"No, not here. I don't have the right lens. I need a—" How could he explain what a macro lens was? He gave it up. "I can't do it here."

"Okay." Hakail grinned and folded the money Teck had given him. The waiter put down a glass of tea and a small plate of hard pastries. "You eat. Eat." Teck took one and bit into it; Hakail happily devoured three while Teck was nibbling at the first, a dry, crumbly biscuit that might have been stale and that tasted oily.

"What happened—" Teck began, and then he paused to

search for a word; there seemed to be no politic way of putting it, so he plunged ahead. "What happened to the body in the harbor?"

"I don't understand."

"The body. The dead man that was pulled in."

Hakail was silent. He looked at his fishhook. "No good," he said softly, seeming to speak of the hook. "No good, that thing."

"Did the police come?"

"Police? Oh, yes, take him away, those police. No good, no good."

Teck leaned forward. "Did they find out who the body, uh, was? Had been?" But Hakail shook his head slowly.

"No good."

"Sorry." Teck leaned back. "How will I get your hook back to you?"

"Tomorrow, okay, bring to place where I fish, yes?"

"Fine. What time?"

Hakail's grin flashed again. "All day. I work hard all day."

He asked without embarrassment if Teck would photograph him, and then he posed as vainly as an actor in rather stilted poses against the backdrop of the lake. He was a handsome man, with something of the late Nasser about his nose and eyes; when Teck mentioned this, he laughed with delight.

Then Teck would have said good-bye, but when he looked up from closing the camera case, he saw two men at the far end of the silly bridge that led to the island. One of them was the man whom he had confronted on the path. Hakail saw the men and frowned.

"Do you know them?" Teck asked. He lowered his voice as if he feared being overheard.

"No good," Hakail murmured. "No good."

The second man started across the bridge.

"Who is he?"

But Hakail said nothing. He made a low humming sound that seemed as if it must end in speech, but it did not and he bit his lower lip and shook his head quickly.

"Waiter!" Teck's voice sounded shrill. He thought of Parduk's hysterical behavior. "Waiter!" Because he wanted to seem casual and because he felt giddy, he sat down.

Hakail popped another of the pastries into his mouth and watched the newcomer pass in front of the teahouse, stopping the old waiter in his tracks with a hand laid against his chest. When he was fifteen feet away, he began a rapid monologue that swung to include Hakail for an even faster, snarling finish. He pressed against the table opposite Teck, the metal edge pushed into the fabric of his trousers just where the seams of the fly ended.

Hakail talked quickly, standing straight and not flinching. When Hakail finished, the newcomer said something and Hakail translated for Teck.

"He says you got something that comes from his friend."

Teck looked at the standing man. He was wide across the shoulders and his belly bulged against his shirt. His shaven head thrust forward on a thick neck.

"Tell him I don't have anything belonging to him."

Hakail spoke. The man answered angrily and his left arm pointed at the bridge as he turned to look and shout at his companion there. When the distant man saw the gesture, he turned away.

"He says you got something from a Parduk, his friend there came behind you from this Parduk's."

"Tell him I have only what is mine."

But before Hakail could speak, the man had reached down to the right side of Teck's chair where the book cover, still in its heavy wrappings, leaned. The fingers closed over the edge of the package, but when he tried to lift it Teck kept his own right arm rigid so that his weight came on the package, and to lift it the man would have had to lift him, as well. They glared at each other for some seconds, their eyes not eighteen inches apart, their hands almost touching.

"Tell him this is mine!"

Hakail translated.

The other man stared into Teck's eyes. Then, as if a decision had been made between them, he let go of the package and stood up straight. His right hand went into his coat pocket as he spoke, more quietly now, to Hakail.

"He say—he want—ah—to look inside this thing there."

It was a humiliating situation, precisely the sort that Teck went to great lengths to avoid. The best solution might well be to give the fellow the package, simply hand it over to him and abandon the book cover that he hadn't really wanted, anyway. Only a hope of humiliating the bully by proving that there was nothing in the package stopped him.

"All right."

The man thumped the metal table with the knuckles of his left hand so that it boomed like a badly tuned drum. Teck laid the package flat between them.

The other's right hand came from his pocket, holding a clasp knife that he opened with great deliberation. He cut the string that bound the package.

"Tell him I'll do it!" Teck shouted shrilly. "Tell him he'll have to pay if it's damaged! It's a gift for my sister!"

Still seated, Teck brushed the man's hand away and parted the brown paper on the top of the package. Under it was a layer of single-faced corrugated cardboard that he pushed to one side; under that, in turn, was a sheet of a thin, stiff board that protected the painted surface of the book cover. He lifted it away, dropping it next to him on the gravel, and with his left hand began to raise the book cover, using its lower edge as a pivot.

His right hand was on the table, holding back the curling corrugated cardboard and the wrapping paper.

When the book cover had been raised to a forty-five-degree angle, Teck hesitated. He could see the undecorated back of the cover, which should have a blank surface of oiled wood.

Instead, he was looing at a black plastic packet that Parduk had fastened there with two strips of tape, which, even as he watched, began to pull away from the wood. Abruptly, the top strio gave way entirely so that the plastic packet swung down like a drawbridge. Then, so slowly that Teck felt he was watching a film, the bottom strip peeled away from left to right and the packet swung lower, angling sideways as it went, and at last it gave up the last corner and fell to the wrapping paper behind the cover.

"What does your friend at the bridge think of this?" Teck's voice was strident and his gesture was so vigorous that it hid the shaking of his hand; together, voice and pointing arm succeeded in making both Hakail and the other man glance toward the bridge. In that instant of distraction, the fingers of Teck's right hand spread over the black packet and pulled it toward him, whispering over the wrapping paper. It shot from the table, still with his hand atop it, to smack down on his left thigh; he slid it forward toward his left knee. The hand came away as the knee rose and pressed the contraband against the underside of the table, exactly as Teck's father, who had loved to cheat at cards if there was no money involved, had taught him to hide a palmed ace.

To hold the packet there, Teck had to prop his left foot on his right instep and extend the toe like a dancer's.

"Well?" His eyes had not left the other man's face.

The bald man grasped the book cover and spun it out of Teck's hand. He examined it, painted surface and plain, and looked along the four edges, then handed it to Hakail, who took it and stood awkwardly by the table. Hastily at first, and then with more care, the man went through the wrappings until he seemed satisfied that what he was searching for was not there. He examined the string that had bound the package and threw it down in disgust.

"Tell him I told the truth and will he please go away."

Hakail translated. The bald man thrust his head forward with his lower lips stuck out and gave some order, but Teck stared directly at him, his arms folded and his chair tilted back, carefully maintaining the contact between his left knee, the packet, and the tabletop.

"He says, your coat. Take off your coat."

But there was a low whistle from the bridge, and the bald man turned to see the young man signaling from the end of the bridge and a group of five people crossing to the island. He hesitated and then closed the knife by pressing the back of the blade against his right hip. He and Teck looked at each other until, with a low rumble of words, he turned and walked quickly away.

"What did he say?"

"He say you are a rich American, uh, son-of-a-bitch—gangster."

Clumsily, Hakail tried to rewrap the book cover, but Teck did it himself without getting up. When he had finished, he reached under the table with his left hand, while with his right he put the package on its edge in his lap; he moved the packet into the protection of the book cover and slipped it inside his jacket and tucked it into the right side of his trousers over the hipbone.

Hakail walked with him to the edge of the Culture Park, where they shook hands and Teck promised to return the fishhook the next morning. There was a taxi stand with three cabs, and Teck, fearing a rebuke from the first driver, got into the second in the line; but the driver was delighted with his choice and he shouted happy abuse at the others as they pulled out into the street.

In the safety of the cab, Teck removed the plastic packet. He opened it far enough to see that the sheets were those he had seen at Parduk's earlier in the day.

Parduk had enclosed one of his regular invoices, a square slip of paper with a legend at the top in Turkish. Below it he had written, "Original MS, V. Nabokov, *The Snow Is Black.* Hold until called for."

Chapter four

TECK'S hotel, the Turisti Pallas, was some blocks from the center of the city among a group of nondescript waterfront buildings. It was most certainly not first-class, and yet Teck liked it, had liked it since he had been billeted there by the Navy years before. He liked it enough to have written about it in a travel article for a popular magazine. Accompanying that article had been a color photograph of the proprietor, Mr. Haydan Hamdar, standing in the doorway of his closet-sized office behind his minuscule registration desk. That picture was now thumbtacked to the front of the desk next to postcards from former guests in Norway and Germany, and Teck was treated as a privileged guest who was given a room with a private bath (one of two in the hotel) and a casement window opening on a view of the harbor. He was fed the best lamb and fish and frequent free drinks in hopes that someday he would write another article.

As usual, Hamdar was behind his desk, frowning.

"Do you have a safe, Mr. Hamdar?"

"What do I need a safe for?"

"I want to lock something up."

"There are many things *I'd* like to lock up, most of them people and one that GODDAMN CAT!" Hamdar's voice rose ferociously as he took a swat at the gigantic yellow cat that had taken up residence in the hotel and was now poised, tail straight up and back end pointed at a potted plant, ready to spray; seeing Hamdar, it darted under a couch.

"What d'you want to lock up?" Hamdar had spent a good part of his life on Cyprus, where the British had taught him a colloquial, sometimes blasphemous English.

"It's, uh, something private."

"Of course, I understand, my dear man, it's your business." He leaned on the reception desk. "I have a strongbox in the office, but it isn't a safe, and confidentially I wouldn't leave anything valuable in it myself. The hotel is like a sieve; I've had three thefts in the last year. Not that it's unsafe, of course!" He smiled reassuringly. "I don't get many guests with the royal jewels, you understand. Yes, nice kitty." The yellow cat, which had successfully sprayed the couch, was now leaning against Hamdar's chest while he stroked its back. "Yes, kitty-kitty. Umm, yes. The best place is the bank, but it's closed."

"Yes, of course." Teck took his upper lip between his front teeth and chewed worriedly. "Could you make a telephone call for me?"

"Of course. Within Izmir City, a nominal charge."

"It's a shop in the bazaar—curios and antiques. Parduk, Ashir Parduk. I don't think it's got a name. Just A. Parduk."

But when Hamdar had found the number and tried to call it, he was forced to tell Teck that the line seemed to be out of order, because he had called twice and asked an operator to check it; and because Teck looked so worried and his hand shook very slightly as he stood there with the large package under his arm, with the knee torn on his trousers and his face flushed from the heat, Hamdar offered to send "the boy," a tiny sixty-year-old man.

"That might be a good idea," Teck said slowly.

"You wish to write a message?"

"Uh, no, no, I—" *What? What do I want to say? Take back your damned manuscript before I'm set upon in the park or in a dark alley?* "No, just tell him that I hope, uh, I hope to hear from him tomorrow."

Hamdar passed this vague message on to the ancient boy, and then he offered to serve Teck a free *raki* of a specially fine brand that only he, Hamdar, in all of Izmir could offer; and was Mr. Teck writing another article about Turkey? So Teck found himself slumped in a chair in the colorless restaurant sipping an anise *raki* and wondering dully why he felt so utterly drained.

"You have been taking photographs?" Hamdar nodded at the camera.

"Yes. I'm working on a book."

"About Turkey?"

"Oh—well, in part. But very ancient Turkey and Greece, you know—some of the very early idylls—"

Hamdar looked distressed because there was no way such a book could help his hotel.

"I was taking photos down along the quay today when they brought a body up." Teck finished the *raki*. "Terrible thing."

"Interesting." Hamdar did not sound very interested. He had confided to Teck that, what with one thing and another, in running a hotel a man saw just about everything, and he was seldom interested in novelties anymore.

"It had been mutilated. With a knife, I think." Teck's face sagged. "Or maybe it was the fish."

"Some sailor. Come ashore, get drunk, go back and cut each other up. Last year two Russians cut each other up so bad they both died." He poured Teck more *raki* and added water to the glass. "When I lived on Cyprus somebody on a ship cut a fellow into pieces—you know, at all the joints—and threw the pieces over for the fish. But they caught him anyway. He'd kept one finger for a souvenir."

Teck rubbed his head. He felt a little sick. When he stood up he listed slightly to the right.

"You won't wait for the boy? Maybe he's got a message for you. Finish your *raki*."

Teck remembered that he had had no lunch. When he told Hamdar this, the man professed to be desolated that Teck had been in his hotel for so long without eating, and he began to put food on the small table: cold spaghetti from the prix fixe lunch; thin bread; cold, mashed beans; and even most of a kebab of lamb with peppers and tomato. Teck was convinced he could not eat, but found he was ravenous, and the food made him feel almost instantly better. He had finished the kebab and was well into another *raki* when the boy returned from the bazaar. After a subdued conversation Hamdar walked slowly to Teck's table, rubbing his bristly chin with one stubby hand. "The boy has been to the bazaar, you know."

"Yes?"

"He says there has been this fire. Your Parduk's shop, it is all burned up, you see."

Teck sat very still with his fork poised over the plate. After a moment he put the fork down slowly and leaned back, blowing out his cheeks in a hiss of frustration.

"Mr. Parduk, he is burned up, too, the boy thinks."

"They're determined to turn me into a bagman, that's all they want me to be—a diplomatic bagman!" Phillip Burrell ground a cigarette into the already littered ashtray.

"That part of it is important, Phil."

"It's a waste of my time. It's not using my skills to their best advantage." Burrell tapped a folded sheet of paper on the edge of the desk.

"I shouldn't have to spend my time running around bribing Senators and third assistant defense secretaries."

"You're supposed to go shooting with the ambassador tomorrow."

"I know, I know."

"It would be *good* for you, Phil."

He frowned. The idea seemed to surprise him. "No, it wouldn't," he said unhappily.

"There should be a report to Wash—"

"I *know*, Sally, I really do know!"

She bent her head in apology. "I only meant that the new people in Washington are—you know. Antsy."

Burrell lit another cigarette. Indeed, he knew exactly how the new people in Washington were, although he had never met them. *Gutless* would have been his word. *Gutless technocrats.* "All right, send them a cable. Tell them about the burning of the Izmir shop. I think *The Book of the Dead* got that far but I'm not sure. And tell them it's paramount that I go to Izmir personally and not off on some cockamamie bird-hunting trip with the ambassador, who can't hit an elephant with a machine gun."

"Shall I say that?" She smiled at her poor joke.

"No." He did not laugh. "Just make it clear that I've got to go to Izmir personally or a very valuable project is going to go down the drain. Okay?"

She smiled and nodded. "I'll let you see the cable after I've drafted it."

"Right." He leaned forward and touched her hand. "You're good for me, Sally." Deep creases had formed between his eyes. He touched her hand again. "Tonight?"

"Yes, Phil." She gently pulled her hand away and left the office. She would draft the cable and he would approve it. Later, after he had left the office, she would draft another cable, reporting on his condition and his attitude.

Burrell was aware that she probably sent reports on him; he would have thought the Agency lax if she had not. In an odd way it made him feel closer to her. To be sure, he did not want to feel *too* close, to "care" for her—caring might lessen his objectivity if ever the need arose—but he was glad for the limited closeness they shared.

He had cared for a woman once (his wife), but she was dead. He had cared for his son, but his son had grown up and they had never been close after the boy had reached adolescence.

He was sure that he had cared for an idea once upon a time. He must have. The idea had been something about a principle and about the United States; now it came down to the banalities of getting a job done. Like his son, the idea had grown up or changed, leaving behind it only the job, as his son had left behind a few photographs and an old toy. He was a little bitter about the idea, as he was a little bitter about his wife's death and his son's growing up. Most of the time he hid his bitterness well.

Anyway, he could still talk as if the idea remained. That seemed sufficient. And he continued to do his job because that was about all there was left.

There were two windows in Teck's hotel room, one looking over a truck storage shed, and the other looking directly over the harbor, whose waters lapped at the very base of the hotel. Under this window, because it let in no direct sunlight to cast harsh shadows, Teck had made a crude photocopying setup. His camera, now equipped with a motor drive and a macro lens, was mounted on a tripod. Directly below it on the floor a suitcase made a crude stand. On top of it were two sheets of white typing paper and the Russian manuscript. Teck focused carefully on the black Cyrillic characters.

Teck's mind was pleasingly clear, despite the *raki* he was still drinking. Indeed, perhaps it was the *raki* that had allowed him to shake off the depression that the news of the fire had brought on and to analyze his problem. *If Parduk is dead,* he had begun, *how will I get the Aelian Fragment now?* He had thought of trying to reach Parduk's wife, but common sense told him that it was the wrong time, that he would only be hurting his own cause. *Or even if Parduk is alive, what will the burning of the shop mean?*

There were 197 sheets in the manuscript.

The camera was loaded with thirty-six exposure rolls of fine-grained color film.

It took him twenty-three minutes, with the camera cycling at four-second intervals, to photograph the entire manuscript on six rolls of film.

Long before he finished, he had reached a conclusion: *If this manuscript was so valuable to Parduk, it is valuable enough to get me the Aelian Fragment.* He suspected that it was even valuable enough to get him the fragment without paying the exorbitant price that had been asked.

When he had finished, he replaced the partially exposed roll on which he had taken the pictures of the quay and of the fisherman. He wound it forward past the exposed frames and shot four pictures of Hakail's fishhook.

He tucked the Russian manuscript into the waistband of his undershorts and buckled his belt tightly over the packet, and, with the six rolls of film in mailing envelopes, walked down the single flight of stairs to the small lobby.

"Could the boy run an errand to the post office for me?"

"Yes, I think, Mr. Teck, if he's not busy." Hamdar glanced at a wall clock that hung behind him. "Just about time for him to get there, just about, although—" Hamdar's right hand hovered in the air like a bird and rocked from side to side. "It will be a near thing."

But with the mailing envelopes and some of Teck's money in his hand, the boy seemed sure that he could reach the post office in time. He left the hotel at a trot; if he got there before the post office closed, the film would arrive at the Agfa-Gevaert laboratory in Turin in two or three days. After processing, it would go to the Princess' apartment in Rome. It would give Teck a useful backup to the manuscript itself, if, for one reason or another, he lost it.

Chapter five

IN Leningrad the long summer twilight had kept people abroad later than usual, as if the cloudless evening were something so valuable it was to be marked with a vigil. Even in the blocks of government flats in the suburbs, birds still sang and people chatted quietly by open windows.

Valeri Seriakin had timed his journey to the meeting place with habitual precision. His walking pace was now moderated so that he would arrive precisely on time. Although his thick body and heavy thighs seemed better suited for weight lifting, he was an almost compulsive walker who could chew up miles of ground with his long stride. He had once thought of going into competition walking seriously, but his father had told him to concentrate on his language study and forget sports, especially one that looked ridiculous and that nobody cared about, anyway.

Seriakin brooded as he walked. He did not think of himself as an introspective man, and certainly not as one who walked in order to think, as some men seemed to do. This evening, however, he had finally admitted to himself that he was tired of the woman with whom he was having an affair, and he was brooding over a way out of it, over his own duplicity in wanting to find a way out of it. *An affair?* A lifetime, rather; they had been lovers longer than many couples had been married.

In the next street a child wailed, and Seriakin sighed lugubriously. He had thought of marrying the woman, of having children around him, as recently as a month ago.

He walked on. In four minutes he would be there.

Across the street a woman was leaning in an open window with her folded arms on the sill. It was too dark to see her face, but she was humming to herself and the clear voice sounded young. A man's voice came from behind her, but she did not pause in her song. Seriakin sighed again. As he passed, he turned to look at her and found that her head was turned toward him. When he swung in at the entrance to a block of apartments, he paused on the steps and looked back. A light had gone on in the room behind her and she was still there, silhouetted now. He raised his hand a little, a gesture that was a form of acknowledgment, but not an insistent one; he saw her toss her head back, and for a moment the side of her face was illuminated. Perhaps she would still be there when he came out.

He knocked at apartment seven.

There was no sound, but after several seconds the door opened and the man whom he had come to meet stood in the doorway.

"Valeri Alexeevich!" The old man embraced him, and Seriakin was pleased and a little embarrassed, as he would have been if his father had lived to greet him with such effusiveness. "Come in, my boy, come in!" Repin laughed and slapped his shoulder. "You look good, Valeri—strong, not too intelligent; the women must worship you!" His deep laughter boomed out again, but there were no answering echoes, for the soundproofed walls absorbed it. There was thick plastic foam underfoot and, covering the walls, an oddly feminine insulation of vivid pink. Except for a long table and five chairs, the apartment was unfurnished.

Repin picked up a light overcoat. He carried the coat despite the weather, perhaps because it was an expensive one with a London label. "Let's go next door, my boy; it's much more comfortable." He linked his arm through Seriakin's and led him back the way they had just come. "You don't say much for yourself, Valeri."

"I'm glad to see you, sir," the younger man said shyly.

The deep laugh turned into an indulgent chuckle as Repin squeezed his arm. He became serious and said, "I am sorry about your father."

"He suffered a great deal." Seriakin had not meant to say anything like that; he usually tried to keep sympathy at arm's length. "He wanted to die at home, he begged me to let him—one night he asked for his pistol—but the pain was so great they had to put him in hospital, under sedation, always sedated. The last coherent thing I heard him say was—oh, you know, about my future. He always worried about me. Not about himself, not enough. For a while they had him on a British treatment for terminal cases—LSD, I think."

Repin closed the door and steered Seriakin down the corridor. "Cancer is terrible, terrible, my boy." He hesitated for a moment. "But many things are terrible. Things he and I saw together, you know. In China we saw things that I wouldn't have believed. Barbarians, the Chinese." They had reached the door of the next apartment. Repin took out a ring of keys and went through them one-handed, his other arm still linked in Seriakin's. "Do you ever read Malraux? He brings it all back. Terrible things." Repin pushed the door open and let Seriakin go in first. "We'll be much more comfortable in here."

The apartment was the architectural twin to the one they had just left. It had been furnished in a consciously opulent style that offended Seriakin. Every upholstered object seemed swollen, as if stuffed beyond any dictate of sense or taste; every fabric was too shiny or too deeply piled; the reds were the purple reds of blood and roses, the pinks the pinks of corals. From the doorway it looked like the insides of something alive. It was a KGB "observation" site, used mostly for the attempted entrapment and blackmail of foreign visitors, who were led to believe that it was a conveniently available rendezvous for convenient affairs with convenient Russian men and women. Next door were listening devices and tape machines. Seriakin's father had been fond of this kind of operation in his later years, and Repin, too, he knew, thought such Graustarkian tactics valuable. To Seriakin, they never seemed to justify the enormous amounts of human energy that went into them.

"I met you next door, Valeri, so that you would see for yourself we were not being overheard." Repin smiled. "I did not want to make you tense." His laughter boomed, faded, rose again as he looked at Seriakin and saw the young man's faint uncertainty. "You are so serious, Valeri! So serious! Ever since you were able to wipe your own bottom." Repin dropped into a pink satin sofa whose soft pillows rose up on each side like water wings. "There is whiskey in the cupboard under the window. Scotch for me."

As he took out two glasses and the bottle, Seriakin asked conversationally, "How is Moscow?"

Repin grunted eloquently. He had never tried to conceal his dislike of Moscow. Repin was a Georgian who had survived several changes of leadership by being, in part, as brash and outspoken as possible, as if the very abrasiveness of his manner were a guarantee of his honesty and fidelity. It was certainly true, Seriakin knew, that he was a ruthless Stalinist who had never really espoused what he had once called the "anti-Stalin fad."

"And Derzhinsky Square?"

"Overcrowded and overbusy, as always. Many people, all making work for each other and none of them accomplishing anything." Repin took the glass, which Seriakin had filled to the brim as in the old days when Repin would visit them. "To your father's memory, my boy. A good man, a dear man." They drank. "A dear, dear man." Repin sighed. He held out his empty glass and Seriakin took it to the liquor cupboard. While he was turned away, Repin put a seemingly innocent question. "How do you like Leningrad, Valeri?"

Seriakin tried to sound casual. "I like it well enough."

"But not in love with it, eh?"

"I prefer Moscow. But we always prefer the place where we were children, perhaps."

"Then you wouldn't object to a temporary post someplace else? As a form of—vacation, as it were. You've been under quite a strain, with your father's illness and all that. Eh?"

Seriakin made a slight sidewise bob with his head, a seemingly grudging admission that the older man was right. In fact he disliked Leningrad and he had thought of asking for a transfer but had put it off, knowing that his immediate superior would mark such a request against him on his fitness report. And he had not wanted it to seem that he had been waiting only for his father's death to make a move.

"How is the work in Disinformation going?"

Seriakin shrugged. "Détente makes some things easier."

"Détente!" Repin smiled cynically. "You make me laugh. Wait until you're my age and see what a word like détente means." Repin finished his second glass of whiskey. "Want to know why we are meeting here and not in your office or someplace else?"

"I'm sure you'll tell me when and if I need to know."

Repin scowled at him and struggled to his feet from the spongy pink mass around him. "Don't use that pious-young-subordinate-to-senior-officer pig manure with me, Valeri. Your father would puke to hear it." He made his way to the liquor cupboard, and with the bottle raised to pour, he stopped and guffawed. "Do you remember the first woman you ever had, Valeri?"

Seriakin did not look at him. Conversation so often came around to sex, the inevitable subject of these once-great old men.

"You are blushing, Valeri! It offends you that Repin should talk of sex, doesn't it? Because the old fool is almost seventy, his cock should have shriveled up, and dropped off, is that it? Well, I remember *my* first woman!" He put his head back and crowed, and the neck of the bottle rang against the glass. "She must have been sixteen, a couple of years older than me. One of those plump girls with little tits like new potatoes, but my God! what legs. It was right here in Leningrad, you see; we had come from Georgia because my father had work here. Out in a field, it was—it was all fields out here then, none of these stupid flats. Maybe, Valeri—maybe it was *right here!* " He stamped on the floor hard, stamped his heavy foot three times so that the glass in the window rattled. "Right down there where the cellar is now, fifty-four years ago, Alexi Grigorovich Repin gave up his virginity!" He raised his glass and drank, still laughing, and choked. Some of the expensive whiskey ran down his suitcoat. He brushed it clumsily with his left hand and wiped the hand on his trousers. Repin was beginning to seem drunk, but Seriakin knew his capacity and knew that the drunkenness was part of his public mask.

"Maybe—maybe, Valeri," he said, dropping his left arm heavily on Seriakin's shoulders, "maybe that is why I have brought you here—to commemorate the loss of my virginity with the loss of yours. Eh?" He hugged Seriakin's shoulders. "Not sexually, my dear boy, but professionally. It's time you came out, so to speak." Repin let go and returned to the pink sofa. "I understand you have a mistress?"

"Well, I—"

"Would you mind leaving her for a while?"

Seriakin hesitated a second too long.

"Ah, so it's like that! Which is it—can't live without her or can't wait to get rid of her?"

Seriakin flushed. "I've decided to break with her."

"Good! Perfect, my boy, couldn't be better! I see it now, just how we'll do it; young Seriakin is tired of his mistress, goes over his superior's head to his father's old friend, the Georgian boor Repin, who pulls strings and gets him an assignment in Turkey. Couldn't be better."

Seriakin filled his own glass. "All my experience is in Scandinavia."

"What experience?" Repin could be brutal. "What experience have you had? Sitting on your ass dreaming up disinformation fantasies! God, you sound like a petty bureaucrat. When I was your age, your father and I were already in Indochina, sabotaging the godamn French, interrogating, living with dysentery—you know, I had to wear a woman's hygienic device, for their period, you know, for three weeks once, the way my bowels ran. Experience!"

Angrily, Seriakin muttered, "Times have changed."

Repin was frighteningly still. "So they tell me," he said slowly. The two men looked at each other in silence until Seriakin lowered his eyes. "I'm sorry," he said simply.

"You must learn, Valeri, that there are times when you must be your own man, and times when you must shut up even if it means biting your tongue out. Anyway, consider it forgotten." Repin stretched his legs out in front of him. "What do you know about Stepan Zhevadze?"

"The writer?"

Repin nodded.

"A poet, a historian of sorts, a Moslem—thought to be a dissident. Gave himself a pseudonym that was something about a horse."

"Yomut. After the stallions they breed in the Kara Kum." Repin's eyes were almost closed. "The Turkman tribes are very fond of their horses. Anything else?"

Seriakin sipped his whiskey. "Well, there's the rumor of something he wrote. We hear of it even up here. Rumors of a list of Moslems who have died in the camps."

"The Book of the Dead."

"That's right." Seriakin was on his own territory now, dealing with the truths and the rumors that filtered across the borders. "We had a report that a publisher in Stockholm was trying to get the manuscript; this was a year or so after Yomut's death. But nothing came of it. All we heard was that Yomut had hidden the manuscript before he died, and that the intellectuals were passing around bits and pieces, and it was mostly smoke and no fire."

"The manuscript left the Soviet Union last Wednesday." Repin gazed gloomily down into the remaining half-inch of whiskey. "It surfaced again this morning in Izmir, Turkey. We thought we had it there, but something went wrong. Now, it has either been burned to ashes, or it is in the hands of someone who will try to get it out of Turkey." His shoulders rose high and then fell as he exhaled a great sigh. "There's reason to believe that Israeli intelligence is active in getting the thing to the West." He passed his right hand over his forehead wearily. "You must know, Valeri, as the child of a KGB official, what goes on in the organization. Rivalries, personal dislike, distrust—you've heard about it all. I hope you have, anyway. You can't be as naïve as you seem. Just at this time it is essential to get *The Book of the Dead* back, but it is also essential that it be done without using the regular people. And very, very tactfully. And that is the real reason that we are meeting in this ridiculous whorehouse."

"Does the secretary know?"

Repin nodded.

"You want me to go to Izmir." Repin nodded again. "My Turkish is rusty. But I could get by; I was going to be posted to a Turkish desk originally, until my father—until I asked to stay with my father."

"Your Turkish will be fine, Valeri. Anyway, you will have plenty of help from the Free Turkey Youth. Finding the manuscript is vital; once found, it has to be recovered. If we are quick, you will find it, bang, and that will be that. If it drags on—well, you know. Your cover is intentionally transparent: you will be going as Scandinavian translator with our delegation to the Trade Fair. Everybody will understand, of course, that you are a KGB overseer; that's the idea, you see. Our own people and the Turks and all the rest expect us to send somebody—but nobody, not even our own people, will assume you're there for the manuscript. You should have about three days' leeway before somebody smells a rat."

"Three days! You could move a book manuscript around the world in a few hours."

"True, if there were no obstacles. But in this case there are obstacles. The Israelis, as I said, want it. The PLO have been working very hard to suppress it; I believe they tortured and killed one Israeli agent already. Some private parties seem to want it for the money it might bring. And the Americans are after it—your greatest obstacle, Valeri. Détente or no détente, watch out for the Americans."

"All right. Three days."

"If you don't have it by then, well, it will be in Washington or Paris or London and some Western publisher will have a new best seller on his hands. And some throats will be slit in Moscow, including mine and yours, my boy."

Then Repin gave him the details of the situation and his means of making contact in Izmir and of reporting. They each had another drink, and when, an hour later, they walked out into the warm night, Seriakin felt slightly wobbly. It was dark now and there were few lights showing.

On the steps of the drab apartment building Repin took his arm.

"My very first, Valeri—right here! Legs like two birch trees!"

He laughed softly.

Seriakin looked up the street where he had seen the woman earlier, but the light was out and she was gone.

Chapter six

IN his room again, Samuel Teck sat for an hour by the open window, his chin resting on the intertwined fingers of both hands, his eyes focused on the distant water. Beside him, yet another glass murky with *raki* (his fifth) was half empty. He was mulling his action in having photographed the Russian manuscript. It surprised him a little, his decision to use it as a lever to acquire the Aelian Fragment.

And yet. And yet, he had never come so close to stealing something before. Oh, to be sure, he had taken a small Olmec figure out of Mexico in the trunk of his car, and he had bought an Asian piece from a Vietnam veteran who would not explain how he had got it. But he had never stolen anything himself. Yet.

And, going beyond the immediate cause for his action, he saw another reason for his behavior: *Because it excited me.* This surprised him a little, too. *And because I am afraid.*

He sighed and rubbed his hands on his trouser legs as if they were sweaty from work. He poured another inch of yellow *raki* into the glass and filled it almost to the top with tap water so that the urine-colored liquid turned milky gray, and with this in his right hand he stood by the bureau, sipping and turning slowly the pages of the curious manuscript that had been forced upon him.

Was Parduk burned for this?

He sipped.

He sipped again, and turned a page, and sipped. *Of course, it's something more than a Nabokov.* When the glass was empty, he filled it again and took a sheet of onionskin paper from his attaché case, noting without surprise that he stumbled against the bed in crossing the room, and he laboriously traced the title of the manuscript (that was supposed to say *The Snow Is Black*).

After that he showered quickly and put on another suit, one without a torn knee in the trouser leg. It was almost dark when he went downstairs with the manuscript again belted into his middle. In the dining room he practiced reproducing the tracing he had made of the Cyrillic characters, writing them again and again until he could do it by rote, a line of meaningless characters in a language he did not understand.

At the end of the meal, Hamdar stopped at his table for a sympathetic word about the state of the hotel business. He hoped that the Trade Fair would help, but he never dared expect too much. "I have two reservations," he said gloomily, "Israelis. Just my luck." He sighed and started after the yellow cat, which was licking the plates on a table that had just been vacated.

It was quite dark when Teck returned to his room. He was more than a little drunk, and he was nervous about where to hide the manuscript.

He rolled the manuscript into a tight cylinder and then wrapped it in the plastic bag that had covered one of his shirts. He taped the bag shut with electrician's tape from his camera bag. The cylinder then went into the heavier black plastic in which the manuscript had arrived, and this, too, was taped. Finally, he put the whole business into yet another shirt bag and tied it up tightly with the stout line that Hakail had given him with the fishhook. Hakail's lead weight was tied in just above the plastic-sealed cylinder; at the other end of the line he tied and then taped an empty film cassette.

With the lights out, he might have been standing at his window to look at the lights of the harbor, pinpoints of bright yellow and blue lengthened into ribbons by their watery reflections. Yet his arm moved, and something dropped toward the water, arcing slightly to land fifty feet out from the hotel wall. It sank immediately. The film can, buoyed by its captive air, rode at the end of its short line a dozen feet below the surface.

Teck stripped. It was a great relief to lie down. He thought of pleasant things that would allow him to sleep: a favorite trout stream, the Princess, and, most of all, the Aelian Fragment, its outline in the tracing filled with glorious colors. He smiled and slept.

He was not waked immediately by the knocking at his door. It had been going on for some seconds before he was conscious, and then he was disoriented. Then he heard, and remembered; he thought of the manuscript, and his putting it into the bay seemed an act of insanity, a drunken folly, and his stomach twisted up with tension.

"Just a minute."

When he stood up his knees were rubbery. According to the clock he had been asleep less than an hour.

Teck pulled on a pair of trousers and carefully opened the door.

It was Hamdar.

"I'm very sorry, Professor Teck," he said. He was embarrassed. "It's the police here, you know?"

He stepped aside for a dark man in a too-tight suit. Teck was taller than the man by several inches, but he felt like a naughty child facing a stern adult.

"I am Inspector Arkadi of the Izmir Police Central." He flipped open a clear plastic wallet; Teck saw a blur of light-blue cardboard with black lettering, and then the identification disappeared. Teck, holding up his trousers with both hands, was embarrassed and frightened.

Inspector Arkadi was grim.

"I am very, very sorry, Professor Teck. It is quite late, I know—forgive me, but I had no idea you would be asleep; it is not yet eleven o'clock—but this is a most unusual event. I am very weary myself." He made a grimace. "May I ask you a few questions?"

Teck looked over his shoulder at Hamdar, whose heavy eyebrows were raised in an expression of resigned cynicism. His cheeks were puffed out and he blew out his breath in short, audible puffs that sounded a little like reproving tut-tuts. When his eyes met Teck's, he raised his shoulders in a shrug, hands still in his pockets, and nodded almost imperceptibly.

Another man in a tight suit stood next to Hamdar.

"Uh—couldn't this wait until morning?"

"I will take a *very* short time, Professor Teck. Besides, I dislike taking you to Police Central tomorrow, making you wait, and so on."

If there was a threat, it was so delicately implied that Teck could have no reason to complain of it.

"Come in."

Inspector Arkadi rapped out something in Turkish with a jerk of his head, and the other man disappeared. Arkadi stepped in and Teck slowly closed the door on Hamdar's disapproval.

"I'm sorry I'm, uh, not very, uh, presentable, Inspector."

The policeman held up a hand that dismissed all etiquette. He was one of those supremely self-confident small men who never realize that they are small and who, being unaware themselves, are able to make others forget their stature. His glare, from under raised eyebrows, the head tilted downward as if he were looking over the tops of eyeglasses, announced quite clearly that he was accustomed to being listened to and obeyed. Teck found himself fearing the man.

"When did you arrive in Turkey, Professor Teck?"

"Yesterday. Today. The nineteenth."

"Where did you enter Turkey?"

"Uh, Istanbul."

"Yesilkoy Airport? Yes. And then you flew to Izmir?"

"Yes."

"Directly?"

"Yes."

"Do you know a Parduk, Ashir?"

Teck's heart pounded. Inadvertently, he glanced at the window that looked over the harbor.

"Uh, well, I've been to his shop. In the bazaar."

"Parduk is dead."

"Oh. Oh, dear."

"He was burned to death in a very tragic fire today. A case of arson. Did you see Parduk today?"

Something in Teck's abdomen rumbled like old plumbing. His bowels were about to disgrace him.

"Yes, I was in his shop today."

Arkadi glanced around the room. His frown was more like that of a concerned parent than an inquisitive policeman. When he looked back at Teck his gaze was very steady. "Now, Professor Teck, I want you to think before you answer my question. Two questions, actually: at what time were you in the shop; and did Parduk give any sign of concern, of worry, of—tension? Those are my questions."

With great haste and minimal courtesy, Teck bolted for the bathroom, where his bowels emptied themselves in noisy and foul-smelling explosions. Each time Teck began to think seriously of returning to the inspector, he was seized by another cramp. At last he flushed the toilet and tried to calm his raging pulse with cold water, and then stepped feebly into the room where the inspector waited. Teck closed the bathroom door behind him, knowing that his own ghastly stench would follow him like some miasma of guilt.

"I'm very sorry," he said weakly.

The inspector did not change expression. Teck reached across him to get a robe from the armoire. As he put it on he was more aware than ever of the room's fouled atmosphere. He opened the harbor side window and then sat on the rumpled bed.

"Well, Professor Teck?"

"What's that?"

"My two questions."

"Oh. Oh. I saw Parduk at around—two o'clock, I guess. For perhaps twenty minutes, maybe half an hour. And, yes, he behaved very strangely."

"Ah, strangely."

"Yes, he seemed preoccupied. Nervous."

"Instead of—"

"I don't understand."

"You say, 'preoccupied.' With what should he have been occupied?"

"Oh. Well, I wanted to buy something. I asked him about such things. Old things—in my field, I mean."

"What is your field, please?"

"Oh, medieval history. Social history. At the moment, I'm interested in games and activities. Sports. Fishing, in particular."

Arkadi nodded, as if a profound interest in such trivia were the most natural thing in the world. He reached into the inner pocket of his suitcoat and pulled out a folded paper. "This falls within your field, I think?" It was a folded rectangle of tracing vellum. He opened it and put the paper on Teck's lap. The deep creases where it had been folded were like vanes that held it in an almost winged shape; the upper half bounced on a current of air from the window. It was the tracing of the four panels from the Aelian Fragment.

"Where did you get this?"

"It was lying right there, on your bureau, Mr. Teck." Arkadi's look was one of bland, unquestionable innocence. Yet Teck knew he had locked the tracing away in one of his suitcases. The suitcase key was on the bureau.

The inspector had methodically searched the room.

"I did *not* leave this on the bureau! It was locked up in my suitcase."

"Are you saying that I have lied?"

"You searched my room!"

Arkadi cocked one eyebrow. "Your proper recourse is to lodge a formal complaint with your consul, Professor Teck. Or you may hire a Turkish lawyer and pursue it through our courts."

"I may do just that!" Teck sounded braver than he felt.

Arkadi nodded. His right elbow was resting on his chair arm, his index-finger knuckle pressed against his upper lip. Before he spoke he moved his hand away from his mouth and pointed it in Teck's direction. "Where did you get this tracing, Mr. Teck?"

"I brought it from Rome," Teck lied.

"It is a tracing of an antiquity?"

"Yes, a, uh, an Italian illuminated manuscript. Sienese, about the thirteenth century."

Arkadi, with a murmured "pardon me" took back the tracing and studied it. "It looks quite distinctly Byzantine to me," he said lightly.

"That's ridiculous," Teck said; he stammered over the *r*. "Well, there may be some influence there. Through the Ravenna mosaics, you know. It's a very involved history."

"I know." Arkadi's knuckles tapped his upper lip again. "You know, Professor Teck, if that were a tracing of a Turkish antiquity, it would be illegal to export such a thing. The penalties for trying to export, or for purchasing for export, are quite severe." Arkadi crossed his legs and glanced at the ceiling. "I don't know what your view of the ethics of exporting art objects from a foreign country are, Professor Teck, but suppose the national holdings of native American paintings were cut to one-third through illegal export. You would not take part in selling your national heritage, surely?"

Teck had been about to say indignantly that his ethics were not in question, when he had a sudden vision of himself, a half-naked man, surrounded by his own excremental stink, who was being told by a little policeman that his status as an academician and a gentleman were a sham, and that he had come to this foreign country because here he could act with blinders on his conscience.

Was that why he had photographed the Russian manuscript—why he had allowed himself to think of using it to trade for the fragment? Because in this exotic place his ethics were on holiday?

"I haven't done anything illegal."

"I believe you have not," the inspector said. He stood up. "But Ashir Parduk interested us. He was a trafficker. You come to Izmir, you visit him; his shop burns and he is dead." He held up the tracing. "I would like to keep this for a day or two. If you object, I will leave it here. If I leave it, of course, your objection goes into my report; if, when I seek it later—with a legal order, if necessary—it cannot be produced, its absence becomes a form of evidence. Please, may I take it?"

Teck's head ached and his bowels were beginning to grind again. "By all means, take it," he said grimly.

Arkadi folded the crisp vellum and put it back in his inner pocket. He crossed to the door. "I am sorry to have disturbed your rest, Professor Teck. It was necessary, however. We will talk again, I think." He stopped with his hand on the doorknob. "Ah, yes, I almost forgot. I was told you were present when a corpse was pulled from the bay this morning, is that true?"

Teck gulped. "Yes."

Arkadi nodded many times, as if some idea had been confirmed. "Just so," he said. "Just so. Interesting. Your stay in

Izmir has been a short but a busy one, Mr. Teck." He opened the door. "Good night."

A few minutes later Teck slumped against the toilet tank with hardly enough strength left to sit upright. He rubbed his eyes with the thumb and first finger of his right hand. He thought of Arkadi, of the tracing, of the manuscript.

His voice was weary. "Oh, dear; oh, dear; oh, dear; oh, dear. . . ."

Chapter seven

ON the morning of the day after the fire in the Izmir bazaar, the Turisti Pallas began to fill. Even the usually melancholy Hamdar looked almost pleased; at best, he had expected his hotel to catch only the overflow of the Trade Fair.

His establishment attracted several Japanese, all ancillary members of the large Oriental delegation; two Israelis who had been added to their country's representation at the last minute; a number of second-level oil people from Libya and Algeria; one Englishman who turned out to be nothing more than a tourist, and who was made to feel somehow like an unwanted vestige of the days of Empire; and eleven Turks from the interior.

The noise level in Teck's room was so much higher that he was annoyed at first, particularly so because of his hangover, but some rueful consideration told him that it was merely common sense that a hotel could not remain silent when it had more than a scattering of guests. At any rate, his own problems went beyond such trivialities as the noisy toilet overhead or the cigarette cough next door.

Teck was beginning to feel remorse. (A hangover is excellent soil for remorse to grow in. It is also good for guilt, regret, and self-recrimination. Taken in the right spirit, it may even be productive of self-knowledge, although Teck did not yet understand how that could be.) He knew only that his head felt as if it were being skillfully opened along a line from the fontanels to the base of the skull; that his mouth and breath were foul; that his stomach would reject anything offered to it; and that his mind, like a bird locked up in a room, flitted self-destructively from guilt to self-hatred and back again, as if trying to smash itself on the glass of those two windows. Could he have raised the Russian manuscript from the water now, he would have done so, but only a diver would be able to locate the tiny film can and the carefully wrapped packet below it. Yet—and the thought caused his stomach to sink—it might be found by a swimmer or a fisherman, its proximity to the hotel and to his window an obvious clue to his guilt.

He understood the expression "sick with worry." He still had a supply of small white pills for diarrhea; two of those with aspirin, washed down with tepid tapwater, would possibly make him feel better in time.

Shortly after ten o'clock he dressed himself with the care of a man handling a fresh egg and walked delicately downstairs. He would walk along the waterfront, taking great breaths of sea air, and return Hakail's hook. What he wanted to do, of course, was leave the city, leave Turkey, but he feared the grim policeman who had visited him the night before. He was impotent: he did not dare leave; he did not dare try to reach Mrs. Parduk about the Aelian Fragment for fear the police would know of it; he had put the Russian manuscript where he could not retrieve it, but where it was a constant threat to him. *How could a man of his intelligence and accomplishments have landed in such a mess?*

"The police did not arrest you?" Hamdar's question was only faintly ironic. He was, of course, concerned for the reputation of his hotel.

"Of course not. There was a misunderstanding. Just a misunderstanding."

Hamdar grunted. "I would not ever take you, Professor, for a man the police could be misunderstood about."

"Thank you." Teck was not certain the remark had been a compliment.

"Still. . . ." The qualification was very evident. "Nobody is what he says anymore."

"Didn't the inspector explain that it was a misunderstanding?"

"You think I'm a confidant of the police?"

Teck tried to sound indignant. "He thought I knew something about that fire in the bazaar!"

Hamdar sighed. He nodded his head very slowly, very wisely. Both he and Teck were thinking, of course, of the "boy's" visit to the bazaar at Teck's command.

"It was a *misunderstanding*, Mr. Hamdar."

"Everything is a misunderstanding, Mr. Teck. I am in the hotel business because of a misunderstanding; it was *my* understanding that I should have been a wealthy Greek with a yatch and a pretty wife. Turkey is a misunderstanding; we thought we were supposed to be the Ottoman Empire." Hamdar squinted through the open doors at a woman who was standing on the opposite curb, waiting for a lull in the traffic. "Prison is a misunderstanding, too, Mr. Teck. But many people wind up there."

Teck's mouth was very dry. "I don't intend to."

"I hope not. It would not make a very good travel story." Then, perhaps because he was aware of how self-righteous he sounded, Hamdar said, "Have a coffee. It's too early for *raki*."

"I couldn't."

"Have a coffee. You need one."

Hamdar looked significantly at him and then led the way to the same restaurant table where Teck had begun drinking the day before.

Teck watched the woman cross the street toward the hotel. Her white dress was tight over a faintly plump belly and generous breasts. A leather shoulder bag, which she kept from swinging by holding tightly to it with her hand, hung from her left shoulder. As she reached the sidewalk in front of the hotel, something about a gesture—brushing her rather wiry hair away from her face while her hand jerked in a quick, impatient motion—seemed familiar.

"My Jewess."

"What?"

Hamdar put a small glass of pear nectar and an empty coffee cup down in front of him. "My female Israeli. I have one of each—man, woman. Here for the fair."

"Do you mind the Jews?"

"I will mind if some mad Palestinian decides to choose my hotel to make an incident." Hamdar shrugged. "Maybe we are all a misunderstanding in God's brain."

The woman crossed the lobby toward the stairs. Seeing Teck, she hesitated—the action was very clear, almost stagelike, the classic double-take—and then she was coming slowly toward the table, the handbag held a little in front of her like a shield.

"Isn't it— Aren't you Professor Teck?"

He rose shakily. Yes, of course, he knew this woman, knew the face and the gesture with the hair. She had once been a student of his, although he couldn't yet place her.

"Yes, but— Oh, dear—"

"You don't remember me, do you?"

Teck could feel Hamdar's utter silence behind him. "Yes, I do. Of course, at, uh, Kentucky, wasn't it? But I'm sorry, your name—" He smiled feebly.

"Sandra Reich." She laughed. "But I'm married now, it's Sandra Lowenstein."

Details fell into place like the symbols on a slot machine: English Medieval Theater; quiet girl, good writer, poor speller; campus activist; blue jeans and a denim shirt, hair longer then; a sweet, almost childlike face that had become pleasant, plump, sensuous. Jackpot.

"Won't you sit down?"

"No, I can't, I really can't now. We're here for the Trade Fair. My husband's a physicist, he's into lasers. But I'd love to talk to you, you know. Howard would love to meet you, he really would."

It was the sort of encounter that Teck despised. Two people with nothing more in common than an accident of place and time meet in a foreign spot, and they must perforce behave as if there were something to be celebrated. It was another sort of misunderstanding, nothing more.

Yet, he agreed that he must meet Howard. He endured Hamdar's scowl as he suggested that they all meet for a drink that afternoon; he even heard himself remark what a pleasant surprise it was to see her again.

When she was gone, Hamdar served his coffee and went to his desk. Teck sipped the coffee slowly, trying to resist the great temptation to lie down on the floor and press his aching head against the cool linoleum.

While Teck wrestled with his hangover, Valeri Seriakin was looking down at Yesilkoy airport from the small window of an Aeroflot jet. Two seats ahead of him, a woman named Olga Leonov was preparing another quiet lecture to deliver when they had a moment of privacy on the ground. She had already made it very plain that she was the designated KGB overseer of the trade delegation. The job had been hers for months; she no doubt feared for her next promotion if she did not seem to perform efficiently and without interference. The sudden introduction of Seriakin into the group had upset her more than she dared show. *What did they think she'd done wrong?*

For his part, Seriakin was already anticipating her lecture. He thought he knew the type—a year or two overage in her grade, worried, overprecise. She would think, of course, that he had come to check on her. That was unfortunate, but it could not be helped.

The wheels screeched against the concrete and the plane slowed. Their bodies were pressed forward against the seat belts. Not entirely to his surprise, Seriakin felt a little sick; he knew, in fact, that he was frightened. *Why did Repin have to pick me? Why must I be a field agent now, when I was hoping to leave the service altogether?*

Teck, feeling that his walk must be an unsteady lurch rather than his accustomed firm stride, moved slowly along the quay, now and again arching his back to try to relieve the tension in his shoulders and neck. He hoped there would be no trouble about explaining away the absence of the weight and the cord that now held the Russian manuscript to the bottom of the bay. He would simply offer to pay for them, if need be.

But when he reached the quay, he did not find Hakail among the other fishermen. There was another man in his place, and when Teck stopped to stare, the other glanced up from his tackle and gave him a steady glare that made Teck turn away. He strolled back along the quay, thinking Hakail might have taken up a new location.

He could feel his undershirt soaked down to his belt on his right side. He wanted to sit down, but he was afraid of the closed faces that stared at him from the terrace of the café.

Still, he recognized one of those faces. It was the policeman who had been with Arkadi the night before, the one who had waited outside the room.

When Teck walked away, the policeman got up and started after him. He made no real attempt to hide what he was doing. Teck's earlier fear congealed into a cold despair and he found that he was actually shaking. The excitement of the day before had turned almost to panic. *Why did I do it? My God, why, why did I do such a stupid thing?*

Perhaps anyone can initiate a crime. It takes a certain mental set, however, to live with the aftermath, the fear of discovery, and the questioning of self. As a boy, Teck had once stolen a bicycle lamp from a store. After the initial thrill had come the same insistent, paralyzing question: *How could I do such a stupid thing?* That time, terrified of being caught, he had not dared to use his prize, and at last he had thrown it into a pond and worried for weeks afterward that it would be found and his fingerprints somehow discovered.

His preoccupation with his own guilt caused him to overlook another, perhaps a more practical question: Why was Hakail not at his post?

Hours later, outside Washington, the events in Izmir were causing other questions to be asked. The two men sat opposite each other again, and each had a small object, a prop with which he played; the younger man had his small notebook, the older an expensive briar pipe.

"Well, so there was a fire." The older man moved the pipe in his fingers, rubbed its smooth bowl. "I'm just trying to see where we are. There's a fire, possibly *The Book of the Dead* is in it, possibly it's burned up—is it unfair to say it might be for the best? Just as conjecture, mind you. I mean, if it's really burned up, where does it leave us? Totally up the creek?"

"Well, no, we're not sure that—"

"What's our paddle here?"

"Well, we're not sure that—"

"You see, Ken, in matters like this, you've got to have a paddle. I mean, my God, you know what will happen if there isn't?"

"Isn't—"

"Any paddle!" He slapped the polished desk with his open hand. "What's our drill on aborting?"

The young man looked at his notebook. There was a silence, and he eased himself into it, his voice so low in the beginning that at first the words were lost. "Well, you see, sir, we're not sure we lost it to begin with. Or other people don't think so. The Russians, they've sent a man in—named"— he turned a page in the notebook —"Valeri Seriakin. We know nothing about him except that his father was a KGB bigwig years back. It seems a little peculiar, them sending in Seriakin, and because it's peculiar, we think it's got something to do with *The Book.* And we have a report of a Free Turkey Youth cadre operating in Izmir; that may be only dicking around, you know, the Trade Fair and all that bull, but it could be a sign, so. . . . Then there's some interest from Tel Aviv. So with that much response, we think it's still there. *The Book of the Dead,* I mean."

The other man looked thoughtful. "You mean, that may be our paddle."

"Sir?"

"Emphasize all this response, really underline it and put it in italics, you know, and—"

"—a sort of 'We did our job but there was this unpredictable overreaction.' Like that?"

"Exactly."

"Oh, right—I can see us saying that."

"Good. Real good, Ken, I buy that. Make me up a report using that line. I like it."

"There's one other thing, sir."

"Shoot."

"Sara Kerrigan's report on the man in Ankara, Burrell. She says he's hot to trot on the Izmir thing."

"Mmmm. Well, keep an eye on him. I don't want him screwing things up if I have to abort. Just let him float a little, see what happens. Is that it?"

"Yes, sir."

"Good." He leaned back. "And make up that report for me. It's not our fault, right? Keep that in mind, Ken. It's not our fault." He rubbed his jaw with the pipe stem. "And get it in someplace that this is only a project that we inherited. My God, we're not going to hang over some spook operation that somebody else thought up."

Teck did not eat lunch again that day. By the time he met Sandra Lowenstein and her husband in the bar of the Buyu Efes Hotel, he had not eaten in almost twenty-four hours, and, despite the occasional rumbling in his belly, he did not feel hungry. He had slept a good part of the afternoon, waking often to fear that the police would be at his door, but he was not disturbed. Still, he needed only to think of the inspector or the manuscript to have his insides plummet sickeningly and then wind themselves up again like a yo-yo.

Sandra had left him a note that directed him to the Buyu Efes. He found the bar crowded with Trade Fair visitors, a Babel-with-booze that spilled into the fierce sunlight of the terrace and made the room throb with noise. It all seemed frantic to him in the beginning, something from a zoo gone wild, but as he started on his second drink he recognized that most of the sound was laughter and that the apparent insanity came from the collision of languages that caromed off one other in noisy disorder. Others of the Israeli group visited their table, and Sandra's husband, a thin, bearded young man who would not have been at all out of place in Berkeley or Champaign-Urbana, was absent more than he was there, visiting other tables.

Sandra pointed out a knot of Japanese, a lone Ugandan, three Egyptians who were chatting amaiably with one of Lowenstein's colleagues. She gestured derisively at eight Russians who formed a tight, cohesive group at a separate table, then nodded her head to the side. "The watchdogs."

"Police?" Teck's voice was husky.

"KGB. You can always tell."

"How?"

She shrugged. "You can tell, that's all."

He turned his head and tried to look as if he were studying the terrace beyond the open doors. The two people she had indicated were a little apart from the other Russians, and they sat like a married couple who were angry with each other, just too far apart for intimacy, decorous and unsmiling and clearly not having a good time. The woman, who was very slender and would have been handsome except for a blotchy complexion, was the unhappier of the two; the man seemed young and almost callow, the sort that Teck classified as a jock and dismissed as a second-rate mind (at best).

"Aren't you a little obvious, Professor?"

"I'm sorry. Was I staring?"

Sandra finished her drink and waved for another. "Not really. But KGB people are very nervous. Watchers don't like being watched." She had changed into a light-green dress of a soft material—crepe, he would have said, although for all he knew the word was hopelessly old-fashioned—and her slight plumpness was attractive. She had vitality and self-confidence and he liked her better than he had when she had been a student.

Then her husband was gone—Teck remembered shaking hands and mumbling something polite—and the bar was emptying, and it seemed inevitable, somehow, that they have dinner together. A taxi took them to the Cosmopolitan Maxim's Restaurant Café, where they encountered the same Babel, now more drunk than before.

She spoke Turkish, he found, as well as Russian and French. She made him laugh. She had an intelligent interest in his research and she asked clever questions about why he had come to Turkey. He found himself telling her about Inspector Arkadi and the fragment, and she said that he had had a terrible experience, and foreign police (by whom she presumably meant police who were neither American nor Israeli) were unpredictable idiots.

"Still pigs?" he said. She had once been involved in a campus clash with the police.

She laughed. "More so than ever." Teck thought she sounded rather drunk, but he remembered that when he thought other people were drunk he was usually that way himself, and he resolved to drink no more wine; but the bottle was almost empty, anyway.

He pushed the remainder of his baklava over to her side of the table. "You've turned into one hell of a handsome woman, Sandra," he found himself saying, and in his voice was a note of—what? Nostalgia? Lust? (*Oh, dear; oh dear.*) "Well, that makes us even," she said as she spooned up honey and a dribble of it ran down her chin. "You're a handsome man, Professor."

So they returned to their hotel, which, as he realized, they so damnably, committedly, intimately shared. He was angry because events seemed to have decided that he would sleep with her, and angrier still because he really *wanted* to sleep with her, and so he said perversely, "I'm afraid I've had too much to drink. I think I'd better sleep it off."

"And just when I was going to invite you for an Israeli brandy!" She took his arm and piloted him into the hotel. "Actually," she murmured, her head tucked in close to his shoulder, "it's Algerian," and she nudged him in the ribs.

On the stairs she let go of him because he did not respond to her, and by the time they had reached the first floor, she was simply solicitous. She offered to unlock his door but he refused, and they said goodnight quite politely.

Teck looked at himself in the mirror above his bureau. He didn't *look* drunk. Certainly, he was aroused; didn't that mean that he was sober, because wasn't alcohol supposed to lower sexual appetite? After a point, at any rate?

Now he regretted having let her go. Perhaps it wasn't too late to go to her room, perhaps. . . . *The hell with it,* he thought, and stripped off his clothes.

He was standing naked in the dark, looking down toward the place where he supposed the Russian manuscript lay, when there was a knock at his door. He thought of Arkadi and his earlier visit and his insides took their yo-yo journey again.

"Just a minute, just a minute!" He pulled on a pair of pants as he had last night and then opened the door about six inches.

It was Sandra.

"How about that brandy?"

She had changed into some sort of pajamas, dark blue now, decent enough for walking about a hotel corridor in the dead of night, perhaps, in this day of pants and evening costumes, but hardly street wear.

"Courtesy of the management?" he said. He winced at the banality of his own tongue.

"Courtesy of me. Can't I come in?"

When he closed the door, he remembered that there were no lights on. *Well, she asked for it,* he thought. *Didn't she?*

He crossed to where she stood with her back to him. He put his hands on her shoulders and pulled her back a little, then slid his hands over the slippery fabric, feeling her breasts as soft as foam pillows.

"I thought you'd never ask," she muttered. After that, there was no hesitation on either side, no restraints left over from the past; they were simply two people meeting willingly on common ground, the present. She wore nothing under the pajamas, a fact that excited him splendidly and that he naïvely credited to her own eagerness. They stood, mouths devouring, while he felt her shake the blouse loose. He moved his pelvis back and unzipped his trousers and they fell to his knees, then his ankles, and he began a slow-motion, stamping dance step to free his feet, rather like a cat kneading a soft blanket before lying down. He clutched her buttocks, the small of her back; his right hand moved around and slid between their bellies.

"Mm-mmp!" she grunted without taking her mouth from his. Her head moved back and she said, "I'll go off like a firecracker." They staggered together to the bed and she crab-walked up it on her back, then pulled him down and they coupled quickly, violently, and it was over in seconds, too soon, too fast.

"I'm sorry," he said after they had lain quietly for a few seconds more.

"For what?"

"That it was—I was so—"

"Christ, man, the night isn't over."

"Oh. Uh—what about your husband?"

"I don't know. What about my husband?"

They drank the Algerian brandy, which was not bad at all. They crouched by the open window for the breeze from the harbor and he pointed out the lights of the places he knew. He lost any accurate sense of time's passage, and one moment he was talking about ships and the next she was talking about Chekhov and Russian literature and then at some point he was kissing her shoulder and caressing one breast, and it evolved into a languorous lovemaking, after which he fell sound asleep.

The telephone waked him.

He was lying on the floor by the window. It was still dark. He thought she was gone, but her voice came from the bed. "Want me to get it?"

"No. No, I'd better get it." He thought somehow it was her husband as he lurched toward the bureau and fell into the stiff armchair there. He picked up the telephone.

It was the Princess, calling from London.

"Sam?"

"Hello, Princess."

"You sound all muffled, Sam."

"You, too. Bad connection."

"What? I can't hear you."

He had been speaking very softly. "It's a bad connection," he said more loudly.

"That's better. How are you, darling?" Somewhere in the background of their conversation he could hear a voice gabbling in French. "Are you alone, Sam?"

"Of course I'm alone. I was asleep."
"You don't have to sound cross."
"I'm sorry, Princess. I've had a difficult day."
"You, too? Oh, God, I can't begin to tell you what I've been through in the past twenty-four hours. Really, Sam—" She told him about her twenty-four hours. She was miserable in London; the weather was impossible; her family was hateful; she wanted to join him at once. She was staying at a hotel but she'd already had too much of her relatives, all of whom had tried to give her advice and borrow money. He let her talk. When she paused, he said that it would be unwise for her to join him, and they would meet in Antalya as planned.
"I knew you'd say that." She did not sound very sorry. Evidently she had simply wanted to complain. "Anyway, we're going to meet some people in Antalya on Saturday."
"People?" He thought of the fragment. If he did manage to get it somehow, he didn't want to have to cope with strangers. "What people?"
A television director she knew was cruising the eastern Mediterranean in a yacht, which they would be boarding at Antalya on Saturday. "It's better than a hotel, Sam, and much more fun! Paul's just bumming around and glad to have us."
Teck said nothing. A possibility had leaped into his mind: *If the worst happened, and he had to leave Turkey in an unorthodox way, a yacht. . . .*
He finished the conversation with the Princess in a state of abstraction, his mind on the yacht and the fragment. He was startled when Sandra's voice came from the bed.
"Female friend?"
"Uh? Oh, I'm sorry."
He stood up, and the sudden change of position made him a little dizzy. Nonetheless, he felt his way to the far wall where there was a light switch. The light seemed very bright and she cried out as if he had struck her.
"What'd you do that for?"
"Oh, I—I thought I might stumble over something."
She seemed angry for a moment; then she smiled up at him. He sat next to her. "I'm sorry I fell asleep."
"You don't want me to talk about your phone call, do you?" She touched his thigh. "It's messy for you, having your female friend call why I'm here."
"Yes, it's a little messy."

"Maybe I'd better go."

Yes, he thought, *you'd better,* but he said just the opposite, from that perverse habit called courtesy and from some sense that he had been unkind to her. As if to make up some slight to her, he decided to flatter her intelligence, and he stood up and said lightly, "How's your Russian?"

"Superb, what else? Why?"

He was silent, sorry now that he hadn't let her go.

"Why?"

"Oh, I came across—in a shop—somebody showed me something, that's all. I was curious about it."

"Why?"

"Oh, the fellow had it for sale; I'm always looking for things, you know—I thought, maybe for the university library. Nothing, really."

"If you could remember some of the characters, maybe I could translate for you. What was it, a medieval book or something?"

"Uh, no, no, more modern. I do remember the characters. Some of them, I mean. Of the title."

"Write them out for me. Come on."

He got a pen from his jacket. When he looked back at her, she was sprawled like an odalisque on the narrow bed, a prodigal display of female lushness on that meager piece of furniture. He smiled at her. When he wrote out the characters that he had memorized, the pen moved as slowly as that of a child just learning to write. Her head was bent over the paper and he could not see her face.

"There, I think I've got it right. Those backward *R*'s may be wrong, I'm not sure. What does it mean?"

"Oh. I guess it's a title."

"What does it say?"

"Oh. *Death Book.* Something like that. *Book of the Dead.*"

"*Book of the Dead?*" Not *The Snow Is Black.* Nothing like the title Parduk had given him.

She leaned back on the wrinkled pillow. "What happened to it?"

He could have told her the truth. He came very close to doing just that, drawn by her warmth and the enormous sense of strength and confidence that she radiated, as if she could be a safe repository for all secrets. But he was too cautious.

"I don't know. They wanted me to buy it, but I had no use for it. I—just left it at the shop."

Then she asked him one or two more questions about it, the sort of idle questions that are asked about some mildly interesting event, and then she let it drop. Teck went into the bathroom; when he came out she was standing by the bed, straightening the sheet. He kissed her, thinking that now she was ready to leave; instead, she pushed him gently down on the bed and began to kiss his chest, his belly, and he was attacked by doubts: *I won't be able to make it again; I can't cut it.* But she was very skilled and very stimulating.

Two hours after she left, there was another knock at his door. He stumbled to it without bothering to put on any clothes. His head ached and his mouth tasted appalling.

The light in the corridor was dim, but he felt blinded.

"Mr. Teck?"

It was Inspector Arkadi.

"I am afraid I must ask you to come with me."

Chapter eight

THE ride through the early-morning streets, at that time when the city has not yet begun to move and the light is thin and cold no matter what the temperature, was made in a sullen silence. Teck was hung over and he had no wish to talk. But the inspector's deliberate silence and the almost brutal driving of the man in the front seat were so intense that Teck was frightened.

He had been allowed to dress. He had not been manhandled, but Arkadi's grip on his arm had been firm, and the second policeman had walked on his other side so that he was boxed between them. They had spoken only a few words: "Am I under arrest?" "Not yet." And, later, "Don't you ever sleep, Inspector?" "Yes."

They made two sharp right turns up narrow passages in a part of the city that Teck did not recognize and pulled up at a doorway with a single, shaded bulb burning over it, the light made bleak by the early daylight. Arkadi waited until the driver had opened the door on the near side and then let Teck get out first. Teck hesitated after he got out of the car; Arkadi passed him. Teck saw them as if frozen there: the driver, one foot now on the single step up to the doorway, his hand on the knob and yet not turning it; Arkadi, between Teck and the other man, the morning light cruel to the fatigue lines that ran down each side of his mouth and to the hollows of his cheeks. Teck even saw himself, as from a distance, shoulders rounded and gaunt head dropped forward, an unprotesting steer at the abattoir.

"In my own country I'd be allowed to call somebody."

"You will."

Arkadi touched his left arm lightly, but there was authority behind the pressure and it turned Teck toward the doorway. He steadied himself on both sides of the doorway as he went in, glad for the support.

Valeri Seriakin dreamed of his father. The old man had played a role in many of his dreams since the funeral, as if themes unresolved at his death must still be acted out on that stage. As in other of the dreams, he and his father were arguing as they never had in life, a noisy, shouted exchange of insults that had the most trivial basis—something about luggage. Carrying his father's luggage on a seemingly endless walk through the Leningrad railway station, searching for a train to Moscow. They argued. Enraged, he threw the old man to the ground and kicked him. The old man wept, then screamed obscenities.

Seriakin woke. He lit a cigarette. He reviewed the dream. *Let us dream—for example, of the life to come. . . .* The idiot Vershinin.

He rolled on his back. He had been attentive to Olga Leonov, the KGB regular, in the hotel bar. She had not responded. Without either of them having to say so, there was no obligation to seduce each other.

In the morning he was to see a man from the Free Turkey Youth. Seriakin was almost certain that it had been they who had burned Parduk's shop; he was now almost certain, too, that they had succeeded in burning *The Book of the Dead* along with it. But there were loose ends to tie up, possibilities to be followed: the police investigation, for example, for which he must bribe their contact in the Izmir police. Then there was talk of an American who had been at Parduk's shop before the fire, perhaps a CIA agent. And then it might be useful to trace backward from Parduk and find the chain that had smuggled

the manuscript to Izmir. He must look at the scene of the fire, take some photos. . . .
Seriakin slept.

They had put Teck into a grubby room. Twelve feet by twelve feet, its plaster walls were dented and gouged like the concrete exteriors of old bunkers, painted over in a disgusting gray-green, both walls and ceiling. A single battered table flanked by two mismatched chairs stood in the middle of the room.

Teck sat in one chair. He had sat there for an hour, at least. A stolid uniformed policeman, paunchy and massive, stood with arms folded by the only door. If he had any interest in Teck, he did not show it.

Teck's mind swung between a numb sense of fright and a deadly repetition of a single theme that ended in a question: *Parduk lied; there is no* Black Snow; *there is* The Book of the Dead. *Why?* Then the pendulum would swing and crazy images of his hiding the black packet from the man at the Gol Café, of photographing the manuscript, of tossing it, weighted and wrapped, into the bay, would tumble through his mind and frighten him.

The door opened. Arkadi motioned for him to follow.

"You are to see something."

Arkadi walked very quickly down the long corridor. Teck lengthened his strides to keep up; the stolid policeman from the grubby room clumped along in their wake. Teck had once been in an Italian police station when a murder was reported, and there had been noise and seeming disorder, but here there was only the eerie emptiness of a De Chirico painting and the hollow clatter of their own footsteps. Once, there was a muffled shout and something like laughter, but it seemed to come from an echoing distance like a sound heard in a tunnel. When they came to a stairway, Arkadi hurled himself at it and his feet tripped down in precise doublets of sound, *tap-tap, tap-tap*, quick as a dancer's. Teck followed by taking the stairs in clumsy skips.

At the bottom of the steps was another door, another corridor, and at the end of it an anteroom where Arkadi had to sign a form for a bored young woman in a white laboratory coat, after which they were allowed through into a cool tunnel of white tile.

The temperature and the smell warned Teck where he was.

Arkadi opened a metal door like a bank vault and stepped through. "Mr. Teck?" he said when Teck hesitated.

There was an empty table on wheels on a far corner. The smell here was almost overpowering and Teck gagged. He knew the smell—dead rats, dead woodchucks, a dead bird in a closed-up house, laboratory cats kept too long in formaldehyde.

Arkadi stood by a wheeled table.

"You are to see this."

Arkadi pulled the cloth from his side of the table by gathering it into pleats in his fingers, eight or ten inches of cloth in a handful, so that the body was revealed in quick jerks—the left arm and shoulder first, then the left side of the torso and the left leg and the first hint of the anomaly in the groin and the ghastly mouth, then the whole head and the right side, and the whole body was visible.

It had been a man before it had died and before the genitals had been cut off and before the face had been butchered.

The worst was the mouth.

Arkadi's voice was expressionless.

"It was done with wire cutters."

Teck was sick.

In the Bulgarian port of Burgas the Soviet merchant ship *Leonid Andreyev* delayed its departure for two hours. It was well after daylight when its passengers were brought out from the dock in a naval launch and delivered with obsequious formality to the captain. After a brief conference the captain opened the sealed orders that one of his passengers brought and the ship got under way. In a few minutes it was gliding out of the Gulf of Burgas and turning south toward the Bosporus.

"You did not recognize the body." It was a statement, not a question, repeated for the third time in twenty minutes.

"No, I told you."

"But you were present when the body was found in the bay."

"I believe I was."

"How do you account for that?"

"What do you mean, how do I account for it? I was there, that's all. I was taking pictures."

"Ah, yes, the pictures." Arkadi whispered to the policeman, who clumped out of the room and left the door open. Someone went by in the corridor and Teck could smell coffee.

"But you don't recognize the man?"

"No, I don't recognize him."

"Did you recognize him then?"

"I didn't see him—the face. Then."

"Then why do you think it is the same body?"

Teck sighed hoarsely. He was acutely aware of his own odor. "The mutilation was the same." He stopped. Arkadi tapped the table with his pencil. "The balls were cut off, all right?"

"Hmm." Arkadi stopped tapping, seemed to consult his notes, then leaned forward and looked directly at Teck. "It *is* the same body. It was taken from the bay by fishermen when you say you were there." He sat back. His thin body was alert and his shoulders were not slumped as Teck's were, but his forehead was furrowed with weariness and concern.

"Odd coincidences you have met with in Izmir, wouldn't you say, Mr. Teck?"

"You mean you don't think they're coincidences. You think I somehow—had something to do with this body."

Arkadi did not answer.

"Am I being charged with something?"

Silence.

"Could I have a glass of water?"

"No."

"For Christ's sake, all I want is—"

Arkadi held up a hand. "Save your objections for the American consul."

"Fine, when?"

"When I call him."

They were back in the gray-green room, Teck on one side of the table and Arkadi on the other. Teck's passport and wallet were in front of the inspector, the papers removed and arranged like a fan of cards. Hakail's fishhook rested on its tissue wrapping. Arkadi's wrist touched the tissue, and Teck saw clearly the frayed threads from his jacket cuff standing out against the white paper.

"Mr. Teck, do you believe that things happen in threes?" He did not wait for an answer. "If you did, you see, we would expect another coincidence, wouldn't we? We have the body in the bay, as yet unidentified—and you were there—and we have the firebombing of the curio shop—and you were *there.* Now, the body in the bay was a professional job, I would say. And the firebombing was a competent job, yes, a professional job, too. Now, if I had reason to expect terrorism in regard to"—he consulted his notes—"Ashir Parduk, I would conclude terrorism. But two such coincidences, Mr. Teck. Shall we look for a third?" Arkadi leafed back through his notebook. "Our interview in your hotel, Mr. Teck. Discussion of a tracing of an illustrated manuscript, which you claim was Sienese, and which I assert is Byzantine." He shook the pencil at Teck. "I know art works, Mr. Teck. Perhaps better than you, although you will not be persuaded of that. Now—is this our third coincidence? Are you a trafficker in stolen Turkish art treasures, Mr. Teck?"

Lie, Teck thought. *Lie, lie. He knows nothing. Let him fish.* "I have nothing to do with stolen goods of any kind."

"Where were you last evening, Mr. Teck?"

"Oh, Christ! Didn't your flunky report after he followed me?"

Arkadi's hand was up and across Teck's face before he had time to ward off the blow. Tears rose in his eyes.

"Don't you ever speak to me like that!" Arkadi's right index finger shook as it pointed at him. "Don't you dare to insult me!" He straightened, folding his arms in apparent disdain, but Teck knew that the man had been betrayed by fatigue into doing something he regretted.

"I ask you again—where were you last evening?"

"I met somebody for a drink, for dinner."

"Who?"

"A Mrs. Sandra Lowenstein."

"Was this by prearrangement?"

"Uh, well, yes, sort of, you see—she's with the Israeli group at the Trade Fair—"

"Yes?"

"She was a student of mine. In the United States."

"Your mistress?"

"No, certainly not. I just happened to meet her yesterday for the first time in four years."

"You just *happened* to meet her."

"We're staying at the same hotel."

"By coincidence, Mr. Teck? *By coincidence?*"

Lamely, Teck muttered, "Yes. Coincidence."

Arkadi asked him about the times, the places—where they had had a drink, whom had they seen, where and when had they eaten, Teck answered as best he could.

"And afterward?"

"We returned to the hotel."

"Is that all?"

"Yes."

Arkadi stared at him. His steady gaze lasted ten seconds, and that can seem a very long time. "Maybe," was all he said, lowering his gaze to his notes.

Head in hand, Arkadi pored over his notebook. As he read, his right hand slipped down the edge of the page to the bottom, then turned the page over; the fingers went to the next page, waited at the top, and then slowly moved down again. When he spoke, his voice was so low that Teck had trouble hearing him.

"When did you last see the fisherman Sayid Hakail?"

"Hmp? Oh, he gave me that hook. On the table."

"*When* did you last see him?"

"Uh—" Had it been only the day before yesterday? It seemed months. "Two days ago. The same day I saw the body in the bay. He was fishing. I was interested in that hook. It's handmade, you see. So I met him at the Gol Café and he let me take the hook back to my hotel for photographing." *Don't mention the weight and the cord. He'll know.*

For the first time in several minutes, Arkadi's head lifted. His right hand covered the lower part of his face.

"This is really why I brought you here, Mr. Teck. To ask you about Sayid Hakail. We went to talk to him, you see, to ask what he knew about the finding of the corpse in the bay." Arkadi sighed. "His wife did not want to let us in. But we insisted. We found her husband in a coma. He had been beaten. Very badly beaten. He is now in a hospital, where he may be able to speak to us or he may not. You see, Mr. Teck, I knew of no connection between you and Sayid Hakail until I talked again to some of the fishermen, and they told me about the American who had shown such interest in the man. And now he is in a hospital, in a coma. What a coincidence, eh?"

Chapter nine

AT some point—Teck would have said about six in the morning, but his sense of time was off and it was closer to seven thirty—Arkadi's place had been taken by the man who had followed Teck the day before. It was like trading an opponent with an épée for one with a saber; where Arkadi probed and feinted and never (with the single angry exception when he had slapped Teck) seemed to let passion affect his skill, the new man slashed and hacked and seemed as likely as not to go after his victim with his bare hands.

"Now, this goddamn business of fisherman," he began.

"I told the inspector—"

"Speak when I say!" The man stood behind Teck. He was bigger than Arkadi and thick in the body, and his face was folded and pouchy in a way that suggested not age or care but dissipation.

"This fisherman, what is the true story?"

Teck hesitated this time.

"Speak!" He gave the back of Teck's head a little push that jarred it forward and brushed the hair the wrong way.

"I borrowed a fishhook from him."

"You were going fishing?"

"No, I wanted a picture of it."

"You take picture on quay, we have this picture, you lie about more pictures. Why did you meet this fisherman at Gol Café?"

And so it would go, until for no good reason the subject would change to Parduk or the fragment tracing.

"Are you a Jew? A Zionist?"

"Certainly not."

"You are a Jewish sympathizer?"

"No. Not the way you mean."

"But you have a Jewish mistress."

"No!"

"How long did you know Parduk?"

"I didn't know him. I visited his shop. Twice before this."

"Dates, please."

The examiner paced behind Teck but insisted that the "guest" look forward, his hands on the table. Sometimes he would pace around the table, seating himself to consult his notebook, only to leap up again at some supposed lie and bellow at Teck, bending low over the table so their faces were close together and the rotten denture smell of his breath flooded out.

He had a list of questions. He would go through the list, sometimes with elaborations or slight deletions, then begin again. By eight o'clock, Teck was stupid with repetition and groggy with fatigue. When it became clear to him that the intention was simply to keep him awake, he was already into that stage of wakefulness when the eyes burn, opened a little too wide, and the body has recovered what seems treacherously like a second burst of energy. After comes real exhaustion.

Between ten and eleven Teck made two admissions that his interrogator thought worth sending messages out of the room about. Each time, he waved the guard aside, put his head out, and handed a folded slip of paper to someone there.

"When did you first visit Turkey?"

"In 1961."

"What were you doing in Turkey?"

"I was in the Navy. U.S. Navy."

"What you did in the Navy? Sixth Fleet? Sailor?"

"I was an—air intelligence officer—we took photographs—"

"Intelligence!" Scribbling of the note, passing of it out the door.

Then, later, for the fifth time, "Did you sleep with the Lowenstein woman? Did you? Wake up—did you sleep with the Lowenstein woman?"

"Yes, for Christ's sake, yes, what difference does it make!" And the man had got the inclusive times of those hours in his room and then another note had been passed out the door.

At eleven twenty-three Inspector Arkadi returned, wearing a clean shirt, shaven, and looking as if he had had a nap. He resumed the questioning without telling Teck that he had informed the acting United States consul in Izmir that an American citizen was being questioned at Police Central.

By eleven thirty Valeri Seriakin had met with a surly representative of the Free Turkey Youth, whose sorry complexion and thin voice did not at all impress him with the potency of the rebel group, but he came away with the knowledge that they had firebombed Parduk's shop.

"Why?" Seriakin had asked pointedly. As the representative of their financial backer (one backer, at any rate; he supposed they got a dribble of excess oil profits from one of the Arab countries, although their file contained plea after plea for more funds), he had the right to ask crudely directed questions.

"He was an Israeli spy."

"Oh, come."

"He was, he was! His wife made three trips to Israel last year."

"Maybe she has relatives there."

"He was a spy, and so is she." According to Repin's files, Parduk was a minor informer who worked for the money; until 1949 he had been mostly in the pay of the British.

"Why did you burn the shop?"

"Something big was going on."

"Why don't you tell me about it like a good boy?" Because he was the principal now, Seriakin shook off his own modesty and tried to take on some of the attributes of Repin.

"We had our reasons."

"You are a very boring fellow." Seriakin stood up to leave the café, but the other stopped him, unwilling to lose his first audience.

"The order came down from the top. From the Black Wolf himself." The Black Wolf, Seriakin was sure, would turn out to be some self-important rebel in his thirties who extended his own youth by dominating these young ones. Behind him would be someone else, and eventually one of the Arab terrorist groups. Seriakin eyed the skinny young man skeptically. "Was it the Black Wolf who told you to get *The Book of the Dead*?"

He flushed. "We had our orders."

"I know. Did you look for it in the shop before you burned the place down?"

"There was no time. We drove up on a scooter and threw the bomb, that was all."

"So the manuscript could be anywhere."

"No, it was burned. One of my people followed an American from the shop, but he didn't have it. We frightened the piss out of him. If he'd had it, we'd know."

Seriakin paid the bill. "You *are* a tedious fellow," he said. "You will make a good waiter one day, or perhaps a dentist. Get out of the intelligence business."

An Izmir policeman was more informative, but his information was somewhat puzzling. He had personally interrogated an American named Teck that morning concerning the Parduk business, and it was his opinion that there was something more to be learned there. The American was shifty, too reserved and yet too free with some information. For example, he admitted he had been visiting Parduk for years. He even admitted that he had been an American intelligence officer. There was, too, the matter of the fisherman who had been beaten after a meeting with this Teck.

"Is there nothing to tie this Teck, and Parduk, and the fisherman together?"

"Inspector Arkadi thinks so. Maybe they're all in some kind of gang?"

"Did the American have anything from Parduk's? Even a wrapping, some little thing he had bought there?"

"A piece of very inferior art work. A fake medieval piece; even I recognized it. But you're not looking for something like that?"

Seriakin was thinking of what the Turkish boy had said about the American at Parduk's shop.

"What *are* you looking for? If I knew, I could be more help."

"If you were more help, you'd be no use; you'd get caught by your Inspector Arkadi." Seriakin did not repeat his father's dictum: *Always keep everybody as ignorant as possible.*

The policeman accepted an English cigarette. "The American screwed a Jewess, one of the Israeli trade group. He says he knew her before. Says he did it three times to her in three hours, but I don't believe him. He's over forty. And an American."

Seriakin paid the man and left through the rear door of the private house where they had met. He crossed the city by taxi to the Bogazici district and made contact with a woman who would relay messages to Repin. She was almost sixty and had had a breast removed because of cancer, Repin had said, but she was utterly reliable. Whether it was the threat of a terminal recurrence or the gratitude for a remission that made her so, no one knew. Seriakin gave her the information he had gathered and asked that she give him any information turned up about Teck or Sandra Lowenstein.

It was four thirty in the morning in Washington.

"I have your call through, Mr. Fellows."

"Are we scrambled?"

"Yes, sir."

There was a long pause, then a low hum and he heard his boss' voice, rendered a thin chirp by the mechanism.

"Well?"

"This is Ken, sir. I've got something here."

"Does this relate to the memo you sent me?"

"Yes, sir."

"Hold on."

He could picture the older man reaching for his glasses and then opening the scuffed leather case he carried from Georgetown each day.

"Ken? Are you there?"

"Yes, sir. Are you ready?"

"Shoot."

"A man named Teck, Samuel Teck. It seems the Izmir police have pulled him in for questioning. There's a possible link with the *Book* business." He glanced at a file in front of him. "This Teck is clean. Did a Navy stint, had a temporary Top Secret clearance, no security connection since. There was a background check in 1971, routine, he's a college professor and we were doing that stuff on some of his students. Nothing on him."

"Keep the domestic stuff out of it, Ken. They could murder us for a detail like that. Well, so?"

"The Izmir police had him for six hours before they informed our consul, which is a really bush thing to do. Strictly in violation of the 1963 Vienna Convention. They seem to be asking him about the Parduk business."

Fellows heard the other man muttering, "Parduk, Parduk," and he could imagine him going through the memo. "Oh, he's the shop owner that got burned. Well, exactly what does this mean, Ken?"

"I don't know, sir. Maybe the Izmir police are on to an angle we don't know about."

The other voice, tinny as it was, sounded shocked. "Is that possible?"

"Gee, I hope not."

"No chance this—what's his name—"

"Teck."

"Teck is ONI or something? One of those leftover NASA spooks with nothing better to do?"

"I don't think it's likely."

"Well, exactly why did you call me at home before daylight, then?"

"Well, sir, I thought that if there was any chance, I mean even a shred, that the Turkish police were on to something here—I mean, I wouldn't want us to get caught with our pants down."

"Christ, no."

"All there is in Izmir is an acting consul, you see, and he's no good from our point of view. Our Ankara man can be there in a matter of hours, but—the President called the ambassador home last evening because of the arms aid business, you know, and—"

"Is that relevant?"

"Well, it explains why our embassy people may be in a flap. They won't do much digging with the Turkish police just now. The Turks always think we're after drugs, you know, hippies, and then our people dig and the Turks just laugh at them."

"Well, you know, Ken, that's something we might use, you know, as a backstop in case we get caught short. You know, lack of cooperation from the embassy. Is that worth pursuing?"

"I'll put it in my report."

"Good boy. Now, about our Ankara man. Now just—excuse me." The voice, more muffled, said, "Yes, dear, only a minute." It became louder again. "Tell our man to put it straight to this—Teck—just flat out. Ask him about *The Book of the Dead.* Things are too messy now to pussyfoot, you follow me?"

"Yes, sir."

"And he can pick up the pieces afterward if he has to. Just flat out, press if he has to, but get an answer. And if this man Teck does know something—"

"Sir?"

"He'll have to be put on the shelf until it's all over. Absolutely. Listen, Ken, you say that the ambassador's back here?"

"Coming back, yes, sir; he should be in in a few hours. I checked; he has a White House meeting at two this P.M."

"Set up an appointment with him. Just to be on the safe side; we can always cancel. You'll have to work through one of those walking corpses at State, but just keep plugging. Then, if we need to, we can bring pressure to bear through the ambassador, right?"

"Right, sir."

"And this way, we can involve them, I mean State, so we're a little covered on that end. Just in case. Wouldn't you say so? And Ken, stay on this tonight, will you? I mean, stay at the shop. I'll give your wife a call; she'll understand. They get used to it, they really do."

Teck was given a bowl of broth shortly after noon, which he ate while the policeman looked on. A few minutes later Arkadi returned to the drab room with two small cups of coffee.

"You will have a visitor in a few minutes. If you wish to clean up, you may follow the guard."

He was led down the corridor to the same smelly washroom where he had been allowed to relieve himself earlier when his bladder hadlbeen throbbing and he had literally begged to be allowed to urinate before he threw over the restraints of a lifetime and messed himself. Yet, there had been one more question before they would let him go, *Did you have any other dealings with Parduk?* and he almost screamed the truth at them before fear whispered that it was better to piss his pants than be accused of involvement in some business he did not even understand, and he said no and had started to let his urine go, but they had motioned toward the door and he had gone out of the room on the run, dribbling as he went.

His hair wet from splashing his face, Teck returned now to the room where Arkadi waited with the cooling coffee. Teck drank it gratefully, savoring the harsh taste after the tepid water he had gulped from his cupped hand.

"I called your acting consul, Mr. Teck. Someone will be here shortly."

"I wish you'd told me."

"I didn't want to deceive you with false comfort." Whether the statement was made ironically or not was unclear.

"You're letting me go, then."

"Why should we let you go?"
"But you said I'm not under arrest."
"That was hours ago."
"Am I under arrest?"
"If you were under arrest, you would be charged. Have you been charged?"
"I don't know!"
Arkadi said nothing more. He was gathering together the notes made by the other policeman and putting them into a brown paper envelope. Teck's transparencies, taken from his camera and processed by the police, went into another. His passport, watch, and wallet were in a third.
A bullet-headed officer leaned through the doorway and spoke to Arkadi very softly. The inspector answered in a single burst of Turkish. He gathered his envelopes into an awkward pile that he had to clasp against his chest with both arms and crossed to the door. From that vantage point, like an actor making an effective exit from a scene, he turned back to Teck.
"There is something you are not telling me, you know. I can smell it. You would be best off to tell me. If you don't, I will find out, and then it will be much worse."
A few minutes later, a rather frightened young man named Rountree from the local office of the U.S. Information Service was brought in. He had no background in law, but he did his best to hide the fact that he was an inexperienced twenty-four-year-old trying to comfort a much older man who was being held on suspicion of involvement in a serious crime.

Shortly before four o'clock that afternoon, Valeri Seriakin was drinking tea in the shadow of the Soviet trade fair building, when Olga Leonov motioned to him from a doorway. He crossed to her, smiling politely in an attempt to counter her frosty look.
"There is a message for you," she said. "They will call again in ten minutes."
That goes into her report, he thought, *the bitch.* He smiled and thanked her.
When the call came again, he was standing by the telephone.
"Valeri Seriakin?"

"Here."

"Your shoes are ready."

He must remember the foolish password. "The black ones?"

"The brown ones with the English toes."

It was a ridiculous rigmarole, but Repin's contact had insisted on it.

At the safe house he was given a message. "Go to the Trattoria di Firenze on Gazi Bulvari. A man carrying the *Abendpost* will contact you."

Carrying my father's luggage the whole way. He wondered if this was Repin's and his father's method, tacking back and forth across foreign cities with mysterious messages about shoes and obscure foreign newspapers and ridiculous stratagems.

In the Trattoria di Firenze, which did, indeed, seem to have a single Italian waiter but which offered mostly Turkish food, the man with the *Abendpost* was reading quietly at a table. He made no signal to Seriakin. After five minutes he got up and went through a door at the back. Seriakin followed, and, squeezed between the filthy washbasin and the lidless toilet, they performed a brief ritual of identification. The stranger handed Seriakin a folded sheet of paper. He never saw the man again.

The information was terse. The American Samuel Teck was an innocuous tourist with a brief background in naval intelligence, merely one more of his country's unenthusiastic military volunteers for the minimum legal period. Nothing further was known.

Sandra Lowenstein, née Reich, however, was from the Mossad—an intelligence agent of the State of Israel. A digest of her dossier was included: married to a nuclear physicist, also with intelligence connections; active in prisoner interrogation after the 1973 October War; now a specialist in disinformation. Her presence in Izmir could not be considered accidental, and her connection with Teck suggested that a revision of the estimate of Teck's role must be made.

Teck was asleep when his second visitor arrived. His surroundings suggested that he was some sort of uninvited guest, for he had been put into an arid closet of a room with a narrow cot made up with one sheet and an unnecessary blanket. He had not questioned his accommodations. Collapsed face down into the trough of the cot's weak springs, he had fallen instantly asleep.

"Mr. Teck? Mr. Teck?" A gentle hand rocked him awake. He turned his head and saw two elegantly clad legs, and, above them, a beautifully cut dark blazer and the rugged, foreshortened face of a man in his fifties. "Hello. You awake now?"

Teck groaned and rolled over, bringing his back into contact with the cool plaster of the wall. A second man was standing behind the one who had waked him.

"This is Mr. Vassanian. Mr. Vassanian is a lawyer." Teck sat up, his legs still stretched out on the cot, and shook hands with the lawyer, whose too-tight suit threatened to split at the seams as he bent forward and exposed a woeful collection of teeth.

"My name is Phillip Burrell." The American showed him a card case with an embassy identification card. While Teck studied it, Burrell and the lawyer spoke quietly together in Turkish, their voices as muted as doctors' discussing a moribund patient. The lawyer shook hands again and abruptly left, a black vinyl folder pinned between his torso and his left arm.

"Now, Mr. Teck, we want to get this business cleared up as soon as possible. I have a memo here from the young chap who visited with you earlier. . . ." The voice continued in the same soothing baritone, its familiar accents those of the educated East Coast, but Teck was distracted by Burrell's behavior, for as the man talked he moved silently about, glancing at the ceiling, at the single light fixture overhead, then into corners and even under the bed. When he noticed Teck's interest, he put a finger to his lips without breaking the even tempo of his monologue and silently mimed someone listening. "—possible embarrassment for our country if there is involvement in a crime, to be sure, but from what I've learned, there is no basis for keeping you here. Turkish law, Mr. Teck, is not like American law, and I warn you that if any crime against Turkish law has been committed, the penalties will be. . . ." He took a folded piece of paper from his breast pocket and held it out. "—but with Mr. Vassanian's help, who is an excellent lawyer, we hope to have you released as soon as—"

Teck unfolded the paper. A single question was printed on it in neat block letters: DOES THE BOOK OF THE DEAD MEAN ANYTHING TO YOU?

Teck hesitated. The hours of grilling had left him paranoid. *Lie* was his first response. Then he thought of where he was and who was asking the question and he changed his mind. He nodded. *Yes.*

Burrell gave him an exaggerated wink. He reached out to tap Teck lightly on the shoulder and retrieved the slip of paper. His monologue never broke stride. "—problem of any foreign national that he must conform to the judicial system of the country in which he is a guest. I think it's best right now if you say nothing further and just let us handle it, at least until we know where we are. Now, I'm going to join your lawyer; in the meantime, I've brought you some things so you can clean up."

Burrell murmured something at the door. A policeman handed in a small plastic travel case, which Burrell opened, placing each item on the cot at Teck's feet so the policeman could see them. When he was finished, Burrell smiled and walked out, leaving Teck to shave and deodorize himself under the policeman's scrutiny.

Forty-five minutes later Teck stood with Burrell and the lawyer at the front door of the Central Investigative Bureau. Of the three, Teck was obviously the only one whom the police could have been detaining. The lawyer was too bouncy, too sleek, and far too familiar with every officer who walked by. Burrell was simply too aristocratic; who would dare to detain such a man? Teck, on the other hand, clutched a little cardboard box with his possessions in it and looked less the American academic than a rather stunned first offender.

He had come a long way in a short time.

No charge had been placed. There had been a bargain, behind which was some official American pressure that Teck did not understand but for which he was grateful. He would not be held, and his detention without notifying the acting U.S. consul would not be protested. *Go and sin no more.*

While he lingered perversely in the Victorian lobby, which seemed more the relic of an outdated hotel than the entrance to a drab Inferno of police work, a polished door at one side opened and Arkadi stepped out. He waved brusquely at a woman waiting on a bench. As she struggled to her feet,

Arkadi saw Teck. He stiffened. Teck raised his hand in an awkward greeting, but Arkadi turned away and went into the office beyond, leaving the door open for the woman. His face had been blank, but Teck thought he had seen contempt there, and in his new paranoia he cringed.

A moment later they stood by the curb. The lawyer apologized for his country's police. Teck responded shakily that they had a job to do, he was sure. He and the lawyer thanked each other; everyone shook hands all around, decided to do it one more time, and then they got into waiting cars and waved their farewells again. Teck sat next to Burrell in a rented Fiat; as they pulled away from the curb into the twilit city, Teck turned his head, half hoping that Arkadi might be there to acknowledge his release, but the massive doorway was empty.

At the same time, in a common dumping ground between two abandoned buildings on the outskirts, an unemployed laborer turned over a rusty sheet of iron that he hoped to salvage for part of his family's shack, which was so far built mostly of flattened tin cans. Under the sheet of iron he found, sticking from the rubble, a hand, which proved, after some digging, to be attached to the mutilated body of Sandra Lowenstein.

Chapter ten

THEY were cramped into the front seat like adults playing with a child's toy, shoulders hunched and knees too high. Teck was acutely conscious of Burrell's right hand when he shifted gears and banged Teck's leg with each move up or down the gears. At first Burrell said nothing, but concentrated on driving; often, he adjusted the rearview mirror, which never seemed quite right for him, and studied the street behind the car. He made small talk. How did Teck like Turkey? What was his academic field? Where had he done his graduate work? The effect was a little eerie, but Teck let himself simply go with the conversation and it relaxed him. He and Burrell found that they had an acquaintance in common. They had gone to the same kind of college. Burrell even knew that Teck had been in the Navy.

The car pulled into a boulevard, down the middle of which a row of overpruned trees marched like hairy dwarfs. Burrell steered the little car into the right-hand lane, where he could go slowly. Traffic was light, and in the early twilight the headlamps of the oncoming cars were as dim as old flashlights, mere tokens that cast no beam on the road.

"I'm not going to ask you what the police are so interested in, Sam," Burrell said as they moved along the boulevard. "I know some of it because, of course, Vassanian had to be told. Now, I don't really care about whatever you may or may not have done, but let me give you a warning: if you're involved in something, get out of it. That inspector won't let go." He smiled. "End of lecture. Now to business." He swung to the left and braked the car to a gentle stop in a turnaround in the median strip. As soon as the car had stopped, he reached behind him, saying, "You know we're being followed, I suppose. That's okay." He turned back to Teck with a small, cigar-shaped microphone in his hand, the black plastic cord trailing down to the floor of the back seat. "Would you mind holding that, Sam? I have to tape this."

They pulled back on the boulevard, heading in the direction opposite to the one they had just come. Burrell was smiling. Every thirty seconds or so the smile was erased by a downward twitch that spread partway into his neck; yet he was an attractive man, one who would spend his last years in Washington and be an asset to hostesses. Teck found himself liking and envying him.

"Tell me about *The Book of the Dead*, Sam."

"I don't know anything about it."

Teck could feel the car slow almost imperceptibly. "You *said* you did. When I showed you the note."

"Well—but I don't *know* anything about it. What it is, I mean. We may not even be talking about the same thing."

"I certainly hope we are." Burrell's voice was grim. His mouth twitched down.

"Well, I've seen a book. A manuscript, actually. I was told it was called *The Death Book* or *The Book of the Dead*."

"By whom?"

"By a—man," Teck lied. "In the shop where I saw it."

"What shop was that, Sam?"

"A man named Parduk, Ashir Parduk, in the bazaar. There was a fire there a day or two ago."

"I know."

Burrell made a U-turn at the end of the boulevard and started back again. "What language was the manuscript in?"

"Russian, I think. I don't read Russian."

"So you accepted this Parduk's word?"

"Of course. Why, was that a bad idea?" Teck was acutely conscious of the microphone, which he held like an ice-cream cone from which melted goo threatened to drip at any moment. He was trying to plan the lies ahead.

"Tell me exactly what this manuscript looked like."

Teck did the best he could, estimating dimensions, the quality of the paper, the color of the ink, the plastic wrappings. "I see. Fine. Well, now tell me how you came to see this manuscript, Sam."

Teck did not mention the Aelian Fragment. They went twice more up and down the boulevard, and Teck had just reached the point where he had definitely refused to buy the manuscript when Burrell turned again into the center mall and stopped the car. "Have to turn the cassette over," he said, and twisted back to work with both hands in the back seat.

Under way again, Teck finished the doctored tale, in which he did *not* find the manuscript with the book cover, did *not* photograph it, and did *not* throw it into the bay. As told, the story seemed to hold together. Teck was pleased.

Burrell reached over and took the microphone from him; he was driving with his left hand. He switched the microphone off and said, "You know what I think, Sam?" He glanced at Teck. "I think you're a liar."

Teck's voice was thin. "Why should I lie?"

"Ashir Parduk wouldn't tell somebody who came into his shop for a contraband art object—that is what you were there for, I suppose—about something like *The Book.* It doesn't wash."

Teck persisted. "I told it exactly the way it happened."

"Oh, Sam!" Burrell steered the car back up the boulevard. "Do you know what *The Book of the Dead* is?" He did not wait for Teck's answer. "It's a Moslem *Gulag Archipelago.* It's a very dangerous, a very subversive work. Do you know who *wants* that book, Sam?" He stared grimly at the now dark road. "The Russians want it. The Israelis want it. The PLO want it. Some private parties want it, because it may be worth half a million dollars. And *I* want it." He adjusted the rearview mirror. "Now, Sam, I want you to tell me the truth. If you *don't* tell me the truth, I'm going to change the embassy's mind about your case, and that will put you back in the Izmir jail. That wouldn't be so bad, if it weren't for all those other people who want *The Book of the Dead.* Because you see, Sam, so long as *The Book* stays in hiding, everybody will have to come to the conclusion that you were the last man to have contact with it. It's obvious! It will take awhile for people to realize it and to believe it, because you're really a most unlikely candidate for the job, but they'll have to admit it in another day or two. And then, with you in the Izmir jail, somebody will put a couple of people inside with you. Maybe it will be the PLO. They did the job on the body that was found in the harbor, you know. Or it might be the Israelis; they're a little more refined; the pain would be the same but you'd look better afterward."

"I don't want to discuss it any further." Teck used his committee-meeting voice, his voice of injured privilege.

"If you don't tell me what happened to *The Book of the Dead,* I'll put you inside a Turkish prison for twenty years. And you won't live five." Burrell's nostrils flared. He was angry.

"I told you, the manuscript must have burned in the fire!"

"It didn't happen that way!" Burrell's conviction was beyond reason and logic. For the first time Burrell frightened him, because suddenly he saw that Burrell was psychologically capable of abandoning him in just the way he said he would.

"You're intelligence, aren't you?" Teck said suddenly.

"With a capital *I*?" Burrell's voice was mocking and the little smile had returned.

"You're an agent, or whatever they're called."

"James Bond in disguise."

"No, how stupid of me! You're some kind of, of—spy or whatever."

Burrell actually laughed. "You should never be allowed to leave the campus, Sam," he said. "They should provide you with a keeper. Now, please tell me the truth about *The Book of the Dead* so I don't have to crucify you. Let me help you a little. Let me make a guess. Parduk slipped the manuscript to you without your even knowing, didn't he? Aren't I right? He had to get rid of it; he knew somebody was on to him and they would be there within minutes and he had to get rid of it. Here was this perfect patsy, this American fantasizing that he was a big-time art finagler, and Parduk just foisted it off on you without your even knowing. Probably planned to pick it up later; hell, he could have hired a black-bag job on your room for peanuts. But then, of course, he got incinerated along with his shop. And the professor was left holding the hot potato. Am I right?"

He drove in silence for thirty seconds. "I'm glad you're thinking carefully, Sam. Because there's a car following us, and I don't think it's a police car anymore. One of the other interested parties. Tell me the truth or the drive ends here." He again pulled the car into the median and stopped.

Teck looked straight ahead. The leaves of a tree were a surprising, plastic green in the light of a streetlamp. An auxiliary policeman walked under the lamp; he blew his whistle and an answering call came from the next street. Teck took a long breath and let it out slowly.

"*The Book of the Dead* is in the water, about fifty feet out from my hotel window. It's wrapped in plastic and held to the bottom with a fishing weight. There's about ten feet of line attached to it, with a film can for a marker."

Burrell smiled on him. "I admire you, Sam. For accepting the inevitable, I mean. Not for diddling around with the manuscript, for which I'd like to beat you silly, but you didn't know any better; your kind never do. What a dumb damned place to hide it!" He let his breath whistle out. "You *are* a schmuck, aren't you! All right, who told you what the title meant? I know it wasn't Parduk."

Teck swallowed. "A woman named Sandra Lowenstein."

Burrell frowned. "Who's she?"

"Part of the Israeli delegation. Staying at my hotel."

"Probably intelligence." Burrell put the car into gear. "Our date is over." He glanced into the rearview mirror and smiled. "Here they come." He turned off the boulevard and headed down a narrow street, then over an intersection busy with pedestrian traffic, where Teck thought he recognized the taxi stand near the Culture Park.

"What's going to happen to me?" Teck said humbly.

"That depends upon whether or not I find the manuscript where you say it is." Burrell negotiated a turn. "It had better be there."

"It *is* there!"

"I'll know in the morning. And, if it's there—you'll be out of the country by noon. If not—" Burrell raised his right eyebrow. "The scenario as before."

The car pulled up at Teck's hotel. Inside, the fluorescent lights looked too bright and cold. "Out you go." Burrell reached across and unlocked Teck's door. "You understand, this is very confidential. You're to talk to no one. Repeat, *no one.*"

"Unless the inspector decides to stop by again."

"You don't talk to *anybody.*" Burrell took the box with Teck's passport, wallet, and camera. "Then, if everything goes well —tomorrow you'll get these things back." Teck reached for the box but Burrell passed it into his left hand and stopped him with a menacing gesture, palm down, fingers stiff and pointed at Teck's eyes. "Tomorrow, Professor. Get out."

Teck scrambled out and stood by the curb. Burrell's face appeared in the passenger window. "Stay in your room until you hear from me. You'll be safe enough—there's a cop in the lobby. Lock your door." He disappeared and then seemed to think of something else and leaned toward Teck again. "The people who want *The Book* are motivated by two things: patriotism and greed. You ought to understand *one* of those things, Professor."

A moment later the little engine spat furiously and the car pulled away.

When Teck entered the bright lobby, he was aware of three people: behind the small desk was Hamdar, bent over the yellow cat, his face raised to study the new arrival; immediately to the left of the door, a small man in a large chair, no doubt the policeman Burrell had told him about; and, leaning against the entrance to the dining room, a red-haired girl with a body so slender it seemed to disappear completely within her short beige dress, leaving only thin arms and legs and neck to suggest that the garment was occupied. Her head swung toward him as Teck took a step inside the lobby; when she saw him, her eyebrows went up slightly and her lips parted. He saw that she wore very little makeup, probably nothing more than a wash of pale green on each eyelid, and she had a dusting of freckles and seemed very young.

"Mr. Teck!" Her voice was happy. Uncommonly happy.

He was still moving toward the desk from the door. Behind him there was a sound as the policeman started to get up.

"I'm so glad to see you again!"
She would intercept him before he reached the desk. Her lips had widened, spread into a smile, their color disappearing, merging with her skin. She was holding something against her small chest.
Teck stopped.
"I've returned your book."
She, too, stopped, an arm's length from him. She turned the book so that its cover was visible to him. Neither Hamdar nor the policeman could see it.
Teck glanced down at the book and saw its title.

Black Snow.

A block from Teck's hotel five men sat in a parked car. They said nothing. One smoked. A man in the back seat idly rubbed a greasy cloth up and down the barrel of an automatic rifle that rested, muzzle down, between his legs, a motion he had been repeating for twenty minutes. Tucked into the map pouches on the backs of the two seats were six hand grenades, three to a pouch.
After two more minutes a light came on in a corner window at the end of the street. The driver of the car saw it, grunted, and nodded his head. The light went out, came on again, then went out to stay.
As the driver put the car into gear, the hand grenades were already being taken from the seat backs and distributed among the three men in the back.
The car drove a block and then turned parallel to the street on which the Turisti Pallas was located. Halfway along, its lights flicked off and on again, and a VW van parked on the other side flicked its own lights and its engine started. A moment later the two cars were moving in opposite directions.
At the ends of the street, both turned so that they were headed toward the hotel block.

Behind Teck, a word had been shouted from the street. It had sounded angry. Another voice said something behind him. The policeman.
Teck stood quite still. He realized that his mouth was open.
"You haven't forgotten about the book, have you?" The girl held the book out to him. "*Black Snow*?"

The Snow is Black. It will be our joke—our password, how is that, eh? The Snow is Black. You will hear that whispered in your ear one day, and you will think of me, eh?

Parduk had said that to him.

Our password.

"I've got the rest of your stuff in the dining room. I didn't want to hold on to them all night, you know." The girl laughed. Her right hand closed around his left wrist and she began tugging him toward the dining room. When Teck looked back, the policeman was being held by a short, heavyset man who was gesturing excitedly out into the street.

There was a large straw basket with handles on a table by the kitchen door.

"I don't understand." A feeble thing to say, but the truth. The stupid truth.

Instead of stopping at the table, the girl whisked up the basket with one hand and bumped the kitchen door open with her narrow backside. "Come on, we haven't got a lot of time."

"Wait a minute!" Teck jerked his arm free. "What's going on? I don't understand."

The girl stopped, her buttocks still thrust back to hold the door open. Her short red hair framed a face that had grown tense; with her smile gone, the wrinkles at the corners of her eyes were no longer gay, but merely anxious.

"The snow is *black,*" she said in a petulant whisper.

"Where are we going?"

She grabbed his sleeve and pulled him into the kitchen.

"Mr. Parduk wants to see you. He wants his manuscript back."

Chapter eleven

INSPECTOR ARKADI was sitting on his terrace (a tarred rooftop below his kitchen window) over which he had stretched a brilliant pink awning that had been faded to the color of sandstone by the sun. When the news came about the Turisti Pallas, he was sitting comfortably, contemplating the cherry tomatoes that grew so luxuriantly thanks to his wife's constant (and expensive) applications of water.

She was in the kitchen now, humming an American song as she sliced an eggplant. He heard the door of their Italian refrigerator open. He was about to shout "Don't hold the door open," as he always did, but it closed again immediately. She was a woman whose every movement seemed to cause money, his money, to flow—water flowed from a hose connected to the kitchen tap; electricity flowed through the lamps; cold flowed from the open refrigerator door like an invisible river—and yet he loved her almost foolishly, as an adolescent might love. It was love that made him angry with her, love that made him shout; he wanted her to be perfect, so that he could love her without first checking the bills.

"Pick me some tomatoes." Her voice was at his shoulder. He swung his head to find her face almost touching his own. Impetuously, he kissed her bare arm. His hand touched her breast.

She drew away. "The children."

"You said the children were playing at the neighbors."

"*Those* children." She gestured with the knife at a building across the street. Two small children leaned on a windowsill, their chins resting on their crossed hands.

Damn children, he thought, although he adored his own. Ever since he had put up the awning, he had wanted to make love out here. Some hot, still night, with the rest of the city asleep—but he had never quite dared to ask her. He would bring out a plastic sheet to put over the tar, and on top of it the satin cover she had never used on the bed, and then—

On that adolescent vision, the telephone rang.

"I'm not here!" he shouted. "Tell them I'm at the café with the other *men!*" He sounded angrier than perhaps he should have. It was a sore point, his failure to behave like the conventional Turkish male. His father laughed at him with open contempt and would not allow his son's wife in his house. He had wanted his son to marry a woman of the old-fashioned kind, one who did not go about in short skirts humming American songs. It was true, Arkadi knew, that if his father had wanted to make love on a roof, he would simply have told the woman to wash herself and lie down.

Arkadi sighed.

"It's for you, Esmen. I couldn't say you were out." His wife's beautiful face—beautiful to him, certainly—was twisted now with concern. "It's the duty sergeant. It's some kind of emergency."

Arkadi grunted angrily and stepped through the window, catching the toe of his trailing foot so that he tripped and almost fell on the kitchen floor; he caught himself on the refrigerator handle and the door swung open and the invisible river began to flow. By the time he reached the telephone he was as angry as a spoiled child.

"Well, what is it?"

"I'm sorry, Inspector, but—"

"Don't you know I'm off duty?"

"Yes, sir, I'm very sorry, Inspector, but you're being called back. A lot of people are."

Arkadi controlled his anger. "What is it?"

"There's been some kind of attack on the Turisti Pallas, down by the harbor. Terrorists, is the first report. Two cars drove up and they used a grenade in the lobby, at least there was an explosion. There's one man dead on the street—" Arkadi listened, but at the same time his mind was retrieving information stored for just this kind of situation. *Turisti Pallas: The American, Teck, is there, plus two Israelis, one Englishman, two Japanese—*

"Who is in charge?"

"Chief Inspector Pandelli. He asked for you personally."

Arkadi had to restrain a groan. *He would, the old fraud. Superb with pickpockets and prostitutes, but lost in this kind of situation.* Arkadi had worked for him for five years in Robbery before being asked to set up the Art Theft Unit.

"Send a car for me."

"I already have, sir."

"Have the military been called in?"

"I was told to wait until Chief Inspector Pandelli gave the order. So far, he has not."

No, he wouldn't. "Keep me informed." He hung up.

"You're going out?"

"You know I am."

He threaded his belt through the loop of a holster so that the gun would rest against his right kidney.

"Bad?"

"Bad enough. That old fool Pandelli is in charge. Some kind of attack where some of the Israelis are staying."

"I'll wait dinner."

"No, eat. You know how these things are."

He looked past her at the kitchen window, where the artificial light made the awning pink and disguised the fading. Beyond it there was only darkness.

"My name's Mickey." The girl shook her head as if she were used to having long hair that had constantly to be flicked out of her eyes. "I know your name, right?" Her head flicked back again.

"I take it you're an American."

"Oh, yes. Sure, what else?"

Her voice was light, almost childish. Her apparent happiness was gone; she seemed shy and insecure now.

"This is all very confusing for me," Teck said. He tried to look out the window of the car but he saw only his own dim reflection and a far-off light. They had passed the limits of the city and were in the rich farmland beyond it now. "How long had you been waiting for me?"

"Oh—all day."

"I thought Parduk was dead."

"Huh? Well—he wants it that way, right?"

"You know, I don't understand—" Teck straightened himself in the seat, trying to concentrate and to keep awake. "Why didn't he get in touch with me before?"

"Search me!" She tried to make a joke of it. "*Don't* search me; there's nothing to find. You'll find out nobody tells me *anything*." She giggled, but it was a lame and nervous sound.

Mickey glanced repeatedly at the rearview mirror. Her nervousness brought him back to the point they had argued earlier. "It *was* an explosion, wasn't it?"

"I told you, I don't know, I never heard an explosion. Why do you keep asking me?"

He was not sure, either. Perhaps it was tension. As they had driven away, two blocks from the hotel, there had been a sound behind them; his first thought had been, *A bomb.* Now he was not sure.

"How much farther?"
"Huh? Oh, a little ways. Not too long."
Teck saw dust-gray poplars in the headlights. There was a flicker of light high up, an airplane or a star.
"Where are we?"
"I told you, I don't know much of anything. Please don't ask me, okay?"
Teck slumped down in the seat and tried to make himself comfortable. When he looked at her, the red-haired girl was sitting bolt upright behind the wheel, her fingers wrapped around it as if she would never let go.

Arkadi told the driver to stop the car before they reached the first barricade. He climbed on the hood so that he could see over the heads of the crowd that had regrouped in the wake of the policemen who had tried to scatter them, apparently oblivious to the fact that they were within range of the Turisti Pallas. He could see the hotel down the street beyond them, its façade lighted by a portable spotlight. *Just like a film opening,* Arkadi thought. *That must be Pandelli's work.*
"Drive on."
The car threaded through the crowd and moved slowly to the next corner, where the driver turned it away from the hotel on a cross street, then back along an intersecting street to a command post. Arkadi saw Chief Inspector Pandelli sitting in a car with the inside light on, under which his bald head gleamed.
"Inspector Arkadi, sir," he said as he leaned through the window.
"Ah, Arkadi! Good. Just like the old days, eh?" Arkadi smiled politely. He knew Pandelli well—a relic of an older way, like Arkadi's father.
"Can I be brought up to date?" Arkadi asked.
"Oh, aren't we grand, Arkadi! Come off it, this isn't one of your faggot art thefts." Pandelli waved a hand impatiently. "Commando raid. Bastards think they can terrorize us in our own houses! It's the Jews, of course, that's what they're after."
"Is there any proof of who they are?" Arkadi asked patiently.
"Nothing. They say they have hostages, won't say how many. Won't say what they want. But we'll get them, the bastards."

"It could be the Jews who are doing it," Arkadi said. "I was thinking about it on the way here. We just identified a body that was found in the harbor two days ago; he was an Israeli agent. Maybe, as reprisal—"

The chief inspector sneered. "The Syrians, that's who it is. Those pricks let them come and go across the border like bugs under a door. Punks—punks, hoodlums, that's what they are. I'd like to have Arafat at Central for a night." As if the picture of what he would do with the man who had not so long ago spoken to the United Nations pleased him, he leaned back with a satisfied smile.

"Sir?"

The chief inspector's glasses flashed. "Well?"

"I'd like to look around. Can I have a man who knows the situation?"

The chief inspector put a hand on Arkadi's arm to move him aside and then barked a command through the open window. A policeman came running. A minute later Arkadi stood behind a police barricade with a sergeant he did not know.

"They arrived in those two cars in front of the hotel." One car, an American sedan, had been driven up on the sidewalk; the other, a VW van, jutted into the street at an angle. "They must have used a grenade right off; we've all kinds of reports of an explosion. You can see the lobby windows are blown out. You can't see from here, but there's a body on the sidewalk, possibly a passerby, and there's a man lying just inside the front door—we're pretty sure he's dead."

"Uniform?"

"Can't tell, the clothes are pretty well gone."

"I had a man in there—plain clothes."

"You expected something like this?"

"No, a different matter." *Or maybe it isn't,* he thought.

They walked back down the side street and struck the waterfront just where a curve in the shoreline gave protection from the hotel. Again there was a barricade and a crowd, but there were more police now and the crowd was being kept back.

"What about the trade delegations? Are we in touch with them?"

"I wouldn't know about that. The chief inspector wants to handle everything himself." *Or seems to,* Arkadi thought; and then, ashamed of his bitterness, he said, "That's as it should be, of course."

The sergeant pointed out an armed launch in the bay, and beyond it a customs boat. Both lay at anchor with lights shining into the water toward the hotel.

"Any sign that they might try to get away by water?"

"Don't see how they possibly could. Of course, with hostages—but aircraft are the things these days."

As they walked back to the command post, Arkadi was told of police snipers on the nearby roofs and of the armored personnel carrier, usually reserved for riot duty, that was standing by to rush the hotel if the chief inspector gave the order. By the time they had reached the car again, Arkadi had a clear idea of their preparations.

"Where are you assigned, Sergeant?"

"Tactical, sir." *Morale-booster,* Arkadi thought, *one of the good ones who moves from unit to unit.* "I don't know you, do I, Sergeant?"

"No, sir. Irmak, Yussif. I've been on detachment in Cyprus for a year, helping to set up the force down there."

"I'd like to have you assigned to me for tonight if that's possible."

"Yes, sir!" Sergeant Irmak would clearly rather work with an inspector than cool his heels waiting for an order that might never come. He started off to ask for his release from Tactical when Arkadi called after him and he turned back. "Get me a list of every ship in the harbor and all arrivals for the next twenty-four hours. Also, if there isn't a helicopter standing by, get one. Get two—one on the ground ready to go and one in the air. I want top men in the helos, no fatties and no short-timers. Take care of that first, then the shipping."

When Arkadi reached the car, Chief Inspector Pandelli was dictating a report to his driver. Arkadi told him he had asked for helicopters.

"You think they're going to sprout wings, Arkadi?" The inspector guffawed. "That's all right, it's a good idea. But with punks like these, it's a fist in the face they understand. Force." He looked at the dashboard clock. "Is that thing right?" The driver assured him that it was. "I'll give them twenty minutes. Then I'm going to give them a five minutes' warning, and then I'm going in with the armored truck—personally."

"They have hostages."

"I know that! They always have hostages. And always, the authorities sit around and scratch their balls and wait for the angels to solve their problems for them. Well, Arkadi, I'm not doing that. I'm not having a Munich in my city!"

Arkadi's heart sank. "Most of the hostages must be foreigners, sir. It could be— Are we in touch with the trade delegations?"

"In touch! The bastards won't stop pestering me! The Japs, the Jews, the Soviets, the whole whining lot keep asking what am I going to do? I've got the lot of them locked in an office over on the next street where they can't bother me."

Arkadi was about to suggest that he soothe the foreigners whom the chief inspector had locked up when he heard running feet. A man was trotting toward the car, shouting.

A hostage had just come out of the hotel waving a white tablecloth.

Valeri Seriakin was being held in an office with the other foreigners. While the others crowded at the windows, from which they could see nothing but the dark street and the taller buildings over the way, Seriakin idly turned the pages of an industrial pamphlet at one of the desks. He was surprised to find that the Turks bought polyvinyl-chloral tubing in Brazil.

"Why don't you *do* something?" It was Lyubin, the nervous second-in-command of the Soviet group.

"What do you suggest I do? Challenge the policeman at the door to a kung fu battle?"

"Agh, what good are you?" Lyubin looked angry and then, appalled by what he had had the temerity to say to the KGB man, he added, "It's not myself I care about, it's our comrades in that hotel."

"What would a sensible Russian be doing in that grubby hotel?" Seriakin asked in a mild voice. "So far as I can tell, six of our people are on duty at the Trade Fair, three are drunk in our hotel, five are enjoying a nightclub under the care of Olga Leonov, and two are in bed together."

"Yes, but—" Lyubin looked worried. *Yes, but. What if.* The petty worries of a bureaucrat. *How do I shift the blame?* That was what concerned Lyubin.

Seriakin was not in a tearing hurry to get out of the office. He could use the time to think. Only moments before Lyubin had begged him to come along to the scene of this terrorist raid, Seriakin had learned that Teck had just been released from police custody, and that the man with whom the professor had left was Phillip Burrell, a CIA officer. It was distressing, because more and more he was convinced that the trail of *The Book of the Dead* led inexplicably to Teck.

The man who waited for Teck was not Parduk. Teck was not surprised. Professor Teck, the arrogant trafficker in small, illegal treasures, might have been surprised; this weary, still paranoid Teck was not. The girl's use of the password, her carrying of *Black Snow* had lured him, and hope had lured him still more strongly—he *wanted* Parduk to be alive—but he was not surprised that it was someone other than Parduk who waited for him.

The girl had driven directly into the garage of what had seemed, by moonlight, to be a Continental country house. A single light had showed at the end away from the garage. She had opened a door; at the far end of an unlighted passage a man had waited, silhouetted in the doorway. It was certainly not Parduk.

"Walk straight ahead, Mr. Teck."

He walked.

"Don't trip over the table. It's on your right."

He watched the man in the doorway as he walked. The voice sounded young. It was a husky tenor, accented with a guttural accent, but not unpleasant. Almost an American voice, but with odd edges.

"I'm glad you could make it. Come on in."

Chapter twelve

THE hostage released from the Turisti Pallas was a young Turk from the interior who had brought his wife with him to the Trade Fair even though his employer—an importer of cheap photographic equipment and office machines—had not paid her expenses. Now, released from immediate danger, he could only repeat over and over. "My wife, my wife is still in there." And each time, as if it explained something otherwise inexplicable, he would add, "They know she's my wife." Arkadi and his sergeant met the man at the first protected corner, where four uniformed policemen with shields and riot helmets formed a ring around him.

"Sergeant, I want the snipers to keep every window of that hotel covered, do you understand?" The sergeant started off. "And send a doctor or a nurse to the chief inspector's car! This man will need something."

Within the protective ring, the man was still repeating, "—is still in there. She's still in there." He appealed to Arkadi. "My wife, she's still in there." And he added, "They know she's my wife." The man looked as if he were about to weep. He still held the white flag that he had waved so vigorously as he had come out of the hotel; Arkadi saw that his flagstaff was a mop handle with a plastic sponge mop still attached to the other end. The white flag itself was a worn tablecloth with TURISTI PALLAS stitched in faded red thread along one hem.

"My wife, she's—"

"It's all right, now, it's all right; they wouldn't send you out if they didn't mean to bargain. Your wife will be all right." Arkadi signaled to the riot police to come with him. "Help him a little, he looks ready to fall on his face," he murmured to one of them, and the hostage was escorted along the street by men who virtually carried him while his tablecloth fluttered overhead and he babbled on about his wife.

Arkadi leaned into the dark automobile. "One of the hostages, Inspector."

"Ah!" The chief inspector crowed with delight. "They're finding out they can't push me around, Arkadi." He leaned over and unlocked the rear door. "Sit up front, Arkadi. Put the hostage back here with me." He gave the door a push with his fingertips and it swung wide. "Sit in the back, please," he said quietly to the man, who looked blank, then glanced down at his flagstaff. He seemed not to know what to do.

"Give that to Sergeant Irmak," Arkadi said, taking away the mop. Gently, he pushed the man into the rear of the car.

"My wife, she's—"

The chief inspector gripped his arm. "It's all right now; we have this situation under control." The man became quiet. It was possible to trust Pandelli in this sort of situation; he sounded strong and self-possessed and his somber confidence was reassuring.

"What's your name?"

"Rafim, Bulent Rafim. I come from—"

The inspector leaned across him and bellowed at the uniformed men who waited beside the car. "Get back to your positions! What the hell do you think this is, a café?" He glared at Arkadi. "Whose men are those?"

Arkadi shrugged. "I could check, I suppose."

The chief inspector turned back to the hostage. "We are in charge of this situation, Rafim. I have men everywhere. Boats in the harbor, men on rooftops,. an armored vehicle—Inspector Arkadi has ordered up a helicopter, isn't that right, Arkadi?"

"That's right, Chief Inspector."

As if to confirm Arkadi's truthfulness, the throbbing of the helicopter's engine could be heard faintly over the rooftops.

"So this situation is under control, and I can give you my personal assurances, Rafim, that your wife is going to come out of there alive and well." *Please* thought Arkadi, *don't let him be such a fool.* But the chief inspector persisted. "My *personal* assurance. Understand?"

"Yes, sir. And thank you." And Bulent Rafim did, indeed, look as if he felt reassured, as if he believed the man and felt better.

"All right, Rafim. You have a message for us?"

"Uh? Oh, yes. Yes, sir. I have this paper—a list of their demands, sorry, their requests, and the names of the hostages. There." He stabbed a finger at the paper that trembled in his hand. "There's my wife's name. And my own, but that's wrong. I'm not there now, but they made up the list earlier. You see?"

The chief inspector squinted at the paper. He tried holding it up under the sickly dome light but he could still not make it out. "Read it to me, Arkadi!" Arkadi scanned the names and nationalities—no Russians, no Americans (*Where is Teck*? he wondered), no Israelis (*Where are the Lowensteins*? for the body of Sandra Lowenstein had not yet been identified, and her husband had not reported her as missing), but six Turks, two Japanese, and an Englishman. The names of the hotel's owner and of his own plainclothesman were not on the list.

"Are there any dead inside?"

Rafim blinked. "I was in my room when the bomb went off.

My wife and I were in the room. There could be—any number. Nobody told me."

"The lobby?"

"There weren't any lights. Only a flashlight one of them had. But a bomb had gone off in the lobby, I knew that."

So if my man and Teck were in the lobby—

"Read it to me, Arkadi!"

He quickly summarized the demands: two cars with drivers, a jet aircraft waiting at the Izmir airport, no armed guards near the hotel or the cars.

The inspector laughed grimly. "Not bloody likely!" he said in heavily accented English. It was a line from a film he had liked, and he always said it when he thought he was challenged. "Not bloody likely!" He laughed again, a single short grunt of grim amusement that seemed to frighten some of the assurance out of Rafim.

"They are giving us thirty minutes to answer. Any refusal and they will"—Arkadi looked at Rafim—"I am sorry. I have to ask you this. They say they have all the hostages in one room that is already fixed with plastic explosive. Is that true?"

"They tied us up and put us into a room at the back. They let the women lie on the bed, and one of the men had a chair. But there was no moving around. I didn't get the chair; I wanted to stand by my wife, but they made me sit on the floor. There was one of them in the doorway with a, what do you call them, an automatic weapon of some kind. A grease gun."

"Any explosive?"

"Stuff like a child's putty, on the walls, wires running into it."

Arkadi sighed. "I'll call Ankara."

"Like hell you will!"

"I'm sorry, Chief Inspector." Arkadi tried to see the man's eyes in the dim light. "I don't think either of us is qualified to negotiate this kind of thing."

Pandelli shot a look at Rafim before he leaned forward and hissed at Arkadi, "There will be no negotiation!"

"Sir, this is not a local—"

"I'm in charge, Arkadi, and I intend to keep this situation under control! If you don't like that, you just quit right now and we can discuss it tomorrow. Clear?"

Arkadi looked at the chief inspector, who was glaring up

under heavily gathered brows in the expression that was supposed to terrify petty criminals and that was much imitated by the young men in the department behind Pandelli's back. He glanced at Rafim, who was cowering into the farthest corner of the car, his eyes flicking from one man to the other as if he thought they might strike him.

"The regulations are quite clear, Chief Inspector—as you know. We need authority."

"Not bloody likely!" One of his pale hands gripped the back of Arkadi's seat. "You know what's wrong today, Arkadi? Nobody's got any guts! Pass it along, send it up the line, guard your own ass. Well, I've got the guts! Those poor bastards of hostages in there are my responsibility and they're going to *stay* my responsibility!"

Now I've done it, Arkadi thought. *I've backed him into his corner.*

Arkadi reached across the chief inspector's hand, his own fingers a little spread, palm forward in a gentle gesture, as of fending something off. "Chief Inspector," he began, "I know this is very important to you; I feel it, too, believe it or not. It's an offense, a sacrilege, a violation. I want to clean it out, too. I'm sick to death of channels and authority and procedures and chains of command, too. But this is too important for us to risk those lives."

The inspector's voice was very flat and final. "If this goes to Ankara, I'll withdraw every man in this command. And I'll have your ass in a meatgrinder."

Neither of the men was looking at Rafim when he spoke. "But my wife is in there. They know that she's my wife."

Teck heard the muffled thump of a car door being closed, and, a few seconds later, the clatter of the red-haired girl's clogs. His temples were tight with fatigue, as if the skin over them had shrunken. His eyes watered and he had to squint to keep the young man in focus.

"I guess I ought to introduce myself, Mr. Teck." His right hand came forward in a curve as if some invisible pillar stood between them. "I'm Ricki."

It seemed absurd to go through polite formalities. Teck avoided looking at the hand and said, "I'm awfully tired. May I see Mr. Parduk?"

Behind Teck, the red-haired girl had stopped in the doorway. In the utter silence Teck could hear the movement as she brushed her hair from her forehead.

"Well, about Mr. Parduk, you see, well, there's been this little slipup." The young man's voice was nasal and his odd accent made the word come out as "slip-UP"; Teck thought he heard something other than Turkish in his speech. "But I'm qualified to act for Mr. Parduk, see; he gave me full authority in this matter. Would you tell me where the manuscript is, please?"

Teck hesitated. *Greed and patriotism.* He had to go over what had happened one step at a time. *I told Burrell about the manuscript. Because I had to. Now I should tell this Ricki about the manuscript. Because he has the password.* All that he said was, "Can I sit down somewhere?"

"Oh, sure, Mr. Teck, sure, sit wherever you like. You want a drink or something?"

"No, thank you." Teck sat in a low chair where he would not have to look into the light. Through his fatigue, something of his professorial self tried to make a comeback. "I'm really exhausted, you know. Perhaps, in the morning—"

Ricki smiled. "The police, they can be very exhausting."

"You knew where I was?"

"Oh, sure, Mr. Teck, we been keeping real good watch over you. Parduk, he was very worried, you know."

"I'd certainly like to see Mr. Parduk."

Ricki smiled again. He seemed to smile a good deal, perhaps because he was a handsome man and he knew it—compact, even short compared to Teck, but slim and consciously graceful, like a dancer. He stood now a few feet from Teck with one hand resting on a little table. Barefoot and dressed in flared trousers and a fitted shirt of a shiny, dark blue material, he seemed very confident and very relaxed.

"Maybe tomorrow you can see Parduk. Tonight I have promised him to get the manuscript for him. Please tell me where it is." When, again, Teck did not answer immediately, he said, "I have the password, Mr. Teck. What more can you ask?"

"Oh, well—" *Oh, well! Oh, well, really,* as he answered graduate students who asked if a grade might be raised. "Perhaps you can tell me more about the password."

"*The Black Snow.* What more is there to tell?"

"Well, uh, who did Mr. Parduk say was the author? Of *Black Snow*?"

Ricki's smile was absolutely dazzling. Teck knew the look. *My paper is going to be late, Professor. I don't know the answer, Professor, but I'm going to fake it.* "What do you mean, the author? You mean, who wrote it? Are we talking about *Black Snow* or about something else?"

"About the work that Parduk told me was called *Black Snow*."

Ricki looked at the red-haired girl. His smile never wavered.

"It is a Russian, okay? Is that enough? A Russian, he wrote it."

"What Russian?"

Ricki laughed. It might have been some delicious joke. "You Americans are such very suspicious folks!" He turned to the girl. "Mickey, would you ask Kamal to come in here, please?" The girl frowned. "Go on, Mickey. Do as I ask."

She hesitated. The ambiguous look she gave Teck before she crossed the room and went out might have been either an appeal or an apology.

"Mickey is my girl, Mr. Teck. You know how girls are when they think you're in love with them. Very stubborn. Very slow to do things." More laughter, more charm, and then a pause as if he were waiting for something else to happen. The pause became awkward, and finally even Ricki's smile subsided to a mere perfunctory little *moue.* Teck remembered what he wanted to say.

"You were going to give me the name of the author."

"No, no I wasn't, Mr. Teck. I have given you all that is necessary. No, now you are going to tell me where the manuscript is."

"I most certainly won't! Not until I have more, well, proof. About the password, I mean. Get in touch with Mr. Parduk and, and have him give you more information."

The door through which the girl had gone opened. A man stepped through. The light from the lamps illuminated only his legs and his shoes and it was impossible to tell how big he was.

Ricki turned slightly to acknowledge the other man and then he looked down at Teck. "You really should have told me, Mr. Teck. It would have been a hell of a lot more pleasanter all around. As it is, you understand, I got a business to run, I can't afford delays. See, I was making a deal with Mr. Parduk for that manuscript, and then somebody threw a firebomb and my business got very messed up. I can't afford that kind of trouble." He nodded sagely and he was no longer smiling. "Kamal."

The man stepped forward into the light.

Ricki opened a drawer in the small table at his side and took out a little automatic pistol, one so small and pretty that it might have been a lady's cigarette lighter or an expensive toy. He stepped back to make way for Kamal, who moved toward Teck with his hands a little in front of him.

His left hand was bare, but he was wrapping a strip of heavy black rubber over the knuckles of his right hand. Teck stood up, aware that nothing in his academic background had prepared him for what was coming.

Phillip Burrell did not learn of the attack on the Turisti Pallas until he had completed a call to an old Navy friend about borrowing a frogman to go down after the manuscript. He was sitting at the desk of the U.S. Information Service office; Rountree, the pink-faced young man who was in charge, had not waited for the receiver to touch the cradle before he blurted out the news. "There's a terrorist attack on a hotel! I just got it from somebody who lives near there. There's been an explosion and there are police all over the place!"

The pink young man had been very excited.

"Which hotel?"

"Uh—oh, Christ, it's one of those places along the water. God, he gave me the name and I had it just a second ago."

Burrell had been calm and slow. "The Turisti Pallas?"

"That's it!" The young man had been dejected. "You already knew."

"Educated guess." Burrell had allowed Rountree a confiding smile and a reassuring squeeze above the elbow, and he had hurried from the office to hide the tic that showed at the right side of his mouth when he was too tense to suppress it.

Now he pulled his car up at the police barricade and turned off the engine before anybody could tell him that the car would have to be moved. When a policeman wearing a helmet and a flak vest put out a hand, Burrell flashed his diplomatic passport, saying in idiomatic Turkish that he was there to negotiate concerning the Americans being held hostage. The policeman looked around for a superior, but Burrell was already over the barricade and striding toward a cluster of men and cars in the middle of the block. *As if he could stop me,* he thought, *as if he'd really try. The good soldier, always ready to pass the buck.*

He was stopped again, but he showed the passport and raised his voice almost to a shout, and a police sergeant appeared.

"What is it, please?"

"I have a diplomatic passport, and—"

"I'm sorry, you can't come any closer."

"I want to see the officer in charge. I'm here to negotiate for the Americans in the hotel."

"There are no Americans in the hotel."

"I'm sorry, I'm afraid I know more about that than you do."

Burrell appraised the sergeant: a tough, knowledgeable veteran who must be somebody's good right hand. Not easily bluffed, probably not bribable. The worst kind.

"Sergeant, I *must* see your superiors. This is a very sensitive matter. Don't exceed your authority."

And the sergeant was not a man to be impressed, either. "My authority is to keep everybody away from the command post. I'm sorry, sir."

"I demand to see your superior!" Burrell's full voice, once effective on a drill field, bounced from the stone walls and rang over the street. Several men looked up from the group around the car. One detached himself and hurried toward them.

"What is it, Irmak?"

"Somebody from the American Embassy, Inspector."

Arkadi moved close to Burrell. They recognized each other from the negotiations to free Teck that afternoon.

"I'm sorry, I've forgotten your name."

"Phillip Burrell. You're Inspector Arkadi, of course. We met this afternoon."

"About the man Teck. Yes."

"Is he in there?"

"I don't know."

"But I left him there an hour ago."

"We don't know."

"Who is in charge here, Inspector?"

"As far as you are concerned, I am. *Don't press,* do you understand?"

The cluster around the car began to break up. Half a dozen uniformed men trotted by on the other side of the street, their boots landing rhythmically.

"Arkadi!" The voice was a bellow. Burrell saw a bulky man step out of the car.

"Here, sir."

"Get your ass up here!"

Burrell stepped forward. He had to shout to be heard over the rising noise, as of a military camp coming to life. A helicopter was swinging low a block or two away; somewhere up ahead a heavy vehicle gunned its engine. "Are you the officer in charge?"

The bulky man took two steps toward them and glowered into the darkness, head down. "Who the hell is that?"

"I'm Phillip Burrell, from the—"

"An American."

The man took another step toward them. Hunched, hands gathered into fists, he looked like an old boxer ready to face one more beating.

"Get that man off this street and up with the other foreigners!"

Sergeant Irmak put his hand under Burrell's elbow. "Come on, before things get worse."

Burrell tried to pull away.

"Get him out of here!"

Burrell found himself being hustled up the street away from the activity. He twisted around to shout back toward the car, "Ankara will hear about this!"

The reply, bellowed out against a chorus of pounding boots and the growl of an engine, was succinct.

"Screw Ankara!"

Chapter thirteen

THERE had never been a place for wanton violence in Teck's life. Violence had been rigorously squeezed from it—even the emotional violence of true passion. The excitements of intellect, such as they are, had sufficed, spiced by the rather timid adventures of adultery (with carefully nonviolent women, of course) and the vicarious passions of Nixon-hating. "Good" public schools and "the better" private colleges had served as funnels for Teck's sensibilities, constrictions that had narrowed his life and delivered him into a class where genuine violence was repressed. He lived in a placid sanctuary, taught on a placid campus in the sanitized air of an expensive classroom building, and the route he traveled between the two places was along expressways that were elevated above the gritty lives of the violent—the strugglers, the loud-voiced and always angry others—Latin, black, poor Irish—who fought with their hands and shouted at strangers, who owned guns and who struck their wives and who cowered in the dock at sordid little trials for manslaughter and assault and car theft.

Violence had always been unseemly.

The shock of abruptly being the victim of violence racked Teck as severely as the pain that the violence caused. With Kamal's first blow, Teck had been utterly degraded, reduced from a man whose every aspect—speech, clothes, manners, thoughts—was a self-assertion, to a mere victim with no self whatsoever. He was no longer Samuel Teck; he was merely an object.

Lying now on his back with Ricki standing over him, he was conscious, even lucid, but his thoughts tumbled recklessly. When Ricki bent down, Teck flinched like a child.

"*The Book of the Dead*, Mr. Teck. I got to have it. You can understand me okay?"

Teck tried to nod his head. The breath had been kicked out of him and there was blood in his mouth and on his lips.

"Now, I want that book, you got to see that. Kamal has gone

easy so far because I hope you're a smart guy who learns quick, right?" Ricki knelt beside him. "If you tell me now, I'll let you go. Out here in the country, so you'll have to walk some, but I'm not the killing type of guy; that isn't my line of business. Okay?"

Teck licked his bruised lips. He tried to think. "Where is Parduk?"

"Parduk is *dead*; he died in that fire, what d'you think, man? Come on, the manuscript, yes or no?"

Burrell, Teck thought. *Burrell will put me in a Turkish prison.* Prison would be violence compressed: Attica. A society of victims, turning on each other. Sodomy. Torture.

Teck whimpered.

"Well?" Ricki said.

"I can't!" Teck pleaded.

"Like hell you can't, man. Like hell." Ricki stood up. He spoke a few words to Kamal, no more than a dozen syllables, and walked to the far end of the room.

Teck saw the large man start to move toward him. It was like the time he had been in an automobile accident: the car had started to skid on a snowy pavement into the other lane; a car was coming from the opposite direction, and Teck had found himself saying silently, *No, no, this isn't happening, this can't be happening to me,* as if something about being Samuel Teck made him immune to mundane accident, and he had gone on thinking that such a thing could not happen to him, must not happen to him, until the two cars had thundered together, bounced apart, and he had seen his side of his own car moving inexorably toward a concrete light pole, still saying, *No, no, it can't be, not to me,* until he had struck and blacked out. Now, he started the *No, no, it can't be,* until abruptly that earlier pain taught him that denying the obvious had been a necessary adaptation to a crisis, but it was the wrong kind now, when he might have some chance of saving himself or at least of delaying; and he pulled himself backward, his feet coming flat on the floor as his knees pulled up to his chest and he swung his torso up to get balance, but Kamal moved quickly and reached him before he could stand.

Teck pushed back with his heels. He escaped Kamal's reaching fingers but landed flat on his back again, and the pain stabbed as sharply as if he had fallen on a piece of glass. He rolled to his left, feeling a glancing kick on the back of his right thigh, and then he had rolled up against a chair and could go no farther. He looked back, and there were Kamal's massive legs and the bulge of his crotch, and Teck wanted to bury his face and hold on and hide from the beating that was coming, but he knew that there was no hiding and that such a move would mean only the full force of those hands on his temples and ears. He pulled himself up the chair, his hands clawing as frantically as a cat's climbing a tree.

Kamal gripped his right shoulder, but he squirmed away and fell over the chair.

Kamal kicked him in the groin from behind. Pain flooded up into his abdomen.

Kamal struck him behind the right ear.

Teck stumbled forward blindly into a wall. He took two steps to his left and spun a floor lamp savagely behind him, where it crashed to the floor.

Motion was everything. If he could keep moving fast enough, Kamal would not catch him. Anything put between them was another stone in a barricade—books from an end table, a sofa pillow, a framed photograph of a group of people who seemed to have been on a picnic when their picture was taken; now, they were rudely separated by long rips where the picture had struck Kamal's upraised fist, and the glass that had protected them for half a century was slivered over the floor. A carved chair was tipped crazily where Teck had passed. The worn carpet was flipped over on itself; he had slipped there and one of Kamal's shoes had caught his left arm, but he had kept his feet and staggered on. Even Ricki had retreated from his wild flight, with his ridiculous little pistol held defensively in front of him.

Teck looked for a fireplace with a poker. There was none. The room had not been furnished for defense.

At last he made a wrong move. Kamal blocked him into a corner. In his last good moments, Teck was pleasantly amazed at the wreckage of the room. He could not remember having broken that large vase, nor having thrown that brass lamp with the rather overweight Diana and her hound. He did not remember striking Kamal, but the man's left sleeve was torn and there was a good flow of blood from a gash on his right forehead.

Kamal feinted with his left hand and struck with his right low down, three inches below the navel. The left hand grasped Teck's throat and pushed him against the wall, the thumb biting in just below the jawbone. Teck made a noise, a screech, such as rabbits make when they are dying and the right hand struck once, twice, three times, on the left side of his head. A knee came up in his groin, and the pain was like nothing Teck had ever experienced, a malignant orgasm that took control of his body away from him.

Teck sobbed and then vomited and choked.

Kamal had struck him once more in his left eye before Teck could beg them to stop and could blabber out the location of the manuscript. Kamal let him go, and Teck, sodden with vomit and the urine that had spurted down his thighs, collapsed and sobbed like a heartbroken child.

It was a minor setback for Phillip Burrell. They were putting him with some other foreigners in an office block two streets from the hotel "for his protection," an expression that had made him smile. He had probably been in more critical situations than any of the police would have dreamed of. He was disappointed that he had not found out where Teck was, of course, but the more important problem was the manuscript. Perhaps there would be a way to get a diver into the harbor near the hotel on some pretext of helping the police. It would have to be considered very carefully. If the terrorists held on, of course, he would have to examine other possibilities.

The sergeant held the door open for him, and behind the sergeant, Arkadi nodded toward the room beyond. Burrell could see several people inside.

"How long will I have to stay here, Inspector?"

"You can go back to your hotel right now if you will stay out of the area, Mr. Burrell."

Burrell shrugged. "I hope your chief inspector knows his job."

Arkadi did not react. "We will keep you informed. Come on, Sergeant." He did not walk away until Burrell had gone into the room. Burrell heard the door close behind him.

He stood very straight. His head turned slowly from left to right, his face masked with a polite half-smile that was useful at receptions and dull parties. As the other foreigners evaluated the newcomer, the room fell silent.

Burrell was the senior man present. In another century he

would have been a British intelligence agent masquerading as a staff man, but he would still have had a public role as an envoy of the most powerful and the most confident of nations. Now, Burrell did what that predecessor might have done: with courtesy and a nice sense of protocol, he went around the room, introducing himself and making the others comfortable.

"How do you do; I am Phillip Burrell, cultural attaché to the United States mission in Ankara." He said it in Japanese, in French, and in German. He gave it a quite different and delightful coloration for the best-looking woman there, the wife of a Belgian textile executive. When he approached the two men who had separated themselves a little from the others, he said it in Russian.

"Lyubin, the Soviet trade delegation." The older of the two was stiff and formal, no doubt ill at ease in the face of Burrell's manner.

Burrell looked at Lyubin's companion. The American extended his hand. "Phillip Burrell."

"Valeri Seriakin."

"Ah." Burrell smiled. The young man was not quite what he would have expected. There was wry amusement in the Russian's manner. Burrell looked at the fashionably cut hair, the clothes, the relaxed manner. *I don't like him,* Burrell concluded.

He would have liked him still less if had guessed Seriakin's thoughts. In notes Seriakin made later, he said of Burrell, *A stringy man like a packet of rubber bands, perhaps many of them about to snap from age or tension; chauvinistic, vain, perhaps a disappointed man. Still dangerous.* He would not write down his private reaction: *I pity him.*

Phillip Burrell held Seriakin's fingers in a prolonged handshake. "I knew your father," he said. It was a delicate thrust.

The young Russian pulled his hand away. "My father died recently." A polite parry.

Burrell smiled sadly. "I know." *Touché.*

They looked at each other.

Seriakin was not surprised. Yet, Burrell's complacency—and the evident assumption that it would be shared by Seriakin—troubled him, was, in fact, one of the elements of the whole system that troubled him; it was a tacit admission that at some level they were men who shared more with each other than they did with the countrymen whose values they were supposedly defending—as if, after a period of probation (shorter in his own case because of his father's eminence), one were admitted to a society, the "intelligence community," that was exclusive and prestigious and as mysterious to laymen as the Jesuits or the Masons. It was very un-Russian, of course, and probably un-American, and it went against the very ctre of Soviet ideology, yet it existed—and Seriakin hated it. It was hypocrisy.

Once, Seriakin had been taken to a party where his father and Repin had hobnobbed with two known British agents and an American; they had been elated and had come away very drunk, and after that his father had referred to one of the Englishmen as "good old Simms," as if he were some companion from a happier past.

Seriakin's smile faded. Deliberately, he did an untoward thing. "Mr. Burrell," he said in English, "I know who you are, and you know who I am, I am confident, and our courtesy disgusts me." He turned away and stood with arms folded looking out the window.

Burrell's tic returned. At first he was in one sense pleased by the young Russian's bad manners, thinking that it was a sign of inexperience and of fear, but then he sensed that he had been outmaneuvered.

Given a moment more, Burrell might have recovered himself and joined Seriakin at the window in order to talk with him again, but just then there was a rattle of automatic fire from the street and an explosion that shook the room, and everyone rushed to the windows.

A late-afternoon downpour was falling on suburban Virginia, and as the cars streamed from the parking lots, many already had their lights on and the end-of-day exodus was slower than usual. There was already a traffic tangle on the parkway, which grew quickly worse when a tractor-trailer jackknifed at five seventeen.

In the corner office, however, there was no sense of the storm, except for the rivulets of water that merged and separated and merged again on the window; inside, it was quiet and the air was artificially dried. When Ken Fellows knocked, his superior was clearing his desk for the evening.

"Can I catch you for a minutes before you leave, sir?"

"I hope it's important, Ken. We're having people at seven."

"It's, uh, something from upstairs."

"From the director?"

"Deputy director's office." The young man looked down modestly. "Actually, a friend of mine shunted it our way before it could go up the pipe."

"Good man." He leaned back. "Smoke if you want, Ken."

The young man laid a typed message copy on the desk. "This was received from ComSubLant this afternoon. It's a priority request for authorization of money for naval personnel and it refs"—he put another paper on the desk—"this set of orders from Sixth Fleet HQ, detaching two frogmen on TAD for something called Grampus."

"Doesn't mean beans to me. Should it?"

"No, sir, I don't think so. I got on to a guy I know over at ONI and he came up with a code word—I think it's obsolete: at least it's not in *my* book—for an operation requested by us for NATO. Well, with a little prying, ComSubLant gave me verbal copy—that's *this* piece of paper—of an attachment to the orders—that's *that* piece of paper—for the two frogmen. It's marked Secret, U.S. Eyes Only, and it says, blah, blah, 'proceed soonest air to Izmir, Turkey, for operation not to exceed forty-eight hours. Upon completion return to, et cetera.' "

"Oh, Jesus."

"Yes, sir. Well, ComSubLant also told me that the orders had been issued by a captain attached to Sixth Fleet staff. Not really normal procedure, and I think that's why we were queried for financial authorization, because—now get this—an *ensign* in Sixth Fleet accounting asked for confirmation that we would foot the bill."

"What the hell kind of thing is that to do? An *ensign*?"

"Well, they're tighter for money than we are. If Congress dickers around much longer with their appropriation, they're strapped."

The man behind the desk reached forward and took a cigarette from the younger one's pack. "Actually, the little son-of-a-bitch was absolutely right. But hell, they don't normally ask us to pay for two-bit jobs like this, do they?"

"No, sir. But if he went by the book, well—"

Both men were silent for several seconds.

"The way I read it, Ken, our man Burrell, he used the

'old-boy' routine to contact somebody at Sixth Fleet; he just finessed around channels and got a quick favor from an old buddy. *Exactly* what's been getting us into trouble on the Hill! And so the buddy issues a set of orders for two frogmen, and everything is clean until an ensign who doesn't know any better decides to go by the book."

"That's about the way I read it, too, sir."

"Did you confirm this with Burrell?"

"You told me to let him hang loose."

The older man carefully tapped out his cigarette in an ashtray. "All right," he said softly. "All *right.* You contact ComSub-Whatever-It-Is and tell them no, N-O, we do not underwrite these costs. Then get on the blower to this Burrell and ask him just what the hell he thinks he's doing, and you tell him from me—and make this very clear, Ken, it's from me direct and you're merely passing on the message, you take no guff from him and if he starts to bitch, let him—you tell him, *from me,* that I want a message request for his frogmen or whatever they are, and I want it spelled out, chapter and verse, *exactly* what he plans and *exactly* what his reasons for every step of this action are. Clear?"

"Very clear, sir. And I appreciate you letting me say it comes direct from you. The field spooks can be pretty rough."

They smiled at each other.

"You're a good boy, Ken." Both men stood up. "And listen, get a file on that ensign. He sounds like a kid we could use over here."

The police assault on the Turisti Pallas was short, ugly, and devastating. Chief Inspector Pandelli, wearing a steel helmet, rode next to the driver of the armored truck. In their wake came twenty men armed with automatic weapons. Hopefully protected by constant fire from the rooftops, the assault force made directly for the front door of the hotel.

The next morning a British correspondent who had been chosen from the pool of reporters covering the Trade Fair stood as close to the ruined hotel as the military guard would allow. A camera from a mobile unit panned over the jeeps clustered at the entrance, over the crowd and the self-conscious soldiers, over the search team probing the rubble, to the third story of the building, where only shattered windows and a bullet-pocked wall showed what had happened inside.

The correspondent's voice, trained to a funereal solemnity for such occasions, was low and hushed. "At least nineteen people, five of them policemen and nine of them civilian hostages, perished in a terrorist attack here last night. Members of the police force, led by Chief Inspector Yussif Pandelli, who was himself one of the first to die, launched a frontal assault on the terrorist-occupied Turisti Pallas hotel shortly after midnight. Within minutes the terrorists and their hostages were dead. An explosion that broke windows three blocks away and could be heard over most of this city ripped the upper floor of the structure as the terrorists engaged in a firefight. Bodies and parts of bodies are still being found, and at this moment identification of the victims is impossible. It is believed that the dead include at least one British visitor, several Turkish and Japanese, and possibly other visitors to the International Trade Fair. An air of pessimism, almost of despair, has gripped this coastal city, which had been trying to put its best foot forward in reestablishing Turkey's international status after recent events in Cyprus. There are army uniforms everywhere and a curfew is rumored. Perhaps worst of all, the nationality, even the goal of the terrorists is unknown, and as of this tragic morning, no group has laid claim to the attack."

When his report was aired some hours later, distance had blunted the edge of the event and none of the watchers was much moved. It happened that three people who knew Samuel Teck heard the report, but none realized that he might be involved. And what did it matter, compared to famine in Africa and the state of Western economy?

And the person who might have cared deeply, the Princess di Paoli, was en route to Antalya by air, and she learned of it only later and almost by accident.

Chapter fourteen

THE deputy chief for crime had a bald, brown skull and a round, brown face that had sagged as he grew older, noticeably so after his last promotion. Seated with his age-spotted hands clasped over his temples, he looked like a man on the verge of despair. Yet, as Arkadi knew, he was simply concentrating on the draft report that lay before him; in a moment, he would turn his face up and his pouched eyes would show, not despair, but cynicism and shrewdness.

He grunted once. Thirty seconds later, he clucked disapprovingly. Arkadi shifted from one weary leg to the other. At last, he looked up.

"Sergeant Irmak will confirm this?"

"Yes, sir."

"The chief inspector *said* you were not to inform Ankara?"

"As it's in the report, sir."

The deputy chief lit a cigarette that he took from his breast pocket. "One hour, Arkadi. One hour, and I have to be ready to tell the great men why we caused—nineteen? twenty?—deaths." He blew smoke out impatiently. "*Could* you have stopped him?"

"I don't know. I was with the foreigners when the attack was started. Or I had just left them; I took an American, the one from their embassy, up to the office where—"

The deputy chief waved his hand, dispersing the smoke and silencing Arkadi at the same time. "I don't want excuses."

"I am not making excuses!" Arkadi stood up to the gaze from the skeptical eyes. "I don't make excuses, not for myself or for anybody else. Maybe I should have contacted Ankara on my own."

"Yes, you should have."

"And if I had been wrong, this morning I'd be standing here explaining why I broke a direct order, and you would be telling me I was through!"

"You're outspoken, Arkadi."

"I'm very tired. I was up all night."

"Well." He scanned the report again. "You can't come out of this looking good. There's just no way out. For an inspector, I mean. What had the attack to do with your unit?"

"Nothing. Pandelli asked for me."

"Hmp." He leaned forward and said earnestly, "Why did he *do* it?"

"Because"—Arkadi thought of Pandelli in the car— "because he was ashamed of being a Turk whose country is treated like a public convenience by other nations."

"Yes. Yes, I can see that. He was impatient, of course. Did

you know he'd been reprimanded for beating a prisoner? That's privileged, of course. But it will come out—there'll be an investigation, the foreign press will dig it up; we can handle our own newspapers, but the foreigners—" The deputy chief closed the cover of the report. "Well, have this typed; I want it in an hour. Three copies, all to my desk. And get some sleep, you look terrible."

Arkadi picked up the report. "There is a man, sir, an American, who might have been in the hotel. I'd like to find out if—"

"American, English, Israeli, what difference does it make? Stay out of it, Arkadi; let the laboratory do its work."

"This is part of another investigation—something I was working on before the—"

"Stay *out* of it, Arkadi! Lie low! No talking to the press, no gossiping around the bureau. Take today off, have a holiday; tomorrow, report to me. There are no 'other' investigations for you until we satisfy *my* superiors that you're fit to go on in your present rank. Is that clear?"

"Yes, sir." Arkadi arched his back against his fatigue. Body straight, he marched out.

The deputy chief made a short note to himself on a desk pad, the gist of which was that Inspector Arkadi was a good and conscientious policeman, but that because of the situation in the department he was allowing himself to be overworked. If he were not stopped, he would lose his effectiveness.

Valeri Seriakin, as the Russian representative to the informal observation group working with the Turkish military at the hotel site, had access to the ruins of the Turisti Pallas. With the American, Burrell, and a solemn Japanese, he had accompanied two Turkish officers through the parts of the building that had been declared safe. No one needed to point out the dark stains on the lobby floor; they did not have to listen to the detailed explanation of why, as yet, it was uncertain just how many people had died. He knew for a certainty that none of the Russian delegation had been involved, but he had not told the Turkish authorities that; instead, he was using the situation to study the hotel where events affecting *The Book of the Dead* had taken place.

He was influenced by Burrell's obvious interest in the place; by the identification that morning of the body of the Israeli agent, Sandra Lowenstein; and by information from a hotel cook (relayed to Seriakin by his informant on the Izmir police) that a red-haired American girl—"of course an American, I could tell, those big shoes and red hair, what else would she be?"—had led a man through the hotel kitchen shortly before the first explosion. The cook had been smoking a cigarette outside by the garbage; he had seen them come out of the back door and run to a small car parked nearby. No, he couldn't say what kind of car. He had walked down to the water to throw his cigarette away, and then the explosion had come.

If Seriakin had had a confidante, if he still had had his Leningrad mistress, he would have offered a speculation:

"Suppose, Varya, suppose that Teck is something more than a professor in some trivial subject. Suppose that he is the buyer of *The Book of the Dead*, not an agent of a government, but a free-lance. Suppose that Teck bought the manuscript from Parduk. He has it, ready to move it out of Turkey; the police hear of this—no, that isn't quite right; they're interested in him, but they don't know about *The Book*; there would be more noise—I must skip something there, something I haven't put together yet—but the Israelis learn he has it. How? I don't know. From Parduk? Unlikely. Perhaps Teck stole it from Parduk and Parduk told the Israelis in retaliation. Perhaps a spy in Parduk's store. His wife, for instance. So, the Israelis send in a woman who has known him before; she seduces him, and—does he tell her about *The Book*? Is he that stupid? No. Let us say that she searches his room while he is asleep, and she finds something. What? How do I know? A wrapping, a receipt from Parduk, something! And she leaves, to inform her contact, and somebody—I am on firmer ground here, Varya, I know the signs—the Palestinians take her, torture her. They learn something. They learn that Teck is the man who has *The Book of the Dead*, which they would like to get their hands on so they may destroy it. And so they attack Teck's hotel, where—where, my darling—they either find Teck and the manuscript or they do not.

"Well, if they do find him, they are all here in the rubble and in the body bags outside. But what if they do not find him? What if the red-haired woman has got him away? But why has she waited so long? Why was she not here yesterday, or the day before? Why is that?"

And Varya would have rolled over, shoving her soft buttocks against his belly, and she would have murmured something about sleep, thus denying him the chance to discuss his other theory, which was that it was the Israelis who attacked the hotel in retaliation for the death of Sandra Lowenstein.

"The hotel records, you understand," a Turkish lieutenant was saying in a quiet voice, "were all destroyed. It is very difficult to tell how many people were staying at this hotel. This room," he continued, gesturing through an open doorway, "was occupied by an American. Somebody ransacked it, but the labels on the clothes, an American paper book in the luggage, such things help us to think the occupant was an American."

"May I go in?" Phillip Burrell was very courteous, but his position in the doorway suggested that as long as he was already partway in, he would go the rest.

"Everything is impounded, sir."

"I won't touch anything. He was an American, after all. The reason that I'm here." Burrell sidled into the room, and when Seriakin followed, the lieutenant merely shrugged at his fellow officer. Fingerprints, evidence—these were problems for the stupid police, who had brought it all on themselves, anyway.

Seriakin crossed to the window. He wondered grimly what would happen when he and Burrell came to open confrontation over *The Book of the Dead.*

Seriakin glanced back at the room. It was impossible to believe that all the damage had been done by the blast that had ruined the upper floor of the hotel. The drawers had been pulled from the bureau and turned upside down; the suitcases had been slashed and their edges slit; the felt mattress had been eviscerated. The clothes were rags; even the photographic case had been dumped out and probed, and a pile of film and filters and lenses lay on the bureau, expensive trifles turned to junk—a stubby Japanese wide-angle lens, a larger one, around whose edge he could read "Steinheil Macro f3:5 Made i-" before the rest was blocked out by the curving edge. Nothing was left intact that was large enough to have hidden *The Book of the Dead.*

The Turkish Coastal Patrol boat had been withdrawn. Below Seriakin, the sunlight sparkled on the rippled water so that he had to squint. A hundred yards out, a small rowboat, painted blue and bright pink, dipped as the fisherman moved toward the stern, trailing a heavy net behind him. Then, between the boat and the shore, there was a dim flash in the water, only a glimmer as if a fish had turned or the sun had struck a wave, and Seriakin thought he had been mistaken. He looked away, then back when the fisherman dropped his net into the bottom of the boat and bent over the far side. Five seconds later, a hand grasped the gunwale and a man's head broke the water. He rested there, gasping for breath, while the fisherman pushed up his face mask.

Sponges? thought Seriakin idly. He knew nothing about the world under the water. If he could believe the flash he had seen earlier, the man had come from the water directly below the hotel.

An idea was forming.

Now he did turn away, just as Phillip Burrell, came from the bathroom. He stopped when he saw Seriakin.

"The poor man had a very pleasant view of the harbor," Seriakin said. He stood squarely in front of the window so that the view was blocked. "Poor man." He smiled at Burrell, although a sick feeling intensified as he sensed their confrontation nearing. Not here, but— "Did you find anything helpful in the bathroom?"

Burrell did not bother to be polite. "No. What would I find?"

"The effects of one of your countryman. To send to his family, I assumed."

"Oh, of course. Yes. Is it a nice view?"

"Lovely. There is even a Soviet ship in the harbor this morning." Seriakin looked out as Burrell came to stand next to him. The fisherman's boat was moving, already a hundred yards farther out. "A lovely view."

Waking, Teck felt that unique psychological ease that sometimes comes in hospital after an operation, when the patient wakes sufficiently to know with absolute certainty that the worst is over. Sometimes the certainty is misplaced; complications may set in later—but at that waking moment he is touched with something like bliss because of his situation and the skill of the anesthetist. The stock question, *Where am I*? is answered, and the ugly question, *How am I*? is not yet asked.

He remembered where he was and he remembered enough of the pain to know that he had been happily released from it. He was lying in a bed, on his back, with his head turned to the right, and when he moved a very little there was no answering pain to restrain him.

There was a table of plain dark wood next to him, and between his eyes and the table was a small area of white cloth, most of it too close to get into focus. It was hard to get even the table into focus because only his right eye was open, and it was still affected by sleep. Teck raised his left arm carefully and swung it toward the table, and the hand floated into his vision as a large, slightly blurred object that moved on and struck the table, although he did not feel it, and something clattered to the floor.

The area beyond the table grew lighter as a door opened behind him and cast its light on the far wall. Instinctively, he drew his left arm close to protect his face.

It was the red-haired girl. She looked swollen, as pregnant women sometimes do, and the side of her face was flushed. She had been sleeping.

"Hey, don't move around!"

She came close to his right side and gently pushed his left arm down to the bed. "How you doing?"

"I—I—" He couldn't speak. His mouth was dry.

"Are you in any pain?"

"No." The word was whispered, a secret. "Could I—have—some water?" But his lips would not close over the *v* and the *m* and it sounded like a comic dialect, "hab sub water."

"Sure." The girl disappeared. It was not worth moving to see where she had gone. Immediately, so far as he knew, she was back; had he slept? She held a glass to his mouth, cradling his head in her left arm. Even though she tipped the glass very slightly, some of the water slopped out over his chin and he smiled crookedly, foolishly. "Sorry." His lips had no feeling and he could not tell when the glass touched them or when he smiled.

"That's okay. Want some more?"

He rehearsed his question before he spoke. "Am—I—still—in—the—same—place?"

"Yeah, we moved you in here, it's supposed to be a maid's room or something. What can I do for you?"

"Out. Get—me—out." His crooked smile curled one side of his mouth.

"I can't. I'm awfully sorry. Gee."

He lay still for several minutes. Her bare arm was still under his head and he enjoyed its warmth. She was wearing a dark green, very tight tank top and he could smell cologne and something more astringent, a deodorant. He turned his head a little to the right and his cheek rested against her upper arm, his chin almost touching the curve of flesh down to her small breast.

"You gave me something for the pain. Didn't you?"

"Ricki said I could."

"What?"

"Demerol and a shot of some stuff. Ricki has all kinds of stuff."

"You're a good girl." He said it desperately; his mind was shying at the memory of the beating.

"Like rape," he said.

"I didn't hear you, I'm sorry, you talk so soft."

"Like rape. Never forget and never—" He shuddered. "Don't let me get too—clearheaded. Keep me under something."

His shoulders began to tremble. His memory cleared, not because of any dissipation of the drugs, but because he could not keep the first images of the beating from his mind, and they intensified and turned into a horror. *Like rape.* Not merely the horror of pain, but the horror of violation and utter helplessness. Teck groaned; the sound turned into a wail. His whole body shook as his breath came in gasps and the wail changed to an inarticulate sob. He said something he had never said to a woman in his life. "Hold me!"

She put her arms around his shoulders and pulled his head into the hollow of her throat, her hand on the back of his head, the mother with a Gargantuan infant. When the sobbing lessened, she lowered his head back to the pillow and bent over his mouth and then moved her head down and over him to whisper in his left ear and kiss his wet eyes. "I've got lots of stuff."

"I'm a coward."

"That doesn't matter." Her hand gripped his left shoulder, hard. She must have known his injuries well, for she knew where he could be touched without hurt. "Everything'll be all right."

In a thousand years. "Please give me something."

She freed her arm and stood up, shaking the hand that had been under his head to restore the circulation. She took a syringe from somewhere, probably the table, and did something with it out of his sight. When she came back, it was to the other side of the bed, where, because of his bad eye, he could not see what she was doing. "This'll put you out pretty fast," she said. "Am I hurting you?"

"It's fine."

"You go to sleep now."

"Please help me get away."

She got up quickly. "I can't. I mean, I don't want to. Don't try to understand it, okay? I just—you wouldn't understand. I owe Ricki, does that make sense?"

His eyes were already closed. He was not unconscious, but he couldn't argue with her.

"Anyways, Ricki and another guy are downstairs. They're waiting for the thing you told them about."

What will Burrell say? What will Arkadi do to me?

He heard her voice again but couldn't make out the words. He slept, this time to dream dreams that were best forgotten when he waked, dreams that made him utter sounds that brought her into the room and that caused him to flail out with his arms, knocking the table askew; and after that, she sat by him, changing a bandage on his left cheek where blood had begun to ooze.

When he waked the second time, she was reading. The light in the room was different and the wall beyond the table was darker. There was a bright spot on the ceiling now, almost over him. He lay awake for several minutes, his good eye open only a slit so that she would not know he was awake. He thought of trying to move from the bed, to escape somehow, but the little effort it took him to shift his legs under the blanket told him that he would not even be able to stand. She put down her book and leaned over him. "Hi."

He did not speak. He put out his right hand and she took it in both of hers.

"Want something?"

"Have—they—got—the—book?"

Mickey frowned. He could see two distinct creases under each eye and a fine webbing at each corner, and perhaps because of the changed light she looked older.

"There was a screwup. But Ricki says they'll get it."

Maybe Burrell got there first.

"What happened?"

"Some Arabs or somebody hit your hotel last night. The radio's got it all screwed up, first one report and then another, but the army moved in there and a lot of people got killed. Kamal couldn't get close enough first try, so they're going after it again now."

He thought of the hotel as he had last seen it—the plainclothes policeman, Hamdar and his cat. "Who was killed?"

"I don't know. I don't like to think about stuff like that."

"How close did we come to being in it?"

She looked away. Her hands gripped his own very tightly. "Close."

So it could have been that and not this. Saved from one for the other. Hobson's choice. He dozed again. The sleep was not deep or steady this time, and he was aware that she seemed restless, moving around him and out into the corridor and back again. She opened the two windows in the wall farthest from his head. He heard distant voices and a motor, perhaps a tractor, and a bird cry like a gull's.

Later, when he was awake again, Mickey brought in a page of a Turkish newspaper from which she puzzled out enough to tell him that his name was on a list of possible victims. A few of the foreign delegations had withdrawn from the Trade Fair, and, in one of those paradoxical shifts that happen when frustrated passions find no outlet, a mob of students had marched to the hotel where the Israelis were staying and then to the United States Information Service library and had stoned the building. There was a hazy picture of the library in ruins, and of Edward Rountree, the young American who had first come to see Teck at the jail. Teck felt sorry for Rountree.

A government spokesman had denied that contingency plans were being made to evacuate foreigners.

"Would you go, Mickey, if they evacuated Americans?" He wanted to talk; it kept the bad images at bay. He still had trouble with some of the sounds—her name came out as "Bickey"—but he was intelligible.

She shrugged one limp shoulder. He realized how like many of his students she was—the ones he never much cared for, the wan and feckless ones. "If I could get away, Mickey, would you come with me?"

"No, man, I couldn't." She lit a cigarette.

"But why do you *stay*?"

"I don't know." She plucked at some bit of lint on the front of her blouse, something invisible to him but seemingly very important to her, for she concentrated on it fiercely. "I owe Ricki a lot, right? I guess that's kind of hard to understand, huh? It isn't love or anything like that, not really—I mean, I know he wouldn't let me go, for one thing. I've been around too much of his business. Anyway, I owe him for this real big favor."

Teck licked his lips. The activity made the split in his upper lip hurt and he was aware of pain in his head and his side. The drugs were beginning to wear off.

"What sort of hold does he have on you? Drugs?"

She laughed. "Oh, come on! Christ, you're so—it's a rotten word, but you're *square!* I smoke some, sure; Ricki has some hash, sure; Ricki has pills and other stuff and if you're down and need an upper, he can help you out—but drugs? No way, man. It's a convenience for him and me."

"And that's what you owe him? Convenience?"

"No, nothing like that." She tipped her head back so that the hair fell away from her forehead. "This guy I met in Kerala a year or so ago persuaded me it would be really cool if I drove this old VW bus from Beirut up to Munich, right? Like it was just an old bus this friend of his had, and I could take a couple of friends along who were broke, and he'd pay me ten dollars a day and gas, right? Well, everything is beautiful until we get into Turkey, and then some Turkish narc rips the ceiling out of the bus and finds all this hard stuff up there, and there I am with my two broke friends, ready to face fifteen to life in a Turkish prison. Nice, huh? Anyway, along comes Ricki, and he talked to the cop, and then he talked to me, and finally the cop made a deal with Ricki, a deal for some of the stuff in the VW, and they let me go."

"Just like that?"

She picked again at the fabric of her blouse. "No, not just exactly like that. The deal was that one of us would get charged, and that it was going to be me because the van was in my name, but Ricki and the cop, they said we'd have to draw straws or flip a coin or something, right? And one of my friends lost. And now she's doing fifteen years at Adana, and I go to visit her and take her food and like that every six weeks when they let you."

"And that's what you owe Ricki."

"That's right."

"And visiting your friend—that's really what keeps you in Turkey."

She shrugged and said nothing.

"And good old Ricki, I'll bet, was just waiting for that shipment from your friend in Kerala."

"No, nothing like that! I mean, they weren't working together. It was more like a hijack, with the narc as the hijacker. Ricki was sorry because I got caught in the middle. He's really a very sensitive person when you know him."

"So I've found out."

"I said he's *sensitive.* I didn't say he was some moral god, all right?"

"Sensitive enough to have rigged the draw when your friend got sent to Adana instead of you?"

Her smile was very sad. "No. I did that myself. I couldn't hack it, the idea of prison. I'd have died."

"And your friend?"

"She's learning to weave from one of the other prisoners there. She practices yoga, you know? She's a very beautiful person."

What a world hers must be, full of sensitive men and beautiful persons. Teck let his head roll to the left so he could no longer see her. After a long silence he heard the rattle of the ashtray as she put it down on the table, and the springs of the bed squeaked and sank as she sat down, the small of her back pressed into his right buttock. Her face was turned away. "You think I'm a really gross person, don't you?" she said.

Teck rolled back to the right. In the slanting light from the windows, he could see each vertebra of her thin back where it mounded up under the fabric. He reached his right hand up awkwardly and ran his middle finger down her spine. "No, I don't. I don't think that at all." He thought of the morning, of her holding him. "No, I couldn't think badly of you."

"But you don't want to make it anymore with me, do you?" Her face was still turned away.

"I couldn't if I wanted to."

"I know that; I undressed you, for Christ's sake." She turned on him. "But it's wanting to that matters! A little while ago, before I told you about myself, you wanted to make it with me, didn't you!"

It was the argot of the young that he used to laugh at. It was the only language she knew, and it no longer seemed comical to him. "I still want to."

"Do you honestly?"

Clumsily, Teck moved his right hand around her arm and closed it over her breast. She clasped her own thin hand over his.

"When you're better," she whispered, "I swear to God—" She touched his chin, his mouth, his cheek, and he heard the raspy noise of her dry fingers moving over his stubble. "You're going to look fantastic in a beard, you know?"

There was a noise downstairs and Teck quickly withdrew his hand. She stood and backed a step away from the bed.

"Mickey!" It was Ricki's voice from downstairs.

"What is it?"

"Here comes Kamal. Get the stuff ready!"

Mickey went to the landing. Below them, a door closed. Teck could hear voices, but the sound was too muffled to make anything out. He looked at Mickey. Her body was tensed; she had raised her thin shoulders and her hands were clenched.

"What stuff?"

"Shh!" She listened. When she pushed her hair back, her hand was trembling.

"Mickey! *What stuff?*"

Her face was haggard. *She must be thirty, at least,* he thought. Not a girl, not the adolescent she seems. Arrested at eighteen or twenty—the last of the flower children, the copouts and dropouts. Far from the Haight and Woodstock in space and time and looking for the way back.

"I've got to give you something, *I've got to.*"

She had left her canvas shoulder bag hanging over the doorknob. Now, she took a slim box from it. In it were another syringe and a long glass tube.

"What is it?"

"It'll put you out for a while. That's all. I swear to God! Ricki *promised* me!"

Teck moved his legs in the bed. Tentatively, he raised himself on his right elbow.

"Mickey, it will kill me."

The filled syringe trembled in her hand. On its tip, a single drop sparkled in a shaft of sunlight reflected from a mirror near the door. Teck thought he might have the strength to get out of the bed now and even to reach the door, but what then? A sound from her would bring Ricki and Kamal. At the thought he sucked in his abdomen. He started to shake.

"Mickey—"

"Come on, man, I wouldn't let anything bad happen to you!"

"Enough has happened already. Mickey, *please!*"

She moved toward him. She carried the syringe point up at shoulder level.

"I've *got* to, you know what I mean?"

"Mickey—"

A door banged downstairs. Quick, angry footsteps pounded over the floor, growing louder, clattering up the stairs two steps at a time. Ricki stopped in the doorway. When he spoke, his mouth was so contorted by rage that he stammered.

"You st-st-stupid son-of-a-bitch! You—oh, my God, you—" He could not express it in mere words. He pounded on the wall with his fist and then turned and flung something at Teck. It missed his head and landed with a murderous thump on the wooden headboard and a spray of water splashed over Teck's face.

"Ricki, what is it?" She put the syringe down on the bedside table and moved toward him.

"What *is* it?"

"Ricki, calm down—"

"Calm *down?* Calm *down?* Do you know what this goddamn son-of-a-bitch has cost me? In gold? Oh, my God!" Astonishingly, Ricki covered his face with tensed hands and burst into tears.

Mickey picked up the thing that he had thrown. It was a sodden roll of paper compacted into a wet mass. Teck could make out the Cyrillic characters, but they were jumbled with others that he could see through pages made transparent by the thorough soaking.

"Is this the book he was after?"

Teck reached for the packet. It was much heavier now than it had been when he had wrapped it up. He tried to peel back the top page, but the paper tore like wet tissue.

"Ricki, oh, Ricki—" The girl embraced the weeping man. He leaned his head back against the door, eyes closed. It was genuine grief. *The passion of the collector,* Teck had said. *Patriotism and greed.* "Ricki, it'll be all right." When she tipped her head back to look at him, there was a bright smear of his tears on her cheekbone. "I'll put it in the oven, Ricki—we'll dry it out; it'll be okay, you'll see—a real low oven, but it'll dry and it'll be okay."

"It won't work."

"Yes, it will! We'll make it work. You can make anything work, if you try hard enough."

"I don't know, I don't know—that son-of-a-bitch has ruined it—"

"It *will* work." She took her arms from his shoulders and came to the side of the bed, reaching out for the sodden mass. "I'll do it right now."

"And you'll bake it into a solid mass, a brick," Teck said. He shifted the paper into his left hand and extended it as far away from her as he could. Ricki's face was wrinkled up again; he pointed a fist at Teck. "You shut up! You shut up before I get Kamal up here to finish you quick!"

Teck could only think that *The Book of the Dead* was the one thing that could keep him alive. He had to save it now. If they ruined it, as they would if they tried to dry it out, they would kill him, if only from the need to vent Ricki's fury.

"You're the stupid one if you bake this mess, not me. I'm sorry that I didn't wrap it well enough. But if I hadn't thrown it into the water, somebody else would have it now. Mickey means well, but she's wrong. If you put these pages into an oven, you're never going to be able to take them apart."

The man and woman looked at each other in silence. Ricki was calmed, but he seemed unsure of himself, and for the first time Teck thought he saw a chance for himself. He did not let himself think of Kamal or the beating.

"What are you, you stupid son-of-a-bitch, some class of expert?"

"Yes, I am."

Mickey moved toward him. "What would you do with it?" She sounded cautious. She wanted to please Ricki by saving the book for him, but she would be desperate if her own idea proved to be the wrong one.

"Freeze it."

Ricki snorted. "And then I got a frozen chunk of paper. Oh, swell! You think my customer is going to buy frozen paper?"

"I'm telling you, if you bake it, you'll get a brick. If you freeze it, the worst that can happen is that when you thaw it out you'll still have just what you've got now."

"And then what, expert? Then what? What do I tell my client to do?"

Teck really did know. He knew what had been done with the manuscripts that had been soaked in the Florence floods. He had watched a museum conservator prepare a box of documents that had become waterlogged in a fire. "Let me go and I'll tell you."

He knew it was a mistake as soon as the words were out. Ricki's eyes squinted and his finger came up again to point at Teck like a pistol. "You son-of-a-bitch, you don't—I don't listen to anything from you!" He came around the bed and took back the manuscript so fast that Teck had no chance to move. "I don't listen to you at all!" As he headed for the stairway he jerked his head toward the bed. "Give him the stuff. Now!"

He had just reached the doorway when the first gunshot sounded downstairs, a booming noise that only a large-caliber pistol could have made. It was followed by three rapid shots from a gun with a sharper report.

Ricki ran to the top of the stairs. The girl called his name and ran after him as several shots overlapped, the boom of the bigger gun drowning the other.

As one more shot sounded and the girl cried out again, Teck felt over the surface of the table until his hand grasped the syringe. His hand was shaking violently. He could not hold it and put his thumb on the plunger, and he jabbed it upright into the mattress and pushed against the plunger with his right palm and emptied it. He tried to put the syringe back on the table but his shaking hand would not obey him, and the syringe fell to the floor.

There were footsteps outside the door. The girl backed into the room; beyond her, Teck saw Ricki flung back against the corridor wall as the large gun boomed again. Ricki sagged to a sitting position in the angle of the doorway and the adjoining wall.

The girl screamed as someone came up the stairs.

Let it be Burrell. Burrell!

The man who pushed past Mickey as she cradled her crumpled lover was not Burrell. Curls of fair hair fell over a broad forehead. He was younger than Teck, and solidly built, and Teck knew he had seen him before but could not place him. *A Slav. Where have I seen a Slav?* He closed his eyes, not wanting to see what would happen to him.

The man called out something, then spoke in Turkish in a normal voice. Teck could hear Mickey sobbing. The man's voice said, in English, "You understand English? Well?"

"You've killed him!"

"No, I do not think so. He bleeds." Teck opened his right eye just enough to see the young man bend down and come up with the soggy mess that had been *The Book of the Dead.* He called down the stairs again, and seconds later another man joined him outside the door to Teck's room, and, after instructions, bent and began to remove Ricki's shirt.

The Slav stood over Teck's bed. Looking at Teck's face, he chewed on his lower lip and grimaced. He stooped down. "You are Teck? Do you hear me? Teck?"

Teck did his best to reproduce the first grating sounds he had made upon coming to that morning.

He rolled his eyes toward the table where the syringe had been.

He had little difficulty in imitating a man falling into a drug-induced coma.

Chapter fifteen

"MR. Burrell's line, Miss Kerrigan here."

"Sally, it's Phil."

"Where *are* you?"

"I'm in Izmir. What have you got for me?"

"Phil, why don't you come back to Ankara? Send somebody

else down there. Anyway, things are kind of piling up here—there are a couple of projects you really ought to sit on. You know the ones I mean. Phil, are you listening?"

"I got a message, Sally. From some little kid at Langley. You know what he told me? You know what he *told* me?"

"All right, Phil, what did he tell you?"

"It was like being slapped in the face, I can tell you. This snotty college boy telling me—he actually told *me* to go through channels. How's that? May I quote? 'Cut out the old-boy *crap*, Mr. Burrell.' How's that? Beautiful, isn't it? 'Cut out the old-boy *crap*!' He said that to *me*."

"Was this in reference to that—deep-sea fishing expedition you were going to make?"

"That's right. That's right! That's just what our young friend was referring to! He blew that one, and he's going to blow any others, unless I'm a proper little Fauntleroy and go through channels. How do you like *that?*"

"Phil, come on back to—"

"There's something very peculiar going on back at the head office, I know that now. I had my suspicions, Sally, but I know it now. That little creep, that little *creep* confirmed what I'd suspected, that there's something very peculiar going on."

"Phil, please—"

"I'm going to call an old friend of mine in CE. I think he'll be very interested in our young friend. And it may go higher, too; he's not acting alone. This is disruption on a pretty fair scale."

"Phil, I'm going to catch the evening flight to Izmir."

"What? Why?"

"Don't you want to see me?"

"Well, of course—"

"I'll be in a little after eight. Where will you be?"

"Oh. Uh, I'm not sure. After that little creep called me, I thought I—I have to keep my options open. I don't like to be a sitting target, anyway."

"A target for what?"

"Never mind."

"Phil, I'll be there after eight. Will you meet me?"

"No. I'll call you. Where will you be?"

"I think I can get the use of an apartment."

"I'll try to call you there."

"Three-nine-seven-seven-three. You *will* call me, Phil?"

"Yes, of course. But if I don't show—I've got to keep my options open."

"Phil—"

"Three-nine-seven-seven-three. I've got it. Bye, Sara."

Two men carried Teck down the stairway and through the room where Kamal had beaten him. Teck, pretending unconsciousness, tried to see through an almost-closed right eyelid. At the top of the stairs, the red-haired girl was trying to staunch the flow of blood from Ricki's shoulder with a sheet from the bed Teck had lain on. A man Teck did not recognize was seated on the floor in a corner of the large downstairs room. He did not spot Kamal until he was almost out of the room, and then he saw only a large shoe and part of a leg sticking out under an overturned chair.

The men who carried him made no attempt to be gentle. It was difficult for him not to make some sound as they shifted his weight or twisted him to maneuver through a doorway. Worst of all was being loaded into the back seat of a small car; the one who carried his upper body simply leaned him against the car, while the other dropped his feet and opened the car door. Then, with little regard for the ways in which the human body normally bends, they forced him into the back seat, head and shoulders first. Teck fell as realistically as possible on the seat, but when his legs were bent to put his feet inside, the pressure on his groin made him moan despite himself.

One of the men said something in Turkish. The door closed, there were footsteps at the back of the car, and then the door on the other side opened. Teck could hear the man's breathing as he bent close, and a foul tobacco smell filled his nostrils.

His good eye was open. He did his best to look glazed by rolling his eyes upward; the movement made the left eye hurt.

The man grunted, withdrew, and closed the door.

The front door on the passenger's side opened. The car sagged under the weight of a new occupant and the door slammed. A voice, which Teck recognized as that of the man who had come into the bedroom, uttered a few terse sentences, evidently to someone standing outside the car. A few seconds later, someone got in the driver's side and the engine started.

As they drove through the fading daylight under a sky that looked at last as if parched Izmir might have rain, Seriakin's thoughts were confused. The thing that he had come to Turkey to get was his. He should have felt triumph, or at least sober satisfaction. Instead, he was depressed. Perhaps it was merely a letdown after days of tension. But whatever the cause, he felt none of the elation he had anticipated, none of the sense of accomplishment he had learned to expect from observing his father. He had always known when some scheme had gone well, even as a boy; his father would drink more, joke more; his mother would get more affection than usual, and the boy knew that at night they made love and drank together. Once, he had heard them taking a bath together at three in the morning, and he had been shocked and ashamed of such behavior from two old people in their thirties.

Too, the American's condition depressed him. Seriakin was not one of the regulars of the torture cells. He did not think of himself as squeamish, to be sure, but he saw no benefit in crushing the frail shell that protected a man. The American had been crudely tortured: one eye was so heavily bandaged that the whole left side of the head was swathed, but blood had soaked through anyway and the stain looked eerily like a rust-brown eye on the bandage itself. One testicle was swollen, and so dark a purple it looked black.

Seriakin looked back at the naked man. He believed that the American had been drugged. His unconsciousness, however, was too perfect. Concussion was a possibility.

He lit a cigarette and glanced at the tense young Turk who was driving. "I will want the car after we get to the clinic."

The driver looked at him, his expression skeptical, even contemptuous. "Clinic! The Soviets must have a new ethic." He concentrated on the road as he passed a bus. "You're very delicate for a Russian."

"I don't believe in waste."

They stretched Teck out on a metal table whose surface felt icy under his bare skin. It frightened him that he shivered and that his skin showed goose bumps. He did not know whether his supposedly drugged body should behave that way or not.

The smells of alcohol and ether were strong. There was no

mistaking where they had brought him, but there was no comfort to be taken from the fact that it was a doctor's office or a hospital, because the men who carried him were the same ones who had been at the house. They might do anything to him.

He was surprised to hear a woman's voice. She spoke in Turkish in answer to questions from the one he had come to think of as The Slav. A Russian, probably Burrell's Soviet counterpart.

A finger delicately touched his body—his ribs, where Kamal had kicked him. The Slav asked a question; the woman answered. The finger touched his right thigh. They must be discussing his genitals; he had not dared look at them himself. Again a question and a tentative answer. Hands raised his head roughly; the Slavic voice spoke sharply and fingers spread under the back of his head and cradled it more carefully. He felt something cold and hard pressed against his left mastoid bone; he heard the scissors cut through the thick bandage that Mickey had wrapped.

When the bandage was pulled away, almost thread by thread at the last, there was a little silence, and then came some word from The Slav that might have been Russian and not Turkish and that sounded like a muttered curse, and the woman's voice murmured four syllables in just the tones he had once heard his mother use when a cake made by somebody else had fallen in the oven: What a shame.

The Slav asked more questions and the woman repeated the same phrase several times. What did it mean? "I do not know"? "I cannot"? "I will not"?

His right eye was pried open. A round circle of light dazzled him before he could roll the eye up. The light moved and turned red as it focused on the retina at one side.

The light receded, but the eye was held open.

The Slav's head appeared, faceless because the light had burned a black spot in his vision.

"Mr. Teck? Can you understand me?"

He opened his mouth and vocalized a breath without shaping it: *uuh.*

"Mr. Teck, I am ordering medical examination for you here. You may have a concussion. I am also ordering a roentgen examination."

Roentgen. X ray.

"I am ordering also, Mr. Teck, an injection of a stimulant drug. As an antidote to drugs given you by those others. If the doctor thinks you do not have a concussion, that is, and the roentgen shows no heavy internal damage. Do you understand me, Mr. Teck? It is quite important."

Teck grunted again and licked his dry lips.

"Good. Your part in all of this is over, finished. There is no reason for you to suppress information. If you give me information freely, I will have you detained only for three days and then you will be released. If you withhold information, I cannot be responsible for what will happen to you."

Teck said nothing. When his eyelid was let go, he allowed it to close slowly and sluggishly, like a venetian blind that is a little askew on one side.

The man and the woman talked, and after what seemed to Teck an interminable time, there were footsteps on a floor of some hard material that made the shoes ring crisply, and a doorknob could be heard turning, and a door hissed and shushed closed against a piston, and the footsteps, sounding mushier now on gravel or some loose material, faded away.

A few words from the woman, and Teck's table began to move. One wheel complained like the wheel of the cart Teck seemed always to get at the supermarket. The whole table bounced convulsively as it rolled over a doorsill.

What information can he hope to get from me? And will he believe me if I say I know nothing? Teck thought of Kamal and the beating. *How much time before he comes back?*

The line crackled with static. Seriakin had spoken over thousands of miles with more ease than he now did over the short distance from the safe house to the Soviet ship in the Izmir harbor. Some of the interference, he supposed, was monitoring by his own people, and some was probably monitoring by Turkish Security; some of it was intentional noise to make the eavesdrops difficult.

"Hello?" a voice said. "Hello? Are you there?"

"Yes, hello?"

The voice was too faint to be heard.

"I'm very sorry," Seriakin said. "I cannot understand you. Hello?"

Distantly, the voice said that it belonged to the deck officer.

"Yes," said Seriakin, "I'd hoped it was. May I speak to Mr. Lopakin, please?"

There was more garbled speech, followed by a long silence. Seriakin said hello twice more, but there was no reply until with a loud clatter the line seemed suddenly clearer and he heard the quite recognizable voice of Repin.

"Well, this is Mr. Lopakin. Hello?"

"Hello, this is Mr. Astrov."

"Ah, yes, how are you today, my dear boy?"

"Fine, thank you. I found a gift for Auntie Masha."

"Splendid! Did you find it at Sears, Roebuck?" (*Did the Americans have it?*)

"No, I found it in the bazaar." (Private parties had it.) "At a damaged goods stall."

After a moment, Repin said, "Auntie Masha will not like it if it is damaged."

"She will like it, I'm sure. It is repairable."

There was a much longer silence, long enough for Repin to repeat the message to someone else. When he returned, he seemed ready to end the conversation. "It was good to talk to you."

"There is something else. I met a friend. He is ill, and I am returning directly to see him at my doctor's."

"Very good, but please leave Auntie Masha's gift with my sister, and stay with her for just thirty minutes to write Auntie a letter, and then you are off, do you understand?"

"To visit my friend at the doctor's."

"Yes, yes, did I not say so?" Repin sounded impatient.

"Yes, I understand. Good-bye."

Seriakin handed the receiver to the lanky woman who stood behind him. He understood without really understanding. He was to leave the manuscript at the safe house, write a brief report, and leave after thirty minutes. After interrogating Teck, his work would be finished.

He handed the woman the manuscript. "This must be frozen until it is called for."

"All right."

"I am to stay here for thirty minutes." He checked his watch.

"Tea?" she said calmly, as if she had expected him to stay.

"Thank you."

He sat at a small table, the steaming tea in front of him, his body twisted against the wall to make the most of the dim light falling over his shoulder. Much of the report was already in his head and only the physical tedium of scribbling it out was needed; yet he hesitated. His mind kept returning to the American. He would be left with the Turks, the Free Turkey Youth terrorists, who would receive their instructions separately. Seriakin had told him that he would be let go after three days; that was the disposition that Seriakin would request in his report. What would actually happen, of course, was another matter. *He asked for it,* Seriakin told himself. *He became involved. He must have known the risks.* But at the same time, he thought of the man's eye, the big bruises on his body, the swollen testicle. Whatever the man had once been, he had become merely a victim—victimized with torture by one group; victimized by Seriakin's interrogation; perhaps to be victimized by murder. It was a waste.

"I have sent out for dry ice," the woman said. "I have no refrigerator."

"Good. Now let me work, please."

He sipped his tea and then began to move a felt-tipped pen across the paper.

> I observed from the window of the American, Samuel Teck, in the ruins of the Turisti Pallas, a skin diver making an apparently clandestine search of the water near the hotel. The room had already been searched. Many of the American's possessions were still there, but none could have contained the manuscript—slashed suitcases, photographic lenses, his—

Seriakin frowned. It was a point he had pondered on the long drive out to the house where he had recovered the manuscript. He had missed something, some connection that would slide across his consciousness like a name that will not quite connect itself with a remembered face. Teck's room. *I was thinking only of the manuscript and I missed something. The American was in the bathroom. The fisherman was carrying his net.* Seriakin continued to write.

> —clothes. Realizing that the skin diver could be searching for something thrown from the window, I left the hotel as soon as possible and ordered one of the Free Turkey

> Youth to keep the diver's boat under surveillance. Within an hour, word reached me that the diver had reached shore. With three members of the Free Turkey Youth, I followed him to a solitary house where—

Not Teck's suitcases. The photographic equipment, a lens, a special lens. . . . Macro. Close-up.

There were photographs among Teck's belongings at Police Central.

What if the American had photographed the manuscript?

Seriakin stood up. He capped the pen and put it in the left inner jacket pocket. Hastily, he gulped half of the remaining tea.

"I am going," he said to the sad-faced woman. She merely scowled.

He was seventeen minutes ahead of the schedule Repin had given him.

In his small cabin on the ship Repin immediately closeted himself with another KGB officer after ending the communication with Seriakin.

"Send a boy to do a man's job and he fools you by doing a man's job."

The other man shrugged. Fifteen years younger than Repin, he was one of those detached, apparently bloodless people who do not much commit their emotions to gestures or tones of voice, but who communicate by shrugs and lifted eyebrows and cool observations. His face was impassive; seemingly the skin was pulled so tight over his skull that there was not enough elasticity to allow for expression.

"Am I to put the substitute manuscript into the line, Repin?"

"We have no choice; he says the original is damaged. If you can, find out who Seriakin got it from; the resident will know. Silence that person. But it must be done quickly; if you can't find him tonight, take the substitute manuscript to Athens yourself and hand it over there—covertly, of course. I want *The Book of the Dead* in the hands of the Paris publisher by tomorrow night."

"And Seriakin?"

"It is all arranged. The Palestinians will intercept him at the clinic. A very clean, Western assassination. It lends credibility, don't you think? Young KGB man, murdered in his attempts to bring back the notorious work of the Turkman dissident? Very convincing."

The other man shrugged, as much as to say that it hardly mattered what he thought—and in fact, it did not.

"Well, you know what to do, do it!"

"Am I to retrieve the damaged manuscript from the resident?"

"Put the substitute into the line first."

"And the American at the clinic?"

"That is for the Turks and the Palestinians to work out. As he is already supposed to have been killed at the hotel, well. . . ."

Teck had been lifted from the wheeled table to a padded surface. When the footsteps of the man and woman seemed to recede a little, he dared to open his right eye to a thin slit, trying to find out where he was. Temporarily disoriented, he could not identify the mass that loomed over his midriff, but when he could focus on it he understood that it was a machine. At its lowest point, close to his right hip, it ended in a plastic cone about four inches long.

X-ray machine.

He could not see the man and woman. When the machine clicked and hummed for two seconds and then clicked again, he knew that they were behind a shield, perhaps out of the room. When the machine had done clicking, he heard their footsteps again.

The man rolled Teck over onto his left side. When he tried to lift Teck too clumsily, the woman spoke angrily. Teck opened his right eye a little more. He seemed acutely aware of sounds and smells, their footsteps and his own breathing, the smell of the sweat-stained coat the man wore and, when the jacket fell open, of the recently fired pistol jammed into the top of his tight, beltless trousers. Teck could see the woman's white smock now, but he did not dare to move his eye to look at her face, and so he was restricted to her torso and one of her plump hands, the left one nervously moving as she slowly twirled a ring around her middle finger with her thumb.

She came so close that the white smock blotted everything

else out. When she leaned over him to adjust the X-ray unit, he smelled medicinal alcohol and some almost herbal perfume.

She spoke. The man and the woman again walked away to some point behind Teck and to his left.

The machine clicked and buzzed and clicked again.

They came back.

He was rolled on his right side. His left arm was lifted so that the inside of the upper arm rested on his head. The machine was pointed at a spot just below his heart.

Click/buzz/click.

Teck was so close to the edge of the padded table that he could see the shelf of medicines set against the wall below normal waist level. On the top shelf was a glass jar about ten inches high, filled with pale purple alcohol and cotton swabs.

They rolled him on his back again. Teck let his right arm drop over the side of the table.

The woman swung the plastic cone until it pointed at a spot just above his pubic hair.

Click/buzz/click.

Before the footsteps started again, before they could move away from whatever shield protected them, Teck groped downward with his right hand until it touched the shelf. Quickly, he found the glass jar. A shoe scuffed on the floor as his hand closed over the glass rim.

When the man stood over him, his abdomen pressing against the padding just at Teck's left shoulder, Teck swung the jar, rolling his body to the left and pushing up with his left arm as he swung. The alcohol and the cotton swabs were driven against the bottom of the jar by centrifugal force, and because the distance of the jar's travel was short, the man did not cry out or dodge or even quite get a hand up to his face before the glass shattered on his left cheekbone and brow and alcohol cascaded into his eyes and his still-open mouth, and then a sharp downward pull of the glass, caused by the pain that struck Teck's back and groin, laid open the man's face from the right corner of his mouth down to the angle of his jaw.

Teck let go of the glass and clutched at the pistol in the man's trouser band, catching the butt just as the man backed away bellowing, and the trigger guard caught and actually held him captive for a moment. Then he lurched backward and struck down with his right hand; Teck pulled, and the top trouser button ripped loose and the zipper opened halfway down. And Teck had the pistol.

The woman was reaching for a tray of surgical instruments. Teck shouted a warning; he sounded concerned, not threatening—and indeed, he disliked guns and would have hesitated to use the one he held. The woman paused. "Don't touch it," Teck pleaded. His voice was shaking.

The woman straightened. She looked at Teck. Her face was angry and frightened as she crossed her forearms over her breasts.

"Do you understand English?" Teck said.

The woman said something in Turkish.

Teck waved the gun at the man, who was trying to feel his way along the wall toward the woman. He moaned. In trying to rub the stinging alcohol from his eyes, he had mixed the blood from his cuts into it and had daubed his face with red, and there were reddening gobs of cotton stuck to him like berls.

"Get his clothes off," Teck said. "Clothes." He sat up straight and pointed at his chest and legs with his bandaged left hand. He felt giddy; he was afraid he might black out. His head seemed to be floating high above the scene, above even his own body, observing events that moved so slowly that he had time to note each smallest detail, as in some kind of time-lapse photography: the injured man's hand moved across his right cheek to wipe away a rivulet of blood there; a dot of blood appeared where the beginning of the rivulet had been, then became a bead, then a drop bulging pregnantly; the drop broke and a new rivulet ran down through the glistening alcohol. Where the drop had broken, a point of light flashed on the edge of a glass shard as the man's cheek moved and it caught the light.

"Clothes," Teck said again from his dizzy eminence.

She hated him. She made her hatred very clear. He could not understand her, but he could hear and dissect each syllable that spat from her full lips.

It seemed an hour before she had the man's bloody shirt off. She paused to wipe his eyes and his cheek before she removed it, despite the threat of the pistol. In the age that it took her to take off his trousers, Teck's heart hammered at his ribs and his pulse rapped upon his eardrums, and he began to tremble.

"The clothes, the clothes!" he said desperately.

Teck felt very sly. Animal-shrewd. Proud of himself for having such instincts. He had remembered the broken glass on the floor and he had remembered his own bare feet. He made the woman hand him the shoes, and, because they were too small, he wore them without socks and left the laces untied. Then, naked except for the shoes, he carefully lowered himself from the padded table.

He put the shirt on first. He was surprised at how easily the buttons broke off. The trousers came next, ill-fitting and baggy and hard to put on over the shoes. He would need a belt. Last, the jacket, which was so tight across the shoulders that Teck was sure he would split it, and so short that it reached only to his wrist when he put his left hand down by his side.

"I make a ridiculous figure," he said to the woman. He was trying to reassure her that he was not a monster, not even a bad man, but merely one driven by necessity. "I'm really a university professor," he said.

She pointed at the injured man and said something. She was pleading.

"You have to stay here and take care of your friend," Teck said. "I'm going out, and if you follow me, I'll shoot you both. Bang-bang—understand?"

Quickly—so quickly that it made him dizzy again and he gasped—he glanced around the room and found nothing else to threaten him.

"Take care of your friend. Face. Sew up."

Teck waved the woman away from her pocketbook and picked it up. "Take care of your friend," he said again, and went out.

He found only two useful things in the pocketbook, a change purse crammed with coins and wadded bills and a pair of Italian-made sunglasses. He was sure that he looked better with the sunglasses on.

He pulled the telephone cord out of the wall.

Teck felt like whistling. He tried to purse up his lips to whistle, but his upper lip hurt. Instead, he hummed to himself.

It was still partly light outdoors. There was no direct sun to cast shadows, but the sky between the buildings was a strong blue. People on the street seemed to be hurrying more than usual, but he could not be sure of his own perception of such things.

Teck looked to his right. There was a military-brown truck at the corner loaded with soldiers.

Teck walked the other way.

At the corner, he looked back.

A car pulled up outside the building he had just come from. The Slav got out, but he did not see Teck. If he saw anything, he saw merely another shabby Turk with sunglasses on.

Teck smiled a little and walked on, humming.

Chapter sixteen

HE could not remember how long it had been since the last drugs that Mickey had given him. Something was happening to him, he knew; his sense of urgency and his curiously heightened perceptions might have been the result of a drug's wearing off. As he moved along the street, the sense of doubled personality continued: his body wanted to rush along (*like Wozzeck, cutting through the world like a razor*) while his mind seemed to want to proceed slowly to avoid attention. He kept his left arm clamped tightly against his side to keep the pistol in place under the coat, and he was aware of what a grotesque figure he made—bent over, one arm drawn in like a cripple's, the eyes hidden. And yet, the few people whom he encountered paid no attention to him; or did they pay the negative attention of *avoiding* him, of actively *not* seeing him, as he had studiously avoided looking at the mad and the deformed and the grotesquely perverse in a place like Times Square? At the least, he did not look like an American professor, and perhaps that was disguise enough.

He saw another military truck from the next corner, this one a block away to his left. Across the street from it a bus was heading toward him; as it came near, Teck waved his right arm. When the bus did not slow, he waved more vigorously.

The driver, with the disdain of bus drivers everywhere, pointed up the street and kept on going. Halfway up the block, two people waited by the curb. The bus slowed; Teck tried to run.

Inexplicably, the driver did not pull away when he saw Teck's ungainly attempt to run; he actually held the bus for several seconds to let him clamber aboard. Teck tried to smile, but the effort was wasted because the driver was concentrating on the street ahead. The bus swung smoothly from the curb and Teck had to clutch a greasy metal bar with his right hand to keep from falling. Once settled in the traffic lane, the driver pointed at the coin box, a glass-fronted contraption like a child's toy that let him see the coins as they clattered down over a flight of baffles. But Teck, not knowing what the fare was, grinned foolishly

The driver said something unpleasant.

Teck grinned more foolishly than ever.

The bus decelerated rapidly and Teck was thrown hipfirst against the metal bar. When he straightened, the bus had come to a stop and the driver sat with his arms folded, looking straight ahead. Teck glanced down the bus. Half a dozen faces frowned back.

He took out some of the change he had stolen from the doctor's pocketbook and held his cupped hand out to the first passenger, a woman in a dark, unfashionably long dress. He tried to make a gentle, deaf-mute's sound, but the ensuing grunt sounded more to his ears like something uttered by Karloff as the monster, and he could only grin more foolishly than ever. The woman pointed at two coins but would not touch them or his hand, so he picked them out like bits of lint, his left elbow still clamped against the pistol, pocketed the other coins, and, after transferring them to his right hand, triumphantly offered them to the bus driver. That eminence continued to look straight ahead, although his right hand and forearm unfolded themselves sufficiently to point disdainfully at the coin box.

Teck tipped the coins into the metal mouth. The bus' gears gnashed at each other murderously and the bus jerked ahead so quickly that Teck fell backward and had to put out his left hand to save himself, reaching across with his right to hold the pistol as he twisted, and the pain in his back overrode whatever had been left of the drugs and he cried out.

The other passengers looked away from him, no doubt hoping that they would disembark before he was seized by epilepsy or a fit of insanity.

He swung his way down the bus from pole to pole, seat back to seat back. In the very rear, he lowered himself into the last wide seat, where he could put his right leg up and ease the growing discomfort of his groin.

It was twenty minutes before he was sure that he was heading out of the city rather than into it. Much later still, in open country, he was sure that a cement factory on the left was the same one he had passed in the car with Mickey, and for a panicky moment he feared that somehow he would end up back at the house with Ricki and Kamal, but the bus continued on until he was in a dreary little town that he did not recognize, and he relaxed a little.

The driver swung the bus in a U-turn in the village street and pulled to a stop in front of a small café. It was almost dusk; within the café, the yellow of incandescent light seemed bright against the building's dark façade. The bus driver stood up and called to Teck, his last passenger. He gestured for Teck to come forward; there was no choice but to do as he commanded. At the front of the bus, Teck looked down at the man who stood in the well by the front door. The driver pointed at his mouth, then at Teck, and Teck nodded and smiled and pointed at his own mouth. The driver pointed again at himself, then at the bus, and then he described a circle in the air and pointed in the direction from which they had come.

Teck nodded and smiled some more. He imitated the driver's actions. The driver pointed at his watch, then brandished the spread fingers of one hand—once, twice, three times. Fifteen minutes.

He waved Teck off the bus, closed the door, and went into the café. Teck lingered by the bus, not daring to follow. Three young men idled by the café door; one spoke and nodded at Teck, who shuffled away a few yards and then followed the scent of cooking meat to an open window at the side of the café. Next to the window a vertical grill was stacked with tiny lamb chops that spat softly and sent up a rich smoke. With gestures, Teck was able to buy three of the chops from the old woman at the window. She wrapped them in a sheet of soft, flat bread and handed them out, and Teck, though he had to pick the food apart with his fingers because he could not chew very well, was able to eat in the deep shadow beside the café. Five minutes after he finished eating and wiped his greasy hands on his too-short jacket, he was huddled again in the deepest corner of the bus, heading back through the darkening countryside toward Izmir.

When Teck was boarding the bus for the first time, Valeri Seriakin was just getting into his car after finding that the professor had escaped from the clinic. He had still some hope of finding Teck then, believing that the man could not move quickly in his condition and without money. In his urgency he had not waited for the woman to check her pocketbook, but he knew that Teck was clothed and armed and he felt ashamed that he had been so easily defeated.

Back in the clinic, the woman finished suturing the slash on her companion's face.

Seriakin drove to the next corner, from which he saw Teck's bus without knowing that Teck was on it. When the bus stopped in the middle of the street because Teck had not put any money in, Seriakin paid no attention and drove off in another direction, looking for a twisted figure in ill-fitting clothes. That was as close as he was to come to Teck that evening.

And when two Palestinian agents of the KGB coasted to a stop in a stolen Fiat 1200 outside the clinic, Seriakin was a quarter of a mile away, driving slowly along strange streets in search of a man who was in actuality on a bus heading into the suburbs. According to their instructions, the Palestinians were five minutes too early to intercept Seriakin. When, fifteen minutes later, their target had not appeared, one of them walked two blocks to a café for a telephone. When he returned, he slid into the seat beside the driver without a word, and with a wave of his right hand signaled the car on its way.

Teck's bus was passing the cement factory.

Seriakin's rented car was parked outside a small hotel near the Culture Park. He was inside in a small closet that contained a public telephone.

"I want to call about the shoes belonging to Mr. Youssif," he said, giving the code term for the Free Turkey Youth.

He was given another telephone number and he rang off.

Ten minutes later, the KGB resident had a message from

Repin, ordering her to lure Seriakin to the safe house and to hold him there, but the message was too late to bring him in that evening. By then, Seriakin had given the Free Turkey Youth a description of Teck and was again cruising the Izmir streets in his car, to be joined ten minutes later by a young man from their headquarters who would help him in the search. They drove, trying to pierce the dusk for a glimpse of a disguised American, while Seriakin thought of the evening in Leningrad when he had seen the woman at the window, now seemingly so long ago and so dreamlike.

Teck was finishing his lamb chops and thinking of the Princess, who must now be at the Hotel Sporting in Antalya.

Teck had been considering his alternatives, and he had come to the depressing conclusion that he *had* no alternatives. He had something like a line of action, and that was all. He would have to get in touch with Burrell.

He could go to Arkadi, of course, but no matter how he explained himself, he would have to admit some act or some intent that the police could jail him for. All things being equal, he would have returned to his hotel, but Mickey said there had been an attack on it and he had no idea of where Hamdar was or how many police might still be around it. No, quite simply, he would have to get in touch with Burrell and ask that he be got out of Turkey. He had one excuse and one persuasive argument: the loss of the manuscript, first to Ricki and then to The Slav, was unfortunate but not entirely his own fault (he would have to accept Burrell's anger at his breaking under torture); and his photocopies of the manuscript, while not as good as the manuscript itself, would be of value. Trade goods. Burrell had his passport, and Burrell would know how to get him out of the country. *A little of the old American muscle, a little droit de seigneur. . . .* Teck would have to resign himself to the loss of the Aelian Fragment, of course. He frowned. He shifted his weight to relieve the tension in his back, which was beginning to ache.

The bus was back in Izmir. He recognized the corner where he had first seen it. The military truck was still there. Nonetheless, the streets seemed busier than they had an hour earlier: men walked arm in arm; cars whizzed back and forth. Teck got out at a brightly lighted corner where, from a distance, he had noticed three taxis lined up in front of a wall covered with tattered movie posters.

"I want to go to the Gol Café," he said to the first driver as he got into the cab. The man expostulated with him excitedly until Teck held out a fistful of paper money.

"No Gol Café!"

"Yes, Gol Café. Take me to the Gol Café." It was the only place he knew in Izmir where he might be able to find some help—namely, the waiter—in using the telephone.

The cabdriver called to the next man in the line, who climbed wearily out of his car and shuffled his heavy body slowly toward them. The two drivers spoke briefly, and the new man leaned in past Teck's driver. "No go to Gol Café, mister, Culture Park all closed up now, damned police close him up for trouble, yes, right?"

"Trouble? Where? The Gol Café?"

Both men spoke at once. He thought he heard his hotel mentioned, and he said, "The Turisti Pallas? Trouble at the Turisti Pallas?"

They both smiled. "Yes, Turisti Pallas. Yes, very bad trouble, then also at USIS, very bad, close down Culture Park at end of day, okay?" The Trade Fair buildings were in the Culture Park.

"You want good café, mister, go Continental, right? Café Continental? Good dance, good drink, plenty whatever you want, okay?"

Teck nodded. Better to go somewhere than nowhere. "Okay, Café Continental."

His driver smiled and, after twice wrestling with the gear lever, got the car moving. As they bucked forward, he smiled back at Teck and the light from a streetlamp winked off a gold tooth in his upper jaw.

"Wait!" Teck shouted suddenly, putting his hand on the driver's right shoulder. The man slowed the car but did not stop, and, with it moving along a line of parked cars, looked back at Teck. "Is the bazaar open? Stores—bazaar?" He searched for the word. *"Carsisi? Carsisi?"* The man nodded vigorously. So long as Teck was willing to pay, he seemed quite ready to drive anywhere. Ten minutes later the car crawled through narrow streets in the bazaar until Teck spotted an outdoor used-clothing rack, and there he gave the driver money and the shoes and the jacket he had taken from his captor, and with much insistence he got the driver to cross the street, hopefully with some understanding of what he was to do. Indeed, he understood too well, for the new jacket, which must have been cut for a Sydney Greenstreet, was large enough to hide in, but its checks of pink and white and black at least did not look like the costume of a hunted man. As there were socks and a rather greasy necktie and a pair of remarkably shiny shoes (whose shine chipped off along the creases like unraveling braid when Teck put them on), he wound up looking rather grotesquely festive. He hoped he could at least attempt the Café Continental without being thrown out by the first bouncer who spotted him.

In fact, it was all easier than he had dared hope. No one seemed to care that he was unshaven, and, since many of the men in the place were wearing glasses as dark and large as his own, no notice was taken of his eye. Too, it was dark—very dark—in the Café Continental.

"Do you speak English?" Teck asked the bartender.

The bartender scowled and shook his head. He signaled a girl in green slacks and very high clogs. She smiled vacantly at Teck until she got close enough to see the beard and the split upper lip.

"Do you speak English?" She did, but only enough to keep a drunk happy. Her French was better, however.

"I want you to help me use the telephone. Can you do that for me?"

She looked so wary he thought she was afraid he might strike her. "Perhaps."

"Good." Teck held out a bill. Behind him, the bartender sucked in his breath. The girl turned away quickly. "I'm sorry. You're afraid somebody will see, aren't you? All I want to do is make a telephone call, truly."

With some difficulty, she was persuaded to find the telephone number of Edward Rountree, the young USIS man who had visited Teck at the jail. As soon as the number was dialed, she handed the instrument to Teck and scurried away.

"Mr. Rountree?"

"Speaking." The voice sounded weary.

"This is Sam Teck. You came to see me at the Izmir police station. Yesterday, I think."

"Oh? Oh, yes, I remember." There was a pause. "Weren't you staying at the Turisti Pallas?"

"I've got to get in touch with Phillip Burrell, Mr. Rountree. It's terribly important. I don't know where he's staying."

"Burrell?" The man sounded vague, not cautious. Teck remembered the account of the attack on the USIS office; no doubt he was worn out. "I'm afraid that Burrell's gone."

"Where?"

"I don't know; he didn't tell me. I really couldn't say."

"Look, this is important! To me, I mean. I don't want to sound melodramatic, but it's a matter of—" Teck resisted the desire to say "life and death," which, although undoubtedly true, was not convincing. "Burrell has my passport."

"Oh, yeah? Gee, that's a shame."

"Rountree, I can't stay where I am. I've got to find a place where I can stay—where I can try to find Burrell. Look, what I'm saying is, I need help."

"Gee, I'd love to ask you up here, but, you know, the baby's just gone to sleep and all. . . ." The voice trailed off, begging for a reprieve. Lamely, he added, "Why don't you find another hotel?"

"Because I'm almost out of money, and— Look, somebody beat me up. Mugged me. I'm hurt, and—goddamnit, you're a representative of the government. *Do* something for me."

"Oh, boy." In the silence Teck could sense the man's dilemma. Standing at the telephone, bone-weary, he must be looking at his wife, who is already tense and worried and confused and who will, paradoxically, become furious with him unless he goes to bed and allows her to take care of him. Still, he is a decent man. "Where are you now?"

"I'm at a public phone. See here, all I want is a safe place to sleep tonight—and a telephone."

"Have you tried the police?"

"I tried the police yesterday, if you remember. Rountree—" Teck flinched at what he was about to say; he thought of his behavior with Mickey. *Hold me.* "*Please* help me."

"Would it help if I loaned you the money to go to a hotel?"

"No!"

"You're not doing much for your own case. Are you a fugitive?"

"No, you know I'm not. Call the police if you think I am. Call Inspector Arkadi."

"I really think that a hotel—"

"No hotels! Look at what happened at the Turisti Pallas."

"Well— Oh, gee—"
"You *must* know of some place I can go."
There was a silence. Teck had the impression that the instrument at the other end had been covered, because there was no sound at all.
"Professor Teck? I'll pick you up myself. Where are you?"
Fifteen minutes later Teck was in the passenger seat of a VW Super Beetle, heading north along the waterfront. Rountree was cautious but apologetic. "You'll just have to be honest with me. This is a very compromising situation. I've got quite a few problems of my own, you know. Tell me why you have to hide. I mean, you do have to hide, right? Just tell me the truth. Then I'll see what I can do."
Teck sighed. He slumped down in the seat and began a slightly laundered history of his experiences with *The Book of the Dead.*

Chapter seventeen

"IT'S pretty basic housing, but it's private." Edward Rountree snapped on a light. "It belongs to this Englishman who works for Exxon. I told him I'd take care of his cat. Uh—" Rountree took a step into the mean little room. "My wife doesn't know about it. I mean, she doesn't dig my helping out somebody this way." *Oho,* thought Teck, *so it's that way,* but then he realized that perhaps it wasn't that way at all; perhaps Rountree was simply one of those decent people who are imposed upon all the time. *Like now.* "You understand, it's my ass if you've lied to me. Izmir is my first assignment. If I blow it—"
"I've told you the truth." Teck removed the sunglasses. "Look."
"Oh, Christ!" Rountree's young face, puffy with fatigue, registered the horror he felt at seeing Teck's left eye. "Holy Christ, you've got to see a doctor."
"No. Unless you can bring one here."
"Not tonight, but there's a hospital about a mile away. We can—"
"I'll go in the morning. I've got to find Burrell."

"God, I'm sorry. That eye— I'm sorry."

That's nothing, you should see my cojones. A sardonic lightheadedness had replaced the urgency of earlier in the evening. He had been amused that the real reason for Rountree's grudging trust had been his discovery that they had friends in common, particularly an attractive woman who had been on the faculty of Rountree's undergraduate college and who was a former graduate student of Teck's. Rountree had even called him "sir" once or twice.

Teck winced as he sat on a bed that proved to be merely a wooden base with a foam mattress. His back hurt constantly now. "Have you got anything for pain?"

"Gee, nothing with me. I can look in the bathroom."

"I can do that myself."

"No, no, stay where you are." Rountree disappeared into a little hallway by the front door. Teck lay back with his head propped up uncomfortably against the wall. He closed his eyes. When he opened them again he found himself being stared at by a large black-and-white cat that was sitting in the archway that separated the room from a minuscule kitchen. The cat neither judged nor questioned; it merely stared. "Same to you, cat," Teck muttered. The cat leaned forward into a walking posture and moved three feet into the room, then sat again and stared some more.

When Rountree returned he had a bottle of English aspirin and a foil envelope of something called MALBAN that had directions in Italian on the back. "Do you read Italian, Professor? They sell stuff over the counter in some countries that you can't get at home. Or here, for that matter."

The ingredients were not translatable in Teck's Renaissance Italian, which was more than adequate for reading Dante, and which usually convulsed the Princess, but he was able to make sure that it was a painkiller. Rountree appeared from the kitchen with a half-empty bottle of Yugoslav plum brandy and a rather scummy glass; Teck took two of the MALBAN from the foil and shook out two of the aspirin and swallowed all four with a dose of the brandy. "Kill me or cure me. Either would be an improvement."

Rountree wrote out the telephone number of the embassy in Ankara and told him how to make a long-distance call. He refused any of the slivovitz himself because he had to drive, and from the way he kept leaning against walls and furniture,

Teck was convinced that Rountree was exhausted. "Go on home," he said almost kindly. "I'll take care of myself now." Teck was anxious to be alone now.

"I guess I understand why you want to call Burrell," Rountree said hesitantly. He yawned. "I know he's more than just an attaché in Ankara. But you know, if there's anything civil involved here—I mean, anything to do with the police—we *are* subject to Turkish law, Professor Teck."

"Call me Sam." Teck turned his head so that he could study Rountree with his good eye. "I won't bring you into it."

"That isn't what I mean." Rountree looked miserable. "The law is the law, after all."

"Nobody knows that better than I do. I'm not a criminal."

"I didn't say that you are, although if you'd taken that manuscript to the police the very first thing, none of this would have happened."

Teck did not answer immediately. He had not told Rountree about the Aelian Fragment. Finally, he said, "The police think I may have been killed at the Turisti Pallas. Let's leave it that way tonight."

"Well, okay. But tomorrow I'll have to notify them. I'll just have to."

Rountree waited for a response, but Teck made none.

"I'll have to call them in the morning, Sam."

"I heard you. Come by here first, will you?"

"You're not going to split or do something dumb, are you?"

"Split? Where? And how?" Teck poured himself another, larger drink of plum brandy. The painkillers were beginning to work. "Just do me the favor of coming here before you call the police."

Rountree turned and moved slowly to the door, hunched over and yawning and half-stumbling into a chair like a sleepy child. "Okay, See you in the morning."

Before he had opened the door, Teck said, "How will I know it's you?" The paranoia had not left him.

"Who else would it be?"

"I don't know; I just want to make sure it's you."

Rountree looked faintly embarrassed. "A signal?"

"Fine. A knock."

Now Rountree was openly embarrassed. "Oh, boy, cops and robbers," he said.

"I just want to make sure. A signal. Just knock twice, then

pause, then again, then the same thing again. Two and two and two. All right?"

Rountree demonstrated the signal for Teck. When he left, he was still embarrassed.

When he was gone, and Teck had bolted the door behind him, he took the gun out and put it on the low table by the bed. The cat had curled up on the bed as far away from him as possible, and when Teck got two pillows from the head to put behind his back, the animal rolled on its side with one paw up and the claws out, ready to battle. "Tough customer," Teck said, and let it be. The telephone just reached from its dusty place on a bookcase to the table. With the pillows behind his back, Teck could sit on the bed, gun in front of him, and make the calls that had to be made.

After a little difficulty in finding an operator who spoke English, he rang the American Embassy in Ankara, where a Turkish switchboard woman assured him that Mr. Burrell was not there. When he asked where Mr. Burrell was, she said coolly that he could be reached during normal business hours.

"I have to speak to Mr. Burrell *now.*"

"I am sorry, he is not here." The words seemed very final.

"Then please tell me where I can find him."

"As of yesterday Mr. Burrell was accepting calls at the United States Information Office in Izmir."

"*I'm* in Izmir. Burrell is not!"

"Please try during business hours, sir."

Teck inhaled slowly and then let the deep breath out with the same deliberation. "Is there somebody at the embassy this evening?"

"*I* don't know who's here."

"Somebody who's in charge, I mean."

"Well, the duty officer, of course."

"May I speak to him, please?"

"But Mr. Burrell is not the duty officer."

"May I speak to the duty officer, please?

"Is this an official call?"

"Will you please give me the duty officer or will I make a formal complaint to the ambassador? During business hours!"

The duty officer seemed unwilling to admit that someone named Burrell was even connected with the embassy, and he was certainly not about to believe Teck's tale of having something important to tell him.

"Well, could you just tell me where Burrell is?"

"I'm afraid I couldn't do that—wouldn't do that, I mean—even if I knew. What is your name, by the way?"

"Is that important?"

"I have to log the call, sir."

Teck did not hesitate. "My name is Higden. Ranulf Higden."

"Did you say Randolph?"

"Uh, yes, Randolph is fine."

"Your passport number, sir?"

"That's the point—Burrell has my passport!"

"Oh, *I* see. Well, that *is* rather important, isn't it."

"Yes, very much so. Now will you tell me where Burrell is?"

"Have you tried the Izmir consulate?"

Teck found it best to be sweetly reasonable. "Yes. Mr. Rountree, the acting consul, has been very helpful. In fact, it was he who gave me your number."

"Ah. Oh, good. In that case, you're getting as much help as I could give you. I hope you see my side of it."

Teck poured himself more brandy.

"No, I don't. I see only my side of it. And if I don't get in touch with Burrell, I'll blab all over Turkey about what his real connection with the embassy is, do you understand that?"

"I'm afraid I don't know what you're talking about, Mr., uh, Higden."

"Like hell you don't! I'm talking about his being a—"

"This is an open line, sir. Please don't say something you'll regret later."

Teck realized that the call could be traced. "I see. That *was* a threat, wasn't it? All the way from Ankara?"

The voice at the other end, no longer young, a little bored, everlastingly patient, grew a little louder, as if the man had pushed his mouth confidingly closer to the telephone. Out of the corner of his eye Teck saw the cat get up at the end of the bed, turn in a full circle, and lie down exactly as it had been.

"Mr. Higden, listen—why don't you give me your number there, and if I hear from Phil, I'll have him call you."

"No, I can't do that. I'm sorry."

"Okay, okay, let's see what else. Look, how would it be if I give you his secretary's home number? She may know whether or not he can be reached." *And she's somebody to pass the buck to.*

"I'll try it."

"Good." The embassy man sounded relieved.

The telephone at the secretary's rang and rang—and rang. The operator came on and asked him if he would like to call the number later. Teck said that he would let it ring a little longer. He intended to let it continue for six more rings. The call was answered on the fifth.

"Allo?"

"Uh, hello, is, uh—" Teck glanced at a sheet of paper next to the gun.

"Is Miss Kerrigan there?"

"No, no here. Nobody here."

"Is this Miss Kerrigan's number?"

"Nobody here."

"Whom am I speaking to?"

"Concierge. Nobody here."

"Is—this—Miss—Kerrigan's—line?" He pronounced the name as if he were French—*Cair-ee-gon.* He waited for a response. None came. Teck sighed and said "Thank you," and started to hang up.

"Allo? Allo?"

"Yes, hello?"

"Boo-rell?"

"I beg your pardon?"

"Boo-rell? You, Boo-rell?"

Lying was becoming so easy Teck did not even have to think about it. "Yes, this is Mr. Burrell." He improvised. "Did Miss Kerrigan leave the number where I can call her?"

The concierge said something quite unintelligible to Teck. He said he did not understand, and the same sounds were repeated. Again his confusion, and again the sounds. This time it occurred to him that he was being given an address or a number—in Turkish. In his own laborious phonetics he wrote out what the concierge gave him. The result was a five-sound set.

"Thank you," Teck said when he was sure that he had been given the entirety of whatever it was the concierge was offering.

There was no sound from the other end. Teck hung up.

He gave the long-distance operator the set of sounds.

"Is that a telephone number?"

"I think so, yes, sir. Do you want to read it to me in English?"

"Uh, no. Is it an Ankara number?"

"No, sir. Ankara numbers have six digits. Istanbul numbers have seven. I believe you will find it is a number in Izmir, sir."

Teck tried the number in Izmir. The telephone rang five times and was picked up and a female voice said, all the words in a clump and without inflection, "Hello-who-is-this-please?"

"Uh"—Teck was suddenly tongue-tied—"I'm trying to reach Phillip Burrell."

"Yes?"

"I called the embassy—in Ankara—and they gave me your number."

There was a pause of about three seconds, and when the woman spoke again, her voice was sharp. "Whyever would they do that?"

Teck's head had begun to ache along a line right down the center of his scalp. "This *is* Mr. Burrell's secretary, isn't it?"

"That's right. But I don't have his itinerary with me. Who is this?"

"My name is Sam Teck." He waited for the name to register with her, but if it did, she gave no indication. "Mr. Burrell and I were working on something together. I have something to tell him. Something quite important."

From the woman's end of the line a blurred voice said something, a voice that was certainly not hers, and then he heard her call out, "I'm on the phone!" A moment later she was saying to Teck, "I'm sorry, I really can't help you."

"But I really have to talk to—"

There was a disturbance at her end. She cried out, "Oh, for Christ's sake!" and the telephone popped loudly as she set it down; after a brief silence he could hear the diminishing taps of her footsteps on a hard surface. Teck strained to hear.

Then the footsteps were approaching the telephone. He thought she was coming back, but as the footsteps grew louder there was a confused jumble and then Teck heard a man's voice say, with perfect, slow-motion clarity, "Hello."

He knew the voice. "Burrell!"

Again, the words that followed were spoken slowly, with a long beat between words that gave each one an eerie isolation. "Who—is—this?"

"Burrell! It's Sam Teck. Remember? Burrell?"

Beat, beat. "Yes?"

And the woman's voice, a little farther away, "For Christ's

sake, Phil!" Footsteps tapping, and the voice, suddenly very loud, "GET OFF THE PHONE, PHIL!"

She must have taken the extension from him and slammed it down, because there was a bang like a gunshot in Teck's ear. His sense of the scene at the other end was abruptly reduced as he could hear only faintly through the telephone that she had first answered.

Her footsteps came close again.

"I'm very sorry . . . hello?"

"Yes, I'm here; now look, that was—"

"I have somebody staying with me who's ill."

"That was Burrell!"

"I'm sorry, you're mistaken."

"It is, it's Burrell!"

He thought she might hang up, but finally she said, "He's very ill, I'm sorry."

"He's drunk!"

And the woman, calm now but stiff, said, "You're very mistaken. Good night."

"No, don't hang up! Give him a message for me—please?"

"Well?"

"Just tell him that Sam Teck has a very important matter to talk over with him. Very important."

"If you'll leave your number I'll have him call tomorrow."

"No. I'll call him, at this same number. Tomorrow morning at six. I assume he'll be sober by then?"

The woman ignored the remark. "I don't want to disturb him before ten."

"You'll have to. If I don't get him at six, I'll be talking to the police. He wouldn't like that."

Teck did not bother with the amenities. After he had hung up he realized that he was shaking and his groin hurt worse than before. He eased himself off the bed and started for the kitchen in hopes of finding food and some ice. The cat, spread-eagled on the bed, was busily licking what was left of its testicles. "Lucky bastard," Teck muttered, trying to walk without increasing his own discomfort. In the ancient refrigerator he found yogurt and cheese and a single ice tray—all that the doorless freezing compartment would hold —with a scattering of cubes and lumps frozen together in the pan. This he broke up on the corner of the tiled drainboard and wrapped in a very suspect tea towel that looked as if it had not been washed since someone's aunt had made the owner a present of it eight or ten years before. Still, with this improvised ice pack resting on his more private wounds, Teck was able to believe that he was getting some relief. On the way back to the bed he picked up a small folding alarm clock from the bookcase. He put it on the table and took up the bottle, which was still a quarter full.

"Well," he said to the cat, "Faint heart ne'er won fair et cetera, right?" The cat minced over and tried to push its head under his ice bag. Teck shouted "Ow!" and the cat withdrew hastily to its own end of the bed.

He asked the head operator to put through one more call, this time to the Hotel Sporting in Antalya. The Princess' voice sounded lazy and cheerful and instead of feeling better, he felt like bursting into tears. "Hello? This is la Principessa di Paoli; are you there?" She loved to roll out the rippling name her estranged husband had given her—all that he had given her, she now said, for she was always pleading poverty, although she lived in a way that Teck found profligate and exhilarating by turns.

"Princess, it's Sam."

"Sam!" The single syllable combined delight with relief. It made him feel worse than ever. "Sam, is it you!" And then, more like a parent scolding a child, "Sam, where have you been?"

"I've been— Oh —" He found to his astonishment that he was choking—the famous frog in the throat, the lump that near-weeping brings—and he tried to swallow and succeeded only in making his throat hurt. "Oh, God, Princess. . . ." That was all he said.

"Sam, what is it!"

"It's— Oh, Christ!" He was angry at himself because he was now weeping in earnest, and the improvised ice bag, as if out of sympathy, was dripping on the bed. With his right hand he tried to wipe the tears from his good eye. Finally, he leaned back on the sofa, face wet, and laughed ruefully into the telephone. "I'm a goddamn mess, Princess."

"What's the matter, Sam?"

"They've busted me all up, Princess. I'm a mess." His voice sank huskily and broke on the last word. He was sobbing.

"Sam, my darling, what is it? What is it?"

"I'll be all right in a minute."

"Where are you, Sam?"

"In Izmir. Not at the hotel. It was bombed or something."

"Yes, I thought you were one of them! No, I didn't really, but I was worried, Sam. I only heard about it today—but in the paper they said your name wasn't on the hostage list, and so I thought—I hoped—I'm coming to Izmir tomorrow."

"No! No, don't!"

"Why not?"

"Because I'm getting out of Izmir. No, don't come here, that's the worst thing you could do."

"What kind of trouble are you in, Sam?"

He laughed. His voice no longer betrayed him when he spoke. "Just about every kind of trouble that there is."

"Have you done something simply awful, darling?"

"No, but I've done something simply stupid. Several things simply stupid. I can't tell you about it, Princess, but— God, it's good to talk to you!"

"I think I ought to come to you, Sam."

"No, definitely not! I'll come to Antalya if I can."

"When?"

"Tomorrow, I hope. I have one—loose end to clean up, and then I'll be there as fast as I can. And you just stay where you are. How are you, by the way?"

"I'm wonderful, horribly frustrated and horny, waiting for you like impatient Grissell. What did you mean about being all busted up?"

"Nothing. A manner of speaking. A turn of phrase. Princess, about your friends with the sailboat."

"It's a yacht, darling. A sailboat is a little thing with teenagers in bikinis and so on."

"All right, the yacht—where is it?"

"Why?"

Teck hesitated. He was afraid to let her know just how desperate he had become. "Because I may need a way of getting out of the country."

It was her turn to hesitate. Then, "Oh, I see." That was all.

"Would your friends take me—that way?"

"All I can do is ask. You come well recommended. Is it about the fragment, Sam?"

"Uh, sort of. In a way."

"You're terribly unspecific. A kind of monumental vagueness, in fact. Rather asking them to take a pig in a poke."

"A well-recommended pig."

"Well, I'll do what I can. Paul's supposed to call me tomorrow; in fact, he should be here tomorrow or next day. He might rather leap at the chance if it sounded dangerous enough. Can I make it sound a bit dangerous?"

"Oh, yes, I think you can do that without stretching the truth too far." He knew that she probably understood fairly well what he was saying. She was still not so very far from Hoxton.

"I'm going to hang up, Princess."

"Oh, dear. Just like that! You wouldn't care to breathe heavily into the telephone or anything?"

"I don't think I'd better. I'll explain when I see you."

"You will call me again, Sam?"

"Yes, tomorrow. And don't mention to anybody else that you talked to me, all right?"

They were both silent. He became banal.

"You'd better get some sleep. Me, too."

"All right."

"Good night, Princess."

"Sam?"

"Yes?"

"I take back what I said at the airport. About your being a stick. Not anymore, at any rate."

A few minutes later he took two more of the Italian pills and more aspirin and the rest of the plum brandy and lay back on the hard bed, displacing the cat. Miraculously, he slept, although fitfully, tormented by dreams and awakened to semiconsciousness by pain whenever he tried to move.

Chapter eighteen

AT eleven that night, a member of the Free Turkey Youth talked to the girl at the Café Continental, who remembered Teck, his ridiculous jacket and his battered face, and who could tell him the name of the American whose number she had found for him.

"Rountree, the United States Information Service man,"

the young man said as he climbed in beside Seriakin. "She remembers Teck and she remembers the name Rountree." He lit a cigarette, trying to let the smoke slide out of the side of his mouth as he had seen Belmondo do it in a film a week before. Sitting with the Russian in a dark car, discussing the pursuit of an American spy, it was difficult not to dramatize oneself.

"You did well," Seriakin said. The young man smiled.

Ten minutes later Seriakin was on the telephone to his contact in the Izmir police department, who assured the Russian that his office had not tapped the telephone of the USIS officer, and why did Seriakin want to know?

"None of your business," was Seriakin's straightforward answer. After a few seconds' thought, during which he made a clucking noise that disturbed the policeman, Seriakin said, "What car does the American drive?"

"How would I know?"

"Find out. I'll call you in ten minutes."

Fifteen minutes later Seriakin and the Turk were headed south along the waterfront road, past the central city to the fringe of American-style apartment houses that had risen there in the 1960's like tall, disapproving faces that frowned down on the crowded Eastern city below them. Seriakin stopped at one of the more modest ones and sent his companion inside to bribe the porter. He hid himself in a janitor's closet on the same floor as Rountree's apartment, while Seriakin drove down the ramp into the garage under the building and parked in a lane marked, in three languages, NO PARKING, and there he spent the night watching Rountree's car, while, outside in the city, others of the Free Turkey Youth watched the train station and the airport for Teck, and the KGB resident and three agents waited for Seriakin himself at the safe house, which was no longer safe for him.

The man to whom Repin had given the responsibility for taking *The Book of the Dead* to Athens was an experienced hand in "wet" missions, a Byelorussian named Yuri Nemchin. Two days before being ordered to join Repin on board the *Leonid Andreyev* he had been in Bulgaria, on leave after three years in Ethiopia. Repin had told him little other than the essentials of the mission, but Nemchin could look at the pieces of the puzzle in his own hands and guess at those that were missing.

The young man from Leningrad, Seriakin, brought in from his desk job; he, Nemchin, thrust in at the last minute instead of one of the KGB area men—it was typical maneuvering, slightly paranoid and very highhanded. It had been set up very carefully, much of it with only the most general kind of authorization, the kind that only someone at Repin's level could manage. He, Nemchin, for example, had been assigned because his area chief was an old Indochina pal of Repin's. "They were on the Long March together" was the ironic saying of one of the young men, inaccurate as historical fact, but quite correct as metaphor.

Nemchin's principal concern was not to compromise himself. He had been ordered; therefore he would act. But he would not act except within the narrow limits of his orders, and his reports would reflect his caution.

At midnight, carrying the passport of a Bulgarian lawyer, he was driven to the Izmir airport to catch the late plane to Yesilkoy; from there he would fly to Athens where the substitute manuscript of *The Book of the Dead* would start its journey to the CIA-supported publishing house of Editions Chaconne in Paris, where it would become an instant sensation. Hopefully, some of the manuscript's history would already be known in Paris, and the book would come with an authentication written in violence.

As the plane banked over the lights of Izmir, Nemchin wondered idly where Seriakin was and how long it would take him to return to the safe house. Off to his left, he could see a faint cluster of lights on the black water—the Soviet ship on which Repin was sleeping. Nemchin did not recognize it, nor would he have much cared if he had.

Phillip Burrell woke to the first morning light, an unfamiliar pink glow on an unfamiliar wall. He picked carefully through his memories of the night before until he had reconstructed enough to know that he was in an apartment in Izmir and that Sally should have been with him, although the other side of the bed was empty. He did not remember coming to bed. He did not remember much after reaching the apartment.

He was nauseated when he rolled over and tried to sit up. The constriction between his eyes worsened and he realized that his head ached fiercely.

He lay in the bed as the light brightened, moving his legs every two or three minutes to find a cooler place on the sheets and half-whimpering, half-groaning each time he moved, his face clammy with cold sweat. He had lain like that for three-quarters of an hour before a door on his right opened and Sally Kerrigan came in. Her hair was brushed and she wore makeup from the night before, the lipstick too livid against the faded color on her cheeks. She was wearing a long blue robe that he had helped her pick out in Ankara.

"Phil?"

"Mmm." He did not move his head.

"How do you feel?"

"Like death."

"Could you drink some tea or some bouillon?"

"Oh, Jesus."

"Or some tomato soup? There's some in a can."

"Oh, Jesus, no." He moved his legs and whimpered.

"Phil, you've got to be ready to talk on the telephone in a few minutes. It's Sam Teck."

"So?"

"He said he has to talk to you. He said it's very important. Phil, do you remember talking to him last night?"

Burrell pulled a pillow down over his eyes. It was cool on his forehead.

"Phil, do you remember talking to him?"

"Un-unh."

"Do you remember what happened last night?"

Burrell lay quite still. He tried to imagine a miraculous surgical operation, one in which a tiny hole could be drilled in the skull and all the pain let out. "I got drunk."

"You took a handful of my sleeping pills. You came out of the bathroom and told me you'd taken my sleeping pills."

"I was drunk."

"Then you threw up all over the living room and passed out. I had a hell of a time getting you to bed."

"I'm sorry."

"Why did you do it, Phil? I mean, you tried to kill yourself."

"I was drunk."

"You took a lot of sleeping pills!"

"I was drunk! Let it go, for Christ's sake!" A few seconds later, his hand moved over the sheet until it found her robe, groped down to her thigh, squeezed it. "Sorry, Sal." It was as well that he could not see her face, which was sullen and almost contemptuous under the faded makeup. *He's through and he knows it,* she was thinking. *It's because of the skin divers getting canceled and things not working out for him. He's all through.*

"You've got to talk to this man, Phil. Maybe he has something to tell you, some kind of news. Can I get you something?"

"No, I'll be fine." He withdrew his hand and pushed the pillow back with his head. His eyes were still closed. "Get me a glass of ice water and a wet towel."

Minutes later, he was propped up in the bed with the wet towel over his forehead and eyes. He sipped ice water. His breathing was hoarse, and each exhalation sounded as if he were emptying his lungs with great difficulty. When the telephone rang at six o'clock, the woman lifted the extension next to the bed, and, when she was certain that it was Teck, passed the instrument to Burrell. His fingers, touching hers, were as cold as the icy glass they had been holding.

"This is Phillip Burrell speaking."

"This is Teck."

"Yes?"

"It would have been nice if I could have talked sensibly with you last night."

"Sorry, I wasn't feeling well. One of those running-at-both-ends things. I think it's best if I call you back from another telephone in a few hours."

"Absolutely not. I want to talk now."

"I don't think it's wise to say anything over this telephone."

"Nothing I do is wise anymore, Burrell."

"If I give you a number, Teck, will you call me there later?"

"No. We'll talk now."

"All right. But I'm warning you, I'll cut you off the moment you start to blab."

"Fine. Do that. I'll call you right back again. Or maybe I'll just pay a call on Inspector Arkadi. Are you listening?"

"So far."

"All right. Somebody lured me away from the Turisti Pallas just before it was attacked. I've been beaten up and I told them where the book was. They got it."

Weakling, Burrell thought, but aloud he said, "Too bad."

"That isn't all."

Yes, Teck, that is all; the rest is just detail. You weakling. "Yes?"
"Somebody else, I think he's a Russian, got the book from the people who beat me. But—before I, uh, jettisoned the book, I, uh, photographed it."
"Why didn't you *tell* me that?"
"What difference would it have made?"
"It makes all the difference!" In his anger Burrell tried to sit up, but he quickly sank back, wiping his face with the wet towel. "You could have saved me—you could have saved a lot of trouble. Good God!" Burrell was silent, trying to make sense of what Teck had said through the fog of his hangover. "Teck, where are the photos?"
"They're being processed."
"Where?"
"I'm sorry, I'm not ready to tell you that."
"Where are they?"
"I'd rather not say."
"You're not planning to do something stupid, I hope, Teck."
"Like what?"
"Nobody would pay you a cent for those photos, Teck."
Teck's sardonic laughter exploded in the telephone. "Burrell, all I want is to get out of Turkey."
"That can be arranged."
"And I want my passport."
"Yes, I still have that."
"Good. When can I leave?"
Burrell spread his legs and drew his knees up. "When can I have the photos?"
"When I'm safe in Italy."
"No, it can't work that way, Teck. This is a very important matter. I'll have to have the photos first."
"Burrell, for Christ's sake, I may be killed! I've been beaten up; some Russian is probably looking for me; Rountree wants me to go to the police—get me out of this goddamn country!"
"Where are you, Teck?"
"Get me out of Turkey. Then you can *have* the goddamn pictures."
"Teck, where are you?"
Teck's breathing was clearly audible over the line. At last he said, "Those pictures are more important than I am, that's what you're saying to me. Right?"

"Absolutely."
"Greed or patriotism?"
"If you have to ask, Teck, you can't afford the answer."
Burrell heard Teck chuckle, a drawn-out, disbelieving sound of slow realization. He was still chuckling softly when he said, "You're almost unbelievable, Burrell. Almost. I really find it hard to believe that this is happening." His voice was quite gay when he added, "You're a really rotten human being. Rotten!"
"You have a lot to learn, Professor. You don't seem to understand that giving me those photos is for your own good."
"But, Burrell, I want to get out of Turkey; chain us together and come with me; just get me out! You owe me that much, goddamnit!"
"For what?"
"For one eye and my pride, not to mention my right testicle, all right?"
Ruthlessly, Burrell said, "Where are you, Teck? We'll need to meet face to face to work out how you're going to get the photos to me."
He heard Teck's sharp inhalation, then nothing, as if the man at the other end were holding his breath. When the answer came, it was pitched so low that Burrell could hardly hear it. "Don't call me, Burrell; I'll call you."
And Teck hung up.
Burrell lifted the wet towel, which was now warm from his own heat, and turned his head so that he could replace the telephone in its cradle. He called Sally.
"Well?"
"Sal, give me an hour—no, it'll take longer than that; give me until ten. I'll sleep if I can. But I'll be all right. A little sleep and I'll be fine. Now, while I'm pulling myself together, I want you to send a couple of cables. Two-cable system, you know the drill. Send them to Billy Hull at the Rome embassy and have him find where Teck stays in Rome. Then ask Billy to put a check on Teck's mail. I want any photos that come for him.
"Then get on the phone to that kid Rountree at USIS here in Izmir. Teck mentioned him, so he may know where Teck is. If he does, get the address and be ready to take me there at ten. And bring me my camera case, the aluminum one."

He lay back with his eyes closed. He felt ill. Worse, he felt that he was suffering a breakdown.

Burrell had had moments before when he had thought that the fabric of his sanity was starting to unravel. Then he would concentrate on his work, and the moment would pass, and the next time he thought he noticed the unraveling, he would be astounded, as shocked and unmanned as if his long-dead wife had walked into the room. Mostly, these nauseating moments would come after drinking too much or when he thought about suicide. Then he would see the unraveling, and his knees would go rubbery and he would pinch the bridge of his nose between thumb and forefinger and concentrate desperately on his work.

He was disproportionately happy when she came back because she brought him work to think about and he could forget the unraveling. She put down a small aluminum case marked PHOTO EQUIPMENT—DO NOT X-RAY and left the room. He frantically dumped the contents on the bed and removed the fiberboard liner from one side. From the recess below it he took out a disassembled nine-millimeter pistol, which he began to put together with slightly trembling hands, his face pale and faintly shiny with chilled sweat.

Teck's hand trembled when he replaced the telephone. When the black-and-white cat leaped into his lap, he brushed it away and stood up so that the normally agile animal stumbled clumsily and then sat down and licked its flank with its back turned to him.

"Sorry, cat," he said, and he bent to touch the animal's head, but when it felt the contact the cat ducked and ran away to the bathroom.

That rotten bastard, thought Teck, meaning Burrell and not the animal. *That bastard!* He remembered the detached man who had visited him at the jail—the picture, he would have said, of the confident and worldly gentleman. *The bastard. What makes a man do things like that? Professional zeal? Ruthlessness? Pride?*

After two angry pacings up and down the room, Teck went into the bathroom. He stripped. The shower was a very poor arrangement, merely a rubber hose with a nozzle and a spray head that was held up by two rusty nails and a bit of electrical cord. There was a circular pipe for a shower curtain, but no curtain. Teck left the pistol on a hamper where he could see it while he showered.

When he finished, he had solved only one small problem—that of his next short-term move. His first problem now was to keep Rountree from going to the police. After that, he would have to decide if he would approach Burrell again; if not, he would pursue the arrangements for the yacht that he had begun with the Princess the night before.

The Englishman's bathroom shelves were stocked with quite a startling assortment of deodorants, colognes, shaving lotions, and hair preparations; whatever his failings as a housekeeper, he was a cosmetic dazzler. Teck shaved with his host's razor and cleaned up his injured eye as best he could with shaving lotion and a towel. It seemed less swollen, although its purples had begun to change to mottled greens and blues and he still could not open it. He dressed in crisply laundered clothes from a rather dusty clothespress in the little hall by the bathroom, and when he was finished at seven o'clock he felt better and looked rather less like a derelict than he had the night before.

The Englishman evidently had some interest in health foods, and, despite the weevils in the brown rice and the mold on the yogurt, Teck was able to feed himself—a kind of mush, cooked up from a mixture of bulgur and walnuts, dripping with honey. Fifteen minutes' cooking made the nuts soft, and he could eat without discomfort.

He fed the cat and gave it water, but it was fastidious and would not eat until he had left the kitchen.

Teck sat again on the bed. He placed the pistol in front of him on the table, his bowl of mush to one side. He set out paper and a ball-point pen from a supply in a rickety desk against the far wall. He began to write an account of his actions that would, he hoped, persuade Rountree to delay going to the Izmir police; Rountree could hold the account for twenty-four hours and then deliver it if Teck did not surrender himself.

To: Inspector Arkadi of the Izmir Police, he wrote. *A summary of my actions in the Parduk affair.* He smiled at the quaint terminology. He began with his visit to Parduk's shop and his unwitting possession of *The Book of the Dead . . . swear I did not know it was in my possession until, at the Gol Café . . . my own folly, insane, stupid, to conceal it . . . was beaten and tortured until I told where the manuscript had been . . . I have committed no crime, but I hoped to commit the crime of buying the Aelian Fragment and taking it out of Turkey. The rest was stupidity and arrogance.*

He looked at the last three words.

He signed his name.

He had meant to write a confession that was also an absolution: *I was the innocent victim.* Instead, he had written a cautionary tale: *The intent to commit a small crime is punished with worse crimes.*

Nor had he intended to write down the truth about his plans for the Aelian Fragment, but it had all come out as he had written, inspired, as he now recognized, by the telephone conversation with Burrell. He had called Burrell a rotten human being, meaning that any man who prized pieces of paper over another human was infected with rot. *And the Aelian Fragment is only a piece of paper.*

Teck read the confession again. It occurred to him suddenly how easily it could be taken as a last message—a suicide note. A confession of guilt, a plea for understanding, and then—expiation?

Suicide, of course, by some serpentine convolution of the law, was also a crime, but one for which the successful criminal did not suffer any burden of guilt. *Not in his present surroundings,* he thought wryly.

He looked at the pistol and shivered.

There were two soft knocks at the door, and Teck, as if caught in some shameful act, hurriedly stacked the small pile of pages on which he had written. The knocks sounded again, and then again.

Teck put the papers down on the ramshackle desk with several blank sheets on top.

"Teck?"

Rountree did not know that he had the gun. Teck glanced around the room and then settled for sliding the pistol under the mattress.

Teck slipped the bolt back. Through the inch-wide opening he saw Rountree, who was alone.

Teck stepped back.

"Come in. Sorry about the idiot signal. I'm a little edgy."

Rountree smiled and stepped toward him. There was a clatter of sound from the corridor to Teck's left; Rountree hesitated and glanced that way, and then, too quickly for Teck to react, Rountree was shoved against him, blocking his view of the corridor.

"Please stand still." The voice was very tense.

Teck looked past Rountree's head. There were two men in the doorway, one a Turk with a ludicrously large automatic, the other The Slav with a small revolver that Teck had seen before.

Chapter nineteen

THE Slav and his ally left Rountree in the Englishman's apartment, tied and gagged and blindfolded. The Slav cut the telephone cord with a knife from the kitchen, and, seeing the cat come from the bathroom in one of those elongated, stretching poses that sometimes follow waking, he put out more food so that the cat would not cry and attract a neighbor. He was careful to make sure that Rountree never saw his face.

The Slav stopped Teck at the door of the building while the Turk scurried away up the street. Teck grew embarrassed in his absence, almost giddily so despite his fear, because the silence between him and the other man was so deliberate. Like two people in an elevator, they looked everywhere but at each other, connected only by the small gun that just brushed Teck's back at waist height. Once, their eyes met, and Teck actually smiled nervously, but the other looked away quickly.

Would he really shoot me if I simply walked away? Or is he simply depending on my playing a part the way I'm supposed to? What if I were simply to push the door open and—

But a Toyota Crown sedan pulled up outside at that moment, blocking the street, and the gun moved forward a little to prod him, and Teck stepped forward without ever testing the other man's willingness to shoot him. On the far side of the car the Turk had got out and was leaning toward them over the hood; his right hand rested inside his coat, undoubtedly on the big pistol he had holstered there.

Through a break between the buildings across the street, Teck could see the mossy green of water, the bay where only days before he had watched the mutilated body of the first victim of *The Book of the Dead* pulled up by the fishermen.

That was the last point at which he could have turned back.

He got into the sedan.

They drove through narrow side streets. Teck was forced to keep his hands locked behind his head, to prevent any quick move toward the doors. When they came to a principal street, the driver slowed until there was a break in the traffic, and The Slav, who was in the back seat with Teck, turned sideways to face him. Once, when an army van turned into the same street and stopped, the Toyota veered left down a covered alley to avoid meeting it. After twenty minutes of driving, the Toyota came to a stop outside a garage in a row of attached buildings. At a sound from the horn, the wooden doors were opened outward by two men, and the car rolled inside; the doors were closed as soon as the rear bumper was clear.

The driver got out, leaving his door open. Teck heard a gibber of voices. Without taking his eyes from Teck, The Slav rolled down the window on his own side and called to someone. A small man about thirty came and looked into the car, first at Teck and then at The Slav. Ignoring what sounded like commands from Teck's captor, he backed away and disappeared. Another man reached in behind the driver and removed the ignition key. He, too, ignored The Slav.

A young man bent down beside The Slav's window and said something in a soft, almost a whispered voice. The Slav replied angrily, but he nodded his head now as if he expected his orders to be listened to and obeyed, and he backed out of the car and motioned for Teck to follow. Side by side they went through a door in the concrete wall of the garage after the young man. Their driver had disappeared. Two other men followed along behind.

At the end of a passage the young man opened a door and went through ahead of them, Teck coming next and The Slav following.

They entered a small room furnished sparsely with out-of-date European furniture. A gaunt woman in an unbecoming black dress stood in front of a massive, mirrored sideboard on the other side of the room. When she spoke, the man nearest The Slav clamped both hands over his wrist, forcing his hand and the gun upward; when The Slav resisted, one of the men behind him dazed him with a blow at the back of the neck.

When he could speak, The Slav sounded angry. He commanded; he demanded. He got no satisfactory answer.

Both Teck and The Slav had to strip to the skin under the woman's dour eye. They were thoroughly searched, even in those orifices where small objects are sometimes hidden by the desperate. When their captors were satisfied, they were given back their underclothes, shirts, and trousers, and, without shoes or socks or belts, they were led down into a cellar to an inner recess dug from the earth there. A heavy wooden door was pushed shut on them and they heard the noise of two heavy bars being pushed across, and after that the cool, dank room was quiet.

The KGB officer Yuri Nemchin completed his part of the transfer of *The Book of the Dead* before noon, Athens time. The substitute manuscript was identical to the original reclaimed by Seriakin, even to the paper on which it was written; no one, even the author, could have told the two apart. It was essential, however, that in starting the substitute on the route to publication in the West, the KGB not be identified with it. Nemchin used, therefore, a blind drop in a public park where the wealthier Athenians came to ride horses. A single telephone call alerted an agent named Stavrides, who thought he was working for the Monarchists; he picked up the small parcel from the drop, and thereafter Nemchin was able to trace its progress with the help of a citywide network of informants. The "Monarchist" agent delivered the manuscript to a physician, a CIA principal who had been compromised three years before and was now more useful to the KGB than to the Americans. The physician made an appointment that afternoon for a journalist, a former apologist for the military junta who had narrowly escaped deportation under the Caramanlis regime and who was allowed to live in Athens only because he had become an agent for State Security, thus making him doubly useful to both CIA and KGB. His credentials with the conservative Western press were impeccable, and in the past he had been useful as a funnel for carefully planted disinformation about the People's Republic of China. In this instance, under orders from the doctor (whom he believed to be his principal in a CIA structure, he easily passed the substitute copy of *The Book of the Dead* to a legitimate, if rightist, literary middleman, from whom it went directly to Les Editions Chaconne, the CIA proprietary in Paris. Near the end of that day, the physical transfer of the manuscript to Paris had not yet been made, but Nemchin knew that the literary agent himself was on the way to the airport and had a reservation on an Air France flight to Orly.

Nemchin went directly to the Soviet Embassy, where he chatted with an old acquaintance from Department V. They spent twenty-five minutes together, during which Nemchin said only two things about the operation he was now engaged in: first, that "he was under the thumb of that superannuated Georgian, old Repin," and second, quite casually and without making any connection with the first, that "it was a pity to see the efficiency of the service undermined by these old men who should have been retired years ago." At the end of their chat, he went to Communications and sent a coded message marked Very Secret to Repin on board the *Leonid Andreyev* reporting on the success of his mission and the failure of the PLO to assassinate Seriakin as Repin had ordered.

He left the embassy at 4:47. At 5:13, as he had hoped, his Department V acquaintance was reading a copy of the Very Secret message. By 5:50 Moscow time it had been read by several men in offices in Dzerzhinsky Square.

At 6:41, orders were issued to the captain of the Soviet freighter to detain Repin until he could be taken into custody by KGB officers, who would board at Varna. The official charge would be misuse of funds and misappropriation of building materials for his country house. When, however, an official had been asked that evening by a subordinate on what charge Repin was to be arrested, he had made a face and said sarcastically, "Zeal."

"You're sure there were *two* men, Mr. Rountree?"

"Yes. I was hit on the head and shoved forward—into Teck—and then I heard somebody say something; that voice was behind me and to the left, and then I'm sure somebody was on my right side. Then I don't remember too much."

Inspector Arkadi rubbed the smooth surface of his desk top. Beyond a narrow strip along the edge where his fingers habitually rubbed, the varnish was crusty with old dirt, soiled by many hands, but here, where his fingers always moved during an interview, the wood was as smoooth and polished as if a butler had worked on it every day for years.

"Does it seem possible in any way that these people were confederates of Teck's, Mr. Rountree?"

Rountree's pleasant young face was dismayed. Across the office, Rountree's pretty wife leaned toward him as if she meant to rush to him.

"I don't see that, Inspector," Rountree said. "Gee, I don't see that at all. I mean, if he'd had confederates, why would he have come to me?"

"Perhaps I am too dramatic. You could tell nothing from the voice you heard?"

"I don't remember *anything* about it. Except that it was a man's voice. It was just a voice."

"Speaking in Turkish?"

"No." Rountree frowned. "No, I'm sure it was English. But there wasn't any accent or anything that I remember."

"An *American* voice."

"Oh, I see, you're still following up the confederate idea. Well, maybe."

"Mr. Rountree, do you think that the account that Teck gave you of his activities was true? All this about a mysterious manuscript, and tortures, and being rescued by sinister Russians, and so on?"

Rountree's face stiffened. "Some of what he told me—which I've told you—involves other governments. It would be unwise of me to comment."

Arkadi looked severe. It was his first day back at his desk and he was aware that the deputy chief would be supremely sensitive to any mistake, particularly one involving an American government official. "Mr. Rountree, did you trust Samuel Teck?"

"Not entirely."

"But you helped him."

"I thought it was the right thing to do."

"Did it occur to you that such a man, in need of a doctor, so very secretive, needing a place to hide—that he might be a fugitive?"

"I felt sorry for him and I thought he sounded a decent sort of man and I thought he'd spent enough time in this building."

"Well, you're very frank."

Arkadi looked more severe than ever. The pretty young wife rose and came across the room to stand behind her husband, one slim hand still on his left shoulder. "He's been under a terrible strain and terrible tension. Why don't you do something about the attack on his office instead of hounding him when he's hurt?"

"Honey—" The young man tried to protest but she could not be stopped. "You know my husband has a diplomatic passport, don't you?"

Arkadi waved a hand wearily. "I am trying to solve a crime, Mrs. Rountree, a whole series of crimes, some violent and horrible. Crime offends me, Mrs. Rountree; it offends my soul—especially crimes that are committed in my country by my country's guests. I do not mean to—what is the word?—to *hound* your husband."

Rountree patted his wife's hand. "We've both been under a strain."

Her childlike face hardened. Arkadi was grateful that he did not face a future with the determined woman who lived inside that clear skin. "My husband and I are leaving here in ten minutes, Inspector. He is *not* well."

Arkadi waved his hand again. "Excellent. Excellent. Yes, he needs his rest. Good. Quickly then, Mr. Rountree, you did help Teck, yes?

"Yes, that's correct."

"And if your English friend had not come home, you would probably still be there, do you think?"

"Well, I think somebody would have heard me eventually. I was kicking the wall."

Arkadi said nothing as he studied his notes. He turned a page and leaned back in his chair. "Do you know about something called *The Book of the Dead*, Mr. Rountree?"

"Only what Teck told me."

"Nothing more?"

"No."

Arkadi rubbed the polished strip of wood along the desk top. "About Mr. Phillip Burrell."

"Yes?" When Arkadi did not follow up his question, Rountree folded his arms and frowned.

Arkadi looked at the pretty wife. "Burrell is from the Central Intelligence Agency, is that correct?" He looked at Rountree in time to see the uneven flush on his smooth cheeks.

"I don't know anything about that."

"Oh, I think you do, Mr. Rountree. Didn't Teck say that Burrell was with the CIA? Surely Burrell himself gave you some indication—an innuendo, a password—"

Rountree's jaw became as set as his wife's. Perhaps they were a good match. "I don't know anything about that." The words were evenly spaced and accented. "You will have to ask the embassy in Ankara." Arkadi tried to stare him down, but it was no good.

When the Rountrees had been formally bowed out, Arkadi called in Sergeant Irmak.

Arkadi swiveled around in his chair and stood up. "Go to the central telephone office. I want everything they have on calls going out of the apartment where Rountree was found. Also any public boxes close by, although I don't think you'll find anything. But from the apartment—calls to Ankara especially, most especially the American Embassy and most especially this man Burrell. Also other calls, anywhere. Washington? Anywhere. He *must* have tried to get help—somebody he could depend on—mustn't he? Go on, go on, get to it!"

He must have tried to get help. Which was to say, in Teck's place Arkadi would have sought help. But Arkadi had never been in his place, alone in a foreign city, not speaking the language, perhaps knowing nobody. He thought of Teck's "confession." *I have committed no crime. . . . The rest was stupidity and arrogance.* The confession painted a picture of a man Arkadi did not know, a man so unaware of his own actions that he had not known when he was planning to do something wrong. Arkadi was familiar with men who knew they were committing crimes and went ahead and committed them anyway, out of desperation, out of passion, out of a need to flout the law. But he did not understand Professor Teck.

"My name is Seriakin, Valeri. Yours I know, of course."

The words floated into the darkness. The dirt cell, hardly more than a cave, muted the sound and made the words seem dead. Like two strangers on a bus the two men had settled at a distance from each other, each with his back to a different wall, and for more than half an hour the only sounds had been their quiet breathing.

"Your name is Teck, Samuel Teck. It would be stupid of me to pretend that I know nothing about you."

Teck did not answer.

"Are you afraid of me, Teck?"

He heard Teck shift his body and exhale heavily, a sigh, a sound of boredom, or exasperation, or despair.

"*I* am afraid, Teck. These Turks are crazy people. Give them guns, they may do anything. That one with the Kalashnilov automatic, he *wants* to shoot somebody. Do you think they take drugs?"

Silence.

"It does no harm to talk to make the time go, Teck."

Silence.

"This is a very serious situation, you understand. I think they have gone mad. Or possibly they think to ransom me—us—or there may be some political situation I know nothing of. What do you think, Teck?"

The silence was relieved only by the scraping of Teck's foot over the floor as he raised one knee. Seriakin, discouraged by his failure to rouse Teck, gave up speaking, but he continued to make small, nervous noises—his tongue against his teeth, the fingers of one hand drumming on the dirt floor. Over the next hour he spoke only as he might have to himself, and then in a flat, resigned voice.

"I wish I had a cigarette."

"Pardon me." (His stomach was rumbling.)

"I'm sorry." (His foot had touched Teck's when he had changed position.)

Without clocks or sun, neither man was certain of the hour, although each could have given a fair estimate of the time. Seriakin's guess now was that they had been in the cell for four hours (and he was wrong by only twenty minutes); he stood up, stamping his feet, and began to move about the cramped space. He felt over the walls trying to find—anything: a listening device, a blocked-up hole, a water pipe. He found nothing. He did exercises. His right hand struck the wall when he flung it out too far. When his foot touched Teck's again he excused himself. He sat down again, breathing more deeply. "Exercise a little," he said. "The cold and the damp, they are very bad for you. Never sit on the ground. My father taught me that. He believed that it affected your liver." He leaned back against the wall. "I wish I had a cigarette. Do you smoke, Teck?"

To his astonishment a small word came back out of the darkness. "No."

"You do not know the discomfort, then. It is a sickness, like alcohol. Bad business, one should never start it, but there you are. It is very hard to go without."

"Oral."

"I am sorry?"

"Oral. Mouth pleasure. Sucking."

"Oh? Oh, yes, you Americans believe in that sort of thing, don't you? Everything going back to infancy. I have read your Freud."

"Freud was Austrian."

"Yes, a Jew, I know. Decadent ideas. Making adults nothing but the products of infancy. Unhealthy." He made the little clucking sound with his tongue against his teeth. "Of childhood, that I understand. But infancy? Do you agree?"

Teck hesitated and then said, "I have no opinion."

Seriakin frowned. Was it possible to have no opinion? It implied such lack of caring, such coldness. Was Teck that sort of man? "I am sure that we are products of the childhood that we remember. Do you remember your childhood, Teck?"

"Yes."

"Happily?"

Teck was silent. What was he thinking? Would he say at last, "I have no opinion"?

"Some of it."

"Where did you grow up?"

"Why do you ask?"

"Curiosity. It helps to pass the time. I, for example, was born in Moscow. But we lived for a time in Bulgaria, and in Vslov and Helsinki—so many places, I have forgotten some. Wherever my father had to go."

"What did he do?"

"He was a journalist." The old lie came easily. "And your father?"

"My father inherited money. And the house I was born in. He was a lawyer, but he didn't practice law all that much. He was very interested in Shakespeare. He wanted to write a book about Shakespeare."

"Did he?"
"Yes, sort of. But nobody would publish it."
"An aristocrat."
"Hardly."
"He sounds like Gaev. In *The Cherry Orchard*, you know."
"My father didn't play billiards."
Seriakin laughed. It was like a spark that had flashed briefly when two wires touched. He said something more about Chekhov and Teck replied more easily than before. *He has an opinion.* They talked quietly, as strangers killing time in airport terminals or on a train will talk. Seriakin knew the strange intimacy that springs up between strangers—the policeman and the criminal, the interrogator and the prisoner. At one point Teck got up and swung his arms, raised his legs, and moved his stiffened joints. With an embarrassed apology he urinated in the farthest corner of the cell. Sometime later, Seriakin did the same.
They talked.
Seriakin learned about Teck's former wife, about his father.
Neither mentioned *The Book of the Dead.*
Teck learned about Seriakin's mistress in Leningrad. Seriakin sighed. "My father died of cancer not long ago. I watched him die. I still have dreams about it. Not happy dreams. Struggle, anxiety. I am made to carry his luggage to a train station in a strange city. . . ."

Chapter twenty

EDWARD Rountree had been found shortly after ten o'clock in the morning. By noon, the gun that Teck had taken from the clinic was in the Izmir police laboratory, where a tentative connection was made with a weapon stolen two years earlier from a private residence in Istanbul. By the time that Yuri Nemchin had left the substitute manuscript at the blind drop in Athens, Arkadi had completed his interview with Rountree, and, in the cavelike cell dug back from the cellar of a house on Buyukedere Street, Valeri Seriakin and Teck were beginning to exchange their first guarded confidences.

At three fifteen, Arkadi sent for tea. He had completed his survey of the cases that had come in during his enforced day off and of those cases he had neglected since preparations for the Trade Fair had begun. After finishing with Rountree, he had studied a weekly Interpol digest, had read two reports of the increasingly brazen purchases of stolen antiquities by American museums ("acquisitions of unverified provenance," as one museum called such purchases) and had filled himself in on a new wave of art forgeries in Europe.

Irmak and the tea arrived almost simultaneously, and Irmak, taking the glass from the uniformed man who had brought it, was grinning when he set it down on Arkadi's desk. "Well?" Arkadi said, suppressing a smile of his own at Irmak's pleased expression.

"I got the telephone records. Of the apartment where Teck spent the night." He put a single sheet with even lines of fine handwriting on the desk. "And maybe something even better—somebody else has been in after the same information. Earlier today."

"Who?"

"She had to leave her name; the office manager required it. An American woman. Diplomatic passport."

Arkadi sat back. "Not Mrs. Rountree!" he said in disbelief.

"No, that's not the one." Irmak had the name written on a slip of paper that he found in his shirt pocket. "Sara Kerrigan."

"Sergeant," Arkadi said slowly, biting on his right thumbnail so that it rode up and down in the small space between his upper front teeth, "call Protocol and Foreign Security in Ankara for me. Ask for Lieutenant Mehvedi; mention my name. Ask if he can find out what this woman does at the American Embassy or wherever she's posted." Arkadi looked at the list of Teck's calls. "I see that Teck made quite a long call to the American Embassy last night. See if Mehvedi can find out what that call was about—the switchboard girl is probably Turkish, so there may be something there for us. I particularly want to know if Teck is trying to get out of the country. In the meantime, I'll ask the Antalya police to find out why Mr. Teck called the Hotel Sporting last evening." His eyes rose skeptically. "For a poor creature without any friends, wallowing in his own stupidity and arrogance, Mr. Teck seems to have run up quite a telephone bill."

Their own bodies and breath had made the air in the cell fetid. The smell of urine was overpowering.

"Strangling in our own effluent," Teck said grimly. "Just like New York."

"Or Leningrad."

"What is this place used for, anyway?"

Seriakin was quiet for a moment. "For this."

"We were expected, then."

"You were, Teck."

"Oh." Teck swallowed. "You mean, when you brought me here, you thought—"

"I meant to question you about the photos."

"Oh. You know about that."

"I guessed."

Teck shifted his position and gasped when he twisted his back too far. When he had settled himself, he said in a low voice, "Tell me, what were you going to do with me after you questioned me?"

"Nothing."

"Difficult to do nothing with somebody. Surely you had something in mind—locking me down here, sending me on a tour of Siberia, stuffing me down a manhole. No?"

"I hadn't given it much thought," Seriakin confessed guiltily.

"Bad habit, not thinking. Leads to all sorts of miseries. Unless, of course, you like to wash your hands afterward and say 'Oh, I hadn't given it a thought,' and leave the dirty work to somebody else."

"You are angry now."

"No. I'm astonished. I'm amazed that I even talk to you. Why don't I swear, or try to kill you, or beat my head on the door? You're my enemy, isn't that right?"

"Am I?"

"Maybe you've just had them lock you in here to make it seem as if you're in trouble. A new way to get at me. Chat a little, share a little hardship, piss in the same corner—bravo, comrades! It may be a better way to get information than torture, yes? Well, spy?"

"I am not a spy. I am an employee of the KGB. I do not spy."

"All right, wonderful, semantically speaking you're not a spy. You're an information-gatherer, how's that? All right, I'll save you a lot of discomfort; you want to know about the photos I took of *The Book of the Dead*? I'll tell you."

"Don't, please! Tell me nothing. I do not want to know what could be taken from me later." Seriakin leaned forward in the darkness. "Do you understand me?"

"I guess so. Very melodramatic."

"I am quite serious. These Turks are crazy. We can only wait to find what they will do."

"I have a pretty good idea what they'll do."

"Hum. So have I, Teck, so have I."

At seven o'clock, Arkadi telephoned his wife to say that he would be staying longer than usual and might even sleep over in the duty room. The Antalya police had not yet interviewed the Princess di Paoli, whose room Teck had called the night before, and Arkadi wanted to wait to hear from them. His wife, too experienced now to hope that his brief holiday might be the prelude to a few easier days, said resignedly that she might take the children on the bus to see her mother. When he hung up, Arkadi rubbed his forehead for a few seconds and then gathered up a bundle of reports and left the office. He crossed the ornate lobby where Teck had last seen him and climbed the Italianate stairs to the second floor. As he passed the teletype room he heard his name called.

"Inspector Arkadi!"

"Yes?"

Arkadi faintly remembered the wiry young man as a former provisional who occasionally appeared in his office with messages. He handed Arkadi a yellow sheet and pointed at one message with an ink-stained finger. "I thought you might want to see this on the way upstairs." Clearly, he knew where Arkadi was headed. "It's about a manuscript, and I thought that would fall in your area, sir. It wouldn't get down to you until tomorrow or the next day. It's routine."

It was a perfectly standard message that would probably appear in the Interpol digest the following week. Datelined Paris, it merely told of an informer's report of the arrival in Paris of a Russian manuscript smuggled from the Soviet Union by way of Turkey and Greece. The report was unconfirmed.

"Thank you." Arkadi looked at the young man. "It may be

quite important." The young man smiled. "Leave a message for your relief that I want anything else connected with this sent down immediately. I'll be here all night. And you might contact Athens and Paris for details." He patted the man's arm and moved down the corridor.

In the few minutes granted him by the deputy chief, he went rapidly through a number of cases and touched on the Interpol digest. His superior's attention wandered. He would be more concerned with the spectacular crimes—the Turisti Pallas, the mutilated bodies of Sandra Lowenstein and the man in the bay—and not in art thefts whose investigations too often wound up in civil litigation in another country with a respected museum as the other litigant.

"Finally," Arkadi said, "I am fairly certain that the American, Teck, was alive this morning."

"Inform his embassy," the deputy chief replied.

"I believe they already know about him."

"Good. You thought at one time he was involved in some smuggling, didn't you?"

"At one time. I'm keeping an eye on the matter."

"Good. That's all we can ask. Work with the American Embassy's security people if it's appropriate. Sing them a nice song—a lullaby, if you know any." He looked directly at Arkadi so that there would be no misunderstanding. "I don't want another incident, Arkadi."

"No, sir."

"Good! Your day off seems to have helped your judgment."

"But there is one thing." Arkadi put the pile of reports on the edge of the desk. "I *think*—but I can't prove it yet—that there's a connection between Teck and the CIA and the KGB."

"Oh, no. Oh, no, no, no. Don't tell me a thing like that, Arkadi!"

"I believe that Federal Security already knows. Maybe they will handle it. I don't know. Maybe they'll sweep it under the rug. I'm never sure whether they're—" Arkadi stopped.

"Well? Say it."

"I'm never sure they're as committed as they seem to be. A report to them is a one-way message. If they were forced to it, and it did turn out that both CIA and KGB were involved—"

"—you think they would do nothing."

"Something of that kind. They might choose to be neutral. They could build up their credit with both sides."

The deputy chief ran his hand over his bald head, and with his head bent and his eyes closed, he said intensely, "What are you asking me, Arkadi? You are asking me something! *What is it?*"

"I simply want your permission to do my duty."

The head came up with a snap. "Are you implying that I would ever keep you from doing your duty?"

Arkadi was ready to plunge in. He had spent his "holiday" thinking about this moment, planning how he would force it, and now he was ready. "You did yesterday, sir."

The deputy chief glared at him angrily. Arkadi, returning the stare, tried to keep his face expressionless. It would not do for him to seem angry or defiant; he was stating a fact, and he was placing his career in jeopardy by doing so. The deputy chief's nostrils flared; he pursed his lips. He tapped the long nail of a finger on the desk top.

"Arkadi, if we were two men in a café, not two policemen and not deputy chief and inspector, I would break your nose for saying something like that. It is rude and offensive and you have the audacity of a beginner, which is wrong, very wrong in a man of your experience." He leveled a finger at Arkadi. "And I will not forget it. Yes, I kept you from your duty, and I would do it again, because you had been put in a compromising position and because you were overworked and your judgment was affected. Because this department has never been in worse shape and because you think that you can be like one of those cops on American television and take all the crimes of the world on your shoulders. Well, I suggest that you make a report and send it to the very top, because I most certainly will!" He sat back and passed his hand over his scalp again. "Now, I say to you again, Arkadi: *What are you asking me?*"

Arkadi had to clear his throat before he could speak. "I am asking for your permission to carry on the investigation of the matters surrounding the American, Teck, even if the case has been handed over to Federal Security."

"*Why?*" Before Arkadi could speak, a fist struck the desk. "I'll tell you why. *Because you're sick of having your country treated like a public convenience by other nations,* am I right? That's how you explained Pandelli's launching of that assault on the Turisti Pallas. Am I right? Well?"

"I am sick of seeing crimes committed against Turkish law that are let go unpunished in the name of international security! I am sick of being frightened off by the magical letters CIA and KGB!"

"And what has that got to do with art theft?"

"The case started with art theft. There is a stolen object involved, an art object of sorts. I can justify my unit's involvement."

"All right, then, involve your unit. You have my permission. *To investigate.* That is all—to investigate! No action, no arrests, no grilling—nothing that can disturb any other nation in the tiniest degree. Clear? Because I want it understood now, Arkadi, if you so much as call down an *inquiry* from another government about what you are doing or why, I'll have you out of this department. Within an hour! Do we understand each other?"

"Yes, sir." Arkadi stood up. "I'm afraid I've run long over my time."

Before he had reached the door, the deputy chief called his name. He was standing behind his desk, his left arm extended to point at Arkadi. "You're arrogant and you don't know it, Arkadi! You can sit behind this desk one day if you're smart. You're a good policeman. You've made the men under you respect you. *Now make me respect you!"*

Arkadi stepped into a toilet on the second floor to splash cold water on his face and let his tension quiet. When he reached his office, outwardly calmer, he found Irmak waiting for him. As offhandedly as possible Arkadi dropped the reports on a cluttered file cabinet and crossed to his desk.

Irmak gave him the report from their contact in Ankara: Teck had spoken to the embassy duty officer after asking for Phillip Burrell, and the duty officer had given him the telephone number of Burrell's secretary, Sara Kerrigan.

Arkadi looked up. "Kerrigan. The same woman who was asking for information at the Izmir Telephone Central."

"Yes, sir."

Arkadi frowned. He remembered the deputy chief's warning. Abruptly, he made a decision.

"Call the Kerrigan woman in for questioning—tell her it's in connection with her visit to the Central Telephone Office. Then set up surveillance on her—very discreet, although she'll probably know it's there. She should lead us to Burrell—and he might lead us to Teck."

Arkadi considered the risk he was taking, then realized that the risk was probably not so very great, after all. Burrell was not likely to make any formal complaint about surveillance; it was more like his sort to pull strings to have it stopped. And Arkadi could cope with that when it happened.

"Then get back to the telephone office, Sergeant. I want to know what calls have been made from the Kerrigan woman's place. I want that information back here as soon as possible, even if you have to drag somebody back from his supper, from the new Charles Bronson film, or from his dying mother's side!" He smiled wryly. "Without offending anybody, of course."

Seriakin and Teck both slept. When one stirred and uneasily woke, it was to the stench from the corner, the foul air, the sound of the other's sleeping.

Once, Teck woke to hear Seriakin's voice. If it spoke words, Teck could not understand them, and he thought it was mere garbled sound, panting breath, and an anguished whimper. He could hear the man's legs move over the damp earth. Finally, the voice cried out in a short, sharp moan, a deaf-mute's appeal for help, and Teck reached over and felt with his hand until it touched Seriakin's chest, moved up to his shoulder and arm. He was astonished to find Seriakin's hand there, tense, the arm bent at the elbow and the muscles of the upper arm rigid, as if he were lifting an enormous weight. The Russian cried out again and clutched Teck's wrist.

"Seriakin!" Teck tried to pull his hand free. "Seriakin!"

Abruptly, the other man sat up. Teck could feel the change in position; he could hear the other's coarse breathing, almost panting, above him. Again he tried to pull his hand away and Seriakin's fingers slowly loosened and the breathing quieted.

"Seriakin?"

The other man gasped.

"You were dreaming. I had to wake you up. You were making noises. Sounds."

"Oh." Scuffing sounds as Seriakin changed position. "Oh. I

had forgotten. I had forgotten you. I thought—I used to sleep with a woman, I would wake like that, she would be holding me. . . . Do you believe in dreams?"

"No. Yes. I believe that we tell ourselves the truth in dreams."

"I was in Helsinki, I knew it was Helsinki, it was not anything like our apartment there, but I knew it was Helsinki." Seriakin needed, in the first moments after waking, to rid himself of the dream. He babbled. "I was in bed with my father, taking care of him, he was dying of his cancer but I was in the bed with him. A little boy. I slept with him during the war sometimes—once when the Germans bombed us. I was in his bed, but it was I who comforted him; I wanted him to take his medicine but he kept saying, 'No no, Valeri, hold me, Valeri. Hold me back,' and he gripped me so tight that I could not breathe, I could not let him go! I want to run away, out into the streets.

"But he held me back. I said we must go, there is a train, I will take you back to Moscow, the luggage is packed, waiting, right at the foot of the bed. But he couldn't get up, he said, he was too weak; and I tried to raise him, tried to lift him off but he was too heavy. I pushed, but he was a big man. Too big to lift. Then I knew he was dead. I was choking—his hair in my mouth, his weight on my chest so I couldn't catch my breath—that's when I woke up."

"The pressing dream. The real nightmare."

"Death, yes."

"That's what they say. The death dream. Did you hate your father very much?"

"I loved him. I loved him. But he is such a weight on me. . . ."

Chapter twenty-one

TECK and Seriakin were slumped in their same places in the dirt cell. Neither man had said anything for an hour. Listless, indifferent to the passage of time, each huddled into his own senses and tried to concentrate on ideas and memories that would make the present disappear.

A thump on the wooden door roused them, but neither man moved. Another thump, and the door swung outward as the light of a powerful lantern stabbed into the cell. Both men turned their heads away and raised their arms as if for a blow.

A voice beyond the light spoke a single syllable; a hand reached through the dazzle and grasped Seriakin's wrist. He was dragged out, resisting, into the cellar. When Teck lowered his arm and moved a little toward the door, he was pushed back and the door slammed shut again, bringing back the darkness and a paradoxical sense of relief. He breathed deeply and slowly to quiet himself. The air was sweeter.

Seriakin was led across the cellar to the flight of steps by which they had come down the day before. Still partly blinded, he had to be guided by disrespectful hands at his elbows. At the top of the stairs, when the door was opened and the full splendor of the morning sun fell on him through an uncurtained window, he made a sound and flung his right arm across his eyes again; the arm was pulled down and he was pushed to the right, into the sunlight, and then past the window and along another corridor to a room larger and more heavily furnished than the one in which they had been forced to strip.

"Seriakin? You *are* Valeri Seriakin?" The skepticism in the Russian words was so rank that the speaker might have been a buyer questioning the authenticity of some particularly outrageous fake. "Valeri *Seriakin?*"

Seriakin could see, although still with discomfort. He looked at his interrogator through squinting eyes: a narrow head, fair hair, close ears, close-cut hair—the whole man seemed to be held close to himself as if to present as small a target as possible to the world. "Yes, I am Seriakin."

The man came close. "What have they *done* to you?" He sniffed. He whirled around stiffly, still erect and his arms tight to his body, like a wind-up toy spinning to strut off in a new direction. "What have you done to him?" he shouted harshly. "Is this any way to treat the man who was in charge here? A *Russian?*" Across the room, the woman who had had breast cancer did not change expression. "He hasn't suffered so much," she said flatly. She spoke as an expert on suffering. "This will go in my report," the Russian said. "Get out. Get out!" She went out by a door at her left, without anger or any sign of shame. Seriakin was left alone with the Russian and one Turkish gunman, who carried an automatic pistol elongated by a silencer.

"I have to apologize, Valeri Alexeevich. This was no way to treat a man of your rank, much less the son of such an illustrious father. Sit down." The last words were a polite command, not a request; if there was irony in the remark about his father, Seriakin missed it.

Next he offers me the cigarette, Seriakin thought. He remembered his own training, the inadequate exposure to interrogation techniques because he had already been assigned to Disinformation and not to field work.

The other man held out a pack of Turkish cigarettes. "Smoke?"

"I've been dying for one."

"Have you eaten?"

"No, nor drunk anything. Not since we were put in there. How long?" His voice was husky. *You're getting a cold,* his mistress would say, *you sound sexy.* She liked him home in bed with colds, in bed and docile.

"Get him water and something to eat." After a sullen look to indicate that such work was really beneath him, the Turkish gunman sighed melodramatically and dragged himself to the door. The Russian turned back to Seriakin. "I am Nemchin, Division V of the First Directorate."

"Yes." *Yes, of course you are. We know each other—comrades, members of the great club. The red fox knows the gray fox.* "Why was I made a prisoner like this?"

"Not on my orders. Not my doing, Valeri Alexeevich. It was done night before last, on the orders of old Repin."

Seriakin said nothing, afraid now that anything he would say would be wrong. The other man might not really be a Russian at all; he could be CIA, or Turkish counterintelligence. Or, as he said, KGB Department V. *My father's line of work.*

"You have no questions?"

The Turkish gunman put a cup of tepid water in Seriakin's left hand. He drank it greedily, glad for its refreshment and glad for the chance to delay. As he had hoped, Nemchin began to speak while he was drinking.

"You should not have been held this way. This was a mistake, a misunderstanding. But, you see, there was an order from Repin that you were to be detained. In fact, there was an order to assassinate you, but the plan did not work."

"Why?"

"Why the orders? This is rather sensitive." Nemchin turned to the Turkish guard. "You, get out!" The man frowned but did not move. "Get out, out—we want to be alone, this fellow and I!" Nemchin's Turkish was comically bad, actually a pidgin mixture of Turkish and Russian; Seriakin was reminded of a film about the British in India. The Turk's frown deepened; finally, he said, holding out the automatic pistol as if it were part of his argument, "It will not be safe." Nemchin appealed to Seriakin with a contemptuous smile. "Get out before I put you out, you moron!" He sounded as if he was angry at a dog that had messed the carpet.

The man went.

Nemchin pulled a chair close to Seriakin's. "How do you feel now? Better?"

"Rotten. I can smell myself. I smell rotten."

"You can think clearly?"

"Certainly."

Nemchin leaned still closer. He made the communication between them seem more important, more confidential, by coming close and by ignoring the fact that Seriakin smelled like a privy.

"Let me tell you something. *I* will tell *you*, because you are still reluctant to tell me anything, because you do not trust me, you do not know if I am really Nemchin of Division V or a Jew spy from Tel Aviv. That is as it should be, and to your credit, and it will go into my report." He was smiling just a little, and his voice was light and whispery as if he was telling a slightly risqué story in mixed company. "So I will tell you. *The Book of the Dead* is now in the hands of a publisher in Paris, a publisher who is funded by the CIA. This surprises you because you took *The Book of the Dead* from somebody two days ago and gave it to Repin. Repin, you were sure, wanted to keep this treasonable and lying work from ever reaching Western hands. How, then, you ask, did it get to this fascist Parisian publishing house?"

Nemchin put two fingers of his right hand on Seriakin's left arm. His lips were so close to Seriakin's left cheek that he might have kissed it with a simple inclination of his head.

"I will tell you the answer. *I* took *The Book of the Dead* to Athens and passed it to somebody who, I knew, would send it to the Parisian fascists. *Exactly* as Repin had set this project up more than two years ago. That surprises you, does it not?"

Seriakin said nothing.

"You have never known our Repin very well, Valeri Alexeevich. You remember him from your childhood—your father's friend. A kind of uncle to you, maybe? Well, you must meet the real Repin now—he is a grinder and men are the meat. All for the greater glory of the Service."

"But why?" Seriakin asked. "No, go back, go back a little in your story—why was *The Book of the Dead* given to the very people I was trying to keep it from?"

Nemchin smiled more broadly. "Because they have waited for a long time to get it, and they are so anxious to have it now that they will splatter the news of their acquisition all over the Western press. A Moslem Solzhenitsyn, they will say!"

"Exactly!"

"Yes, exactly. Just as they planned when the CIA forged it in the first place." Nemchin leaned back six inches so he could see Seriakin's face. "Now are you surprised?"

"I don't think I believe you."

"No, of course you don't. You are conditioned to believe what Repin has led you to believe. How did you first hear of *The Book of the Dead*?"

"I'm not sure. A rumor. It came over the desk from Stockholm, I think. Not regular disinformation material."

"No, of course not, because it was planted. Repin has worked on this for almost three years—two, at the very least. Think of it from another point of view, Valeri—think of it as if you knew for a fact that *The Book of the Dead* is a CIA forgery, smuggled into Russia to be passed covertly from hand to hand by dissidents who think it genuine. Disinformation of a very black kind. Now, as a member of the KGB, you know one thing that the CIA do not. What do you think that is?"

Seriakin did not have to think long. "That it is a forgery."

"Only in part. You know that, but you know it is a forgery *because you can ask the author himself.* The CIA dared to create the forgery because they believed the author, this Turkman poet, this Yomut, was safely out of the way, dead of a heart attack three years ago. But Repin knows that the author is alive, and, in fact, he can talk to him every day in the Lubyanka if he chooses."

"But he *is* dead. Everybody knew that. Repin told me. . . ." His voice trailed off under Nemchin's quiet laughter.

"Repin told you he was dead, exactly. Actually, he is quite alive, quite reconciled to being a loyal Soviet citizen, and quite ready to fly to the PEN International Congress in two days to deny authorship of *The Book of the Dead.* To point out errors in it, to denounce it to the assembled literary world as a fraud and a forgery—in short, to smear the pitiful cheat perpetrated by the CIA upon the Russian intelligentsia, to reaffirm our ties with our Moslem friends in the Middle East, to make suspect every underground manuscript that appears inside the Soviet Union."

Seriakin looked away from the face that was too close to his, too flushed, too eager. He knew the convolutions of disinformation—lies twisted like pretzels to become truth, then made to seem lies again, and presented finally as brilliant truths. Nemchin's story was eminently plausible.

"Then I was not supposed to intercept the manuscript."

"No. Your corpse was to be the proof of the efforts of some group—the PLO, the CIA—to get the manuscript for themselves. Your body was to be the book's *bona fides*—the loyal KGB officer shot down while trying to recover this searing exposé of his country's evils. Unfortunately, you succeeded too well in your dummy mission; you were sent out as a pawn and you captured the queen."

"Meat for the grinder."

"Yes, exactly. But cheer up, Seriakin, so was I."

"Am I still to be killed?"

"Why should we kill you? My orders are to take you back to Moscow."

"To be handed over to Repin?"

"Oh, no. Repin is under arrest, you see." Nemchin stood up. "You need more water; how thoughtless I have been. And food, where is the food I asked for?" He went to the far door and handed the cup out while talking to someone there. When he came back he held a cigarette out to Seriakin. "This will carry you until the food comes." He lit both cigarettes. "This operation was tainted. I knew that when I was brought into it. When you have been in the field long enough, you *know.*

Three years ago when Repin started all this, it might have been politically acceptable. Now, it runs directly counter to the desires of the Politburo. It is anti-détente and it is too public. It sought to make policy rather than to follow it—and however highly we value ourselves, Seriakin, we live in a nation in which the intelligence community does *not* make national policy, and for that I am supremely grateful."

As this piety was uttered without a hint of sarcasm, Seriakin did not make the caustic remark that came to mind. Nemchin, of course, was thinking of what Seriakin might say under questioning in Moscow. *Was Nemchin involved in this plot? No, he was not. What did he say about it? He thought it an offense to national policy and to the intelligence service. . . .*

"What will happen to Repin?"

"He is an old man; he has done notable things. At this time, there is merely a charge of misusing his position, something about funds."

Seriakin was hesitant. "What will happen to me?"

"As I said, I am to take you back to Moscow. There will be an aircraft at Yesilkoy tomorrow."

"And?"

"I don't understand, Valeri Alexeevich. What 'and'?"

"*And* what will happen in Moscow?"

Nemchin tapped another cigarette from the pack. "You must understand, you are not blameless in this. I speak of the meat grinder and of Repin's ruthlessness, but the facts look like collusion. Oh, I'm not saying the prosecutor will call it collusion, but you know that when somebody in our work makes an error, the error is either buried by his friends within the service or he has to be punished. Such friends as you have can't bury this."

"But that's stupid. I didn't make an error; I was deceived!"

Nemchin put a hand on Seriakin's shoulder. "Exactly. But we are like soldiers. Discipline and obedience. Deviations from discipline and obedience, even unwitting ones, must be dealt with. Admit it, now—at some point when you first got into this, you knew it was contrary to current policy."

Seriakin remembered his meeting with Repin in Leningrad, the talk about détente. He realized suddenly, as surely as if Repin himself had told him, that that entire meeting had been taped by Repin himself; he would have done it as a matter of habit, because at some unknown time in the future he might need a record. That tape would still exist.

Seriakin took a step away to shake off Nemchin's hand. "Prison?"

"I would think so, yes."

"How long?"

Nemchin shrugged. "Three years at the most. More likely only one. And when it's finished, you might have a new role, Seriakin—a prison background can be an excellent cover. I'd suggest that you discuss this with the prosecutor; you could transfer to the Fifth Directorate after your release and be a very valuable man."

The Fifth Directorate. The witch-hunters. Investigation and betrayal of dissidents, subversives, political deviates. "Three years where?"

"Not where you're thinking." Nemchin chuckled. "Not somewhere east of the Urals. We can't risk one of our own, you know." Seriakin knew. A KGB man in one of the Siberian camps would die, horribly, at the hands of other prisoners. He might try to hide his identity, but they would know. "It isn't fair, Nemchin!"

"No, it *isn't* fair. Many things are not fair. Your father's cancer was not fair. Losing a woman that I had to leave behind in Addis Ababa was not fair. But these things happen. If you think of it as punishment for a wrong you did not commit, you will make yourself bitter and useless, Seriakin. Think of it as something that was done to you because you were not alert enough, not suspicious enough when you should have been—and vow never to be that way again." He patted Seriakin's shoulder. "Come on, I think I can get you a warm bath and a decent bed upstairs. It's disgusting the way these people have treated you."

As Nemchin crossed the room to the door through which the woman and the guard had gone out, Seriakin considered the Russian's behavior. *Why is he being so careful?* And the answer was obvious. *Because he wants me to go back without any trouble; I am his prize, his bona fides.* Seriakin remained where he was. "What about the American?"

"What about him?" Nemchin was waiting like some rather formal host at the door, his hand on the knob.

"Is he going with us?"

"What an idea! Of course not." Nemchin frowned. "You are too concerned about him; that would go against you, you know. In fact, somebody is bound to ask you why you ever brought him back from that house where you found the manuscript."

"I intended to question him."

"You even left this place before you were supposed to; that's why you weren't assassinated on schedule, by the way. Why did you leave?"

"Something had occurred to me."

"What?"

Seriakin knew that it would do no good to hide the fact of the photographs; they were bound to surface sometime, and he would be asked so many questions in Moscow that he was bound to reveal their existence. Better now than later. "I realized that the American had made a photographic copy of *The Book of the Dead.*"

"When?"

"When he first had it, I believe."

"You believe? Don't you know?"

"I didn't ask him."

It seemed that Nemchin might have been about to smile, even to laugh. He did neither, however, but said with a mildness that hid the interrogator's intent, "You didn't ask him?"

"I am not an interrogator!" Seriakin answered angrily. "We were down in that hole together, thanks to the Turks!"

"I would have found it a perfect time to get information," Nemchin murmured. He took his hand from the doorknob and with his forefinger traced a line from his earlobe down to the corner of his mouth. The finger rested there pensively and then sprang forward to point at Seriakin. "Together in such a place, comrades, two against their oppressors—really, it's the kind of opportunity a man might work for months to set up. Does he seem to trust you? Does he confide in you?"

It was I who confided in him, Seriakin thought. *I babbled and had the nightmare, not he.* "We weren't antagonists down there, if that's what you mean."

"And yet you didn't question him. You surprise me, Valeri Alexeevich." Nemchin came back into the center of the room. The door—to comfort, to a shower and bed, to Moscow—remained closed. "You should have, you know."

Seriakin looked back at him as unflinchingly as he had learned to glare back at his father during one of their infrequent arguments. "No, I should not have! I didn't know who my real captors were; to have had that information would have made me that much more vulnerable."

"Still, you know, it would help you in Moscow if you had all of the American's information—now that you know who your 'captors' are."

"I thought *The Book of the Dead* project had been disavowed."

"It has been disavowed as too clumsy and too arrogant on Repin's part. But it is a fact now, you see; *The Book of the Dead* will be made public tomorrow in Paris. The First Directorate would like to close the matter quickly, but without embarrassment."

Seriakin hesitated. "Then they will go ahead with Repin's plan and reveal that *The Book of the Dead* is a forgery?"

"Of course."

Seriakin shrugged. "Then I'm sorry I didn't interrogate the American." In the face of the bitter news of his probable imprisonment, such a detail seemed unimportant.

"But you still can, Seriakin!"

"What, take on the role of interrogator? Offer the cigarette, alternately rage and despair, have him beaten again? Yes, perhaps I could create a little Lubyanka right here in Izmir."

"Now you are bitter. Bitterness always sits poorly on a young man. You have a great deal to be grateful for."

"One to three years in a prison?"

"A lifetime of favored treatment because you are your father's son!"

Seriakin smiled wanly. "Bitterness sits as poorly on you as it does on me, Nemchin."

Nemchin walked to the door through which Seriakin had come from the cellar. After some seconds he took out another cigarette and lit it, his back to Seriakin. Then, still without looking around, he said, "I recommend that you return to the cellar and continue to pretend to the American that you are a prisoner. Learn everything that he has to tell."

"And when I'm through, what will happen to him then?"

"That is up to the Turks. Something has been said about keeping him for a time. To trade, I suppose."

Seriakin was silent, but his expression caused Nemchin to say, "You must not have compassion for such men, Valeri Alexeevich. If you once start, there is no end."

"Compassion? Is that what it is?"

Nemchin moved to the center of the room, inhaling fiercely on the cigarette. He planted himself firmly, like a man about to utter an important declaration, and blew the smoke out in a long, steady stream. With his head tipped back and his hands clasped in front of him, the cigarette in a corner of his mouth, he said, "I knew a woman once in Cairo; she saved a starving kitten from a sewer. A month after that she found a female cat that had a broken leg. Then she found more starving and sick and hurt animals until her room was full of them, her garden was full, her family were all sick of her, and the police had to be called in by the neighbors. Hundreds of miserable animals that woman helped! And you know what? It didn't make a bit of difference in the number of miserable animals in Cairo." He tipped his head forward to peer at Seriakin through the smoke. "Don't let your victims tempt you, Valeri Alexeevich. Sometimes—sometimes the urge to have compassion is as strong as the urge to make love. But don't yield—*because it makes no difference!*"

A dog was barking somewhere in the house. Seriakin heard the woman's voice, but whether she was scolding it or soothing it, he could not tell. The barking stopped. Seriakin pressed the fingers of his right hand into his eyes. "I hate going back into that place."

Nemchin came to him. His hand on Seriakin's shoulder urged him toward the cellar. "It will be uncomfortable. But you are doing the *right thing*. And it will help your case in Moscow. Do you want another cigarette?"

"No, the American might smell it."

"Just so. You must invent a story of what happened up here. The simplest will be the best—that you are a prisoner of the Turks and they questioned you. Naturally, I won't be mentioned."

"Naturally."

Nemchin summoned the gunman and instructed him to put Seriakin back into the cell with the American. Seriakin had to translate into good Turkish the rather complicated instructions about his being an interrogator and not a real prisoner any longer. In Russian Nemchin said, "Knock on the cell door when you are finished—three knocks, pause, three knocks. The guard will bring you to me."

"How long do I have?"

"About twenty hours. We leave tomorrow evening."

Seriakin nodded. "This is a rotten business," he murmured.

He went ahead of the gunman down the corridor. At the cellar door the gunman pushed him back against the wall and then pounded on the door, three blows, a pause, and three more. After some seconds Seriakin heard the other guard mounting the steps from the cellar. The gunman opened a bolt on his side of the door and the guard did the same on the other. With the guard leading and the gunman following, Seriakin went down the stairs, ducking his head under the low, whitewashed beams. The only lights were the gunman's powerful flashlight and a portable propane lantern that hung from a ceiling hook next to the guard's stool. A book had been left face down on the stool; Seriakin could not make out the title, but the cover was illustrated with a man with a smoking pistol and a girl with breasts like beehives.

The cell door was held shut by two wooden bars, each as thick as Seriakin's calf. Each had to be lifted entirely away from the door before it could be swung outward. Seriakin watched as the guard removed the top bar, balanced it on his hands, and then bent to his left to lean it against the cellar wall. He did the same with the second bar.

Seriakin took a last look around him. The cellar seemed almost spacious compared to the hole he would enter, the tufa walls reflecting the warm yellow light of the lantern and stretching softly into deeper brown shadows under the low ceiling. Half of the cellar farthest from the light was taken up with boxes and barrels, and from a pile at one side there was a golden flash, as from the side of a fish, from a liter can of Italian olive oil. The place smelled of brine and earth. Seriakin breathed deeply.

The gunman moved him into the open doorway. Seriakin ducked his head, moved through, and the door closed behind him.

He had seen Teck in the moments when the flashlight had fallen on him. His arm had been raised against the light again. Seriakin had been surprised to see how little the man's ordeal showed. He had expected to be shocked, but Teck looked merely dirty and unshaven.

But it has been only twenty-four hours. Imagine one to three years. He allowed himself to think of the thing he rarely dared think of. *Imagine ten years in one of the camps.*

He sat on the floor in his old place. Outside, the guard replaced the second bar, and there was no more sound.

"Welcome back." Teck's voice was a croak. He cleared his throat. "Are you all right?" When Seriakin did not answer, he said, "Can you talk?"

"I am thinking."

"Did they—do anything to you?"

"No."

"Did they feed you? Did you get any water?"

"I had a cup of water. And a cigarette."

"Did they say anything about me?"

"No, not really. No."

The two men sat in the darkness for ten minutes; Seriakin changed his position and was still again and the ten minutes became twenty, then half an hour. Teck had slipped back into his lethargy. After almost an hour, Seriakin spoke. "It's all a waste, Teck."

"What?"

"You and me. This hole. Waste."

The answer was a mere grunt.

"It is a rotten waste! You and I, we have been dupes—pawns—fools." His voice became low and conspiratorial. "*The Book of the Dead* is a fraud. A forgery, made by your CIA to fool my KGB; smuggled out by my KGB to fool your CIA. And you and I are sitting in this hole because we are little pawns who are not supposed to have wills of our own, who are supposed to respond when a button is pushed, who are supposed to be little machines like cheap watches. But I do not want to be like that!" He stood up.

"What are you going to do?" Teck said hoarsely.

"I am going to help a starving kitten."

Chapter twenty-two

ARKADI lay limply in his office chair, a deflated balloon with a face painted on it. Sara Kerrigan, who had seemed to gain in energy and high spirits as he had been drained of them, had just bounced out of Police Central.

"Maybe—maybe if I'd been *tougher*, Inspector, I could have got her to break."

"You did what you could, Irmak. You went through the questions; she went through the answers."

"But she's lying."

"Only sometimes. She admits she went to the telephone exchange to get information; she denies that it has anything to do with police matters. She admits that Burrell flew to Antalya this morning; she denies that it has anything to do with a man named Samuel Teck. She denies that Burrell's work is anything but that of a cultural attaché. She knows nothing about a smuggled manuscript. She knows nothing about any Russians. In short, she knows nothing!"

Arkadi leaned forward to pick up a sheet of paper from the desk. "This came in while you were questioning her: Burrell left the Hotel Sporting in Antalya twenty minutes ago—and Teck's female friend did not accompany him. The policeman who made the report says here that she seemed 'haughty, cold and angry' throughout what was a very brief meeting." He dropped the paper on the desk. "Burrell has an airplane reservation that will take him from Antalya to Ankara at one, then a four-hour layover, and back here a little after nine this evening. I want him met at the airport, and courteously—courteously, Irmak, but firmly—no, let's not bring him here. We'll find some kind of place to meet with him at the airport. Get anything; I don't care if it's a mop closet. But we'll meet him, you see, we won't detain him, only a polite formality and so on and so on, and then I am going to put the screws to him!" Arkadi made a vigorous gesture of forcing in a corkscrew. "But courteously, of course."

The inspector inhaled deeply and slowly, as if he were

reinflating himself. "I am reasonably certain that Burrell learned no more from the Principessa than the Antalya police did."

"Anything new on Teck's 'Slav'?"

"Not much. Immigration and Aliens had nothing. Some of the Soviet delegation are going home, some today, some tomorrow. Only one is unaccounted for, the fellow we put in with the other foreigners the night of the raid on the Turisti Pallas. There's a description."

Irmak read. "I remember him. Young, fair complexion. Not unpleasant for a Russian."

Arkadi grunted. "The Russians get pleasanter; the Americans get the other way. Myself, I could live without all of them."

"Do you think he's Teck's 'Slav'?"

"Possibly. He checked out of his hotel last night. Or at least his baggage is gone and he *has been* checked out. The hotel clerks are confused about whether he checked out personally or whether one of the other Russians did it for him."

"He could be holed up with Teck somewhere."

"I know. I'm going to ask for authority to stop him if he appears at any frontier. Courteously, of course."

When Phillip Burrell arrived at the American Embassy buildings in Ankara, he did not pause in the elegant structure that was nominally the home of the United States mission; rather, he passed quickly through it into the recently built modern wing that lay behind, and was mostly hidden by, the old rococo building. Burrell was still in a foul mood because of his rebuff by the Princess di Paoli, and he scarcely spoke to the people who greeted him.

There were four messages for which Burrell had to sign. All had been coded and classified. One concerned an Iranian gift of air-to-air heat-seeking missiles to Saudi Arabia; one was a routine summary of Near East intelligence data; and two concerned *The Book of the Dead.*

The first of these confirmed what Burrell knew from rumor: a copy of *The Book of the Dead* was in Paris and would be made public at a press conference tomorrow. Excerpts would be read, and longer sections would be published in *L'Exprès* and an unspecified English-language weekly. The second message was a complete surprise: Yomut, the purported author of *The Book of the Dead*, reliably reported to have died three years before, had been issued a tourist visa for travel to the Netherlands, Denmark, and Sweden.

The report of Yomut's visa was shattering. Why, if the manuscript now in Paris was the one that had been smuggled out of Russia, had the Soviets pretended that he was dead? He had been a gadfly, a Turkman nationalist and an avowed Moslem; why now, if he were really alive, would they grant him an exit visa?

It was not the possible answers to such simple questions that caused Burrell's insides to knot with tension. It was the fear of what Yomut would say when he arrived in the West. He could not be expected to admit *The Book of the Dead*'s authorship, after all. Not when the epic poem of Moslem suffering under the Soviets was largely the work of a Central Intelligence Agency disinformation enthusiast named Phillip Burrell.

"Well, what do *you* think it means, Ken?"

"I don't know, sir. I hate to plead ignorance, but this whole business predates my tenure here. I wasn't on board when this Yomut was supposed to have died. I mean, I had to look the whole business up, sir."

The man behind the desk made a sonorous growling noise like some machine threatening to malfunction. "It's your job to know things, Ken. Even if you have to look them up."

"Well, sir, in my own defense I'd like to point out that there has been subterfuge here."

"Intentionally?"

"I don't want to respond to that without going back for more input, sir. I want to be fair."

"But you think Burrell has—"

"—flown by his own personal guidance system? Yes, sir."

"Mmm. Well, I don't get it. Burrell dealt them this *Book of the Dead* over two years ago; now they deal it back and suddenly the ace of spades turns up."

"The author. Yes, sir. Yomut. It's a blow."

"If he's genuine."

"Or even if he *seems* genuine. Hell, a man is more convincing than a manuscript. All things being—"

"—equal. Hmm, yes. The hell of it is he can blow the whistle and this damned *Book of the Dead* is shot down in flames, and like every other goddamn time when something smells a little ripe in the goddamn world, our agency will get blamed!"

"We'll just have to deny, sir."

The older man's face folded up in disgust. "With every bonehead Congressman and every goddamn media person in the whole country blaming us for every goddamn operation that surfaces this side of the moon? If goddamn Yassir Arafat came down with the flu, for Christ's sake, they'd say we were using germ warfare! Use your head, Ken."

"There is one thing we have to keep in mind, sir. We *are* responsible this time. For *The Book of the Dead,* I mean."

The other man's head sank lower. "I know it, Ken. That's the tragedy of it. For once those bastards will be right when they accuse us of something." He paused to take an oversized briar pipe from a rack. "Where is Burrell now?"

"He acknowledged a batch of messages from Ankara about thirty minutes ago. That's—four twenty their time, P.M."

"What'd the woman say about him?"

"Sara Kerrigan? The gist of it is that she thinks he's going to pieces. I took it on myself to check in with Medical Services, and their last report is not particularly good news in the light of what we're hearing now. This is his last field assignment, of course."

"Swan song."

"Sir?"

"*Book of the Dead* business. They always like to go out on a big operation. All right, Ken, is it absolutely clear on the records that the assignment was made by my predecessor—and that the psychological profile was available to him?"

"Yes, sir. His signature is on the assignment order."

"Okay. Get Burrell back here. Urgent, Immediate, Super-quick. No delays to close up the apartment, no good-byes, do not pass go, just get your ass back to Washington, preferably within twenty-four hours. Then bury him somewhere. Stick him in Historical if you can. If not, find him a nice, quiet corner with the winos in one of the backwaters."

"I'll try, sir. He's still got a lot of friends in Operations."

The older man's voice was very low as he concentrated on the filling of the pipe from a cobalt-blue bowl. "Don't try, Ken. *Do it.* That's what you're paid for." He put the pipe in the corner of his mouth, struck a match, and looked up through the heat ripples at his assistant. "I want to go to work on two fronts now. First, I want something ready for the Press Office. Something Press can use, I mean—brainstorm it a bit, then we'll get together at—let's say three thirty, I think I'm free then—" He glanced at a folio-sized appointment book. "Yes, that'll do, and get in somebody from the Israel desk; I think there may be an Israeli angle here, ease it off on them without seeming to. You know, 'Gee, fellas, faking *The Book of the Dead* sounds like a swell idea, we wish we'd thought of it before Tel Aviv did.' Something like that. Then—" He puffed; the match flame was sucked down into the pipe bowl and smoke gusted out. "I want absolute readiness on a story to discredit this Yomut. If he denies writing *The Book of the Dead*, I mean—knock the ground right out from under his feet. He's a fraud, he's a fairy, he's been brainwashed, something on that track."

"I don't think we can ever make the foreign press believe that he wrote it if he denies it in person."

"We won't try to. All I want is to discredit him. Cut our losses, that's what I want. If he denies, we raise a smoke screen. Leaves everybody wrangling about what really happened—nobody wins, nobody loses. Feasible doubt, that's what I want. Who'd handle the story for us?"

"Without our hand showing, you mean?"

"Well, of course."

"People's Republic of China, most likely. They'd buy it if the source was good—nice anti-Russian angle, but not too direct. I think we might send it up through Aden, sir. Reliable Arab sources say, and so forth. Lot of Chinese Communist journalists working out of Aden. They'd get it pretty quick."

"Good. Good. It's neat. Tied up with its own ribbon. I like it, Ken. You get Burrell back here within twenty-four hours, and tuck him away someplace, and I think we can come out of this one all even. Deuce."

To the east, against the black mountain heights, the sky was dark, shading to a deep-water green overhead; to the west, a line of fire showed where the sun had disappeared behind Izmir, and a bank of green clouds was underlined with orange. Arkadi leaned against his car with his left forearm propped on the top of the door to cool the sweat that trickled down his side. When the lights of the incoming airplane dropped toward the runway, he straightened and adjusted his necktie. Then, bending down so he could speak through the car window, he said to his wife, "Stay here. I won't be long. This is just routine."

"Be careful," she said tonelessly, uttering the same unnecessary warning that went unheard each time he left her. She knew that she said it as a ritual for her own comfort and not for his.

Arkadi skirted two parked cars and crossed the pavement to the rear door of a cargo area. A minute's walk took him to the employees' section of the terminal, where he nodded to a plainclothes officer before signaling for two uniformed men to follow him. Together they crossed to the waiting room; he saw Sara Kerrigan stand up as the plane's arrival was announced, and at the same moment Sergeant Irmak appeared at her side and spoke to her, gesturing toward a door on the far side of the building, away from the arrival gate. A needless move, probably, but there might be something gained by not letting Burrell talk to her before Arkadi could get to him.

When Phillip Burrell stepped through the door into the arrival lounge, Arkadi moved to his right side while one of the uniformed men stepped behind him and deftly directed the other arriving passengers around them.

"Inspector Arkadi, Izmir police," Arkadi said softly, presenting his identification and making a polite bow. "We met the night of the unfortunate business at the Turisti Pallas. Probably you don't remember me."

"I remember very well," Burrell said, although he studied Arkadi's identification with great care. "Is something wrong?"

"It is a continuing investigation, Mr. Burrell. There are still many mysteries. I would like to ask you to give me a little time, a very little time. I want to ask a very few questions." Burrell pursed his lips. "I realize," Arkadi continued, "that you carry a diplomatic passport. Of course, it goes without saying that the investigation does not touch on yourself, Mr. Burrell. Oh, no. Not in any way." Arkadi lowered his voice. "Let me be perfectly frank. It has to do with Samuel Teck. I know that you spoke with a woman this morning in Antalya who received a telephone call from Teck two nights ago. That is why I took the trouble to come to the airport; I did not want to ask you to come to my office—the delay, the probability of attention from journalists—if you could spare me a few minutes, I have a private area reserved for us."

Burrell murmured that he would be happy to help the police if he could, of course, and he moved in step with Arkadi, swinging an aluminum photographic case marked FILM—DO NOT X-RAY at his right side.

"Are you in charge of the Turisti Pallas investigation, Inspector?" Burrell asked. The note of curiosity was just right.

"No," Arkadi answered as he stepped back to hold a door for Burrell. "I happened to be called to second the officer in command that night."

"Dreadful thing. Appalling."

"We lost five men," Arkadi said grimly. "One died in the hospital this morning."

"Are you, uh, connected with some special crimes unit, then, Inspector? Special Branch?"

"No. I am part of the Art Thefts Unit."

"Oh." Burrell seemed puzzled. Over his shoulder as he walked through another door Burrell said, "I don't quite see how the Turisti Pallas disaster connects with art theft."

"Neither do I," said Arkadi enigmatically. He did not explain further, and thirty seconds later they were in the small lounge reserved for officials of Turkish Airways, where Arkadi waved Burrell to a chair and then ordered the uniformed men to wait outside. He sat in a vinyl-covered armchair facing Burrell, who sat with legs crossed and with one arm stretched out along the back of a small sofa.

He looks sick, Arkadi thought, *and fighting hard to hide it. Purple shadows under his eyes like an old woman. Terrible color, looks as if he'd just puked.* He offered Burrell a cigarette, but the American took out a pipe. When he held it by the bowl, Arkadi could see the stem quivering in the tense grip of his fingers.

"I will come right to the point of our meeting, Mr. Burrell." Arkadi looked out the large window at the jeweled runway. Against the black of the mountains he could see Burrell's reflection, its shadows deepened by the glass and the night so that he seemed more a lean death's-head than a living man. "I asked Miss Sara Kerrigan, who, I understand, is your assistant—please, if you wish to correct me, wait until I have finished—to come to my office this morning. Yesterday, she had inquired at the central telephone headquarters concerning calls made by Samuel Teck. I do not think I have to identify Teck for you. Now, Mr. Burrell, my question is this: Did you ask Miss Kerrigan to make these inquiries at the telephone headquarters?" Arkadi swung around to look at Burrell.

"Yes, of course I did." Burrell had loaded his pipe from a black pouch and was holding a cylindrical lighter in his left hand. "Shouldn't I have done so?"

Arkadi ignored the question. "Did you want the inquiries made in order to learn more—no, let me make it even more general—was it to trace Samuel Teck?"

"Yes."

"Do you *know* that he is now alive, Mr. Burrell?"

"He was alive yesterday morning."

"At what time? This could be important." So far as Arkadi could see, the time was of no importance at all, but he felt he should behave like Burrell's idea of a local policeman. He took out his notebook.

"Shortly after six. Six A.M."

Arkadi dutifully wrote down the time.

"You're sure it was Teck?"

"Oh, yes, no doubt about it."

"How did you know?"

"Oh, a number of things. The voice. He mentioned his passport, which he'd left with me. And another private matter we discussed."

Arkadi wrote. "Did Teck tell you where he was, Mr. Burrell?"

"No. And before you ask the next question, I traced the place he'd telephoned from by calling Edward Rountree, the USIS boy. Teck mentioned him during the call."

"Rountree . . . phone," Arkadi muttered, scribbling away at things he already knew. "I see! Of course. Well." He consulted what seemed to be a list of questions on another page. "Did Teck mention any fears he had, any sense of—danger, threats—you know what I mean." Arkadi leaned forward, eyebrows up innocently, lower lip thrust out. *Am I overdoing it? No, he's beginning to relax and enjoy himself.*

"As a matter of fact, Inspector, he did. To be perfectly honest—well, he wanted my help in getting out of Turkey."

Arkadi cluck-clucked with his tongue. "Illegally, you mean."

"Well—I think he had some daft idea that it could be done extralegally. American citizens sometimes have an inflated idea of the power of their embassy."

Arkadi nodded. "You told him that such a thing was impossible?"

"Oh, of course! Good God, from what he seemed to be saying, it sounded to me as if he wanted to get out because he was in trouble with you people."

"We people? The Art Thefts Unit?"

"The police."

"Ah! I see. Ah, yes, there it is." Arkadi nodded and then stood up. "You've been a great help to us."

"Have you found Teck?"

But Arkadi seemed to be deep in his notes. "A great help." He looked up. "Investigation is a very complicated business, Mr. Burrell. Maybe you don't know that, not being in police work. Your work at the embassy is—"

"Cultural affairs."

"Ah! What sort of cultural affairs do you deal with? Films, dancing, musicians?"

"At the moment we have nine track and field athletes competing in Ankara."

"In that heat! Wonderful! I admire that, I really do. Very impressive!"

He shook hands with Burrell again and successfully talked through the other's attempts to ask more questions about Teck. They moved out into the waiting room where Arkadi saw Irmak and Sara Kerrigan. She started toward them.

"Thank you. A great help," Arkadi said. He turned Burrell to face Sara Kerrigan, then waited until they had come together fifteen feet away from him.

"Oh, Mr. Burrell," he called. "One more thing!" Burrell looked back, his face pasty under the fluorescent lighting. The side of his face was dragged down by a sudden tic.

Arkadi flipped through his notebook. At last he seemed to find his place. He raised one finger.

"*The Book of the Dead!*" he shouted, so that everyone in the waiting room could hear. "Did Teck describe the Russian who took it away from him?"

On the drive into Izmir, Phillip Burrell said virtually nothing. He let Sara Kerrigan talk and did not look at her.

Twice he twisted around to look out the rear window, and when she murmured, "Is anybody back there?" he grimaced as if it were a stupid question. She told him of her visit to Arkadi's office; now, she was a little unsure of herself and she apologized to him, although for what error she could not have said. When they were in the city's evening traffic she asked, "How did your meeting with Teck's girl friend go?"

"Badly."

He did not elaborate.

He had reserved a room at the Buyu Efes. He got out of the car at the hotel door and took his case from the back seat without another word to her. When she had parked and entered the hotel, he was not in sight. She took the elevator upstairs.

He did not answer her knock at first. After the second knock, however, the door opened a scant two inches and his left eye, red as if from weeping, looked out.

"What do you want?"

"We've got to talk, Phil."

"We'll talk tomorrow."

"I've got to talk to you tonight. It's important."

"How did you get up here?"

"By the elevator, like everybody else. Phil, let me in." She pushed. He held the door in place and it would not budge.

"They shouldn't have let you up. They can make a lot of trouble here if a woman goes up to a man's room."

"I bribed the clerk. Come *on*, Phil, let me in!" The eye stared fixedly at her.

"Five minutes. That's all I can give you, Sally." There was an unhealthy tension in his voice.

She pushed the door open, stepped through, and shut it behind her. Burrell was carrying a pistol with a silencer, and clearly he had been holding it while he talked to her at the door.

"All right, what is it? I've got a big night ahead of me." He sat in a straight chair by a small desk, on which he put the pistol. The fingers of his right hand curled over the desk's edge six inches from the gun.

"Phil, you're pushing yourself too hard."

"I know that." A proud little smile touched the corners of his mouth. "I've pushed myself too hard all my life. Do you think that things get done because they're easy?" He pointed at a manila envelope on the bed. "Hand me that, please."

She fetched it, although she despised being made a mere clerk by him. When she handed him the envelope, their fingers touched and her arm jerked at the contact.

"Some things are worth doing and pushing yourself for, and some things aren't worth doing at all," he said. "When they matter, what good are you if you don't push and push? Get me a glass from the bathroom."

She wanted to tell him not to drink, but she knew perfectly well that she would only make things worse. When she came back with the glass, he already had a pint of scotch open on the desk next to him. He reached for the glass without taking his eyes from a thick sheaf of papers in his lap.

"Was that all you wanted to say, Sally?"

She leaned forward. To her, the papers in his lap were upside down, but she recognized them by the patterns of blocks of type. "Phil, isn't that the daily intelligence summary?" He said nothing. He was reading, although he succeeded in pouring himself a glass of scotch. "Phil, that's classified!"

"I still know what is classified and what is not, no matter what the Izmir police think of my intellect."

"Phil, those papers shouldn't have left the Ankara office."

"I signed for them."

"The security officer will report you."

"He'd damn well better; that's his job."

"But, Phil—" She sat on the foot of the bed. She was wearing a sleeveless white dress that had seemed too warm in the outside heat; now, she was cold and she wrapped her hands over her bare upper arms. She leaned toward him again. "Phil—we've been pretty close, haven't we? I mean, closer than just hopping into bed together, right?" He took a felt-tipped pen from his breast pocket and made a mark on the sheet in his lap. The glass that had held the scotch was empty. "Can't you look at me, Phil?"

"I'm *trying* to work."

"Why are you doing this to me?"

"Doing what, Sally?"

"Why have you turned on me all of a sudden? What's happened? Phil, could you please in the name of God give me a minute of your precious male time so that I can find out what's going on?"

He poured himself more scotch. "No, I can't." Reasonable, measured, steady. Not rising to the bait.

"*Why*? What's *happened?*"

He drank. "You saw that cop's performance at the airport. Wasn't that cute? Didn't you enjoy that? Right out of a bush-league thriller, a real cute cop! He thought he had me suckered right down the line, he was just going to spring the old whammo at the end there, 'Oh, by the way.' Real *cute!*" The voice was no longer reasonable or steady; the hand that held the glass quivered.

"Phil, did you already know that the Russians had got the *Book of the Dead* from Teck?"

"Oh, use your head, for Christ's sake! *The Book of the Dead* is in Paris at a publishing outfit that's in our pocket! The cute cop was trying to get a rise out of me. Real *cute!*" He sipped the scotch, then put it down quickly. "Your five minutes are up."

"That isn't all that's upset you, Phil. I know you better than that."

He pushed himself back in the chair and sat rigid, as if the force of his body alone kept the chair from folding up around him. His stare was direct and prolonged. The fingers of his right hand felt for the edge of the desk and the gun. "I've been ordered home."

Thank God, was her first thought, *it's over.* She had not liked reporting on a man who was supposed to be her lover; instead of giving her the sense of superiority she had wanted, it had made her feel cheapened and humiliated, used by the men in Washington because she was a woman. *Thank God.* "When?"

"Twenty-four hours." The words were spoken rapidly but very clearly, each one set off with a meticulous precision of consonants that made them seem sarcastic. "Twenty-four hours from five thirty this afternoon local time, that is. So, now you know what's 'turned me against you,' Sally."

Does he know? she wondered. She glanced at the hand that was so close to the pistol. He was wound up very tight, and he believed in guns, believed in their dangerous explosion as a release for his own tension.

"What are you talking about, Phil?"

As suddenly as he had been angry, he was tender. He took her hands between his own and spoke very softly. To her astonishment, tears were running down his sallow cheeks. "I can't involve you any more, Sally. You're too good—too precious—" He was as maudlin as he had been imperious before: she was the best thing that had ever happened to him; he adored her; she was his life, except for the Agency. "I can't ask you to share what I've got to do, Sally."

"Do you want me to stay here tonight?" she said softly, hating both of them.

"No. Absolutely not." He sat back. His cheeks were wet but his expression had stiffened again. "Too much to be done."

"Are you going back to Ankara, Phil?"

"Not yet."

"But you *are* going to Washington."

"Like hell!" The voice was contemptuous and he poured himself more scotch. "My job is here. I know from experience—something's about to burst; I can feel it, smell it—there are signs. I'm close to something, Sally—*that's* why they ordered me home. Getting too close." He sat back again. "I've suspected it for some time—something funny in Washington, I mean, in the Agency. Treason—" He held up the glass and squinted at it as if a sample of that deadly toxin, treason, were in it to be analyzed. "Treason catches even some of *us*. Those disappointed, gutless wonders in their swivel chairs in Washington—they're prime targets for a good foreign contact. . . ." His intelligence was still there, but it was coupled with something that made it sly and mean—fear or hatred. "They think they'll order me off this job, just like that. Bring me home to wait out my pension. But it won't work."

"But if they've ordered you, Phil—"

"I take my orders from the Agency, not *them*, not some swivel-chair driver who's been subverted. I'll put it all in my report." He bent over the papers again.

"Can't I help?"

"No. I have to do this myself." He began to stuff the papers back into the manila envelope. "I really need to be alone now."

She became quiet, intense. "I'm going back to Ankara, first thing tomorrow. I'll take the classified papers back."

"You're worried about me, aren't you, Sal!"

She lied. "I'm worried about *us*, Phil."

"You'd really take the classified things just to help me?"

"You know I would."

He handed her the envelope and she wrote out a receipt on a piece of hotel stationery; he saw the letterhead and said that it was too revealing, and she burned the paper and dropped it into the toilet and then wrote a new receipt on a small sheet of paper from her appointment book. She picked up the manila envelope and went to the door, where he kissed her, but without emotion. When she was in the corridor, she heard the bolt drop into place.

She was frowning when she left the hotel and got into her car, and she did not notice the plainclothes policeman who watched her from across the street. In her own apartment she went through the intelligence summary and found that Burrell had checked two items: a report of the sudden departure from a Bulgarian resort city of a KGB officer named Yuri Nemchin and of his appearance at the port of Varna; and a brief mention of the departure from Varna of a Soviet freighter that subsequently had passed through the Dardanelles and anchored off Izmir.

Half an hour later Phillip Burrell came out of his hotel. The plainclothes officer followed him to a restaurant, where after spending only a few minutes at a table, Burrell went to a telephone. Unheard by the policeman, he called an Iranian who was a known free-lance passer of low-level information, a man used by both the Soviets and the Americans. Burrell asked him to locate a Russian named Yuri Nemchin. They agreed on a price, and Burrell returned to his table, knowing that, within hours, the word would be everywhere. With any luck, Nemchin himself would hear of it.

As he ate, he drafted two cables to a man in Amsterdam. The first, which seemed to be concerned with the sudden illness of a mutual uncle, was merely a dummy; the second, which continued the history of uncle's woes, contained a single coded name, which, deciphered, was Yomut.

Chapter twenty-three

"TECK?"

"What is it?"

"Why did you do it?"

"The manuscript?"

"Yes, the manuscript, the photos—all of it."

"I thought. . . ." Teck's voice trailed off. His eyes had been closed, now he opened them to the same darkness. "I had some idea that I might make a trade for something else I wanted."

"What?"

"Oh, part of an old book."

Seriakin was speechless for some seconds. "An old *book?*" he said in disbelief. "It must be very rare to take such a chance."

"The only one of its kind in the world."

"Would you have hidden the manuscript and taken those photos if you had known how dangerous it was?"

Teck sighed. "Not if I had it to do again, but my values— When I did it, it seemed to matter very much; now—it wouldn't matter much now."

Seriakin thought of a morose Finn whom he had met in Helsinki. It had been a casual meeting; they had not even exchanged names. But something of moment had been discussed—the famine in the Sahel, perhaps, or the depletion of fish stocks—and the Finn, his arms resting on a stone parapet overlooking a small lake, had said grimly, "It doesn't matter, anyway."

"Certainly it matters," Seriakin had said stiffly.

The Finn had smiled knowingly. "Nothing matters. Nothing ever matters."

Seriakin had been shocked then. Now, he had got over the philosophic shock, but he still had to ask: What matters? What does not matter? *What if nothing matters?*

"Some things must matter to a man," he said aloud to Teck.

"What matters to you?" Teck's voice was openly curious. Seriakin thought he could hear the echo of another question: *What matters to a KGB officer?*

"Places I have been, lived in. People I have known. Love, I suppose. Laugh at me if you like. As an employee of the KGB, I am supposed to be an unprincipled villain, is that not right? Your Central Intelligence Agency gentlemen can be romantic men of principle. The very British gentlemen of MI-6 can be. But KGB are despicable bullies and gangsters, are we not? We have the Lubyanka and the infamous Archipelago; we suppress freedom and destroy initiative, that is what you believe, no? Your men of romantic principle are not like that, of course." Hearing his own words, Seriakin was surprised to hear the bitterness that Nemchin had heard there. "I am sorry, Teck. I am talking too much about myself."

Both men were silent for a quarter of an hour. It was Teck who finally spoke. "Will we have to kill somebody to get out of here?"

"Maybe. Maybe. Can you do it?"

"I don't know." He sighed heavily. "It's a change from the usual demands put on a medieval scholar."

Ten minutes later Seriakin asked Teck what time he thought it was. Teck thought it was well after midnight; Seriakin thought it was as late as two. "In any case," he said grimly, "we will wait another hour. Then I will knock on the door. Then I think we will find out what really matters."

Time moved erratically. Seriakin had to concentrate to sense its movement. The beating of his heart, his own measured breathing, and Teck's slight snore as he dozed were clocks. Sometimes his mind would stray and the clocks would stop, and he would find, some immeasurable moment later—seconds? minutes?—that he had been thinking of Leningrad, of his mistress, of a cabin in the country where he had spent a week one summer. He became sleepy, desperately so, and staying awake became a physical ordeal like climbing a steep hill.

He stood up and stretched. He did exercises. When he sat down again with his back against the dirt wall, he was as sleepy as ever.

At last he could bear it no longer. It was important only to get on with it. If not, time would become as plastic as dough, and he would wake to find it was full noon and it would be too late.

He touched Teck's right foot. "It's time," he said. He shook the foot gently.

"I'm awake."

"Good."

"What time is it, do you think?"

"I hope it is three in the morning. About that. The low tide of life." Seriakin stood up and bent his knees to rid them of their stiffness. "They say it is the hour when the most men die. Old men, the sick, infants in their beds."

He heard Teck stand up; his breathing was close to Seriakin's left ear.

"In the Middle Ages," Teck said, "they thought that the soul might leave the body after midnight. Ghosts walked. The dead came out of their graves."

"Like us." Seriakin touched the rough wood of the door. "I am going to give the signal. You understand what we are to do?"

"Yes."

"I think the guard will go up the stairs and knock there for the other guard. But perhaps he will open this door at once. I do not know. We must be ready."

"All right. Go ahead."

Seriakin put both hands on the door. He moved his feet back a little so that he was leaning against it. "I am ready," he said quietly. He felt Teck touch his left side. Teck moved around behind him, his hands on Seriakin's hips. "Lower," Seriakin said. "You must push from my bottom, understand?" The hands moved down over his buttocks. The pressure increased.

"Is that all right?" Teck whispered.

"Good. Do not get too tense. If your muscles stiffen, you will not move quickly enough. I am going to give the signal."

He raised his hands to knock and then turned back toward Teck. "Can you start an automobile without the key?"

"No. I'm sorry."

"I will do it." He raised his hand again. "If we get as far as the garage."

He knocked three times, paused, and knocked three more times. His ear against the door, he strained to hear the sounds from the cellar. "Nothing," he whispered.

"Maybe nobody's there."

"There has to be somebody there." He waited. "That bastard is asleep." After another wait he repeated the knocking, this time as loud as he could pound on the door. A second later he heard a sound. "Ah," Seriakin breathed. Both men tensed.

"Footsteps. He's going to the stair. Yes, now he goes up. Wait—he is knocking. He will be talking to the guard at the top of the stairs. What is taking so long? Perhaps he has to wake Nemchin, or— No, they are coming down. Be ready, Teck. It will happen now."

Seriakin pushed against the door. Teck's palms thrust

against his buttocks. A loud clatter from the door itself, which Seriakin could feel as a vibration in his hands, signaled the removal of the first bar; Seriakin visualized the movements as the guard lifted the first bar out and then bent down and to his left to lean it against the wall on the hinge side of the door. Then he would straighten, and the second bar would be grasped, lifted, and the moment that it came free of its restraints—

The door burst outward. Seriakin's impetus banged it against the guard and swung both door and man back against the cellar wall, and then Teck's push moved Seriakin through the opening and toward the man who held the flashlight only five feet away.

There were only two men waiting in the cellar. They expected him to come as a docile ally; they did not expect him to catapult out with such speed that the gunman had time to raise his pistol only partway to his hip before Seriakin crashed into his chest. With a vindictive spat the pistol went off once, and then Seriakin and the guard were falling toward the floor together.

The guard tried to swing the heavy light at Seriakin's head, but the very weight of it made the movement too slow and clumsy. Seriakin's left hand had caught his forearm; the hand with the pistol twisted in his grasp like a snake's head, trying to aim the weapon. It fired again. Seriakin struck the man in the face and then twisted to his left and raised his torso to get more purchase on the gun hand. He glanced over his shoulder to see Teck and the other guard locked together, seemingly immobile. Too late, he saw the heavy flashlight swinging again toward his head, and he caught the blow above his ear. Momentarily blinded, he struck again at the other man's face, and behind him he heard a half-strangled shout in Turkish.

Seriakin put his right forearm across his opponent's throat. He leaned forward to bring as much weight as possible over it, his head tucked down next to the other man's for protection. The light struck his back twice, and then the man was straining to free his throat from the arm that crushed his larynx. Seriakin moved his left hand down the other's arm until he held the pistol by its barrel. The man gurgled and Seriakin pressed harder.

The hand that held the pistol let go and tried to push Seriakin away.

Seriakin turned the heavy pistol in his left hand until his finger was around the trigger, and then he pressed its muzzle into the other man's armpit and fired.

When he rolled off the dying man, he saw Teck and the other guard still locked together. Each had one hand on the other's throat and one hand on the other's wrist. Teck was trying to keep the guard from reaching for the heavy revolver at his belt.

Seriakin swayed from the blows when he stood up. Two steps put him behind the Turk. Seriakin kicked up between the legs, then straight at the right kidney with his heel.

"Revolver, money, and a knife," he panted as Teck lowered the unconscious man to the cellar floor. Seriakin took down the propane lantern from its hook and smashed the globe with the silencer of the pistol. The fragile mantel ruptured and the flame burned blue. Seriakin put the lantern on a pile of cloth bags and almost immediately a thick plume of smoke went up. He returned to the man he had shot, and, without looking at the man's face, felt through his pockets until he found a folding knife.

"Ready, Teck."

He picked up the flashlight. A small sound distracted him. The man he had shot was still alive. The lips opened and a red bit of tongue appeared between them, tried to lick them. The eyes slewed toward him and killer and victim looked squarely at each other.

Seriakin thought of the Cairo woman and her cats. *And it made no difference.*

Seriakin went first up the stairs, the automatic pistol held a little in front of him. At the top, the door was slightly open. To his right a corridor ran at right angles to the doorway; to his left, another led to the garage. There was no one in sight, but he could not guess who might be awake on the other side of the three doors that he could see.

He stepped out and turned to the left.

Teck came behind him.

Seriakin had taken one step toward the garage when a door opened on the other arm of the T; just half of it was visible past the corner from where Seriakin stood. Teck was in full view, and, as the man who had opened it came through, his sleep-swollen eyes suddenly widened.

Behind him, Nemchin was just visible, in blue pajamas and a light, almost feminine robe.

Teck raised his revolver and fired. It was an English-made thirty-eight, virtually an antique, and it made a sound like a cannon in the enclosed space.

The four men moved at the same time. Halfway to the garage, Teck turned and fired again, although there was no one there. Seriakin had been prepared to find the door to the garage locked, but it was not and he held it while Teck ran through. He could hear Nemchin shouting behind the closed door at the far end of the corridor and, overhead, feet shook the house as someone pounded across the floor.

The green Toyota was still in the garage.

"Stay at the door," he said to Teck. "Use the gun if you have to." He did not add that Teck should have saved his ammunition, because the shooting he had already done had only waked the other people in the house. In the light from the corridor Teck's face was strained and, he thought, frightened, but it might have shown only heightened awareness.

Seriakin opened the driver's door. Within seconds he had exposed the ignition wires. When the engine roared he felt an unexpected surge of self-congratulation.

"Teck!"

But Teck was firing the noisy revolver. He emptied the weapon from a prone position on the garage floor, his body protected by the cement step; then he ducked his head and rolled back so he could catch the bottom of the door and slam it closed on their attackers.

"Get in, Teck!"

A spot of light appeared where a bullet had gone through the thin door.

Teck clambered into the passenger seat. Seriakin handed him the automatic pistol and shouted, "Keep your head down!" As Teck ducked, Seriakin gunned the engine and let out the clutch; the car jerked backward and slammed into the double doors that separated them from the street.

Instead of opening in the middle as they were made to do, the wooden doors remained locked together with a heavy chain. The hinges burst on the right side and the doors swung like a single door, only to catch again on a hump in the paving outside. Seriakin pressed down on the accelerator, but the car had lost its momentum and the wheels spun on the greasy garage floor with a hideous, high-pitched squeal, and Seriakin, cursing in Russian, crashed the gears back into low and moved six feet into the garage, the doors following like the wings of a great butterfly. As the car came to a stop, the door through which they had come from the house opened and a man leaped through. He fired wildly. Seriakin bent to his right so that his cheek rested on Teck's left arm and shifted into reverse. As he again jammed down the accelerator, another shot came, hitting the windshield high up on the driver's side. As the car surged backward, small chunks of glass, like coarse sugar, cascaded over the two men and the hood of the car.

They roared backward. The garage doors were ripped off the remaining pair of hinges; they bounced off the lump in the pavement and rose slightly, were struck again by the car, and bounced up and to the side as the car charged under them. When they fell, they struck the hood on the passenger side, and then the car was free of them and it rushed across the narrow street, over a stone curbing, and into the wall of another building.

Seriakin again shifted into first. He turned the wheel and let in the clutch, and the Toyota pulled away from the wall and swung back into the street. Something was dragging noisily, but the car responded.

Two men appeared at the end of the street. As they fired, Teck opened the passenger door and fired through the crack between it and the post beside the windshield; the Toyota completed its turn, headed toward them, and the two men jumped for the same side, firing as the car sped past. Three seconds later, Seriakin had turned a corner and was accelerating away from them.

He turned again in order to be out of the line of fire from the house. Three blocks farther, he turned into a wider street that led them to a boulevard, and Seriakin used the boulevard to move smoothly and put distance between them and their captors. He recognized the area; after three more turns he drove for two minutes along a road where the buildings began to thin out and he knew they were leaving the city. He pulled into a side road that was hardly more than a lane and stopped the car.

"You'll have to drive," he said calmly.

"What's the matter?"

Seriakin opened his door. "I've been shot," he said. In the feeble dome light, the glass chunks from the windshield sparkled like ice, and under his left leg they were red with the blood that had saturated his trouser leg below the knee and run down over his shoeless foot.

Chapter twenty-four

"SEE what is dragging from the back end as you go around," Seriakin said. Teck closed the passenger door and walked to the rear of the car, and Seriakin laboriously lifted his right leg over the gearshift lever and slid his bottom into the passenger seat, then dragged his left leg over.

Teck peered through the driver's door. "Are you going to need a doctor?"

"No. That is, yes, of course I do, but I cannot." He propped the injured leg up on the dashboard and felt blood trickling back down his thigh. "It is very curious; I don't know when I was hit." He pressed his thumbs behind his left knee. "What is the trouble in the back?"

"I can't see without a light. I think it's the tailpipe. I'll have to get the trunk open to get tools, though." He disappeared. Seriakin took the guard's clasp knife and slit the pant leg, thinking of the day he had bought the suit and how pleased he had been with it, a smoky-gray raw silk made for him in Hong Kong. In the feeble light the bloody fabric looked almost black.

He cut it into strips and tied a tourniquet just below the knee, inches above the dark hole where the bullet had entered. When he tightened the cloth by twisting it around the knife handle, the welling blood subsided, but the drops wrung from the cloth itself ran down to his wrist. *A vein. A vein and not an artery. That should be good.*

"The trunk's jammed and I can't see what the hell I'm doing back there," Teck said angrily. The excitement that had carried him through the escape was going, and Seriakin could hear a jagged tremor in his voice. "It's the tailpipe, all right, but the goddamn thing's too hot for me to hold on to it." He sat in the driver's seat and reached across Seriakin to put the automatic pistol on the dashboard. "Are you going to be all right?"

"I hope so."

Teck opened the glove compartment. There was a box of ancient candy, melted now into a lump; a pair of eyeglasses; several booklets having to do with the car; and a small flashlight. He flicked the switch. Nothing happened and he smashed the flashlight against the dashboard.

"Teck!" Seriakin's voice stopped him before he hurled the flashlight into the road. "Rest a moment. Lean back and breathe deeply. Don't think; rest a moment." Teck slumped back into the seat, breathing heavily. Seriakin took the little flashlight and shook it; when he tried the switch, it glowed. "The cells are almost exhausted. You must do what you can." He held out the rest of the blood-soaked pant leg. "Tie it up with this." After a hesitant moment Teck took the cloth and the light and disappeared. Seriakin turned off the dome light.

When Teck returned, Seriakin had found the lever beside the seat that allowed it to recline, and he lay back with his left leg elevated on the dash and the long pistol concealed between his right thigh and the door.

"Could you do it?"

"There was nothing to tie it to. I broke the damned pipe off. At least it won't drag." Teck wiped his hand on his shirt, then bent and wiped his fingers on the grass that grew along the road.

Teck sat in the driver's seat.

"*Can* you drive?" Seriakin said.

Teck rested his head on the oily curve of the steering wheel. "God, I hope so!" The tremor had left his voice and he was breathing more easily. "How much chance the car will be recognized?"

"In Izmir, every chance; the KGB have a net over the city. Nemchin will know within minutes if we are on the main streets. Outside the city we have a chance."

Teck did not remark on the word "we." Before Seriakin had been shot, he had thought they would separate. He sat staring through the space where the windshield had been, then sat suddenly upright and, after shaking his head as if to clear it, put the car into reverse and swiveled about, ready to back up.

Seriakin's right hand came up with the pistol in it. "Where are you going?"

"A little town called Antalya. I've got a friend who—" Teck saw the automatic pistol. He said nothing. After a moment he backed the car to the end of the lane and pulled into the roadway. When he had shifted gears again and was ready to move forward, he said quietly, "The gun wasn't necessary, you know."

Seriakin tried to smile. This time it was his voice that was unsteady as he murmured, "I couldn't be sure. I'm sorry, Teck."

At 4:30 in the morning Yuri Nemchin left the safe house and crossed the city. Behind him, the safe house was still smoldering, but most of the damage was limited to the cellar and part of the first floor. Nemchin had been forced to leave before the firemen arrived, taking with him only a suit and a pair of shoes and a small case that held his forged identity papers.

It remained to be seen what the firemen would make of the corpse in the cellar.

At the apartment Nemchin heard of Phillip Burrell's search for him. A panicky Turk advised him to flee, but Nemchin believed that Burrell was sending him a signal.

At 4:49 Nemchin entered Burrell's hotel with the kitchen help, who were just going to work. He was dressed nondescriptly in Turkish clothes. A small bribe caused the lone watchman to look the other way.

At 4:53 Nemchin stood by a house telephone in the basement, just outside the kitchen where coffee was being made.

"Yes?" Burrell's voice was hoarse.

"Am I speaking to Phillip Burrell?" Nemchin said in English.

"Yes." The voice was clearer.

"I think you have been looking for me. I have a message from an Iranian colleague."

After a moment's silence Burrell said, "Do I know you?"

"We met in Tehran, I believe." They had never met, but they had heard of each other.

Burrell said cautiously, "I think we have a common interest in the French literary world."

"Yes, perhaps we have. Shall we discuss it over coffee?"

"Where?"

"Stay where you are. I will come to you."

At 5:07 Yuri Nemchin carried a coffee tray to Burrell's floor, preceded by one of the Free Turkey Youth, who quickly scouted the corridor before signaling to him that it was safe. When Nemchin entered the room the young man stood guard in a stairwell nearby.

Burrell closed the door behind Nemchin, who walked straight in and put the tray on a small desk. "It is French coffee; I hope you don't mind?" The smell of the bitter coffee was very strong.

"I prefer it."

Burrell had brushed his gray hair and splashed on some musky cologne that Nemchin found himself liking. The American looked pale and a little tense.

"We were in Tehran at the same time," Nemchin said.

"Yes. How is Kondroshnoi?" The old man, then Nemchin's ambassador, was now retired.

"Quite well. He gardens and writes his official memoirs, I understand. And Ambassador Monhegan?"

"Returned to banking, I believe."

"Ah, yes." Nemchin smiled and handed him a cup. "May I come to business?"

"Please do."

"A man named Teck."

Noncommittally, Burrell said "Yes?" and reached across Nemchin for sugar. He turned it slowly into the coffee and began to stir with a tiny spoon.

"He is supposed to have been killed in the tragedy at the Turisti Pallas."

"That was a theory."

"Just so. May I be frank? I know that Teck is still alive."

"Oh? I'm a little surprised; I thought you had kidnapped him," said Burrell.

"Good, we are both frank. Now, however, I must be a little circumspect. I did not until recently think that Teck was one of your professional connections, but now—" He left the conclusion of the sentence hanging; one eyebrow rose and his head dipped speculatively to the side. "I should like to know if you sent me a message in order to arrange a discussion of some sort of . . . exchange concerning this Teck."

"An exchange of what for what?"

Nemchin glanced at the window, whose centerpost was dimly silhouetted against the first daylight. He studied Burrell's face but could not read it.

"Burrell, my Turkish friends think you sent out word in order to trap me here. I think that is a foolish notion because we both know there is no need to be so crude as that."

"Thank you." Burrell smiled.

"But I must know if we are leading up to a negotiation of some kind. My time is very short and I cannot linger."

"All right." Burrell set down his cup and it rattled very slightly against the saucer. "I think that you have a message for me from Teck. Is that possible?"

Nemchin was bewildered. "If I had a message, *I* would have got into contact with *you*." He had thought that Teck, once escaped, would be in contact with Burrell, and he thought it likely that Seriakin would do the same. He could not understand Burrell's delays. "May I ask a direct question?"

"Please do."

Nemchin moved forward in his chair. His extended forefinger almost touched the silky lapel of Burrell's robe. "Have you received a message from Teck in the last twenty-four hours?"

"Absolutely not."

Nemchin touched Burrell's left wrist. "What is the time, please?"

"Five eighteen. More coffee?"

"Yes, if you will."

The escape had been made shortly after three. Two hours ago. Nemchin was convinced that the two men would not have waited so long if they had meant to make contact with Burrell.

"Is your telephone tapped?"

"No. I checked, of course."

"If Teck wanted to contact you, would anyone be able to prevent him?"

"Other than your own people, you mean?"

"Forget my people."

Burrell shook his head. "The police have had some interest

in him, but I don't see—" He refilled Nemchin's cup and handed it to him. "You don't have him, then?"

Nemchin stirred the coffee and considered his choices. The important thing, of course, was to protect himself from Moscow's wrath over the loss of Seriakin; Teck was merely a detail. Moscow would be especially angry if Seriakin popped up in the wrong place, saying the wrong things—or, even worse, if he failed to pop up anywhere and it would have to be assumed that he was saying the wrong things in secret. For years, information would have to be evaluated in light of the *possibility* that a KGB defector was coaching another intelligence service. It was a gloomy prospect—especially for the man from whom he had escaped.

Seriakin was, of course, only a desk driver. Still, if he were lost. . . .

Nemchin looked at Burrell. *That man,* he thought, *does not really care about Teck. He cares about something else. And that can be only* The Book of the Dead. *That millstone for his agency and for mine. That old man's foolishness.* And then he looked more closely at Burrell and realized that he was more Repin's contemporary than his own, and perhaps more Repin's sort of man. *An American Stalinist.*

He put down his cup and spoke decisively. "Look here, Burrell, let us face facts. We are both worried sick over *The Book of the Dead.* In a few hours the poet Yomut will descend from an aircraft in Amsterdam and the battle of propaganda will be joined." He saw a reaction in Burrell's face, but he went on without pausing. "We have both done our parts in this operation, each from his own side of the barrier. We both know it is an elaborate hoax. You and I, and a few people in Moscow and in Langley know the truth, but we will all hold our tongues. All of the opening moves have been made; now, we rest and wait to see which side wins the end game." Again, he moved forward and almost touched Burrell's robe. He did not meet Burrell's eyes, but seemed intent on the first knuckle of his own index finger. "But there are two men who can terribly confuse the end game—like pawns that reach the end square, they can become new and powerful pieces—and you and I, and our employers, will be the losers."

Nemchin looked up, directly into Burrell's eyes. "Those two men are Teck and a Russian named Seriakin."

"I thought you had Teck."

"I did. Two hours ago Seriakin helped him to escape. If they have not been in contact with you, then they are out there someplace"—Nemchin jabbed a finger at the window—"moving toward the end square."

The right side of Burrell's mouth twitched downward. He put the tips of the fingers and thumbs of both hands together, the thumbs touching his chin, the tips of the third fingers tapping his lower lip. He sat thus for fifteen seconds; then he said, "I met Seriakin once. He was rather rude. Uncouth. Certainly not one of your better men. But why did he help Teck to escape?"

Nemchin gave a brief account of Repin's use of Seriakin.

"Then suppose I forget Teck and Seriakin and use what you have just told me to discredit you and Repin and your manipulation of *The Book of the Dead*?"

Nemchin shook his head. "By all means, write a report! Your superiors will believe you. But the world, Burrell—the world! I am concerned with today, with an hour or five or ten from this minute, when those two fools begin to babble. They will be so believable!"

"All right." They looked steadily at each other. "All right. We'll . . . consult each other on this. But only on this matter, is that understood?"

Nemchin looked astonished. "Of course! Did you think I was trying to recruit you?"

"And we stay together. No individual action."

"Most certainly. I trust you no better than you trust me."

"And only so long as the balance is even. If there is some new factor—an incident, a new KGB ploy—that ends it instantly. Agreed?"

"Agreed. But time is short, Burrell. We must find where those two idiots have gone."

Burrell tapped the coffeepot idly. "I think I know. Teck has a woman in one of the coastal cities. We'll have to get an airplane."

After a night of unsatisfying sleep, Arkadi was at his office at a little after seven. The absence of any news about the case that most interested him was not surprising. He turned to other cases. The first taste of coffee was sour in his mouth, and when the hot liquid hit his stomach it caused a cramp that made him hunch over his desk and massage his abdomen with one hand. He was afraid he had an ulcer, but he told himself it was only his imagination.

At seven forty-five Arkadi received a telephone report from the man who had been on duty at Burrell's hotel. So far as the man could tell, Burrell was still asleep.

"Check with the hotel for any telephone calls and let me know." Arkadi hung up.

Sergeant Irmak appeared just at eight. Arkadi pushed a pile of reports across the desk toward him. "I think they've located the opium runner who supposedly has Mr. Teck's precious Aelian Fragment. They hope to pull him in today." He made a comment on another report and put it on a pile of material to be circulated in the department. "How are you at surveillance, Irmak?"

"Good enough, I think, sir."

"How would you like to take charge of keeping track of Burrell? The man who reported in this morning sounded so sleepy I think I might as well have got him a bed at Burrell's hotel. Get over there, would you?"

"Yes, sir. Shall I take these along?" He put one hand on the reports.

"Yes, but don't get too involved in them. Get over there now—there's a chit for a car—and look things over. Find out about telephone calls, in or out of Burrell's room. I just can't believe he's doing nothing at all."

For another hour Arkadi worked on matters unrelated to *The Book of the Dead.* By nine fifteen he had formed a theory of how certain artifacts from Cyprus that had begun to appear in mainland Turkey were being smuggled to France. When his desk telephone rang, he was so engrossed in a report of the routing of contraband artifacts that he momentarily resented the interruption.

"Arkadi here. Well?"

"Sergeant Irmak, sir. I am at the Buyu Efes."

"Well?"

"The American's telephone just rang—twelve times. No answer. Two minutes later it rang again—same thing. But nobody answered in Burrell's room."

"This just happened?"

"Yes, sir."

"Get on it, Irmak. Go knock on his door with some pretext—if there's still no answer ask the manager to open the door. Tell him we're concerned about Burrell's health."

"I'll try, Inspector."

"Try hard."

Irmak called back in ten minutes.

"He's gone, sir. Can't say how. The room's empty, looks undisturbed—his things are there, but no sign of any trouble. I found a tray with two coffee cups; they'd been drunk from and so forth. Two, sir."

"Good, stay with it." Arkadi massaged his stomach, which still burned. "Talk to the kitchen staff. Try to find how long ago it might have been drunk. If you think somebody's lying, put it to him; I'll back you all the way. Come down heavy if you have to."

"Yes, sir!"

Arkadi asked for two men to join Irmak at the Buyu Efes. A few minutes later he learned that the Antalya police were waiting to speak to him. He listened to a series of clicks and pops as the call was put through.

"This is Arkadi!"

"Lieutenant Halkavi here, Antalya police." The static was terrible, but Arkadi could make out the words. "About the Italian woman."

"Yes, the Princess di Paoli."

"She had a telephone call. From out of town; the hotel clerk is certain. Speaking English. Not the same as the one who called last night."

"What call last night? I wasn't told!"

There was a garbled explanation of a mixup in responsibilities. Arkadi massaged his abdomen. "All right, what was the call last night?"

"From the quayside hookup—the boat anchorage."

"What sort of boat?"

"I don't know, there are many boats in Antalya harbor—cruise ships, yachts, fishing boats."

Arkadi frowned. "All right, when did this new call from out of town come in?"

"It was still going on when I placed this call." Even through the static the man at the other end made the delay seem like Arkadi's fault. "It's probably over by now."

And the call was, indeed, finished. Teck was waiting beside

a telephone kiosk on the outskirts of Demre, a village less than twenty miles west of Antalya. Seriakin sat close by in the car. Both men were filthy and exhausted, and Seriakin shifted his position often as if he were feverish. Their attitudes were listless. Neither spoke.

The roadside telephone rang.

"Sam?"

"Yes. You didn't take long."

"I'm at the café. I wasn't followed, I'm sure. I did feel a fool, skulking about like somebody in a Bond film while the chambermaid pranced off in my best dress."

"Well." Teck had given her no idea of the seriousness of his situation when he had called her at the Hotel Sporting, nor did he intend to tell her the truth now. "I just think it's wise to be cautious."

"Of *course*, love! It's really quite fun, although I do think it's tedious when nothing happens for days at a time. Where have you been?"

"In hiding."

"Are the police—what does one say—on your tail, if you'll pardon my descent into Hoxtonese?"

"No. At least I don't think so. But we do have to move quickly, Princess. I have to get on that boat."

"Did you get your passport back?"

"No."

"Paul said you probably wouldn't. He thinks it's best if he picks you up along the coast at a spot he knows and go merrily off to the Aegean as if he hadn't a care in the world. Although he couldn't understand all this fuss about a medieval manuscript."

"I'll explain when I see him. Where do I meet the boat?"

"Paul will tell you about it. You're to phone this number." She dictated the number of the quayside hookup. "The yacht's called the *Gone to Ground*, if you can imagine. Paul will tell you everything. And, Sam?"

"Yes?"

"Do be careful crossing the street and so forth? I shan't see you until you reach Greece, you know. It would look a bit off if I packed my bags now and got on the yacht."

"Yes. That's wise. I'll call him now."

Neither spoke for several seconds.

"*Do* say something appropriate," she said softly.

Teck looked at Seriakin. The Russian shifted his body, and the movement made him wince.

"I'm dying to see you," Teck said.

He hung up. A little later he was drawing a crude map on the back of the Toyota Owner's Instruction Manual, at Paul's dictation. When he hung up the second time he knew where he would rendezvous with the *Gone to Ground* that afternoon, at the tip of a little peninsula called Cape Atriani.

For her part the Princess had left the café with a triumphant smile on her little cat's mouth. A large kerchief partly hid the upper half of her face, and, despite the coarse apron that hid her figure, her chin was lifted too happily for her to be a hotel chambermaid returning to work.

She did not pay any attention to the tieless young man who got up from a table as she left the café. He spoke briefly with the old waiter who had placed her call to Demre, and then he gave the old man money. Using the same telephone, he called a member of the Free Turkey Youth in Izmir and told him to pass along the word that the Englishwoman with the Italian name had called her American at the village of Demre.

Thirty minutes later, when Burrell and Yuri Nemchin landed at the Antalya airport, Nemchin called the same Izmir number and was given the new information. He and Burrell were on the road in ten minutes in a black Daimler whose age hid a responsive and powerful machine; and in Demre itself, three members of the Free Turkey Youth searched the narrow streets in the summer rain, looking for a green Toyota Crown sedan with signs of recent damage to the rear end.

Chapter twenty-five

THE coastal road from Demre to Antalya winds down into little sheltered harbors and up again to the heights above them, sometimes hugging the rock hillsides to escape the sea that threatens directly below the road, and sometimes arching more comfortably over the landward end of the small peninsulas that jut out every few miles. Demre itself is the city where the man who became known as Saint Nicholas made his first gifts. Alexander came this way, and Saint Paul, and the Emperor Hadrian. Behind the ancient coastal towns, the Taurus mountains provide backdrop to the scenery of the Turkish Riviera, and a refreshing alternative to its semitropical shores; there are cold-water rivers there, and snow on the mountaintops, and alpine views.

Insignificant roads run out from the coastal highway along the peninsulas. The Demre-Antalya highway is modern and well suited to automobiles; the peninsular roads are more often than not mere rocky tracks to now-ruined towns that flourished when Greek and Roman ships sailed the clear waters beyond. The towns are only rubble, hardly traceable anymore, and the roads to them are better for walking than for driving.

The road around Cape Atriani is a narrow loop, each end of which joins the coast highway. Only the eastern segment is paved; the authorities wished to make the spectacular view from the cape's headland more accessible to the foreign visitors who are just discovering what Alexander and Hadrian and Saint Paul discovered long ago. The western strip, however, which must be driven over in coming from Demre, is still a track of unpaved boulders; and at the headland, as if resting from its labors, a huge American road-grading machine sits twenty yards off the right-of-way where the black new asphalt so abruptly ends.

Rain had started to fall shortly after Teck had finished the telephone call to the yacht. Teck and Seriakin huddled in the car in a small clump of trees that screened an automobile turnaround a few miles outside of Demre.

"Nobody will see us here," Teck said.

Seriakin grunted. "Nemchin will have the dogs out. This is not America, Teck."

Teck glanced at Seriakin's swollen leg. "How are you doing?"

"I am terribly thirsty."

Teck reached into the back seat for a paper bundle of food they had bought early that morning. "There's still one bottle of beer. And more *ayran*."

Seriakin grimaced but said nothing.

Teck handed him the container.

"Is it still bleeding?"

"If I let it."

"They'll have a first aid kit on the boat."

"It will have to be cauterized. And the bullet got out somehow." Seriakin turned the calf to show the dark bruise on the side. "Another two or three millimeters, and I could have taken it out with my fingers. Maybe I should cut it out now with the knife."

"You've got a lot of guts, you know."

"Guts." Seriakin smiled wanly. *In one of the Siberian camps a prisoner chopped off one of his hands so they would have to put him in hospital.*

"You still think it's worth it?"

Seriakin loosened the tourniquet. "Yes." He watched the blood begin to flow like thick paint. "Survival is a statement."

"And if you die?"

"That is a statement, too." He twisted the cloth up again. Next to him, Teck shook his head but said nothing.

Arkadi put the telephone back in its cradle. "Two men chartered a small airplane this morning at shortly before nine. Quite legal. One was certainly Burrell. The other gave the name of Tlgahsli, a lawyer from Bulgaria; I'm checking the name with Customs and Immigration. The flight plan has them already in Antalya." He had not taken his hand from the telephone, and now he picked the instrument up again. "Get me the Antalya police." He glanced at Irmak. "The fingerprints from the coffee cups in Burrell's hotel room have gone to Interpol?"

Irmak nodded. Arkadi spoke into the telephone. "Yes, I'll wait." He looked up again. "Burrell could have been abducted, but I don't believe it. What exactly did the hotel watchman say?"

Irmak opened his notebook. " '*Question*: Who bribed you? *Answer*: I accepted twenty liras to turn my back while some fellow made a call on the hotel telephone. He swore—' "

Arkadi held up his hand and spoke into the telephone. "Very good of you to give me so much time, Lieutenant. Two foreigners hired an airplane to fly to Antalya this morning; we think there is a direct connection. Yes, quite a dangerous trip over the mountains, I agree. Strong motivation, wouldn't you say? Yes, it was a two-engined French Hirondelle, Turkish registration and a Turkish pilot. Hold on." Arkadi read off the aircraft's numbers and the estimated arrival time. After another exchange of courtesies he hung up.

"He's going to check it. They don't have anything on the boat yet other than the fact the woman had a call from one. Could be coincidence, but—" Arkadi stroked his chin. "You know, Irmak, if Teck is trying to make a rendezvous with a boat, he doesn't need Burrell's help. So why is Burrell flying down there?"

Irmak, who had no theory, looked apologetic.

"Well, what else did you get from the hotel watchman?"

Irmak reread the watchman's statement. " 'He swore it was a woman that was trying to make trouble at home. He swore to me there would be no trouble. *Question*: Did you recognize the man who made the call? *Answer*: No, he was just a foreigner. He spoke Turkish pretty well. But he was not a Turk. *Question*: How could you tell: *Answer*: He smelled. He had on perfume. Maybe that was to cover the other smell. *Question*: What other smell: *Answer*: The woodsmoke smell. He smelled like a woman when she has been cooking on a wood fire. *Question*: Did you know—' "

Arkadi held up his hand. "Woodsmoke. A European. Let us speculate—I know, Irmak, speculation is dangerous—let us speculate about the Bulgarian lawyer who turns up at the airport with Burrell some hours later. Did *he* smell like woodsmoke? Hum. Check on the fires last night. Maybe there is a connection there."

Half an hour later he heard from the Antalya police that the two men who had hired the Hirondelle had left Antalya airport in an unidentified automobile.

Shortly after that he sent a formal request to the deputy chief that the Coastal Patrol intensify surveillance on the stretch of coast from Finike to Manavgat for any boats anchoring close in to shore.

At noon Burrell and Nemchin met with the three young people who had been coordinating the search for the green sedan. One of the men, a twenty-year-old with a deep voice, leaned in through the car window.

"The Toyota is coming along the coast road toward Antalya."

"Excellent." Burrell started the engine. "We'll meet them halfway."

"We will come with you," a fierce-faced woman said commandingly. Nemchin and Burrell looked at each other, then at her. In English Nemchin said softly, "No witnesses." To the woman, he said, "We will take care of them ourselves. Keep track of their car; we will check with your people along the road." He slammed the door and started off.

Teck steered the car over the balky track that pretended to be the western road from the coast highway to the tip of Cape Atriani. Ahead, two ruts led on, and between them and on both sides rose rounded boulders. The track itself was narrower than the sedan's axle width, and he had to drive with one wheel in a groove and the other on the rocky shoulder. Each time a wheel came down from a boulder, Teck had to brake to avoid a plunge that would jar something loose, and he had to maneuver constantly to avoid rocks that threatened the car's underside.

Seriakin's face was damp and pale. "You have gone a kilometer on this, at least, Teck," he murmured.

Teck glanced at the odometer. "One point three," he said.

"Halfway." Seriakin winced as the right wheel struck a boulder and his left foot was jarred loose from the dashboard. "Don't slow down!" he said angrily. "I will be all right." He lowered the foot to the floor.

Teck maneuvered the car out of the ruts and tried driving with one wheel on the side and one in the center of the track, but he had to swing constantly from side to side to keep on the flat places.

"You drive very well."

Teck almost smiled. "My father taught me."

"You drove well through the mountains. *Very* well through the mountains." Seriakin sat upright, although the back of his seat was still reclined, and without its support his upper body swayed back and forth. "I am sorry about the pistol, Teck," he said suddenly. The Walther was still in his right hand.

Teck steered to the left, away from a gnarled tree whose roots seemed to spring directly out of the right-hand rut. "It doesn't matter now." He gunned the car over a hump, then took his foot off the accelerator to minimize the drop on the other side.

"I didn't think I could trust you."

"Neither did I."

Teck's eyes hurt. Driving without a windshield made them burn. One eyelid pulsed to the beat of his heart and he kept opening his eyes as wide as possible to ease them. He rubbed his right eye with a grimy hand and then had to grab the steering wheel quickly and swing the car to the other side of the track.

"Look ahead, Teck. Maybe the end of the cape."

Ahead, the road climbed steeply, and at its top it seemed to meet the leaden sky.

"It must be." Seriakin put his left hand on the back of the seat to steady himself. "Can you make it?"

The slope ahead was abrupt, with no lead-in, and the wet rocks were slippery. Teck accelerated, banging in and out of the ruts as he steered across the high places. He saw a glimpse of gray ocean through a break in the trees to his right; on his left, a wall of boulders, glistening with the rain that fell like fine, stinging mist now, cut off the rest of Cape Atriani. The sedan hurled itself at the hill. A third of the way up the incline he shifted down as the tires began to spin and the car lurched to the right. It jerked forward as Teck straightened it, and the car clawed its way uphill until the worst of the slope was over and he could shift up again, trying to gain all the speed he could for a last, short pitch at the top.

The car shot over the rise, still accelerating, with Teck's foot jammed down to the floor. They were fifty yards from the end of the cape on a little plateau that was edged on the ocean side with the tops of trees that grew halfway down the steep slope to the water. Between the road and the trees was the gigantic, pistachio-green road-grading machine, and Teck saw it and felt the tires strike the slick new asphalt road surface at the same moment, and as the car began to spin counterclockwise, he lost sight of the machine for an instant.

He touched the brakes. The skid was corrected, then over-corrected, and they were in an uncontrolled spin that took the sedan end-for-end until it reached the hairpin curve at the very tip of Cape Atriani, where the Toyota left the road going sideways. They slid down the slope, threatening to roll, until the right rear panel smashed the road grader and the impact straightened the car; there was a brief feeling of flight, a shudder as something caught the undercarriage, and a sickening deceleration as the car came to a stop against a house-sized boulder.

Teck was held down by his seat and shoulder belts. His right hand had struck something and was numb, but he felt no real pain.

He looked at Seriakin, who seemed to be sitting on the floor. *Where are his legs?* Blood was running down Seriakin's face from a wafer-sized mess at his hairline. His right hand must have been thrown up to guard his face at the moment of impact; now it lay across his chest. The gun was not in it.

"Seriakin."

Teck unclasped the belts. He bent forward and felt over the floor on his own side for the gun.

"Are you all right, Seriakin?"

The Russian's eyes were open. The right side of his mouth curled up ruefully. "My legs. I can't move my legs."

Teck opened his door, surprised to find it undamaged. He stepped out into knee-high grass. He had to support himself on the side of the car and, when he grew dizzier and he thought he would faint, he sat on the doorsill and put his head down between his knees. When the vertigo passed, he could smell some sweet flower brought by the damp breeze and feel the spray of rain on the back of his neck.

He looked at the floor on the driver's side. The gun was not there. He put his right hand on the driver's seat and leaned into the car very close to Seriakin. When his left hand touched one of Seriakin's legs, the man groaned.

The pistol was there, under the leg; Teck could feel the end of the barrel.

"Go on, Teck," Seriakin whispered. "Go to the boat."

"I'm going to try to lift you." He braced himself against the floor on the driver's side and put both hands around Seriakin's arm at the shoulder, one from the back and one from the front. When he lifted, Seriakin cried out like an animal and Teck let him go.

"I've got to get you out."

"No, I am caught. Something is holding both my lower legs." Seriakin said something in Russian that Teck could not understand.

Teck walked around to the other side of the car. The door could not be opened. The front end on that side was crumpled and the wheel was bent under as if the car were making a curtsy to its master, the rock.

Teck returned to the driver's side. "I want to lift you out."

"For the gun? Yes. Good, for the gun. Yes, you may need it. Go on."

"It's not for the gun. Not just the gun." He braced himself again and tried to lift Seriakin by the shoulders. He ignored the moan of pain until he knew he could not move the heavy body, and then he let Seriakin slump against the seat again. When he felt for the pistol again, he found he could move it. After several seconds of wiggling it over the gritty floor, he could grasp the butt and pull it free.

"I've got it!"

He put it on the driver's seat. "In case—you know."

"Take it, Teck."

"I couldn't hit anything anyway." He nodded at the gun. "Just in case."

Seriakin took out the clip. There were two cartridges left.

"Go on, Teck. Go find your boat."

Teck stood up beside the car. He could hear the waves striking at the base of the slope. He ducked down to look at Seriakin. "I'll come back for you."

"Of course."

Teck went around the huge boulder on its landward side, and as he came out of the trees and found himself at the top of a cliff that fell directly to the water, he heard the sound of an automobile engine on the road above him. He moved more quickly, trying to find a vantage point from which he could find the little pocket harbor Paul had told him about; to find it, he would have to get over the bulge of the hillside ahead of him. The only way to do so was to climb up the slope and cross the tip of the cape just below the road.

The car above him slowed. It continued on past the point where the Toyota had left the pavement, then stopped. Then it backed slowly toward him again. Seconds after it had stopped the second time, he heard two doors slam.

Teck climbed around a granite ledge. He pressed his back into the unyielding ridges of another block of stone and began to inch along its face. Below him and to his left, beyond the outward bulge of the slope, two stunted arms of rock, with here and there a stunted bush, embraced the pocket anchorage, and from it the tip of a black mast poked up like a marker. He heard a man's voice and a soft splash. To his left a rough path wound between the rocky outcrops and the gray-green foliage down toward the water's edge.

He took three steps along the path and, realizing that he might be seen, crouched low. Two more sliding, crouching steps put him behind a low mound of rock. He could now look past its seaward edge at the slope from which he had just come—and at the bottom of which the sedan lay.

He saw two men, and beyond them, the road grader. One of the men was Burrell. Both were peering cautiously down the hill like hunters waiting for the crack of a twig or the flicker of movement through foliage that is the sign of the quarry. Burrell gestured warily toward the bottom of the slope, where the green sedan would be—where Seriakin would be, with the Walther and the two cartridges. They began to move down the slope and away from each other, moving sideways and down with their eyes on that spot that Teck could not see, Burrell moving away from Teck and the other circling toward him so that his back was partly turned.

The yacht's mast seemed so close now he could easily have tossed a stone, he thought, and it would have landed on the deck below. He heard a voice from the cove, and he glanced quickly at the armed man sidling down the hill. But he hadn't heard.

Teck took another step down the path.

He looked across the little rocky saddle. Burrell's companion was walking, crouched, toward the clump of trees that Teck had come through; Burrell himself was farther up the slope and moving away. He was visible only from his knees up because of the hill's crest, and as Teck watched him he became a legless trunk, and then a disembodied head seemingly moving through the grass.

The nearer man now had his back completely to Teck. He stopped and crouched lower. He raised his automatic pistol, gripping his right wrist with his left hand, and Teck remembered that he had left the driver's door of the Toyota open. He would be able to see Seriakin.

Teck did not hear either of Seriakin's shots, but the crouching man fell to both knees suddenly as if he had been smacked hard between the shoulders, and then the second shot knocked him over backward so that he seemed to be looking at

Teck now, upside down, and his right leg twitched as if it were trying to get him to his feet again.

Burrell's head was gone from the hill, and Teck was sure he would be in the trees on the far side of the car. If he went all the way through the trees and around the seaward side of the boulder, he would be able to approach Seriakin safely.

Two shots. Two cartridges.

The yacht's mast dipped. He heard a rope moving through its blocks.

Teck sidled around the wet rock face and trotted across the saddle that lay between him and the slope. When he reached it he could look to his right and see the dead man, and beyond him a black car and the road grader, and down to his left he could see the green sedan nuzzling the huge rock. Burrell was not yet in view. Teck felt hideously alone and vulnerable, and when he moved stealthily to the dead man and glanced at his half-closed eyes, he felt utterly helpless. He knelt a few feet up the slope and began looking for the dead man's gun; from that vantage point he could see the green sedan from its right rear quarter, but he could not see Seriakin.

He found the pistol ten feet away in the wet grass. He lay down and rubbed his face on the grass because he felt sick and weak. *Survival is a statement,* Seriakin had said, but there seemed to be no statement that could be made for survival at this high a cost. If it did not stop now, it would simply get worse. Burrell would kill Seriakin, and then, not finding Teck in the car, he would go on— There had to be an end.

The clump of trees looked flat; unshadowed, grayed by the rain, they were like a stage drop. The scene was all of muted greens and browns, all but the dead man's shirt, which was close by and was vivid.

Something flickered in the scene, and Teck saw one pale hand appear on the dashboard as Seriakin tried once more to pull himself up. When Teck looked back at the trees, Burrell was crouched in front of them, the gun at eye level and his right arm extended almost straight in front of him. He, too, saw the hand; he began to move slowly toward the car around a screen of scraggly bushes.

Teck extended the dead man's gun in front of him and then held it with both hands.

"Burrell!"

Burrell turned to face the sound and crouched lower.

"Burrell, it's Teck!"
"I know that."
"It isn't worth it."
"Not on your life!"
Burrell began to run toward the green sedan. Teck could not swing the gun because of the grass, and he had to scramble into a squatting position; when Teck was exposed, Burrell stopped and fired. Teck pulled the trigger and the recoil of the gun boosted his hands two inches and blocked out Burrell. Teck tried to move to the side and his left foot was knocked from under him as if it had been struck with a club; he fell heavily on his right shoulder and then he felt a terrific concussion in his right ear, and his mouth and his eyes were full of grit and his nose was bleeding. He tried to stand but his left foot would not support him, and he lay on his back with his torso swiveled to the right and his arm almost on the ground, looking down his arm and the length of the gun to see Burrell, who was supporting himself on the side of the car because he was oddly hunched over, aim through the space where the windshield had been. Teck fired again and kept firing, seeing Burrell spin toward him and feeling an impact in his hip that caused him to lose his aim, but he fired until the gun would fire no more and the trigger clicked helplessly.
The air thrummed. It was a beating of wings, as percussive as a distant tympanum, and he thought it was the sound of his own dying. He could no longer see Burrell because he was lying on his back, looking up at the featureless silver sky, but as the thrumming grew louder he understood that it was only a helicopter, and not the wings of mortality, after all.

Three hours later the door of a Washington office burst open and a young man hurried in without knocking.
"You've heard the news? The word just came through—Yomut's been assassinated—at the Amsterdam airport!"
"Oh, God! Who?"
"No word yet. But I'd think—the Israelis, maybe?"
"Mm, could be. Or the PLO, hard to know about them—check with Mother's boys, they'd know. Unless—uh, it couldn't be—uh, we didn't—"
"Oh, no, sir. Well, if it was handled a certain way out of Ops, we wouldn't hear, but—unless. . . ."
They were thinking the same thing. *Burrell?*

"Better not to know, Ken. Whatever the source, it's for the best. Couldn't be better. What's the word on Burrell?"

"He died on the way to the hospital."

"Tragic. Family?"

"There's a son at Princeton. I'm getting data now."

"Good. We'll want to do the right thing, of course. He didn't say anything before he died?"

"We'll have to hope he didn't. The Turkish cops were with him. Sara Kerrigan's bringing him home."

"Right. I'll want to see her, of course. Make a note about a new assignment for her, Ken; I don't want to lose her. Hell of a fine person. What else do we worry about?"

"The Russian, sir. The Turks have him and I guess he's opting for asylum. Rebuffed any contact from the Russian Embassy. He refused Russian protection, even." Ken Fellows ran a hand through his hair. "The Turks are standing by their threat to expel three people from our embassy and the Soviets'. They're pretty antsy about the whole business."

"I know, I know, Ken!" The voice was almost a groan. "Turkey could have everything from us, arms, support, money—it's tragic. But it's their loss, not ours. History will show that."

"Yes, sir."

"If only once they could sit at this desk and see it our way. Just once. Of course, I suppose they'd say, if we could just— Well."

"Sir?"

"Never mind."

The Antalya hospital at one in the morning was almost serene, and the few nurses moved unhurried along dimly lighted corridors. To Arkadi, who had had to fly to the city by way of Ankara, the silence was a welcome balm. He had slept a little on the plane, but the awesome throbbing of the engines had been always with him. The local policeman who had brought him from the Antalya airport now led him through the hospital to a small office.

"Inspector Arkadi. Thank you so much for coming." The bearded man had the silky voice and an effusive manner that sometimes are associated with effeminacy, although his large body moved with a ponderous lack of grace that was almost bearlike. "Irmun, National Security." The two men exchanged credentials. The bearded one was younger than Arkadi and it was evident that he was better rested. His courtesy to Arkadi was almost ceremonial, and the inspector guessed correctly that he had been told to deal carefully with the Izmir cop who had so much information on this bizarre and potentially explosive affair.

"Naturally, Inspector, we want to share information with you." The statement masked a question: would Arkadi share information with Security?

"I'm not a policeman because I want to *create* secrets, Irmun. But you know, selfishly, I'd like to think that in the future you'd share with me. More than in the past."

"You're in Drug Control, Inspector?"

"Art Thefts."

Irmun blew cigarette smoke through his nose. Arkadi doubted that the man saw much connection between art theft and counterespionage. Still, he was conciliatory. "Why don't we discuss a liaison? When this is over, I mean. You might come to Ankara from time to time—even on a regular basis. Or we might channel some of our reports your way. It would have to be worked out very carefully."

"Yes, of course. But you *can* help me, that's the point." Arkadi accepted a cigarette and stood with it in his fingers, unlighted, rubbing his eyes with his other hand.

"You're exhausted, Inspector."

"I am."

"We've got a bed for you here if you like. Or you can be driven to a hotel."

"I'd hoped to see the American and the Russian."

"The Russian's sedated. I'm sorry."

"Sedated" may have been a polite word for "on the shelf," but Arkadi did not argue the point. "And the American?"

"We'll see what the nurse says."

"I *will* be able to talk to the Russian, won't I?"

"Mmm, well—yes, of course you will. But, uh, we have to insist that one of our people always—you know—"

"Be with me? But of course. I only want to know what happened. And why."

Irmun guided the inspector along a corridor. At the far end two armed men stood on each side of a door; around the corner two more men guarded another door. Arkadi dropped the cigarette that he had just lighted into a metal ashtray.

"And the CIA man? Burrell?"

"He died in a matter of hours. Massive injuries—an expanding bullet. He never spoke."

While they waited for the nurse they strolled to the end of the corridor and looked at the two stolid soldiers who stood guard there. The bearded man pointed out his other precautions—guards on the hospital grounds, armed men in the stairwells, a military truck at the gate. They turned and started back along the corridor.

"Do you know exactly what happened out there, Irmun?"

"Well, it's fairly clear that Teck and Burrell shot each other. Teck says that the Russian killed the third one in self-defense; he had a Bulgarian passport, but he's actually a Russian named Nemchin. KGB. That's all confidential, of course. The other Russian—Seriakin—had a bullet in his leg—bad shape, static gangrene had started—and we'll get that from him later. But it's still very confused."

They paused at the door to Teck's room. The nurse nodded curtly and let them in. Teck's unshaven face looked out of place in the clean, spare room; he seemed almost healthy to Arkadi's eye, and the bandage over part of his head seemed more rakish than pitiful. Arkadi glanced at the other people in the room—a man in civilian clothes, obviously another guard; and a very handsome, very tense woman of about thirty-five. Arkadi looked questioningly at Irmun.

"La Principessa di Paoli," Irmun said softly.

"Ah." Arkadi and the Princess exchanged a look—mutual distrust, mutual interest.

Arkadi approached the bed.

"I am not really here in a professional capacity tonight, Mr. Teck. I know you have been injured."

Teck smiled groggily. "I'm not quite ready to try to run away." His voice was husky and his tongue tripped over some of the consonants.

"I suppose your consul has been notified, and so on?"

Irmun spoke up. "Mr. Teck has refused to see *any* of the representatives of the American government." His odd emphasis on "any" was revealing. "The Princess di Paoli is hiring a Turkish lawyer for Mr. Teck."

"Good." He tried not to sound harsh. "You're going to need one, I'm afraid."

"I understand, Inspector." Teck licked his lips. "How is Seriakin?"

Arkadi looked at Irmun, who raised his eyebrows as if he were just as puzzled as the inspector. Arkadi looked down at Teck. "Sleeping, I am told. As you should be. After all, you and I have many days ahead of us to talk, I think." Arkadi's voice was very serious. "But understand—you must be sensible this time. *All* the truth, yes?"

Teck nodded.

Arkadi started to turn away, then thought better of it and looked at Teck with a little grin. "Ah, yes, Professor, I have a surprise for you. I had meant to put it off, but—" He took a thin packet from his coat and laid it on Teck's chest. "A present for you."

Teck glanced at the Princess; Arkadi, without looking at her, was aware that she had stood up.

"What is it?"

"It is your Aelian Fragment. Remember? I took it from your opium dealer today."

Arkadi unfolded the waterproofed cloth in which the fragment was wrapped. He knew the Princess was standing close to him, and when the first illuminated sheet was visible, her little inhalation of breath was audible.

Arkadi held it up where Teck could see it. "Is it not beautiful?"

Teck was smiling. "It's—everything I expected."

"It's yours." Arkadi saw Teck's quick frown. "After all, you have earned it. And it's very fitting."

It was his turn to smile.

"It's a fake, you see."